THE WRATH OF LEANDER WELLES

ASHLYN DREWEK

FOX HOLLOW BOOKS

Cover design by Teresa Conner at Wolf Sparrow Creations

For Amy,

Thank you for all that you do. I can't even begin to describe how amazing you are. This journey has only gotten better with having you in my corner.

FOREWORD

This book contains references to alcohol/drug use, various mental health issues, self-harm, suicide, and on-page torture. Reader discretion is advised.

1

BENNETT

There wasn't anywhere left to go.

Our quarry was trapped — Leander at one end of the alley; I at the other. The man darted back and forth, as if to see which of us would be easier to escape. The answer was neither.

"Poor little mouse," Leander purred, closing the distance in fluid strides.

I tsked the man, matching Leander's steps. "Didn't run fast enough."

"Or far enough."

The thief backed up until he could go no further, cornering himself against a mint-green wall.

"Wrong pocket, amigo," I said with a dark smile.

"You *do* know how much I hate thieves," Leander concurred.

"Almost as much as liars."

"Now that we've caught him, whatever shall we do with him?" Leander cocked his head, a chilling smile on his lips.

I glanced up in faux thought, drumming the tips of my fingers on my chin. "He did make us run all this way…"

"And interrupted a perfectly pleasant evening."

"So rude."

"I abhor rudeness."

The man flung Leander's wallet on the ground and held up his hands, blubbering in a string of Spanish and snotty tears. Something about kids. Food. Hurricanes. Blah blah blah. Woe is me.

"How can he make amends to you, my love?" I asked, taking a step closer to the man.

Leander studied him with narrowed eyes, his head held high, like the dark prince he was. "Historically speaking, what was the punishment for theft?"

"When caught in the act?" I replied with a feral smile. "Muerto."

The man's eyes widened, renewing the blubbering.

Leander's smile spread wider, matching mine. "Ah, yes. Death."

"Lo siento," the man pleaded, clasping his hands together. "Por favor."

Up close, he was even more pathetic. Half a foot shorter than either of us and as scrawny as a teenager, despite being twice as old. If he'd simply asked for assistance, his fate would have been much, much different. Both of us could afford to be charitable in the right situation. But getting a little handsy with Leander's back pocket, taking what wasn't his? Assuming we'd be none the wiser because my tongue was down down Leander's throat? Unacceptable.

But that wasn't even the worst of it. No, the worst part was making me run with a fucking hard-on. Was there no decency left in the world?

"Alright then," I sighed, looking at the man sadly. "If you insist." Pulling a steak knife from the small of my back, I plunged it into the center of his abdomen, all the way to the handle.

He grabbed my hand with both of his, a stunned expression on his face. If he thought the move would stop me from twisting the blade viciously or from yanking it sideways to sever more of his internal organs, he was wrong. A wave of blood gushed over my hand, letting me know I'd hit the artery.

"Vaya con Dios," I murmured to the dying man. Ripping the knife out, I took a step backward, away from the spurts of blood. Without me literally pinning him in place, the man slid down the wall, leaving behind a streak of glistening black on the pale stucco.

I started to reach for my handkerchief when Leander strode forward. He grabbed me by the back of the neck and yanked me in, kissing me hard. His forward momentum and the force of the kiss drove me backward. I nearly tripped over the dead man's feet before Leander slammed into the wall, knocking the knife from my hand.

My newly-freed hands caught Leander's face, as much to steady myself as it was to pull him closer. He didn't seem to mind the blood smeared on his jaw, just as I couldn't have cared less about the fact we were in the middle of San Juan, where anyone could waltz up and find us.

Leander grabbed my hips and pushed me up two steps, into an arched doorway.

"What are you doing?" I didn't recognize the sound of my own voice, raspy as it was.

Tearing open the front of my pants, his hand slipped inside, fisting my rapidly hardening cock. "What I should have done in Venice."

Eyes closed, my head thumped against the door. "Oh my God — Leander!"

"Should I stop?" he asked, blazing a trail of kisses, alternating with bite marks, down the side of my neck, all the while torturing me with his hand.

I could barely comprehend the question, let alone answer it.

"No?" He chuckled darkly before his mouth covered mine, his teeth sinking into my lower lip.

Still riding the high of bloodshed, it wasn't long before his mouth and his hand pushed me over the edge. I collapsed against him, muffling my cry into his shoulder as I came. He nuzzled the side of my face, a Cheshire grin on his lips. Meanwhile I tried to catch my breath and come back down out of fucking orbit.

"We should leave before someone sees us," Leander said with another quick kiss before slinking away, as nonchalant as could be. Stepping over the corpse, he leaned down and plucked his wallet off of the ground, thumbing through its contents quickly.

"Oh, *now* you're concerned?" I shook my head with a laugh, trying to make myself presentable again. Wiping what was left of the dried blood from my hand, I frowned at the dampness on my sleeve. There went another jacket. At least it was dark, so hopefully no one would see it on the walk back to the hotel.

As soon as I caught sight of Leander, I cringed. "Whoops. Come here."

He met me halfway, his brows furrowed. "What's wrong?"

Licking the corner of the handkerchief, I did my best to clean the bloody streaks off of his face. "I'm starting to think I've been a bad influence on you."

"The worst." The corner of his mouth ticked up into a sly smile.

"My mission in life is fulfilled, then." Snickering to myself, I picked up the knife one more time and wiped the fingerprints off of it before throwing it in the closest trashcan.

"Where did you get that from anyway?" He smoothed down the front of his suit jacket while we stepped over the river of blood trickling through the cobblestones, strolling away into the balmy summer night.

"I snagged a couple from the restaurant. Want one?" I opened my suit jacket like a peddler, revealing a row of knives carefully pierced through the lining.

He shot me a look out of the corner of his eye before his beautiful gaze rolled away in exasperation. He did a shitty job hiding his smile, though.

"I'm just saying… One can never be *too* careful. Haven't you heard? Murders are on the rise around here," I said with utter seriousness, adding a serene smile when he looked at me again.

He smirked, shaking his head. "I don't need a knife. I have you."

"Always." I slung my arm around his shoulders, bonking my forehead against his.

THE TWITCHING WOKE me before the whimpering. With one leg hooked around Leander's and my arm draped across his waist, each jerk he made registered along the length of my body.

I reached for his face in the dark, caressing his cheek. "*Easy, my love. You're dreaming. That's all,*" I murmured in Italian. In truth I could have spoken Klingon. It wasn't anything that I said, so much as the sound of my voice.

Still asleep, he turned his face toward me and grew quiet.

I'd nearly drifted off again when a sharp pain landed in the center of my diaphragm. If that wasn't enough, Leander's scream reverberated through my skull at the same time. I was still trying to figure out how to breathe when he shot upright, scrambling away from me to the far side of the bed.

Rubbing the sore spot beneath my sternum, I leaned over and turned the light on, hoping it would snap him out of it.

It took a minute, but eventually his chest stopped heaving. His fingers loosened from the tangled sheets and he blinked himself into the present.

"What happened?" I asked, knowing perfectly well it was another nightmare. Even if he denied it, I had the bruises to prove it, collected over the weeks of our otherwise blissful vacation.

"Nothing." He whipped the covers off and darted to the bathroom, like I was going to take him at his word and just roll over and go back to sleep.

Scrubbing a hand over my face, I sighed and climbed out of the bed. I padded after him quietly and leaned against the bathroom doorframe, watching him.

He stood at the sink, staring in the mirror while the shower ran. I doubted he even saw himself, or me, in the reflection. He had that haunted look again, the one I couldn't erase no matter what I did or how hard I did it.

For the most part, our time in Puerto Rico had been relaxing. Yet it seemed like every night, *this* happened. He tried to brush it all off and tell me he'd always been like this, but not once in the two weeks we were in Venice did this happen. When I reminded him of that, he ceased talking altogether, retreating even further inside himself.

Wordlessly, I moved forward, taking him by the wrist and pulling him into the shower. The water was on as hot as it would go, another indication it was more than "nothing." If it was a regular shower, he wouldn't feel the need to burn off the top layer of his skin, like it was possible to scrub away the memories if he tried hard enough.

Turning the temperature down, I adjusted all of the shower heads so they were directed at him. If he noticed the water wasn't scalding, he didn't say anything as he slumped against the wall. Tipping his head back, he closed his eyes, letting the water spray over him like an Italian statue in a rainstorm. Michelangelo would have cried to have him as a model. With hard, straight lines and smooth skin, he looked like he was carved from alabaster. The scars all over his arms were his only "flaw," but even they were perfect in my eyes simply because they were his.

I squirted an oily body wash onto my hands and slid them over the back of his neck. Moving downward over his body, half-cleansing and half-massaging as I went, I took my time kneading his tense muscles and working out any knots as the scent of neroli filled the steamy shower.

"Easton? Or Parkview?" I asked quietly.

"Parkview." He exhaled the word and ran his hand over his face, dashing water out of his eyes.

Every time he mentioned that fucking psych ward, it was like a little bit of him disappeared. It wasn't just the mind games he played with *all* of his doctors, or any guilt he might be harboring over the whole thing with one blonde in particular. It was the abusive staff, the grueling psych tests, and the memories that were unleashed as a result. Like Pandora's box, now that they were out, they refused to go back in.

"Will you ever tell me what happened?" I asked, hoping he didn't hear the growl in my voice. I hated that he refused to talk about it, that I was helpless to *do* anything while he was in turmoil. If there was one thing I was looking forward to about eventually returning to the mainland, it would be hunting down every single person from that fucking place and ending them once and for all. It might not undo the damage they did, but it was a start. More importantly, it gave me a mission instead of sitting on the sidelines while the love of my life fought a war inside his head every single night.

He swallowed thickly before answering. "No."

"I've read the complaints, you know. In the lawsuit." It

was one thing to read about it — I wanted to hear it from him. I needed details the court papers couldn't provide, so I'd know how painful their punishment had to be.

Ignoring me like usual, he closed his eyes again and ducked his head under one of the shower heads. If he thought his silence equaled another "No," he clearly forgot he wasn't the only ruthless one in the relationship. I was tired of being ignored, just like I was tired of seeing him suffer in silence.

Sliding my hands around his narrow waist and down to his ass, I grabbed him and yanked him against my chest. Ignoring his glare, I kissed the pulse in his neck, up to his jaw.

I made it to his cheek when he angled his face toward me. His green eyes flashed, a warning to drop the subject. "We won. There's no reason to revisit it."

"Except they continue to torment you. And that's my job." My hand slipped between us, wrapping around his dick. Sliding up and down easily with whatever body wash was left in my palm, I arched a brow at him, daring him to stop me.

A soft moan escaped his lips and his eyes drifted shut. Biting his lip, he looked like he was torn between arguing and letting me continue. Regardless of whatever direction his head was going, his cock was thickening by the second, swaying things in my favor.

Stroking him harder, I grazed the side of his neck with my teeth before sucking at the red mark. "Consider this payback for the alley."

"I didn't hear you complain." He drew in a surprised gasp when the fingers of my other hand slid along the curve of his ass and slipped down the crease, teasing his hole. That was one avenue we hadn't crossed yet and one I certainly wasn't going to force, but it didn't stop me from pushing the boundaries of his newfound sexuality. Just a little bit.

"How could I? You had your tongue in my mouth the entire time." To emphasize my point, I licked the seam of his lips. As soon as they parted, my tongue found his and tangled together, tasting every part of him.

When his hand encircled my cock, I broke our kiss sharply and shook my head. "No."

He frowned, his brows drawn. I know it wasn't a word he was used to hearing, especially from me, but I had other ideas in mind.

Swatting his hand away, I placed my palm in the center of his chest and walked him backward to the tiled bench. "Sit."

Swallowing his reply, he obeyed nonetheless, watching my every move. It was always interesting to see who'd take the lead in any given tryst. Just because you started out in control didn't mean that's how it ended — a fact he'd learned over the course of our sexcapades.

Kneeling between his legs, I gave him a devilish smirk before I continued to extract sexual retribution. It's not that we kept score, per se, but I hated the idea he'd one-upped me. And in public, no less. That was *my* move, not his.

Pressing my tongue flat against the underside of his shaft, I licked him from base to tip, pulling a rewarding groan out of him. But that's not what I wanted.

Swirling his head once as a distraction, I promptly swallowed the entire length and sucked. Hard.

"Oh, fuck!"

There it was. His body tense, his hand in my hair, and that mouth. I don't know why his swearing turned me on so much, but it did. I didn't consider it a job well done unless I got a certain number of verbal outbursts. When applicable, that is. In the restaurant last week, under the table, I accepted dropped silverware, stifled swearing, and nearly upending said table as proof I was on the right track. *Goddamn it, Bennett* had never sounded so sexy.

Using my hands and mouth, I brought him to the brink, again and again, until he growled and seized my throat in one hand. The movement forced me to pop off his dick, even though I was nowhere near done with him.

"Enough edging," he said between clenched teeth.

I narrowed my eyes, a challenging twitch playing at the corner of my mouth.

Maintaining a hold on my neck, he shifted forward off the bench and knelt between my legs. He kissed me hard, one hand in my hair and the other shifting up to hold my jaw. I was completely at his mercy, to kiss — or not kiss — as he so desired.

When the hand in my hair released, the one on my jaw pushed me down until I was laying on my back, my legs draped over his thighs. Thankfully the tile was warm from all the hot water otherwise it would have been far less enjoyable.

He let go of my face, trailing his fingers down my chest, down my abdomen and then disappearing altogether. In their absence, he bent down and kissed my wet skin, working upward to my mouth again.

As soon as I heard a distinctive cap flip open, I cupped my palm for him and spread the lubricant over us both.

"I love you," I whispered against his lips.

"God, I love you." His lips reclaimed mine as he pushed his cock inside slowly. I cradled his face between my hands, deepening the kiss, savoring the feel of him. All of him. Not just his dick, but the way his hands touched me, the bruising way he kissed me, the way his hair dripped water from up above. Everything.

Steadily the rhythm increased, once he knew I'd adjusted. But there was still something off. He kissed me and he touched me, but he wasn't *connected* like normal. It was hard to pinpoint. Maybe it was the tile. The rough surface was scraping the hell out of my back, so I was sure his knees were probably on fire. Time to change tactics.

I pushed him back, trying to catch my breath in the process. "Now fuck me like you hate me."

A dark smile curled his lips. "Stand up."

He didn't have to tell me twice. I was on my feet and bracing against the tiled bench in a flash. Leander was seconds behind me, one hand on my hip while the other guided his cock back inside until he was in all the way.

"Goddamn, you feel amazing," I exhaled, shifting one hand up to the wall for a more stable foundation.

"It's what you wanted, isn't it?" He had both hands on my hips now, holding me firmly. Before I could answer, he rocked back and thrust in again. Slow, hard movements, his fingers digging into my slippery skin.

"Fuck yes it is."

One of his hands swept up along my spine, probably distracted by the tile outline undoubtedly embossed on my back. If that's what it was, it didn't last long, since he grabbed my shoulder and pulled me down against his pelvis, making each thrust that much harder, deeper.

His pace quickened, but the intensity didn't slow at all. The hand on my shoulder slid over to my throat and clamped down, forcing me to stand straighter. Thank God we were nearly the same height. It made situations like this so much easier.

Since I didn't have to brace myself against the wall anymore, I put my empty hands to work. One reached behind me and tangled in his wet hair, while the other jerked my cock in tandem with him.

When he bit the back of my neck, I was done for.

I managed to get out "I'm going to—" before coming all

over the bench like a teenager with no self-control. Pretty sure the hand job earlier had something to do with it.

"Fuck, Bennett!" His grip on my throat tightened, almost a little too much, and he groaned into my shoulder. "Where do you want it?"

"I don't care," I said, gasping in a short breath between each word. That was the perk of the shower — cleanup was a breeze and the least of my concerns at the moment.

He gave a final thrust, burying himself inside of me, a strangled cry reverberating off the tile. Breathing hard, he pulled out carefully and staggered to the side of the shower, slumping against the wall.

Turning toward him, I tried to keep my expression neutral, even though I was on some level between "Um, ok," and "What the fuck?!" This wasn't right. Other than the mutually-assured orgasms, this wasn't *us* — it wasn't *him*. He didn't pull out and just walk away. Ever. Even if he was, technically, still in the same space as me, the distance may as well have been as wide as the Grand Canyon.

"Leander?" I didn't know what the hell I was going to say, but I had to fill the silence up with *something*.

He opened his eyes, but only gave me a quick glance before they dropped to the floor. "I didn't hurt you?"

Mutely shaking my head, I let neutrality fall by the wayside, replacing it with full-blown confusion. It was a fair question, I suppose. But also unnecessary since we'd been far more aggressive with each other in the past and I'd never had an issue with it. It's not like I was one to keep my mouth shut about, well, *anything*.

Closing his eyes again, he tipped his head against the wall. Even in that position, his brow was furrowed, the muscles in his jaw constricting. Usually sex cleared his mind, or at least quieted it, but he looked as troubled now as he did before.

Crossing the short distance, I pulled him against me and kissed the side of his neck. “My love...”

He didn’t answer the dozens of unasked questions in those two words. He simply wrapped his arms around me and leaned his head against mine, exhaling softly into the curve of my shoulder. “Mon coeur.”

2

LEANDER

Sculptures, paintings, photographs — it didn't matter. Bennett was a walking encyclopedia, chattering on about various artists and time periods as we moved through the museum. My own personal docent, it seemed. Though anyone who happened to be in the vicinity lingered to listen to him and his colorful explanations.

It had been that way almost the entire trip to Puerto Rico. Every historic site, every cultural highlight — he had a slew of information to pass along, his hazel eyes bright and his ringed-hands gesticulating with the dramatic flair he was so known for.

Not a single day passed that he didn't amaze me in one way or another. The simple fact that he was there, everyday, never ceased to amaze me.

More than once I'd woken from the throes of yet another nightmare to see him right next to me. Even if I could never bring myself to tell him why there were days I couldn't eat, why sleep was so fleeting, the fact he was *there* meant more than I could ever fully articulate.

I treasured the levity he brought to my waking hours as much as the quiet comfort he provided every night through his mere presence alone.

"—and supposedly that's why he chose photography over…" Bennett cocked his head as we strolled through the gallery, glancing at me out of the corner of his eye. "Are you ok? You've hardly spoken since breakfast."

"How many times have you been here?" I asked, stopping when he did, my hands clasped behind my back.

"Here? As in, the museum?"

"I meant Puerto Rico, but sure. The museum."

He furrowed his brows at me, the corner of his mouth ticking up into an amused smirk. "This is my first time. Why?"

"Then how can you possibly know all of this? Venice was one thing, but here?"

He laughed quietly and took a step closer so we were nearly chest-to-chest. Licking his lips, he inclined his head slightly, his voice low. "The answer is quite scandalous... Are you sure you really want to know?"

"I wouldn't have asked if I didn't want to know." I met his wry grin with a smirk of my own. "Besides, I'm no stranger to scandal, Mr. Reeve. Unless you've already forgotten I stood accused of murder not that long ago."

Shifting forward, he circled behind me, dragging his fingers from one shoulder to the other, across my back. "I can't forget anything when it comes to you, which is why I'll tell you my secret, my love, even though the ramifications will be costly." He leaned in again, on the other side from where he started, and skimmed his lips across my jaw. "I read a guidebook at the airport."

Mouth agape, I gasped in outrage that wasn't entirely faked. He laughed and slipped his hands around my waist, pulling me close to nuzzle my neck. "You had a guidebook and you didn't let me read it? How could you? Of all the loathsome things..."

"I wanted to spend this time with *you* — not you *and* a book. Sue me." He snickered at his own lawyer joke.

"That's it. I've had enough of looking at art." I pulled out of his arms and started toward the exit. "We're going to a bookstore *right* now."

"Whatever you want, my love."

We made our way out of the museum and after Bennett ascertained the location of the nearest bookstore, we were off. The way Spanish rolled off his tongue was just as mesmerizing as the Italian he spoke, or the French. Even Latin.

He was mesmerizing. I could spend hours watching him, and I did. For the past three weeks, I'd been by his side every waking moment, making up for the years we'd already lost due to time, circumstances, and stupidity. I certainly wasn't about to waste any more.

Watching Bennett bask in sunlight on the beach, study the Spanish colonial architecture in town, or charm the old women in the marketplace were all things I observed from afar and locked away in my memories. My hope was that if I collected enough of them, they'd eventually replace the evil that lurked in the corners of my mind. During the day, it worked. Nighttime was when I lost control.

The horrific dreams were a constant, needling reminder that my family's curse was still there, waiting to claim its next victim. I felt the weight of it daily, doubly burdened by the knowledge that I had responsibilities at home requiring my attention. My company, for starters, demanded I return at some point before it fell into complete ruin. The terms of my grandmother's exacting trust also ensured I eventually had to go back to Easton or I'd forfeit everything.

Then there was Lorelei.

I had neither seen nor spoken to her the whole time we'd been gone. It wasn't entirely by choice. In our — *my* — spur of the moment decision to be completely selfish and run away, Bennett and I left our cell phones behind. To truly escape from the demands in both our lives, we had to be unreachable.

And it worked.

In the rare moments I wasn't thinking about reality, things were perfect. It was just Bennett and I, together, unstoppable — the way it should have always been from the beginning.

But, Lorelei cast a shadow over our summer escape.

Bennett must have felt it too. He asked about her, on occasion, a thread of hostility woven through every word, however innocent. Thus far I'd been mostly successful in deflecting the questions, but I knew I couldn't hold him off forever. Soon, he'd stop asking and would simply demand answers. But answers might chase him away and that was the very last thing I wanted now that I had him back. So I avoided anything that could remotely bring her up in conversation and when she haunted my dreams, I lied to the love of my life and told him it was nothing. Because it *was* nothing. *She* was nothing. She'd been something — or the possibility of something — once before, but none of that mattered compared to what I had with Bennett. As much as I'd wanted her to fill the void he left behind, it was impossible. No one could replace him. No one could even come close.

Arms crossed and leaning against a a shelf, Bennett watched me browse through the bookstore, much as he had in Venice. While I could have certainly purchased a dozen or more, I humored him and only picked a couple. It was mostly to occupy myself whenever we went boating. As relaxing as the water was, it gave me too much time to think and at present thinking was the last thing I wanted to do.

"Do you have enough?" he asked, brows raised.

"Never." I shot him a smirk.

"What about the store?" Sidling up to me, he pushed me backward against the bookcase. He caught his lower lip between his teeth, openly staring at my mouth. The conversation may have centered around books, but the look on his face indicated they were the furthest thing from what was really on his mind.

I cast a cautious glance from side to side. Thankfully, we were alone. "What about the store?"

"Say the word, and it's yours." His hips pushed into mine while his fingers ran through my hair, pulling me closer to his waiting mouth.

"I don't need you to buy me a bookstore," I replied in a near-whisper as he kissed and nipped my jaw and throat, sliding his hands up and down my body. "I just need you."

"You have me" — he pulled back, his expression solemn as he caressed the side of my face — "for as long as you want me."

"All of eternity?"

"And then some." He pressed his lips to mine, grinding his hard-on into me.

Pulling away with a small groan, I did my best to arrange my features into something of a stern look. Not that Bennett cared about propriety. At all. "We are in public."

"Didn't stop *you* the other night." He unzipped my pants and worked his hand inside, shamelessly stroking my length. Dragging his tongue up the side of my throat, he sucked on the soft skin just beneath my jaw.

"Bennett…"

"Yes, my love?" he breathed between kisses, working me

harder, faster, and in total view of anyone who happened to turn the corner. Luckily the rare books section wasn't exactly popular with today's society.

I forgot what I was even going to say. He didn't seem to care since he reclaimed my mouth with voracity, his tongue as unrelenting as his hand.

Tearing my mouth free, I squeezed my eyes shut and threw my head back. The books I'd been holding as a last-ditch effort to keep Bennett at bay, tipped out of my hand and crashed to the floor. I grabbed the shelf before I fell along with them. "Oh, fuck. I don't know if I can hold out much longer."

I should have known my admission wouldn't make him stop. Rather, he dropped to his knees, right there in the store, and took my cock into his mouth. Raking his hands up and down my abdomen, his tongue swirled and massaged every place he could reach.

"Bennett..." I bit my lip, trying to listen for the sound of footsteps, but it was impossible over my own ragged breathing.

Completely unconcerned, Bennett carried on. One of his hands grabbed my ass, holding me firmly while the other slid up and down my shaft.

A string of swear words was on the tip of my tongue, just dying to come out until I bit down, hard. My orgasm rushed down my spine and flew out of me. A split second before my legs buckled, I shored up my grip on the shelves with both hands.

Bennett kept his lips wrapped around me, somehow chuckling as he swallowed every bit of my release. Licking his lips, he rose to his feet and brushed a curl off my forehead. "Now don't you feel better?"

Breathing hard I readjusted myself and my clothing, torn

between glaring and smiling like a blissful idiot. "You are the Devil. You know that, right?"

He stooped to gather my books and tucked them under his arm, as nonchalant as ever. Giving me a wink as he rounded the corner, he strolled away, whistling to himself.

3

BENNETT

"You can open your eyes now," I said, hoping my voice didn't betray the volley of butterflies darting around my stomach.

Why was I so nervous?

I'd never been nervous on water, even at night. Unlike most people, I didn't fear heights or speed or sailing into the abyss with zero navigation. The credit for that, I think, went to the lightning bolt I took to the brain as a kid, but that was neither here nor there. The fact was, for whatever reason, I felt like I was moments away from hurling my dinner into the water, which would *definitely* spoil the night.

Rubbing my palms over my thighs, I focused on Leander instead of trying to figure out whatever the hell my problem was. Between his never-ending nightmares and the disconcerting tryst in the shower, I decided I had to do something spectacular. Something out of this world to draw him out of the shell he was retreating into like a little hermit crab.

Leander did as instructed, his dark brows coming together ever so slightly as he glanced around. "Um... Where are we?"

After rowing for a good amount of time, our kayak floated in the middle of nowhere. The water was pitch black as far as the eye could see, shining only with the pale starlight from above. It had taken some persuading to even get him in the boat in the first place considering how dark it was with the new moon. Not to mention the fact the last time I commandeered a boat, I purposely crashed it. Apparently he was still a little sore over that whole incident.

Instead of giving him a verbal answer, I leaned over the side and ran my fingers through the water. Brilliant blue flashed over my hand, dripping back into the sea to rejoin the blackness.

"A bio bay," he gasped, trailing his hand along the water. The ripples lit up in the wake.

"Do you like it?"

"Who could possibly say no?" he quipped.

I chuckled quietly, peeling off my t-shirt. A second later, I was in the water, a larger burst of light erupting all around me. Surfacing with a sigh, I swiped water and hair out of my eyes. "Are you coming?"

I didn't need to ask a second time. He dropped the anchor before unbuttoning his shirt. Tossing it aside, he dove past me, disappearing under the surface. The water lit up in gentle waves, illuminating his path straight back to me.

His hands slid up my sides, like a diver skimming along a tether to the surface. As soon as he emerged, I pressed my lips to his. The glowing blue water around us lit up his smirk when he pulled away from me. "Why is it every time we're in a boat, you make get me out of it?"

"I like seeing you wet." I brushed the long, sopping curls out of his eyes before kissing him again. Thankfully, we were close enough to the kayak that I could grab it to stay afloat. In return, he captured my jaw and kissed me hard, the salty water on his lips mingling with the mint left over on his tongue from his mojito.

My fingers scraped along his ribs, doing my best to pull his body closer to mine. Tearing my mouth from his, I kissed my way down the side of his neck, biting the juncture of his shoulder.

"You better not be trying to start something," he said sternly, rolling his shoulder away from me.

"I'm not *trying* anything." Flashing him an impish grin, I slid my leg between his and hooked it behind his calf to make sure my sea otter didn't float away.

"I believe that as much as I believe you when you say you're looking forward to domesticity."

"I am!" It was probably the last thing he ever thought would come out of *my* mouth, but it was true. Being with him — *really* being with him — reined in my wild side and made me yearn for things I'd once avoided at all costs. I still wanted to travel and marvel at the world, but I also wanted to make him crepes on Sunday mornings and argue about how to properly load the dishwasher.

There was a disbelieving smirk on his face, accompanied by an arched brow. "You'll get bored."

"I won't."

"You always do."

"Not this time." I nuzzled the side of his neck, pressing soft kisses upward, until I reached his ear. "You're all I need. All I'll *ever* need. All I'll *ever* want."

He hummed his skepticism, but tilted his head to the side regardless, exposing more of his throat.

"Marry me," I breathed against his wet skin.

Oh, fuck… Bennett!

I didn't intend to blurt it out quite like that, but my brain suddenly lost control over my mouth. Now it was out in the open and there wasn't a damn thing I could do to call it back.

"What?!" He recoiled so fast he sent a wave of shimmering blue across the surface of the water, lighting up his bewildered expression. I don't think I'd ever seen his eyes as big as they were, which meant I had *no* idea what was going through his mind. Nothing caught Leander Welles off guard. Except, apparently, a marriage proposal.

The plan was to ask *sometime* during this trip, to declare my intentions publicly and without reserve. After everything, I never wanted him to doubt my commitment, but words weren't enough. Especially *my* words, words that were infamous for spinning webs upon webs of lies. Marriage was the only thing I could offer to demonstrate the magnitude of my feelings, the sincerity of my vow to never be parted from him ever again.

"Marry me, Leander," I repeated, trying my best to scrutinize his expression in the near-dark. "Say you'll be mine for the rest of our lives. God knows, I'm not a poet. I can't describe how perfect you are or credit the stars for bringing us together. All I can do is promise to love you as no one has ever been loved before until I take my last breath."

His lips parted and shifted just so, enough that I knew he was biting the inside corner of his mouth. Save for the rocking of the waves, he was utterly still — and silent.

So silent.

Shit!

The butterflies in my stomach dropped like stones, one by one, with each passing heartbeat. How many horrible scenarios had he already gone through in his head? How many reasons had he come up with to say no? How would we — how would *I* — ever recover such a fucking misstep?

Marriage? Who was I kidding? I swore I'd never get married after seeing the shit show Camille put on over the course of my life. I even made sure kids were out of the picture by getting a vasectomy at the ripe old age of eighteen, cutting off the baby-mama drama at the pass.

Children were obviously not a problem with Leander. But marriage? Not once in all of our time together did he express *any* desire to get married. Ever. To anyone. Least of all to a man.

So why the *fuck* did I think this was a good idea, again? I would have been better off tattooing his name across my chest as a sign of my commitment. But nope. Instead, I asked him to take the biggest leap of faith there was with another human. I asked the man with a ridiculous amount of childhood trauma and abandonment issues to marry *me*, a man who lies, drinks, and murders his way through life and historically hightails it to the hills when the going gets tough.

Marry me. Oh, yeah. Great idea. Bennett, you fucking moron!

At last, Leander saw fit to put me out of my misery.

Nodding, he licked his lips, his reply barely audible. "Yes."

"Yes?" I wanted to make sure I heard him over the wild beating of my own heart and the waves smacking the bottom of the kayak.

"The answer is yes, Bennett. I'll marry you."

Relief, love, euphoria — whatever fucking emotion it was exploded inside my chest. We crashed together again, our tongues and bodies twisting together until I couldn't tell where I stopped and he began. All around us, the water glimmered and glowed. If I could have stopped time, I would have. I wanted this moment, this indescribable feeling of pure happiness, to last for an eternity.

THE HOTEL LOBBY was mostly empty when we strolled in, still damp and disheveled from our little illegal dip in the bay.

I, for one, was on Cloud Nine. From the impish smirks and sideways glances Leander kept giving me, I was pretty sure he was too. I'd spent most of the drive back daydreaming about our future together. It was full of endless possibilities and I couldn't wait to see what adventure was waiting for us after this one. Maybe I'd finally get to take him to Malta and show him the palazzo. Or we could go to Paris. Of course, we'd probably have to stop and see Allegra in Barcelona, even if that meant meeting her — ugh — "boyfriend."

My happiness popped like a soap bubble the minute I heard someone else say Leander's name. Not the cordial "Señor Welles" I was accustomed to hearing or even an accented "Leandro," but straight-up American "Leander Welles."

Stopping dead in my tracks, I looked around for the source. It was another male, so it was easy to skip past the few women I saw. My gaze zeroed in on the TV, catching a glimpse of dark curls on the screen before it cut back to the news anchor.

"The search for missing millionaire Leander Welles continues into its third week," the man said, shuffling through a stack of index cards.

Without even looking, I clawed the air until I grabbed ahold of Leander's arm and dragged him to my side.

"What's the matter?" he asked.

My jaw dropped when they flashed Leander's picture on the screen again. It wasn't a hallucination or some freak coincidence. They were talking about *my* Leander, the one who was most certainly *not* missing.

For once, the picture the media used was actually flattering, versus the ones the *Easton Sentinel* ran leading up to his murder trial. On TV, Leander was every bit the charming and dapper CEO you'd expect. The picture featured him smiling politely as he shook hands with the mayor, right after he'd donated a fuck ton of money to the school system.

Leander followed my gaze to the TV. "Oh, shit."

"His vehicle was located at a private airstrip outside Chicago," the news anchor continued, "along with his cell phone and other personal effects. As of yet, police have not advised if there have been any ransom demands. Investigators are still searching for anyone with information."

"You didn't tell anyone where we were?" he asked, both brows raised and his eyes wide.

I gave the same incredulous look right back at him, tinged with irritation. "Uh… no. I thought *you* told them?"

Groaning, he pinched the bridge of his nose, his eyes closing. "God, this is going to be a nightmare."

Before either of us could speak again, a familiar face popped up on the TV. A face I, frankly, never wanted to see again.

Her.

Lorelei.

"And now, a heartfelt plea to the public from Leander's girlfriend," the newscaster said in a voiceover as she changed positions with whatever detective spoke before her.

I inhaled sharply, seething in silence.

Leander opened his eyes and looked at the TV again, his head canting to the side.

Silently, we watched her approach the microphones with trepidation. Given the fact it was daylight on the TV and it was currently after midnight in the real world, it was obviously the replay of some sort of press conference outside the Cook County Sheriff's Office. Besides the gaggle of suits and uniforms, she appeared to be the only civilian on the "stage."

It struck me that no one from Easton was there, or at least not on camera. If anyone was going to be concerned for Leander's wellbeing, it would be one of the inner circle.

Since there was nary a peep about me, I had a feeling their involvement in this "case" was nil. Not to mention the fact they were smart enough to investigate his disappearance on their own and *not* turn to the police.

She drew herself upright, gripping the podium. The only sound was the rapid clicking of cameras. It took a century for her to work up the nerve to speak, since she cleared her throat and blinked away a handful of tears half a dozen times. "I'm here today to ask for the public's help. If you saw anything, heard anything, or know something, please call the Cook County Sheriff's Office. You can remain anonymous. All we care about is getting Leander back. And Leander? If you see this, please come home. I miss—"

A stream of nearly incomprehensible Italian flew out of my mouth at the same time I threw my hands in the air, spinning away from the TV before I broke something.

Marching straight into the hotel bar seemed like the safest bet for everyone in a twenty-foot radius of me. The last thing I needed was to hear *Her* pleading to some imaginary kidnappers and sobbing about how much Leander meant to her. Suddenly, everything that happened an hour ago seemed absolutely pointless. In one weepy statement, Lorelei managed to stab me in the heart with the heel of her fucking Louboutin and destroy everything I'd hoped for.

Before I even made it to the stool at the end of the bar, the bartender had a strawberry piña colada waiting.

"Needs more rum," I said, throwing a couple bills on the polished wood. It would have been rude to refuse the national drink entirely, but I wasn't in the mood for something refreshing — I was in the mood to erase a snivelly blonde from existence. Since I couldn't technically do anything to her from Puerto Rico, I could at least get blackout drunk. Pretty much the same thing.

"Claro." Manuel chuckled and nodded, retrieving a bottle

from behind the bar. He poured a glass of dark rum and tossed in an ice cube.

I chugged half of the piña colada and dumped the glass of rum into it, stirring them together with the straw.

By the time I reached the bottom of the glass, Manuel placed another tumbler of rum and ice in front of me, sans fruit. I slid him another bill for his foresight and slipped off the barstool, making my way to the bank of windows overlooking Old San Juan.

What the fuck was I expecting? Of course she would miss him. Who wouldn't? Not to mention, he up and disappeared on a whim. Leaving our cell phones behind for much-needed R&R, we boarded the private plane with only the clothes on our backs. The freedom was intoxicating. But freedom always came with a price. I knew that. So, why did I think this time to be any different?

Leander's girlfriend. For fuck's sake.

At some point, a full bottle of rum appeared on the window ledge next to me with a fresh glass of ice. God bless that man.

Topping off my tumbler again, I was halfway through it when fingertips grazed my back. A moment later, Leander materialized at my side, his face unreadable. From the quirk of his mouth, I got the feeling he wasn't happy. His gaze narrowed on my glass immediately.

I gave him a sidelong look, waiting to see if he had the nerve to say something about how much alcohol I'd managed to consume in such a short period. I also refused to be the first one to address the blonde elephant in the room. Purposely taking another sip, or gulp, I raised my brows at him.

His fingers curled around my glass, slowly pulling it out of my hand as if daring me to try and stop him. Lifting a dark brow, he sipped it before setting it down on the window ledge, just out of my reach. Guess he didn't see the half-empty bottle behind me.

"I arranged for our return flight," he said, his voice soft and controlled.

It shouldn't have been shocking, but it still felt like someone knocked the wind out of me. As soon as I saw that blonde bitch on TV I knew he'd regret his decision to up and leave... his company, the mainland — *Her*. It was a dark, niggling feeling that had been lurking from the moment he told me we were running away. Maybe that's why he was so weird the other day in the shower. Maybe he'd been missing her. Maybe he'd been trying to figure out a way to get home and now he had the perfect excuse.

I exhaled and braced both hands against the window ledge, hanging my head to try and alleviate the rising nausea. This was it. This was him rescinding his answer, this was him telling me he was going back to her. That it was all a mistake. If he told me we could still be friends, I was going to immediately walk to the Castillo and hurl myself from the wall.

"We're leaving Sunday," he continued, apparently unperturbed by the turn of events or the fact I was on the verge of falling to fucking pieces.

My head snapped up in time to see him shift his attention to the window and the skyline beyond. Perfectly poised, he radiated a steady calm. The departure date was three days away, which surprised me more than his first announcement. I straightened slowly, watching his reflection in the glass.

When he didn't elaborate, I cleared my throat softly, hoping I didn't sound as bitter as I felt. "Why the delay?"

He met my eyes in the dark glass, his chin lifted regally. "Because we have an appointment tomorrow at ten."

I furrowed my brows. My buzz kicked in two glasses ago,

but I knew I wasn't drunk enough to have missed the obvious strategy in delaying. "For what?"

A curl fell across his forehead when he tilted his head to the side, turning on the ball of his foot to face me. "Do you want to leave sooner?"

"I figured you would."

His mouth turned down for the briefest moment. "Are you angry, mon coeur?"

"No." I realized that sounded entirely too pouty, so I clarified. "I'm annoyed."

"Don't be. I called the police in Chicago and informed them I'm perfectly fine. It was all a misunderstanding. I offered to reimburse them for their time and effort, but they declined. Surprisingly. Still, we should probably make some sort of donation when we get back."

I squinted at him, trying to suss out what was going on in his brain. He called the *police*, not *Her*. Or so he said... Then again, despite everything that he was, he wasn't a liar, least of all to me. Maybe. I don't know. He did basically lie to my face for months instead of telling me he was in love with me, only to turn around and do the Mexican Hat Dance on my heart.

"Why are you so calm right now?" I asked, choosing to focus on the present and not the time we were apart. "This is a PR shit storm. You know that. You said it" — I had no concept of time, so I waved toward the lobby — "over there."

"Let's not talk about business right now." He gave me a predatory smile and threw a slow glance toward the stairs. "Shall we?"

"What are you up to?" As tempting as it was to gloss over this little hiccup, I still wasn't buying it. He was up to something. He had his scheming face on.

His fingertips skimmed down the length of my arm, toying with the edge of my fingers. Before I could fully capture his hand in mind, he slipped away with a smirk, clasping one wrist casually behind his back.

I pivoted in a half-circle, watching him.

When he got to the threshold of the bar, he paused and looked over his shoulder giving me a look — *that* look — the one that left me lightheaded and my heart stuttering. The one I'd spent years telling myself meant nothing, when it had meant everything.

I had all I could do to contain myself when what I really wanted to do was sprint across the way and kiss the hell out of him. He'd kill me, of course. Despite what he did in the alley, his tolerance for PDA was practically non-existent.

As if proving my point, he darted up the stairs the minute I got too close to him. I gave chase, narrowing the distance on him in the hallway outside our room.

He spun and grabbed the front of my shirt, yanking me against him. We fell against the door in a frenzy of kisses. I twisted my hands in his hair, biting his lower lip while he groped my pockets with both hands. It wasn't my dick he was after, because that was front and center and hard to miss. It was the keycard, I realized, after he pulled it out and stabbed blindly behind him for the slot.

I swiped it from him and jammed it in the card-reader. As soon as I got a green light, I cranked the handle and shoved him inside, kicking the door shut behind me.

If I only had three more days with him, alone, away from reality, then I was going to make the most of every fucking second.

4

BENNETT

The return trip to Chicago was entirely different than the original flight four weeks ago. Every hour we flew closer to home added another brick to the pile of obligations on our backs. After the whole cluster created by She Who Shall Not Be Named, we both knew we were returning to a firestorm. In typical Leander fashion, he seemed bound and determined to avoid *any* conversation involving *Her*.

But trapped on an airplane for five hours, he didn't have much choice when I brought it up.

"What are you going to do about *Her*?" I asked, spinning the onyx ring on my index finger.

He didn't even take his eyes off his book. "What do you mean?"

I gave him a minute to look up. When he didn't, I swatted the book downward, into his lap. "You *know* what I mean."

His jaw shifted as he looked away, staring daggers at the empty seat across from him.

"She was living with you when you disappeared," I continued. Even if he refused to look at me, I watched him like a hawk, waiting for any flicker of emotion to reveal itself so I could dissect it.

"Point?"

"Pretty sure the news said she was your girlfriend. Which means she's still *identifying* as your girlfriend to the police. So..."

"We never labeled it as anything," he said loftily, finally deigning to face me with an infuriatingly blank expression. "It means nothing."

"Neither did we," I shot back, mocking his tone. "By that same logic, you're implying *we're* nothing."

"Don't be ridiculous."

"Ridiculous? More like confused. Concerned. Arrabbiato..." The rest of my Italian adjectives trailed off when he huffed. I was pretty sure I heard his teeth snap together, too. Throwing out another language wasn't exactly fair, but I shouldn't have to spell out how angry I was in English if he couldn't pick up on the fucking context clues.

"Why don't you ask me whatever it is you want to know? Preferably in a language I actually understand."

"So you can shut down, like you always do?" I asked in French with a faux smile, just to be an asshole. The final word I spat out in English. "Pass."

He pinched the bridge of his nose, squeezing his eyes shut. "I don't know why we keep circling back to Lorelei."

I ignored his muttering and the fact he was probably getting a migraine. If his head was throbbing, maybe he'd be more inclined to answer whatever questions I threw at him, just so I'd stop talking. "What are you going to do if you go home and she's still there?"

"Politely ask her to leave?"

I glowered at him. For once I wasn't in the mood for sarcasm.

When I didn't audibly react, he opened his eyes and

looked at me. His brows drew together, exasperation written all over his face. "What would you like me to say?"

What I *wanted* him to say and what he *would* say were two entirely different things. In the hope of avoiding an actual fight, I took a slightly less hostile route. Slightly, being the operative word. "This trip was *your* idea, so excuse me for wondering what your plan is for doing damage control when we get home. Unless you regret the whole thing already, in which case we need to have an entirely *different* conversation."

He turned his glare on his book, like an irritated cat ignoring a human, and lowered his voice. "Do you regret going?"

"Do you regret asking?"

"Do *you* regret asking?"

Turning back to the window, I propped my elbow on the arm of the chair and bit my knuckle to keep from screaming. Way to take my question and use it against me, dick. Going on a month-long vacay without telling your girlfriend about it and a marriage proposal were *not* the same thing, yet he had the balls to try and compare them. I shouldn't have expected anything less from the King of Deflection.

I tried not to growl out the next question, but I knew I did a shit job the second the words rolled off my tongue. "You *are* going to break it off with her, aren't you?"

In the most maddeningly serene manner, he picked up his book again and turned the page. "No. I figured, given your feelings on adultery, you'd be *perfectly* willing to accommodate an open relationship at my bequest. I hear that is acceptable within the LGBTQ community, even expected in some circles. But you're the expert, so I defer to you, mon coeur." Each perfectly enunciated syllable dripped with sarcasm, even his French.

Before I strangled him with his tie, I exhaled slowly and

turned away from him. Forcing my gaze out the window once more, I tried to focus on the fluffy clouds streaming by, looking for shapes or animals like when I was a child.

It didn't work. All I saw was a leggy blonde dying in a multitude of ways.

Poison was too nice, too clean, for the amount of rage she called up from the depth of my soul. Likewise, an ice pick was too clean. Too smooth. It was going to be a knife. A serrated knife. Maybe that would clue her in on how fucking furious I was. But not too big... couldn't let her bleed out too quickly, because that wouldn't be very cathartic, either. She needed to suffer.

After another minute of silence, the book dropped again. "You won, Bennett. *You*. Not her. There's no reason to sulk."

"I'm not sulking," I replied through clenched teeth, refusing to reward him with a heated glare.

His hand slipped into mine. I still refused to look at him, even when he lifted our joined hands and pressed a kiss to the onyx ring he gave me last Christmas. "Do you have any idea how much you mean to me?"

I cut a quick glance in his direction, fully committing to the role of the silent martyr. I was too far gone to quit.

"She won't be there," Leander continued. "I'll make sure of it."

"How reassuring. Making sure the mistress is gone before the lord of the manor returns." I snatched my hand from his and stood, striding to the bar. It shouldn't have bothered me so much, but it did. Maybe because I was used to being the interloper in other peoples' relationships. Now, in a twist of fate, *I* was the cuckold. Neither the hypocrisy nor the sense of karmic justice were lost on me.

"Am I to be punished forever?" His voice may have been soft, but I detected the edge creeping in.

Dropping a couple of ice cubes into a tumbler, I blatantly

ignored him while I emptied the rest of the bourbon into the glass. I swatted the bottle into the garbage can and carried my drink to the couch — conveniently located at the other end of the plane.

I wasn't trying to be an asshole, but since he'd been fairly mum about his time with *Her* I was left to fill in the blanks on my own. With an imagination like mine, it wasn't a very pretty picture. Despite the events of the past month, uncertainty remained about where each of us stood in Leander's affections. He wasn't exactly helping his case by refusing to give any clear-cut answers.

Halfway through my bourbon, his fingers grazed my shoulder. He circled around in front of me slowly, a dark brow lifted.

I continued ignoring him in favor of my drink. He had his book. I had bourbon. We could spend the rest of the ride relaxing with our preferred method instead of devolving into a full-on fight.

Without warning, he kicked my feet apart. Smirking at my narrowed gaze, he stepped into the space he created and knelt between my legs. If he thought a blowjob would get him out of answering, he was dead wrong. I mean, he was welcome to try and persuade me, but my mind was fairly well made up.

"Talk to me," he purred, his hands gliding up my thighs.

"So you can keep trying to pacify me with vague answers?"

"So I can try to understand why you're so angry about something that means nothing. I'm here, with you."

I glared at the shifting ice cubes instead of him. "Do you love her?"

"No." He answered too quickly, which only made me more suspicious.

"Did you?" Lifting my gaze again, I watched each minute

tic on his face. His brow furrowing, his lips pursing, eyes narrowing. All in a split second before they were gone again, wrangled into submission by his incredible control.

He exhaled quietly, the angles of his face softening. "I tried."

I asked the question, but like a rookie lawyer I wasn't prepared for the answer. My chest seized, a figurative ice pick right through the heart. I tried to override the sensation by burning it out with another gulp of bourbon.

"I said I tried," he repeated, like I didn't hear him as clear as day the first time around. "But I couldn't."

My molars ground together so hard I was sure they were about to crack. I knew I had no right to be mad at him for doing what he had to do. He was so invested in his plan for revenge, he probably believed his own lies. If anything, it made him all the more convincing.

Besides, I practically drove him to her. I wasn't there and she was, as he'd oh-so-helpfully reminded me. But fuck if I was going to admit to any of that.

His hands slid up to my hips as he leaned forward, his eyes locked on mine. "I never stopped loving you."

"And yet, you seemed quite content to go on playing house with the little missus while pretending I ceased to exist." I lifted the tumbler for another sip. He intercepted it, plucking it out of my hand.

"You were always with me," he murmured, not baited by my rampant insecurity. "Always."

Setting the glass to the side, he stood. Wedging one knee between my thighs and forcing them apart, he balanced carefully on the edge of the seat. Leaning down, he cradled my face between his hands and kissed me softly, slowly.

My resistance was half-hearted at best. As much as I wanted to be mad at him, I was furious at myself. I'd nearly lost him once and now here I was purposely picking fights instead of accepting what he was saying.

I meant to return his kiss gently, tenderly. And I did, for a minute. Then, somehow, I ended up grabbing him around the waist and slamming him backward onto the couch, intent on devouring every part of him.

Clawing at his throat desperately, I yanked his tie loose and began fighting the buttons on his shirt. I loved the fact that nine times out of ten he was in a suit, but not when it took forever to get him naked.

Since I hadn't gone through the trouble of dressing up, he peeled off my button-up and jeans before I even got his goddamn cufflinks undone.

"I can't lose you again," I breathed, finally ripping his shirt off and throwing it over my shoulder. My hands tangled in his dark curls, crushing my mouth against his.

His tongue caressed mine in earnest, distracting me from the fact he was sliding up into a sitting position. Before I knew it, he had enough leverage to pounce. I was the one on my back before I even knew what hit me.

"I'm yours," Leander whispered against my lips. "I've always been, and always will be, yours."

As soon as we made it to my Chicago apartment, Leander and I sat on opposite ends of the couch, each with a cell phone in hand. Exchanging a glance and resigned sighs, it was time to get the verbal lashings done and over with.

"Are you telling them?" I asked.

He studied me for a minute, blinking solemnly. I couldn't tell which way he was leaning. We never exactly discussed it beforehand, so who knew what his answer would be. "Do *you* want to?"

"I mean..." I licked my lips, giving him a small shrug. "They're going to find out eventually."

"I thought, perhaps, we would do it in person?" Both brows quirked up, like he was worried it was the wrong answer.

"No, that's a good idea." Since he wasn't close by, I flashed him a reassuring smile.

Nodding, he turned his attention to his phone, starting with Elijah. It was a safe place to begin, since Elijah was unequivocally the most understanding of the bunch. There was minimal explanation on Leander's part, and once Elijah established Leander was "ok" they moved on to business as usual.

The rest of his phone calls were similar, except for Olivia who threw in an ass-chewing before she filled him in on whatever she had to say. I *also* got an ass-chewing from her, through the speaker on his phone. No business, just a solid fifteen minutes of being told what a self-centered asshole I was. Noted, Kitten. Duly noted.

Since his last known location was Chicago, meeting me, they weren't too surprised when we both became suddenly unreachable. And given everything Leander endured with the murder trial and imprisonment for five months, they'd assumed correctly he was simply off regrouping.

According to Elijah, they tried to get The Blonde One to back off the whole "missing person" bit, but *she* had other ideas. Cole even followed her to Chicago to try and talk some sense into her, but she wouldn't listen and went sobbing to the police immediately thereafter. Fucking drama queen.

As for my phone calls, I started with my sister. Del was happy with a text, but I knew she would demand a full explanation, just like Gavin and Olivia.

"Bennett?" Damn. Allegra didn't even say "Hello." Instead,

she launched into a combination of Italian and Spanish so fast I could hardly keep up until she ended her rant with *"I am so mad at you!"* in Italian.

"Didn't you get my email?" I asked with a wince.

"The one where you said you'd be out of town for a while? Yeah. Thanks. That was hugely comforting."

I bit my lip, cringing again. Allegra wasn't sarcastic. She didn't sling barbs like the rest of our fucked-up family.

"I didn't have my phone. It was the best I could do from the hotel."

"And how was I supposed to know that was actually you? What if that was someone pretending to be you? What if you were really in the hospital again? Or worse?!"

Ah, fuck. Didn't even think about that. "Allegra," I sighed, searching for the right words.

"No! You don't get to talk your way out of this! I am mad at you, Bennett. Do you hear me?"

"Yes, Mother."

"Don't start! You're lucky I didn't tell her. Again, I might add! I hate keeping secrets."

"It's not a secret. She just doesn't need to know."

"She's still your mother."

Insert eye roll here. At least I managed to keep my sigh to myself. *"How can I make it up to you?"*

"Come to Barcelona."

Groaning, I smashed the heel of my hand into my eye. She didn't hesitate at all before throwing out that particular demand, which meant it had clearly been brewing in the back of her head for a while. I knew going to Venice for Christmas was a bad idea. Now I had no excuse *not* to go to Barcelona and meet her stupid boyfriend. *"I just got home. And now you want me to fly across the Atlantic?"*

"Not now, you jerk. For my birthday." I opened my mouth to answer, but she cut me off abruptly. *"And don't even think*

about coming up with some excuse why you can't! You have plenty of time to make whatever arrangements you need to make."

"Fine. I'll make sure Leander doesn't have anything important scheduled that week."

"Leander?" In the blink of an eye, the storm clouds parted and I could feel her practically beaming from across the pond. *"You're talking again? Since when?"*

Automatically, my gaze slid down the couch, taking in his profile. He had a half-smile on his face, listening intently to whoever was on the other line. As if he knew the moment I looked at him, he turned toward me, his smile widening. God, he was breathtaking.

"Yeah," I answered distractedly.

"Good. Bring him with you if that means you'll actually come."

"You mean bring him with so you'l have an ally for whatever lecture you have planned?"

"No, I mean bring him with so you don't kill Sergio."

"How do you know he won't help me?"

"Very funny."

I wasn't exactly kidding, but I decided to drop it. She was the one person in the world who absolutely did *not* need to know about my particular way of handling problems. *"I have to go. I'll email you the reservations when I have them."*

"You better."

Rolling my eyes, I smiled nonetheless as I hung up. She was getting feisty the older she got. It made me so proud.

Gavin was next on the list of phone calls. Unlike Allegra, he didn't let the whole thing go. Instead, he proceeded to read me the Riot Act for the next *hour*. An hour of my life I would literally never get back.

As the keeper of my finances, he was smart enough to track my credit card purchases, which meant he a) knew I wasn't dead and b) had a month to stew about the fact I didn't inform him of my impromptu vacation, as if it was on some secret agenda of mine. Given the fact he managed my personal *and* professional calendars, I don't know where he got the idea I'd plan anything on my own. That was literally part of his job.

"I had to clear our your *entire* schedule," Gavin ranted. "Do you know how many fucking people I had to reschedule? I pushed everyone out until September because I didn't know when the hell you were coming home!"

My head hit the back of the couch and I closed my eyes, rubbing away the budding headache with my thumb and forefinger. "Speaking of September, can you book two flights to Barcelona for Allegra's birthday?"

I doubted he even heard me, since he didn't skip a beat. "The FBI was here I don't know how many times looking for you! And what was I supposed to tell them? That you're off sunning yourself on a beach somewhere when they expected your ass in court? The federal prosecutor is *pissed*, Bennett! He had to postpone the whole Marchese case. Not to mention the fact *I* had to be the one to tell Olivia what was going on since Leander didn't bother telling *anyone* what you two were doing either. What the hell were you doing in Puerto Rico for a month, anyway?!"

"Uh, vacation?"

"Who the fuck leaves their cell phones behind when they go on vacation?"

"Someone who doesn't want to be bothered by shit like this?"

"Oh, so now I'm *bothering* you, your majesty? Keeping your accounts paid and the lights turned on is suddenly a *bother* to you? Well, then, perhaps you should find yourself another assistant — one who doesn't *bother* you so much!"

"Would an apology suffice?" I asked, gingerly putting the phone closer to my ear again.

"An apology?! You think an apology is going to make up

for the fact I had Sergei fucking Sidorov send his thugs to *my* apartment at two in the morning to drag me to one of his clubs? I thought I was going to *die*, Bennett! You know how Russians feel about gay people!"

I pulled the phone away again with a grimace.

Leander appeared behind me, setting a cup of coffee on the side table and pressing a kiss to my temple at the same time.

I turned toward him quickly, trying to catch another kiss, but he stepped away with a smirk. The bastard made it through four people and had the time to make coffee in the time it was taking me to text one and call two.

"I don't get paid enough to deal with this bullshit!" Gavin huffed. "*I* need an assistant just to help me keep track of all your escapades. Between Bancroft's and your Chicago clients, plus everything back at the Welles Corporation, I don't know if you're coming or going. Bennett? Are you even listening to me?"

"No," I replied, tracking Leander as he moved across the open space. He paused at the edge of the hallway and threw a look over his shoulder. *That* look, sending a bolt of electricity straight to my dick.

"Are you kid—"

I hung up on Gavin and threw the phone to the side, hurrying after Leander.

5

BENNETT

If Gavin was pissed about my disappearance, the FBI and the federal prosecutor were even more pissed.

We were only back in Chicago for a day when two agents arrived at my apartment to "escort me" to the downtown building. Leander wisely stayed behind to work remotely and catch up on administrative duties at the Welles Corporation while I went to slay the mafia dragon.

I thought I'd at least get in some verbal sparring with my FBI besties, Diefendorf and Denning, while I was there. Sadly, they were nowhere to be found. I admit, I was actually a little disappointed. The rookies they sent to babysit me were nowhere near as fun to toy with.

Plopped in a boring, gray interview room, I recounted all of the dirt on Giovanni Marchese *again*, clarifying some aspect of the organization that apparently wasn't clear enough from the flow-charts or piles of sticky notes.

After a lengthy lecture about the seriousness of this case from a pencil-neck lawyer in an unflattering brown suit, I was dismissed with a new court date and a remonstration I'd better be there. The "or else" part of the threat hung awkwardly in the air. I mean, what were they going to do? I already had a signed guarantee that Leander and his company were off limits. And if they thought *I* was stupid enough to let them pin everything on me, they clearly didn't know who they were dealing with.

"So you'll be there?" the lawyer repeated, staring at me over the top of his wire-frame glasses.

"I'll try," I said, saluting him with his business card.

"No, you *will*, Mr. Reeve."

"Yes, I *will* try. Scout's honor." I held up two fingers in a peace sign, quickly reversing it into a V with a smirk as the elevator doors closed. Even if he didn't recognize the Brits' version of "Fuck you," I'm sure he got the gist of it. Dickhead.

As I descended to the main floor, I sent Leander a text, happily informing him I was on my way home. Finally. When they picked me up, the agents said it was a "briefing." But I forgot — everything on Federal time took ten times as long as the regular world, so of course I was there all day.

When I got to the sidewalk, I flicked the prosecutor's business card into the planter with the rest of the crumpled cigarette butts and bottle tops.

"Mr. Reeve," a deep, rumbly voice said behind me.

Busted.

"It's biodegradable," I sighed as I turned, expecting to find another sour-puss agent yelling at me for ruining our planet, despite the millions of trees the Feds killed every year with their mountains of redundant paperwork.

Except, it wasn't an agent. It was a pair of oversized, tattooed Russians.

"Come with us," the darker of the two said, gesturing to the Escalade behind his partner. On cue, the second man opened the door.

"You don't look like my Uber driver," I said, taking a cautious step backward.

"Get in," the other one barked.

"Umm, no... Mommy said I'm not supposed to get in the car with strangers. If you need help looking for your puppy, you should ask another adult."

"Bennett. Get in." It was a third male, only this time the voice was coming from inside the car.

Taking a cautious step forward, I ducked my head and looked at the occupant in the backseat. It was Mikhail — aka: Misha — the beautiful, blue-eyed killing machine Sergei sent on special missions. That either meant I was precious cargo or in for a really shitty night.

"Is this a good meeting, or a bad meeting?" I asked, stupidly hopeful Misha would have the answer.

Misha didn't say anything, he just glanced pointedly at the seat.

"Good talk." I slid in next to him and slipped my phone out again. So much for making it home on time for dinner.

I'd no more than pulled up the text message to Leander when Misha leaned over, snatching the phone out of my hand.

"Hey! What the fuck?" I swiped for it, but he was faster, tucking it in his inner jacket pocket. His large hand caught my wrist before I could yank it away. In the process, I inadvertently came way too close to his face. I held my breath as we stared at each other. Whatever thoughts were going through his head were carefully concealed behind a stony expression.

Finally, he pushed my hand toward me, releasing it with a surprising gentleness. "You'll get it back." He held my gaze while he spoke, giving a nearly imperceptible nod. As he pulled his hand away, he stroked the length of my fingers.

I masked my shiver with a fleeting smile and leaned back

into my seat as far as I could go. Facing the window, I closed my eyes, swearing silently in my head. Instead of being flattered Misha obviously recalled our night together or worrying about how furious Leander would be if he found out (even if it *was* two years ago), I kicked my lawyer-brain into gear and tried to prepare for the absolute worst-case scenario.

The SUV hurtled through the city in relative silence until it rolled to a stop in front of Delirium, a place I was intimately familiar with. Aside from being Sergei Sidorov's main club, it was one of the best spots to score whatever you were in the mood for, be it drugs, alcohol, or kinks.

Misha hopped out first and circled around the car while one of his henchmen opened my door and gestured me out impatiently.

"Jesus. The Feds move like molasses and you move like your ass is on fire. Something I should know about, fellas?" I glanced at the trio of Russians as we made our way inside.

"Nyet," was the only grunted reply I got and I wasn't even sure who said it.

Not surprisingly, Delirium was empty, except for the staff getting ready to open. It was too early for someone to have OD'ed. Maybe it was another alderman looking for a handout. Or something to do with the Italians and Marchese's upcoming case.

Marching up the curved staircase, we made our way past all of the private rooms to Sergei's personal VIP area — *not* the kitchen where people were tortured and dismembered. So, things were looking up.

Sergei was already there, deep in conversation with a pair of tight blonde beauties. The one in red was stroking the tuft of gray chest hair poking out of his shirt, while the one in blue rubbed his thigh... and then some. Neither of them stopped when we walked in.

"Bennett," Sergei acknowledged with a smile. Smiling didn't guarantee jack shit, so I tempered my enthusiasm.

"Sergei," I replied with a nod. "It's been a while."

"Sit."

I knew better than to argue, so like a good little doggie, I took a seat on the couch across from him. "I've been meaning to call, but we just got back and I've been swamped playing catch up."

"Are you thirsty?"

Before I could answer, he snapped his fingers. Red-dress popped up and sashayed to the bar.

I held up an apologetic hand, trying to wave him off. "I'm fine. Really. I've got dinner plans" — I flicked open my pocket watch and cringed — "well, *now*. But what's up?"

The girl returned with a chilled bottle of vodka and a glass. Instead of depositing them on the table next to me and leaving, she draped herself across my lap, grinding against me in the process.

"Ok then. One drink it is." I took the glass from her and planted my other hand firmly on the arm of the couch. She proceeded to use that arm as a pillow, stroking my jaw and throat with a featherlight touch.

Sergei waved his hand in a little circle, prompting me to drink.

I lifted the glass toward him and tossed back the vodka with a wince. I'd been on a rum kick for so long I forgot how potent grain alcohol could be.

Sergei nodded his approval and motioned to the girl. She promptly refilled my glass.

Like riding a bike, Reeve. A rusty bike with a wobbly tire, but a bike nonetheless.

I downed the next *nine* shots without complaint. It wasn't until I was ready to puke that I risked Stalin's wrath by saying "No." The impossible was suddenly possible — I actually reached my alcohol limit for the first time since I was twenty and hurled a gallon of Tequila Sunrise into a fish tank on Spring Break.

"Look," I said, retching behind my fist and turning to the side. Once I was sure the vomit was safely contained in my GI tract, I lowered my hand. "I know what you're doing. I'll tell you whatever you want. Just drop the pretense and ask."

The blonde's hand slipped inside my mostly-open shirt. Her nails raked over my chest and back up to my throat, as if it would somehow distract me from the fact I could breathe fire if I wanted to.

"What are you talking about?" Sergei laughed, spreading his hands innocently. "We're celebrating."

I tried to smile, but I knew it was more of a grimace. "What, exactly, are we celebrating?" We passed celebration status five shots ago. Plus *he* wasn't drinking.

"That fucking dago Marchese is no longer problem. Da?" Sergei's smile widened, his perfect white teeth gleaming behind his salt-and-pepper beard.

"Yeah, I've been meaning to send a gift basket for all that work you guys did. Did you want bath salts or wine of the month? Jams and jellies?"

He leaned forward, gesturing to himself and then to me as he spoke. "Friends help friends. It's America, no?"

"Mhmm." I jerked my head away from the girl in my lap. She'd moved from my chest to toying with my ear. Like a goddamn gnat at a barbecue. "I assume you had no problems claiming your new turf?"

Sergei laughed again, either at my irritation or the question. It was hard to tell. Once upon a time, I watched him laugh, one of those deep belly laughs, two seconds before he shot his cousin between the eyes. "Nyet. Business is good."

"Wonderful." So, at least I wasn't going to die today.

The blonde in my lap ran her hand through my hair

and sat up, nuzzling along my jaw. Trying to figure out a polite way to get her off of me, I kept turning away every time her lips came anywhere near mine. She settled for my throat, kissing and sucking different spots like a leech. Her cotton-candy perfume was particularly nauseating in my current state, not to mention I had no interest in providing whatever she was after. Not anymore.

"I want to keep it good. Keep it safe." Sergei's eyes narrowed, like a Siberian snowstorm on the horizon. He leaned forward, bracing his elbows on his knees. "You were with FBI a long time."

"I was gone for a while. Out of town, I mean. There was a lot to catch up on."

His gray brows shot up, sending a chill down my spine.

"Calm down. Nothing about you," I said with a chuckle, hoping it made me sound at ease, despite the flip-flopping in my stomach. "Implicating you would implicate my partner and I'm not about to see him go back to jail."

Sergei nodded and leaned back, apparently satisfied. "I heard he was free. I was hoping to meet with him but his schedule is busier than yours, it seems. Both of you have been out of touch for weeks. Coincidence, no?" His icy gaze was back, piercing me to the couch.

"We had, uh, business. A lot to catch up on since he got out. You know?"

"Mhmm. A lot to catch up with your *partner*."

I didn't like the way he emphasized partner. My gaze snapped toward Misha. He stood in the back of the room, surveying everything. His expression yielded zero hints as to where his boss was headed with this conversation. But he said I'd get my phone back, which wouldn't matter if I was a corpse. It wasn't much to go on in terms of reassurances, but it was all I had.

Sergei continued, gesturing widely. "A lot to catch up with the FBI. A lot to catch up with everyone, it seems."

"Land the plane, comrade." I tossed my head, shaking hair out of my eyes and dislodging the suckerfish from my throat. When in doubt, bravado was the best option.

"No one asks questions about us? No more deals for you and your partner at my expense?"

"Nyet." I gave him a reassuring smile. "Just Marchese."

"Good."

"Anything else?"

He shook his head with another smile, squeezing Bluedress's thigh. "Just here to have good time. That's all. Relax. Finish your drink."

As if it was some sort of cue, the blonde on my lap fished a packet of pills out of her bra. She placed a tiny white circle on the edge of her tongue and curled it in a second before her lips were on me. Wasting no time invading my mouth, she transferred the drug from her tongue to mine with one swipe.

Between the heat and moisture, the pill was already on its way to dissolving, which meant I couldn't even try to squirrel it away to spit out later. Not that I had the chance with the girl's tongue still in my mouth.

The moment I felt her ease up on the intensity, I pulled back as fast as I could, while still being slow enough to not be offensive. I'm sure it hadn't escaped Sergei's attention I wasn't interested in his "gift." Hopefully I could play it off as being jet lagged.

She smiled and licked her lips, removing what remained of her lip gloss and any pill residue.

"If you'll excuse me a moment." I shifted her off my lap and stood, immediately regretting my attempt to flee.

The moment I was vertical, the world spun. It was too

soon to be the pill, whatever the hell it was, so it had to be the vodka.

A bike, Reeve. Just like that time I took my finals completely wasted. I passed back then, I could certainly hold my own now. It just required complete concentration.

Inhaling a fortifying breath, I focused on the door at the far end of the room and started toward it with slow, purposeful strides. Some water and some air. That's all I needed. I'd be fine. I was a fucking professional.

I all but crashed through the door to the private bathroom. Yanking off my suit jacket, I snarled at it when it wouldn't come off my arm. Flapping it as hard as I could, I finally freed it from the silver cuff on my wrist and threw it at the sink.

Collapsing against the black marble basin, I hung my head, trying my damndest not to puke.

Water. I needed water.

Turning on the faucet, I cranked the right side and waited until I was sure it was as cold as it was going to get. By the time I was done splashing frigid water on my face, the top part of my shirt was soaked, along with the hair that kept getting in the way.

Well, that was pointless. Still felt like heaving my guts out and now I was cold and wet on top of it.

Staggering toward the window, I shoved it open and leaned against the sill, closing my eyes and inhaling the lovely city air. It smelled like fried food and exhaust, which made me both hungry and nauseated.

Leander was going to be so fucking pissed. I had *no* idea what time it was. The numbers on my pocket watch were a blur. Nope. Pretty sure the tiny hands stopped moving altogether. Shaking it and smacking it against my palm didn't help, so I stuffed it back in my vest pocket. We hadn't even been home a week and I was already back to my old ways. Not by choice, but I was going to get an earful nevertheless.

Unless I made it home. Now.

Popping the screen out of the window, I leaned forward and watched it fall to the concrete below, like it was in slow motion. Hanging onto either side of the window frame, I leaned out even further, glancing up and down the alley. I was only a couple floors up. I could totally jump. I'd survive. I'd probably break my leg, but I'd be alive and maybe Leander would be merciful when he saw how desperate I'd been. Unless he broke my other leg. Some days I wouldn't put it past him. He really was a violent prick when he wanted to be.

The door opened behind me, immediately halting any ideas I had about flinging myself from the window.

I didn't bother leaving my perch. I probably couldn't have even if I wanted to. My hands somehow attached themselves to the window frame like it was a life preserver.

"I'll be out in a second," I mumbled.

"Take your time."

The sound of Misha's voice made me jump and whirl around.

We stared at each other across the tiled space, with only my pounding heart to fill the silence. The last time we were alone in a room together, I got a furtive blowjob behind the bar before we went back to his apartment for some privacy. Even if I was half in the bag — or completely in the bag, it was hard to tell with each minute that passed — I knew my dick was officially off limits this time around.

"What's up?" I squeaked out the question, still hanging onto the window for some support.

He shrugged, walking forward slowly. "Been a long time."

"I mean…" I sputtered, gesturing helplessly. What was I supposed to say to that?

I didn't have time to ponder the answer. Letting go of the sill was a bad idea. I tipped backward, cracking the back of my head against the frosted glass. "Fuck!"

Blond brows furrowed, Misha darted forward and grabbed my shoulders. He pulled me upright again, his big hands drifting downward to hold on to my biceps. "Are you ok?"

"Yeah." I cleared my throat, trying to sound more sober than I was. "Why?"

"You don't look so good." He was directly in front of me now, so close I could smell his body wash. It smelled like the ocean. If I concentrated hard enough, I could hear waves crashing.

No, it was me crashing. Right into Misha's broad chest. My legs were heavy, like sandbags instead of limbs. They refused to obey my brain's command, whether I told them to stand, or walk, or anything.

"What's happening?" I asked, clinging to the front of his shirt. Thank God he was so strong. If he hadn't secured his arms around me, I would have face-planted on the floor by now.

"It's probably the pill."

"What? What pill? I'm not allowed to do pills anymore. I said no more pills. He hates pills. I promised! What pill, Misha?!"

"Special K," Misha replied over the top of my muttering.

Goddamn that girl. "What happened to molly?" It had been years since I had molly, but at least I knew what to expect. I knew how long the rush lasted. This? This was new territory.

"Sergei moved into a new market." Bravely taking one of his hands from my waist, Misha peeled back one of my eyelids. I blinked rapidly and yanked my face away from his hand. He promptly grabbed my chin and turned my face this way and that, his sky-blue eyes narrowed. “Stick out your tongue.”

I shook my head, or at least as much as I could with my chin still under his control. I wasn’t a damn horse up for auction. If his next move was to try and check my teeth, I had no qualms in biting him. Although from what I recalled, he liked it rough.

He glowered at me, his eyes even icier. “Can you breathe?”

“Am I *not* breathing?” I thought I was. My chest rose and fell in quick succession, but maybe I wasn’t actually getting any air. Maybe this entire conversation was a figment of my dying imagination. But if it was, where was Leander? As hot as Misha was, I didn’t want to die with *him* on my mind. I wanted my brooding little otter, driving me insane with his sexy smirk while he recited Poe and gave me smoldering looks.

“Come.” Misha draped one of my arms over his shoulder, holding on to my waist tightly as he basically dragged me to the door.

“No, I need to sit down. Here. Right here.” I reached for my jacket as we passed, nearly falling over in the process. “Son of a…” The world around me spun. All of the black marble suddenly looked like a galaxy. No, a sinkhole, where the cracks and fissures were going to swallow me whole.

“You can sit out there, where I can watch you.”

“I don’t want you to watch me. I don’t want to be here. I want to leave.”

“You can’t leave.”

“I *need* to leave. Right now.”

“Nyet. Sergei has more business.”

“Fuck his business!”

“Shh. Don’t say that.”

With my free hand, I gestured as emphatically as I could

while I switched to Italian. At least, in my brain it was Italian. I couldn't really be sure what was actually coming out of my mouth, or if they were even individual words anymore.

"Fuck him and fuck his business! He drugged me, Misha. I could have a heart condition. I could die! Am I going to die? I'm going to die. You just implied I was dying. Fucking backstabbing Russians! I can't breathe. Why can't I breathe? Leander is going to kill me. Oh my God... Leander. Where is my otter? You have to go find him! Tell him I didn't mean to! Oh my God. I can't breathe anymore."

Misha ignored me and my babbling, so I must have picked the right language. Or, it was completely unintelligible. Either way, he hauled me back to my seat out front with only the barest assistance from my uncooperative legs.

Sergei said something in Russian, chuckling, to which Misha replied with a shrug and two grunts that I think were supposed to be words.

The blonde in the red dress was still there. I smelled her before she even came into view. Thankfully, she'd turned her attention to another guest and was in the midst of stroking the man's porcelain skin. A man dressed in an all-black suit wearing a severe look on his perfectly chiseled face.

"Perfect timing. Look who joined us," Sergei said happily, gesturing to the most beautiful man I'd ever seen.

I gasped out loud, staring at the new addition with wide eyes. *"Oh my God..."*

Leander snatched the girl's hand and flung it away from his face before he stood, his eyes locked on me, burning with the heat of a thousand suns. "Bennett."

"Is it really you? How? What are you doing here, my love? You shouldn't be here. Fuck me twice over with this goddamn day. Did he kidnap you too? Are you ok? Are you hurt at all?"

"Want to try that again in English?" Leander's question was practically a snarl. Even if it was technically a question, I knew better than to answer. I also knew murderous rage when I saw it. He was so pissed, tendrils of red and black danced around him, like hellfire.

The world tilted on its axis. I crumbled under Leander's dark gaze, clinging to Misha again. "I'm going to be sick. I need to sit down. Now."

Misha steered me toward the couch and gave a little push, sending me off across the ocean of carpet that took me all of three steps to traverse. I crashed into the corner, hanging on to the black leather with both hands.

Leander snapped his fingers at the blonde and jerked his thumb over his shoulder. She scurried away without a peep. As soon as the path was clear, he sat next to me.

The couch cushion dipped under his weight. I teetered to the right, slamming into him. He grabbed me by the back of my neck, forcing my head backward so he could look at me.

"You're so pretty." I breathed the words in pure awe, touching his face gently.

"What are you on?" His gaze bored straight into mine, his beautiful mouth pressed into a hard line.

"The couch," I replied with the utmost seriousness. Boom. If these were the types of questions he had, I was golden. What the hell was I worried for?

Leander's displeasure turned toward Sergei while he maintained a hold on my neck. "What did he take?"

I scooted closer to Leander, nuzzling his shoulder and inhaling the scent of his cologne. He smelled so fucking good. Like sex in the middle of some ancient forest, while it poured rain and poisonous flowers bloomed. At night. Naturally.

His fingers tightened on the back of my neck, but he didn't shove me away. The subtle, controlling gesture only stoked the wild fantasy playing out in my head. If I could find a forest like that, I would fuck the shit out of him there.

It was my new travel goal in life — track down the magical forest and have a sex marathon unlike anything humanly possible.

"He'll be fine," Sergei said with a chuckle. "Let's get down to business."

Leander caught my hand as it crept across his thigh. He squeezed it, hard, all while keeping his gaze fixed on Sergei. "I'd rather wait until my lawyer is in his right frame of mind."

Sergei scoffed. "You came all this way. At least have a drink."

"I'm afraid I'm not feeling very social at the moment. And it looks like Mr. Reeve has had his fill for the evening. I wouldn't want either of us to overstay our welcome. I'll see him home." Leander stood again, leaving zero room for argument. His hand dropped from my neck and hooked around my waist. He hauled me to my feet roughly, his fingers digging into my hip.

"Do you need help?" Misha asked, stepping forward.

Leander's voice was barely above a growl, matching the lethal look etched on his face. "No, thank you."

My head swiveled toward Leander, brows raised. A shiver ran along my spine despite the sweat rolling down the small of my back.

Misha knew a hint when he heard one, stepping back with a nod.

"Welcome home, gentlemen," Sergei said, raising his glass to us as we made our way to the door. "We'll talk soon."

The club was in full swing outside of Sergei's private room. Strobe lights and neon colors assaulted me as soon as we stepped foot in the hallway. My head thumped, beyond the usual amount of pain I'd lived with ever since my little brain bleed a few months back. Speaking of which, it felt like a blood vessel was one techno beat away from exploding.

I yanked away from Leander as soon as we approached

the main door. Bursting through it, I clawed open the rest of the buttons on my shirt, peeling the damp fabric away from my skin. I couldn't count my heartbeats if I tried. Despite a cool summer night, Chicago felt like it was at the center of the goddamn equator.

"Get in the car," Leander snapped, yanking open the passenger door on a waiting sedan.

I knew it. He was going to murder me right then and there. If I got in that car, it would be the last time anyone saw me alive. I wasn't supposed to die like this. I was supposed to die in the magical forest, fucked to death, drained of my life force and bodily fluids. Not beaten to death with a crow bar by the most beautiful murderer to ever walk the Earth. Besides me, that is.

"*Now*, Bennett!"

As I turned to go, resolved to my fate, Misha appeared, tugging on my arm gently. "Bennett?"

I glanced between the two men, frozen in place. On one side, there was a panther, all-black and graceful lines. Silent and deadly. On the other, a bear, a force of nature, capable of crushing anyone or anything. Currently, their attention was on me. If they turned it to one another, who knew how bloody it would get.

Misha fished my cell phone out of his pocket and held it out to me, giving another small nod. An apology? A farewell? Good luck? I had no idea. Russians were so hard to read.

"Dasvidaniya," he murmured. A formal goodbye, then. I was dead. I was fucking dead and Misha knew it.

Before I could dredge up any parting words, a hand seized the back of my neck in a vice grip and shoved me into the car.

Leander climbed in after me, slamming the door.

Curling up in the corner of my seat, I stared at him, afraid if I blinked it would be the last thing I ever did.

He paid me no attention. His gaze was fixed forward, as rigid as an onyx statute, his hands resting in his lap.

"Are you going to kill me?" I whispered.

His head angled toward me slowly, but his glance was fleeting. A muscle in his cheek twitched, right beneath one furious green eye. "What do you think?"

"I think you're going to kill me."

Leander's gaze shifted out the window. He was silent the rest of the ride. Only by watching the cords in his throat tighten every so often did I know he, himself, was still alive.

The city lights flashed by at warp speed. Even though I squeezed my eyes shut, I could still see it behind my eyelids. The light, then the dark. Light and dark. Lightanddark. Like another strobe, flashing away.

As soon as the car rocked to a stop, I threw the door open and launched myself onto the sidewalk, gasping for fresh air. A whiff of cotton candy sent spasms through my stomach and my hand flew to my mouth. I could only contain the vomit for two steps before I collapsed and threw up in the giant concrete planter.

Fucking Sergei.

As soon as I crawled out of this goddamn K-hole, I was going to kill him. Or at least send him a strongly worded email. No, no. A carrier pigeon. That was safer. Maybe not for the pigeon. But who gives a fuck about pigeons?

Until then, I just had to survive the night.

6

BENNETT

I couldn't move. My body was paralyzed from the neck down. Fucking Christ. I'd been here before, in a Venetian hospital to be exact. The same weighted feeling. Being aware of my surroundings but unable to interact or communicate in any way. The doctors didn't expect the sedation to wear off so fast, so I laid there, in utter terror, for an eternity until someone realized I was conscious.

Just remembering it made my heart rate skyrocket. My breathing came in short pants, exacerbating the dryness in my mouth. Squeezing my eyes shut, I screamed internally at my central nervous system.

My fingers responded, curling around something warm and kind of squishy. No, hard. So I wasn't completely paralyzed.

Leander's voice was in my ear, his breath warm against my neck. "How are you feeling?"

Glancing down at the same time he propped himself up, I saw our fingers were laced together. The fear dissipated in an instant, chased away by his mere presence. My body moved under its own command, hurling itself toward him while my arms wrapped around his neck.

"I thought I was dead. Or paralyzed."

He stroked my hair, holding me tightly with the other arm. "You pretty much were."

"What?" I jerked back, blinking.

A dark brow lifted. "You don't remember last night?"

I shook my head.

He ran his tongue over his teeth, scooting backward so he was leaning against the headboard. "You were at Delirium."

Well, shit. That was never a good start to any conversation. Sergei's flagship club was the location of many, *many* of my less than moral escapades — not to mention the illegal ones. From the look on Leander's face, I was in for one of two things: a) getting yelled at or b) getting the silent treatment. Sometimes I didn't know which was worse.

"What were you doing there?" Leander asked, both brows raising slightly. His tone was surprisingly calm, given the irritation in his eyes.

"I... don't remember." I watched him carefully, hoping for a clue. "What were *you* doing there?"

"Looking for you." As I tried piecing the night together in confounded silence, he continued. "You texted that you left the FBI's office and were on your way home. And then you failed to return."

I nodded, remembering that bit clearly. "Yes, I did. I was. Literally, walking out the door."

"Do you remember what happened after that?" Leander asked softly, like an attorney trying to lead a witness without the rest of the court catching on.

Raking my teeth across my lower lip, I focused on the flashes in my brain, trying to pick a solid one. They were hazy and disjointed, which got me nowhere. "I talked to Sergei."

"About?"

"I don't know."

"And then what happened?"

"I woke up." I blinked at him, trying to figure out what, exactly, he was getting at. I clearly did something to piss him off, but damned if I knew what it was.

He sighed, raking a hand through his dark curls. "You were *on* something, Bennett. Not to mention it smells like you bathed in vodka."

"You cannot be mad at me for doing a shot or two to keep a Russian boss happy. It's insulting to refuse their hospitality."

He scoffed. "A shot or two? Really? You expect me to believe that?"

"I don't know why you're so pissed."

"You nearly gave us away because you couldn't keep your hands to yourself! I'm surprised your mouth didn't ruin everything."

"Gave us aw—" The lightbulb clicked. "Oh, fuck."

Leander gave me a tight smile as the realization hit home. "Yes, well, hopefully Sergei will think it was whatever you took."

"I didn't take anything!"

He scowled at me, folding his arms. "Do you want to rethink that position?"

"I didn't take anything!" Like repeating it would help. To say I was feeling more than a little insulted was an understatement. "I've been clean since you came back."

He arched a challenging brow, his scowl deepening.

"Except alcohol," I conceded. "You can't crucify me over that. You drink too!"

"Not to excess. And not to the point where I'm crawling all over some Bratva henchman in front of the boss!"

Despite the fact I had zero recollection of crawling all over *anyone,* I cringed more at the anger in his tone. "What?"

"I don't know if I should be more irritated with that or whatever female managed to leave her mark on you before my arrival. If she sucked you off as well as she left a hickey, I'm sure you had a great night." He scraped the tip of one finger along my jaw and held it up, showing a smear of pink and silver sparkles. "I didn't realize when you said you were bi, what you meant was you would continue sleeping with both sexes, regardless of your relationship status."

I wiped at the underside of my jaw in the same spot and stared at the sticky mess on my hand. "I don't know where that shit came from, but I didn't sleep with anyone last night, male *or* female."

"And you had the audacity to be mad at me over Lorelei when you and I weren't even together!" He flung the comforter back and jumped out of bed, stalking out of the bedroom.

"Leander, wait!" Scrambling after him, the sheets tangled around my feet in my haste. I hopped on one foot, kicking them away. "I'll prove it! Just wait a goddamn second!"

By the time I made it to the walk-in closet, he'd changed into a sweater and dress pants. "I thought we were past this. I thought the lying would finally stop, that this was the start of something new. I thought, after Puerto Rico, you wouldn't feel the need to—"

"I'm not lying!" I held my hands up, blocking his attempt to sneak by me in the doorway. At the moment, I wasn't above locking him in here to prove a point. "I swear to God. I wouldn't do that to you. I *didn't* do that to you!"

He glared at me, his arms crossed again, as unconvinced as ever.

"Where's my phone?" I asked.

"Kitchen."

"Don't leave." I held a finger up and darted to the kitchen as quickly as I could. Swiping my phone off the counter, I scrolled through the contacts, hurrying back to him. I intercepted him as he rounded the corner from the hallway. "So much for waiting."

He rolled his eyes, unfazed by my glare, and looked away.

I dialed Misha's number and switched over to speakerphone while we waited. In one of the flashes of color, I saw his distinctly sky-blue eyes. He had to have been there. Even if he wasn't, he could at least get me the security footage to prove my innocence in the court of Leander.

After a few rings, Misha answered. "Privet?"

"It's Bennett Reeve," I said, hoping a second too late he didn't say something wholly inappropriate. Considering Misha and I had a past, however brief, there was always the possibility I *did* do something stupid. The only thing I had going for me was my deep-seated conviction that I didn't. At least, not intentionally.

"Is everything ok?" Misha sounded genuinely concerned, which was both touching and a tally in the "Not Good for Bennett" column.

Leander's scowl tightened.

I ignored that for the time being. "What happened last night? Did I take something?"

"Yes." Fuck me.

Leander went to walk around me. I grabbed a fistful of his sweater and pushed him against the wall, keeping him there despite the murderous look he gave me.

"What was it?" I asked.

Misha sighed. "I told you. Special K. It's Sergei's new product." Well, that explained why I couldn't remember shit. It was a goddamn horse tranquilizer.

"Ok… Did *I* take it? Willingly?" Please say no. Please say no…

Misha made an unsure noise, which I hoped was due to his translation process and not an indication I was going to be in more hot water. "Sveta gave it to you."

Oh thank God. As relieved as I was, I kept my celebration to a minimum. I made sure Leander was looking at me when I asked my follow-up question. "Did I *do* anything while I was there? Go anywhere with anyone? *Privately*?"

"No. Why are you asking?"

"Thank you!" I hung up and faced Leander expectantly. He was still pinned to the wall, my hand planted in the center of his chest, looking no more convinced than he had prior to the exonerating phone call. I backed off, holding my hands up, trying to take the high road. "See? I didn't lie."

He took a step forward and swiped his hand down the front of his sweater, removing the wrinkles. The gesture was a giant "Fuck you," as loud as if he'd screamed it in my face. "Regardless, I'm leaving as soon as I'm packed."

"You just heard him! How can you seriously still be mad at me for something I didn't intentionally do?"

"There are things that need my attention at home. Unlike you, my job doesn't consist of getting high in clubs and nearly choking on my own vomit."

Low blow, dick. "That's *not* my job — not anymore. And you know that!"

"All I know is this city is a fucking cesspool," Leander shot back, his eyes flashing as he took another step forward. "Every time you're here, something horrible happens. Say what you will about Easton, but at least I don't have to worry about you *dying* there."

"No, but *I* have to deal with the fallout from your love affair with your fucking doctor!" So much for the high road. I waved at it as I plummeted by on my way to the lowest of the low roads.

He shook his head, his face a mixture of disbelief and

anger. "You really are going to hold that over my head forever, aren't you?"

"No different than you and whatever the hell happened last night."

"You nearly gave us away," he repeated, enunciating each syllable. "Or at the very least, you nearly gave *yourself* away. Between pawing at me and latching on to Misha, I'm surprised Sergei didn't have you beaten on the spot."

"While we're on the topic of taboo relationships — have you even called your girlfriend?" I crossed my arms, completely ignoring his point in favor of my own interrogation. He wasn't wrong about Sergei, but hopefully the Pahkan realized I was worth far more to him alive than dead, especially over something that literally had nothing to do with him or the money I made his organization.

Rolling his eyes, Leander shook his head and stalked away, muttering under his breath.

"I'll take that as a 'No!'" I shouted after him.

He whirled around and marched back up to me, his hands balled at his sides. "I have had other concerns!"

"Name one!" I came nose-to-nose with him, refusing to back off. We'd never actually gotten into a physical fight over the course of knowing one another, so it would be interesting to see how it all played out. After the years of abuse he endured, he didn't feel pain like regular people. And he didn't surrender, even if it was in his best interests. I was sure I could ultimately win, but at what cost?

"You!" Leander yelled, bringing me back to the heart of the fight. "The house. My company. Irene's fucking will! The police. Now the FBI and the Russians in the middle of my business. Of everything I have going on in my life, Lorelei is the *least* of my fucking concerns!"

"Just like getting high and fucking my way through a club

full of mail-order brides is the *least* of mine! Nice to know you trust me."

"The same way you trust me?"

"I made you a promise! Does that mean nothing?"

"Actions speak louder than words." He gave me a pointed once-over, his lip curled. "You, of all people, know that."

"What do I need to do to convince you I'm not going anywhere? Hmm? I've killed for you, Leander. I nearly died to keep you out of harm's way. Do you want me to bleed again to prove how far I'm willing to go to make you happy?"

I didn't wait for an answer. Without even thinking, I grabbed a knife from the wooden block on the counter and sliced across my forearm. Blood rushed out, hot and stinging, eliciting an involuntary hiss.

"Christ!" Leander gaped at me for a split second before grabbing the knife away from me and launching it in the sink.

"Sincere enough for you? Want to go draw up a contract? I'll sign with this so you have no more reasons to doubt me." I swiped my fingers across the stream of red and flicked it on the tile, adding to the splatter mosaic at my feet.

He ripped a towel out of the drawer and pressed it over my arm, clamping down on it with both hands. "You *are* a fucking lunatic, you know that?! Jesus Christ, Bennett..."

"'I was never really insane except upon occasions when my heart was touched.'" I'll see your insult, asshole, and raise you one Poe quote.

His green eyes flashed up to mine, brimming with a mixture of emotions. Anger, primarily, but also understanding. There was even a fleeting glimpse of fear. Perhaps a touch of nostalgia? After all, "fucking lunatic" was the same insult he lobbed at me in Venice after I crashed the boat.

I swept a curl off of his forehead, tucking it behind his ear. They say love makes you do crazy things. "They" had no idea. Crazy didn't even scratch the surface of what I was willing to do for him. I hoped he saw that now.

We leaned in at the same time, lips brushing against the other's. Once the ice was broken, we plunged in head-first, kissing each other roughly, as much a punishment as it was a reconciliation. Our hands tangled in each other's hair, our clothing, pulling the other closer and closer, regardless of the blood running down my arm. It wasn't until I swayed in a moment of dizziness that either of us pulled back.

"We have to go to the hospital," Leander said, resting his forehead against mine.

"Not a chance."

"Don't be an idiot. You need stitches."

"I know someone that makes house calls."

"Of course you do..."

I smirked and kissed him gently. Even though my arm was throbbing and I couldn't really feel my fingers anymore, I chalked the whole incident up to a win.

7

BENNETT

I hadn't been to Leander's mansion since he was in Stratford under house arrest. In the intermittent weeks, it became foreign territory to me. Then once he was back, with *Her*, it went from foreign to hostile.

Even though Olivia assured me Lorelei moved out of the house weeks ago, I dreaded crossing the threshold. Who knew what would be there. Who knew what Leander's reaction would be to whatever was there — or *not* there.

But I couldn't put it off forever. Out of the frying pan and all that.

Thankfully, the house was empty when we strolled through the back door. *She* was gone, but her presence lingered everywhere I looked, crashing against my own memories. I questioned what happened in each and every room, wondering what their relatively short time together had been like. It was torture, but I couldn't stop.

Leander dropped his luggage at the base of the servant stairs and disappeared deeper into the house. "Annabel?"

Annabel?!

"Who's Annabel?" I asked, following after him.

"My cat."

"Oh." Did he really just say cat? How many more bombs was he going to drop in the first ten seconds? "When the hell did you have time to get a cat?"

"It's a long story." Stalking down the hallway, he called her name as he went, clicking his tongue now and again. He rounded the corner for the library and stopped short, spinning to face me in the doorway. "Don't tell me you don't like cats."

"I'm allergic," I answered with a grim smile.

"Of course you are." He sighed, like it was some personal choice of mine instead of fucking genetics, and carried on.

I was sure there was more he wanted to say on the matter, but I let it go in favor of keeping the peace. The four-hour drive from the city in our separate vehicles had given us both space and time to think. In the driveway, he promised to let drug thing go — again, as if I had a fucking choice in the matter — and I agreed to a tad less salty about how he was handling, or *not* handling, his former mistress.

Checking behind curtains and every sunny spot we could locate, we wove through the rooms on the ground floor quickly. Leander's frown deepened as he climbed the stairs.

"Maybe she's up here," I offered weakly.

On the second floor, he took the west wing, while I took the east. Even though most of the doors were shut, there was no telling if the cat snuck in somewhere while Yolanda was cleaning, like his grandmother's room.

Pushing the door open, I assessed Irene's former bedroom quickly. White sheets covered all of the furniture with no obvious dips from a cat trying to walk across them. The screen in front of the green, marble fireplace was securely in place, which meant it didn't somehow make its way up the chimney. All of the heavy drapes were tied back and I couldn't spy a single cat silhouette behind the lace curtains.

I was re-emerging from the master bathroom when Leander appeared, his jaw set.

"I can't find her," he said, his worried tone matching the crease between his eyebrows.

"How many thousands of square feet are there? I'm sure she's here. She's probably chasing mice in the basement or something."

He shook his head, about to say something, when he recoiled, as if he suddenly remembered what room we were standing in. Without another word, he spun on his heel and strode out, not even bothering to see if I was behind him.

I was, but I lingered in the doorway. Glancing back at the bed, I studied the spot where his grandmother had been beaten to a bloody pulp a decade ago. It might as well have been yesterday with how viscerally he reacted any time he went near her room.

If there was a way to purge her from his memory, I'd do it in a heartbeat, just like I would rid him of the memories from Parkview. With a sigh, I closed Irene's door behind me and followed the sound of Leander's voice to the second-floor landing.

He had his phone pressed to his ear, his scowl back in full force. "Where is Annabel? Sí. La gata."

Ah, Yolanda. Hopefully she had an answer so he would calm down. He hadn't eaten all day and with the amount of brisk pacing he was doing, it didn't look like he had any plans for the evening, either.

"She what?!" Leander snarled into the phone. Oh fuck…

Keeping my expression neutral, I folded my arms and watched his face darken. Nope. He definitely wasn't eating now. Looked like I was on my own. Maybe Cole would want to go grab something somewhere with a lot of fucking alcohol.

"Gracias." Hanging up, Leander exhaled slowly and closed his eyes. "She took my cat."

"Yolanda?"

His eyes flew open, pupils narrowed to pinpricks. "Lorelei! She took my goddamn cat!" He launched the phone across the hallway, pegging one of the solid oak doors and shattering the screen.

"Feel better?" I asked in a monotone voice. If only he'd shown a fraction of that possessiveness over humans, perhaps we wouldn't be in this situation. But, c'est la vie. Keep it on the high road, Reeve...

He shot me a glare before jogging down the main staircase and disappearing around the corner. If I had to guess, he was en route to the library. At least he had the foresight to keep a stash of burners for occasions such as this, when he destroyed his current phone or needed to plan a murder on the fly.

Sighing, I pulled out my own phone and called Gavin. Time to do what I did best — getting my clients what they wanted.

"No, I haven't scheduled to have your shit picked up from the St. Louis apartment yet," Gavin huffed instead of a normal greeting.

"That's actually not why I'm calling." I strolled down the hallway, stepping inside Leander's room. Our room? We'd have to discuss sleeping arrangements. In fact, I wanted to discuss an entire house remodel, if he'd let me. Anything to get rid of Lorelei's apparition haunting me from every room.

Despite the fact she cleared out weeks ago, I could still smell an alien perfume in the air. I wrinkled my nose, trying to figure out what brand it was. Whatever it was, it was bland, boring, and entirely fitting from what I knew of her unexciting personality.

Even if Yolanda changed the sheets and bleached every inch of this room, I wasn't sleeping in that bed until there was a new mattress. My formerly broken ribs would come in handy as reasonable excuse for wanting a new, "more supportive" bed.

"Can you put me through to Lorelei Clayton? Doctor, Stratford," I said to Gavin as I pulled open the door to the armoire, relieved to see nothing but black. I wasn't above burning her shit in the backyard if she happened to leave a wardrobe full of clothing behind. Or anything else, for that matter.

There was an unimpressed grunt and a flurry of typing on the other side of the phone. "Don't forget you're supposed to be at that auction on Thursday. Sergei has more pieces to move."

"Yes, I know. It's in the calendar." I rolled my eyes and picked a long, blonde hair off the sleeve of one of Leander's suits. Flicking it away with a sneer, I made a note to have everything dry cleaned. Immediately. I'd triple Yolanda's salary to make sure it was done within the next twenty-four hours.

"Oh, happy to see you're finally using it for a change. Not that you'd, like, I don't know, put your vacation plans in it or anything. Or tell your assistant. Or your family. Or anyone. Just up and disappear with your—"

"Wasn't there something you were supposed to be doing?" I snapped. He was worse than a nagging wife sometimes.

"Here she comes, your majesty," Gavin snipped in return before the line fell silent.

Steeling myself for a confrontation, I exhaled slowly as it rang. And rang. I was preparing for a voicemail when she picked up, sounding as exhausted as she had on TV. I hoped she looked equally shitty. "Dr. Lorelei Clayton."

"Dr. Clayton, my name is Bennett Reeve. I'm calling on behalf of Leander Welles."

There was a pause. "You're one of his lawyers, right?"

So, she at least knew I existed. "Indeed. I'm calling about his cat."

"Is he... is he dead?"

I blinked, but managed to spit out, "Uh, no." That was quite the leap. If he was truly dead, it would be the police or the coroner calling her dumb ass, not a lawyer. Unless she thought she was already in the will? God she was presumptuous.

There was an audible sigh of relief, followed by a little laugh. "Thank God. I've been so worried about him."

Refusing to engage in the small-talk bullshit, I waited until she circled back around to more important things — like why I was calling.

"Is he there with you?" she asked, sounding way too eager. "Can I talk to him?"

"I'm sure if he wants to speak to you, he'll call. I, on the other hand, am only concerned with the whereabouts of the cat."

"Yes, yes, she's here. I... I'm sorry, have you *seen* Leander? Is he ok?"

Oh my God. Two seconds on the phone with this broad and I was ready to open a vein. How the hell did she counsel crazy people for a living?

"Dr. Clayton, I'll keep it brief since you seem rather... distracted. It's in your best interests to return the cat as soon as possible. If you cannot accommodate that request, I'll make arrangements to have the cat picked up."

"I'm sorry, what? I'm just..." She exhaled and sniffed quickly. Fuck me. She was crying. Why the hell was she crying? Wasn't she supposed to be a goddamn professional? "I'm trying to understand what's happening."

I spoke slowly, so hopefully each word sunk into her thick head. "He's home. He wants his cat back. Got it?"

"But I—"

"Failure to return said cat will result in theft charges being filed against you. I promise you, I'll go for a Class Three felony. I'm sure this cat has lived in the lap of luxury since Leander got it and boy do those vet bills add up. At the very least I'm guaranteed a misdemeanor."

She gasped. "What?! I didn't steal her! I didn't know where the hell he was or if he was even coming back!"

I rolled my eyes, doing my best not to let her yapping get under my skin. "You are currently exerting unauthorized control over his property and if you refuse to return the cat, you're intending to deprive him of it forever. That is the textbook definition of theft. Would you like me to provide the statute number so you can Google it?"

There was a long pause, filled only with her short, rapid breaths. When she spoke again, her voice was hard. "I want to talk to him."

"As I said, if he wants to speak to you, I'm sure he'll be in contact."

"Are you with him?"

"Whether I am or not has zero relevance to this conversation. Any further questions?"

There was another sniff, this one longer and wetter. I could only imagine the waterworks taking place on the other end. "No."

"Good." I was just about to hang up when she spoke again.

"Can you tell him something for me?"

I wanted to tell her "No." I wanted to tell her to fuck off. But my sick curiosity was stronger than my anger. "What?"

"Tell him I love him, and that I understand."

The fuck she did! I disconnected without acknowledging her request. I was pretty sure she heard my disgusted scoff, but I didn't care. There was no way in hell I was passing that little message along. Ever.

"Feel better?" Leander's voice asked behind me, mimicking my tone from earlier.

"No," I replied loftily, turning with a bright, but bitter, smile. "How much of that did you hear?"

He was leaning against the doorframe, his arms crossed. If he was mad, it didn't show. Nor did I detect any amusement. "Enough."

I crossed the room to him in slow, measured strides. As I did, he unfolded his arms and pressed himself into the doorframe to let me pass. Except, I didn't. I stopped directly in front of him and leaned in close, my lips hovering above his, the promise of a kiss hanging in the air. "She's in love with you."

"I know." His voice was steady, but there was a slight shift in his shoulders as if he was mentally preparing for a brawl. I didn't blame him. Every time her stupid name came up, we ended up fighting — just not physically.

"Until she accepts it's over between you, don't expect me to be ok with any of this."

He kept his eyes locked on mine, the muscle along his jaw tightening. "Shall I call her right now?"

"No." Grabbing the knot in his tie, I slid my hand down the length of it slowly. His breath caught at the same time my hand stopped, right above his belt. "You can tell her when she drops off the damn cat."

"Since it troubles you so much, why wait?"

"I want to see the look on her face when you crush her little heart." My hand slid even further, past the end of his tie, until the black silk slipped out of my grasp. It floated backward gently and my hand fell to my side, all without ever touching him directly.

His gaze dropped and he swallowed whatever reply he might have had.

With a smirk, I pivoted, venturing back down the hallway to the red guest room. It was the only room that didn't reek of the blonde bitch.

Pulling out my phone again, I ordered a new mattress, pillows, and bedding in the matter of seconds. Leander wasn't the only one who could erase a person's existence in the blink of an eye. Lucky for him, my method didn't involve an axe or a giant fucking fire.

8

LEANDER

There was no gentle way to settle back into my old life. It was more akin to ripping off a bandaid, or kicking a baby bird out of its nest. As soon as we returned to Easton, I had a million things waiting for me — people demanding my time, my money; the house; and of course, Bennett.

I wasn't oblivious to the fact he was rankled by the knowledge Lorelei had lived in the mansion, however briefly. A few weeks was nothing compared to the years Bennett had come and gone at will, and hopefully the years we had in store for us. A part of me wanted to point that out — that he had no reason to eye each room with suspicion, like he was flipping through a mental catalogue of the way things used to be and assessing the changes, however minute.

In the hope of avoiding another fight, I didn't say anything. It was practically all we'd done since we came back. Chicago was a disaster, a fact which I was reminded of every time I saw the scar on Bennett's forearm. It was almost identical to the one on my own arm, though their meanings couldn't have been more different. Mine was part of my master plan for revenge — his was an insane declaration of love, as insane as his marriage proposal. And yet, there was no way I could possibly doubt the sentiment behind either action.

My brief memories of Lorelei floated through the house like dust motes, nothing more than glimpses of moments we shared. I tried to leave it alone, to ignore it. Bennett, in an attempt to eradicate her from existence, stirred it all up, much like yanking a sheet off abandoned furniture and shaking the particles free.

Subtly was not exactly his strong suit. I got the message loud and clear when he set up his things in the red guest room instead of my bedroom. Still favoring his broken ribs, he said. The luxury memory foam he ordered would be much better for both of us, he said. I agreed.

Likewise, his sudden urge to clean out the pantry didn't go unnoticed. He threw out an entire garbage bag full of any ingredient he knew did not belong to me. Even the items he remotely suspected of being tainted by her influence were immediately binned. I had to rescue both a tin of earl grey and a bottle of imported truffle oil as they sailed through the air. We needed to make healthier choices, he said. Some items were expired, he said. I agreed.

He asked Yolanda to send everything in my armoire out for dry cleaning, despite the fact it had been weeks since I'd worn any of it. And room-by-room, every drape, curtain, or scrap of cloth was taken down or taken out to be cleaned, despite being cleaned in the spring as per schedule. The flu virus, he said, never mind the fact it was late summer. Dust mites. Allergens. He thought it would help with my headaches, he said. Again, I agreed. I agreed to anything and everything he wanted in the hope it would assuage his anger at the past.

In the midst of purifying the house of all its imaginary

toxins, Bennett also developed an obsessive candle habit out of nowhere. Still ignoring the fact it was summer, the house continually smelled like mahogany, teakwood, and amber — clearly masculine scents. I wasn't complaining, it was just… odd, to see him actually making an effort at domesticity, like he said he wanted. Even if he had ulterior motives, I took comfort in the knowledge he was making the house his own. If he made it his own, then maybe he wouldn't leave.

Sometimes I still didn't quite believe it, that he was really here with promises to stay forever. I wanted to believe him. I wanted to believe the love between us would last an eternity. The cynic in me knew better.

Beyond the curse that afflicted every member of the Welles family, there was another thing standing in our way — Lorelei. She was wholly my responsibility to deal with but for reasons I couldn't explain, I kept putting it off. It wasn't to hurt Bennett, as he sometimes accused. Nor was it to protect *her*, as he alternatively claimed. There was no valid excuse for my reluctance beyond my own fear.

"So what's the deal with Malibu Barbie?" Olivia asked on the phone one day.

"What do you mean?"

"Bennett said you still haven't broken up with her."

I couldn't help the sigh that escaped me as I turned the bacon-wrapped asparagus on the grill pan. I shouldn't have been surprised he talked to Olivia about it — Olivia hated Lorelei as much as Bennett did. Or, nearly, at any rate.

"He's the one who told me he wanted me to do it in person," I said in my defense. If it made him happy I would have called her that very minute, or driven to Stratford immediately. But no. That's not what he wanted.

Part of me thought it was his form of punishing her. She knew I was alive, that I was home, but I remained a distant figure in her life, much like he had been in mine those heart-wrenching months. Or maybe it was a test, to see if I would make a liar out of myself and break my vow to him.

Olivia didn't sound convinced. "And when is that going to be?"

"Whenever she brings Annabel back. By the way, how could you let her take my cat?"

"I didn't *let* her do jack shit," Olivia snapped. "She just did. Like reporting you as missing. That was all her brainchild, not ours."

"Other than giving me more grief about Lorelei, was there another reason you called?"

"Yeah, the trust lawyer has been poking around. I tried to put him off as long as possible, but I think he knows you were out of town. So I'd expect a meeting in the near future."

"Shit..." A jolt of tension shot through my brain. Pinching the bridge of my nose, I closed my eyes and tried to exhale a slow breath.

"It's probably just a coincidence."

"I don't believe in coincidences. And neither do you." The other line beeped and I stole a quick glance at the screen. "I have another call."

"Talk to you tomorrow."

I cleared my throat and clicked over, praying for better news. "And?"

"I got it all set up," Cole said. "Going up there next week during visiting hours."

"Make sure you don't use your real name."

"You have to sign in with something — they check everyone who comes in for warrants."

"Then use Jake's alias from Parkview. You know it's clean."

"Yeah, sure. I'll see if he's still got his ID. My guy can probably swap the pictures real quick."

The way he said it, the flatness of his tone, made me stop

and take notice. I turned the burners off and removed the asparagus from the grill before giving him my full attention. "What is the matter?"

He was quiet for a moment. "Are you sure you don't want to tell the others?"

"Absolutely not. The less people who know, the better."

"What happens if they get you, like they got Bennett? What am I supposed to tell them? What am I supposed to tell *him?*"

I sighed again, rubbing my forehead. The tension in my head had gone from a sudden pang to a steady throbbing. "They won't. That's why we're striking first. Our Russian friends already have them on the run. This is the final death knell."

"Whatever the fuck that is."

"Endgame."

"Ah, ok. Oh, shit! Olivia just walked in." The phone rustled and disconnected quickly.

Shaking my head, I tossed my phone on the counter and stooped down to check on the steaks in the oven.

As soon as I straightened, the cast-iron skillet in hand, Bennett pulled me against him. I had just enough time to set it on the stove before I accidentally sloshed melted butter all over the place. And he accused me of being cat-like.

"You almost made me spill," I chided, leaning back against him.

Brushing my hair away from my shirt collar, he kissed the back of my neck, sending a wave of goosebumps over my skin. "How much longer?"

"They have to rest."

"Good. Come see." He slipped his hand into mine and tugged me toward the front of the house.

"What have you done now?"

He laughed, but conveniently did not supply an answer.

As we rounded the corner for the parlor, I expected the furniture to be rearranged, or new drapery installed. Instead, a giant photograph hung over the fireplace, replacing the oil painting of the mansion that previously hung there.

It was us, on one of our last nights in Puerto Rico. We'd gone to the Ruins and managed to capture an amazing picture at sunset. Now, here it was, in a stunning frame on full display.

More than commemorating a trip, the photograph summed up our entire relationship. I was dressed in my customary all-black suit and tie. Bennett was also in a black suit, though he paired it with a bright red shirt. As usual, he opted for no tie and left the shirt unbuttoned most of the way, showcasing the jangle of necklaces laying on his smooth chest. We were surrounded by the beauty of a crumbling nineteenth-century lighthouse and a windswept beach, but for all that, we only had eyes for each other.

Without a doubt, that picture confirmed how much I loved him — how much he loved me. It was in every facet of our body language, from the genuine smiles to the way our hands intertwined. Like any photograph, it was only a fraction of a moment, a mere glimpse at a feeling I'd been chasing my entire life. Before Bennett, love was something I only ever read about in books.

And it terrified me.

From the moment I confessed my love, or maybe even before, a countdown began, a silent bomb waiting to go off. How long until his love turned to hate? How long before Fate decided to intervene, giving me this chance at genuine happiness only to take it away, as had happened to so many of my family members? Worse yet — how long until I became too much for him? Until he decided he'd made a mistake? Until he ultimately left?

"Do you like it?" Bennett murmured over my shoulder,

hugging me from behind again.

Swallowing the knot in my throat, I nodded, forcing a smile to my lips. “It’s perfect.”

9

BENNETT

It was just one of *those* days. The kind where you regretted getting up the minute you opened your eyes. A day full of meetings and paperwork left me with a raging headache and a desperation for some oxy. I knew I'd have to settle for something over-the-counter, which made me even crankier when I pulled in the driveway. I could have stayed in Chicago another night, but I just wanted to be home. And home was on the opposite side of the damn state.

"Fuck."

Parked in front of the house was a silver car I didn't recognize. Leander didn't say anything about having a dinner guest, but who knew. He'd been out of touch all day. Maybe he didn't get my last text where I said I was on my way.

I tried to muster up some semblance of civility as I climbed the back stairs.

Surprisingly, the kitchen was empty and there were zero signs of a dinner in progress. No pots, no pans. No dirty dishes. Not even a bottle of wine. He always served wine. God knew there was enough in the cellar to serve the entire town.

Furrowing my brows, I made my way down the hallway toward the front of the house. Maybe they were just having drinks. Unlikely, but possible.

"My love?"

No answer.

There weren't any signs of life in the parlor, the library, or the conservatory. The music room was still off limits, since Leander destroyed it and we'd yet to decide if we were going to replace the piano. Where the fuck was he?

Inexplicable dread filled me as I glanced up at the ceiling. Maybe they were in the billiard's room. Or on the terrace. The third-floor ballroom. The tower. Anywhere but the west wing.

I climbed the stairs at a snail's pace.

Each step down the western hallway made my pulse beat that much faster. The pounding in my head matched the spasms in my chest until I wasn't sure which would explode first.

I was almost to Leander's room when I jerked to a halt. The smell of sex and distinct groaning hit me at the same time. Male *and* female.

"You son of a bitch," I snarled, storming through the open door and nearly tripping over his discarded black clothes and a ripped red dress.

As I'd feared — as I'd *known* — would happen, Leander was there. With Lorelei. She was on all fours in front of him, gripping the footboard while he fucked her from behind.

At my arrival, he at least had the decency to stop. But then he smiled at me. The bastard smiled! One of his dark, sexy "I know I'm fucking evil" smiles.

"Mon coeur. You're home earlier than I anticipated."

"Clearly!" Frankly, I didn't know who I was more furious with — him, or myself. That was the problem when you opened up to someone, when you confessed your deepest fears and darkest hatreds. When they were so inclined, they had the power to ruin you with the very things that blackened your soul, the things they said they'd protect you from.

Lorelei faced me with wide eyes, covering herself with the sheet as if I didn't just see everything two seconds before.

"I can't believe you." I was at a loss for anything else. For once, I didn't know what to say. What to do. All I could do was stand there, marinating in the pain and humiliation of the ultimate betrayal. The *one* thing he knew I hated above everything else, just as he detested liars.

"Don't be angry," he said, somewhere between a pout and a purr. He slipped off the bed and walked forward slowly, his hair shifting over his eye as he canted his head, the picture of innocence.

I scoffed and shook my head, biting the inside of my cheek. "You're fucking incredible, you know that?" As soon as he was within arm's reach, I grabbed him by the throat and slammed him into the closest wall as hard as I could. "Anger doesn't even come close to what I'm feeling right now."

He didn't look worried in the slightest, even when my fingertips pressed harder against each artery. Rubbing my dick in slow strokes through my pants, his pale eyes locked on mine, that little smirk playing on his lips.

"Don't," I growled, swatting his hand away. It returned immediately, except this time he slipped it down the front of my pants and caressed me directly.

"I can't help myself." Even though my hand was still around his throat, I seemed to have lost the power to fucking strangle him. He leaned forward without much effort, brushing his lips along my jaw. "I need you both, Bennett. Can't you see that?"

"I don't share, Leander. I told you that." I tried to hang on to my anger, but my dick had other ideas. Traitor.

He pressed kisses to my throat while his free hand threaded through my hair. "One time. Just give me this one time. That's all I'm asking."

"Oh that's all?" Shaking my head again, I tried to push away from him, but he held on this time. He grabbed the back of my neck and pulled my face closer until his mouth covered mine. Forcing his tongue past my lips, he greedily took what he wanted while he continued stroking my length.

I hated him so much in that moment, for manipulating me like the blonde bitch on the bed. More than that, I hated myself for allowing it. I was blinded when it came to him. I'd give him whatever he wanted and he damn well knew it.

After a moment, the hand in my hair disappeared and I heard a snap. There was a rustling of satin and quiet footsteps. Then she was there, like an obedient little dog. Leander pulled his mouth from mine and gave it to her, even as his hand gripped my cock in long, slow strokes.

I bit the curve of his shoulder, marking him as mine with the jolt of pain. He moaned and broke his kiss with Lorelei, reclaiming my mouth. I felt her hand slip between us. Before I knew it, her hand was down my pants, replacing Leander's, while she stroked him with the other.

With both of his hands now free, Leander gripped each of us by the back of the neck, drawing us in closer. Slowly, so slowly I didn't realize it was happening, he backed away and guided my mouth straight to Lorelei's.

I should have hated it. No, I *did* hate it. I hated her pillowy lips, her velvet tongue, the soft throaty noises she made. I hated the way her hand tightened on my cock when Leander kissed her breasts, doing God knew what else with his other hand. I hated every bit of it. But I didn't stop.

Lorelei broke her kiss with me, gasping. With only a

nod from Leander, she started undressing me. And because I was an idiot, I let her. With each layer of clothing that came off, Leander was there, kissing and biting the newly exposed skin. Once I was completely naked, he seized my face in his hands and kissed me, hard.

I was only vaguely aware Lorelei dropped to her knees, a cock in each hand. When her mouth encased the length of me, I couldn't help but groan. It was fine, I told myself, grinding my molars together. It was a mouth. That was all. It didn't have to be *Her* mouth — it could have been anyone's. It could have been Leander's if it weren't for the fact his was currently biting my shoulder so hard I thought he was going to draw blood.

She switched off between us, alternating her mouth and her hands. I hated the fact she could make me feel so good, just like I hated hearing Leander's appreciative moans. Seeing her blonde head bobbing with each of his thrusts was simultaneously arousing and infuriating as fuck.

"Get on the bed," Leander breathed, lifting Lorelei by her chin with only the tips of his fingers.

She wiped the saliva from her mouth and turned, doing as she was told.

Leander took a step after her and stopped, looking back at me. He held his hand out, palm up, a silent invitation — no, a plea. Just as mine had been all those months ago, when his heart was fighting with his head.

I didn't move, his words replaying in my mind. *One time. Just give me this one time.*

His beautiful eyes locked on mine, predatory but patient. He knew I'd cave before I did. He knew, because he always knew. He knew me more than I knew myself.

Against my better judgement, I relented. I took his hand. My moral compass only had two points and here I was, trashing one of them, all out of sheer desperation to hold on to the beautiful and cruel love of my life.

When we reached the bed he kissed me again, gently, almost apologetically. He *knew* the magnitude of what he was asking, but he asked anyway. How could I refuse when he never asked for anything? At the end of the day, what was more important? His love, or my integrity?

Breaking away slowly, Leander caressed my cheek before climbing onto the bed and settling on his back. When he motioned to her, Lorelei scooted forward, straddling his lap with a practiced ease. Inch by inch, his cock disappeared inside of her. She threw her head back and clawed his abdomen with a groan. I wanted to snap her fucking neck.

Biting his lower lip, Leander's attention turned to me. He beckoned me with the crook of one finger. Once I got closer, he held out his hands. As soon as he had a hold on both of them, he pulled me forward, right behind Lorelei, and placed my hands on her hips.

"Leander, I—" she said softly, but he shushed her and placed a finger against her lips.

"Just this one time," he purred, rocking beneath her.

She sighed, her hips rolling with his movements.

Leander's gaze shifted past her shoulder to mine, waiting. Demanding. Fucking bastard.

I put my hand between her shoulder blades and pushed her down so she was laying on his chest with her ass in the air.

"I fucking hate you," I ground out. Even in Italian, the meaning was clear.

He didn't even flinch. "I know."

I worked up a good amount of saliva in my mouth before tipping my face downward and spitting onto my cock. I smeared it around the head before guiding it between Lorelei's smooth ass cheeks.

Leander's movements below stilled and he kissed her, both hands in her hair, as I pushed into her ass as quickly as I could, not even giving her the courtesy of letting her adjust before I was fully seated inside her.

She cried out and her legs started to quiver, her nails digging into Leander's arms.

I kept one hand pressed on her back, keeping her flat, while my other hand squeezed her hip. There'd be no escaping for either one of us. She was as committed to this course as I was, whether she fucking wanted it or not.

As soon her trembling subsided, I rocked back, thrusting in again. Not gentle. Not concerned for her welfare or pleasure, or even mine, for that matter. This was all about hate and proving a fucking point.

Leander let me set the pace before he joined in. Lorelei moaned and whimpered, hardly moving as the two of us thrust in and out of her.

"I'll never fucking forgive you for this," I panted, this time in French so *I* knew *he* knew how pissed I was. The fact I had a hard-on was completely irrelevant for this argument. The wind changing directions could give me a hard-on. It had nothing to do with Lorelei — or *him*, or *anything* that was happening at that point in time.

"I know," he groaned, squeezing his eyes shut. He kissed Lorelei roughly and then shoved her upwards, toward me.

She gasped with the sudden change in angles, but she adjusted quickly and the rhythm resumed.

I snaked an arm around her torso and pulled her against my chest. Palming her breast, I kissed her over her shoulder, fucking into her as hard as I could. It's what he wanted, wasn't it? To see his two pets using each other for his enjoyment?

Leander's hand grazed up my thigh, along with something cold and hard. His fingers twined with mine as he transferred the object, never once slowing his thrusting from below.

I let go of her breast in favor of her throat, squeezing tightly and tipping her head back so my mouth was right at her ear.

"He was never yours," I hissed.

Her eyes flew open when the filet knife plunged between her ribs. She sucked in a sharp breath, frozen in disbelief. I twisted the blade to drive home the message. My reward was a strangled cry and a spray of hot blood across my abdomen. As she started to slump forward, I ripped the knife out and pushed her off the side of the bed. She landed in a heap, blood rushing out around her on the oriental carpet, twitching as her life drained away.

Leander gazed up at me, lips parted and a lascivious glint in his eye. His breathing was heavy and of course he was still hard — maybe even harder than before. "Mon coeur…"

Lorelei's blood coated my hand and dripped down my bare skin, but I didn't care. I lunged forward on top of him, pressing the knife to his throat. My face was a whisper away from his, all but snarling my response. "Do not call me that."

"What shall I call you, then?" He smirked, tracing his tongue across my lower lip. "Mon diable?"

"If you ever do anything like this to me again, I'll fucking kill you." I put more pressure behind the knife, until tiny beads of red appeared on his pale skin.

"I'd expect nothing less," he replied with a sigh, tipping his head back, as if daring me to cut him again. For a minute, I wanted to. But it would have been tantamount to slitting my own throat.

Throwing the knife to the side, I bent down and dragged my tongue over his neck, soothing the sting and licking away the blood.

He seized a handful of hair and yanked me up again,

crushing his lips to mine in a bruising kiss, the scent of blood and bergamot floating in the air.

JERKING UPRIGHT WITH A GASP, my heart slammed against the inside of my ribcage and I swore my lungs stopped inflating. Adding insult to injury, something inside my neck tweaked, seizing a muscle painfully.

"Goddamn it!" Rubbing the sore spot gently, I grimaced and closed my eyes again. I didn't know which was worse, the pounding headache or the now-pulled muscle.

Headache.

The same headache I had right before the worst threesome of my life.

My heart rate went into overdrive at the memory. Dream? Whatever it was, rage prickled along my skin like needles. All of the blood, or the hot, sticky sensation of it, made me shudder.

Opening my eyes slowly, I expelled a few quick breaths and forced myself to look down.

My torso was bare — naked *and* clean.

There was no blood.

No knife.

And certainly no body next to the bed.

I wasn't even in Leander's bed. I was in the red guest room, covered with crimson and gold bedding instead of black.

Exhaling a couple of steadying breaths, I turned to my right, still wary of who I'd find in the bed beside me. Or what.

Leander was the only one there, dressed as he had been hours earlier, but fast asleep. A book laid on his stomach, rising and falling with his slow, even breaths. It was after midnight when I called it quits and left him to his insomnia, so there was no telling when he crept in.

Swiping a hand over my face, I eased out of bed and down the hall. A freezing cold shower would have been the better option, so of course I went for the *other* recovery method.

Descending the stairs on shaking legs, I headed straight for the butler's pantry.

Grabbing a bottle of bourbon out of the cabinet, I didn't even bother with a glass. I twisted the cap off and drank straight from the bottle until I nearly gagged on the fiery taste and the sudden volume of liquid in my stomach.

What the fuck was wrong with me? It was anxiety. That's all. Stress-induced anxiety. Nothing a little Xanax couldn't fix. Hell, I might even have some oxy stashed somewhere if I looked hard enough. I'd do it in the morning, when I wasn't so jacked up from that dream — no, *nightmare*. That way I wouldn't take the whole damn bottle in a desperate attempt to get that blonde bitch out of my head. But Xanax was ok. Especially with a little alcohol chaser. I was an expert when it came to that combo.

Chugging another few gulps from the bourbon, I made my way to the kitchen. Most people tended to keep their drugs in the bathroom, but mine were right next to the kitchen sink. Easier to access at any point in the day and easier to throw down the garbage disposal if the need ever arose, such as the cops showing up unexpectedly.

I tossed back a couple of pills and washed them down with more bourbon. Sighing, I slumped against the counter and cradled the bottle against my chest, though the cool glass did little to relieve the heat radiating out of me.

Without even meaning to, I glanced at the knife block on the island. All of the knives were there. I double-checked the ones hanging on the magnetic strip by the stove. They, too, were all accounted for. The logical part of my brain told me

Leander would never risk ruining one of his kitchen knives to murder someone, but the darker side of my brain couldn't rule out the possibility. He tended to use weapons of opportunity — hence, the crowbar that became something of a signature.

I should have quit drinking while I was ahead, but I couldn't. Even if it was a dream, I swore I could still taste Lorelei, something sickly sweet and sharply bitter. It overpowered the bourbon no matter how much I drank. Worst of all, I could *feel* her all over me, scratching beneath my skin like a rat trying to chew its way out of a cage.

Rolling my head in slow circles, I grimaced, rubbing the back of my neck again. A shower. Definitely in need of a shower. Maybe two. And some bleach.

Taking one last pull from the bottle, I shoved it in the closest cabinet, making a note to put it back in the pantry later. Leander had a thing about the counters being clear and him coming down in the morning to find evidence of a three a.m. drinking session was going to lead to questions, questions which I did *not* want to answer.

On my way out of the kitchen, I stopped abruptly. My gaze landed on Leander's cell phone, laying innocently on a silver tray. He left it on the center island next to his keys and a pile of bills. Same as he did most nights. With how shitty he slept, it wasn't like he needed an alarm clock to wake up.

I picked it up, watching the lock screen light up with the motion. There was no picture. No notifications. Just the time and date, glowing from a black screen. Even if his aesthetic was totally Victorian Gothic, he was a minimalist at heart.

Put the phone down, Bennett… Walk away before you do something stupid.

No.

I *had* to know.

I had to know if my subconscious was telling me something my waking self refused to see. He promised me she meant nothing, that he would end it properly. But… what if? The Devil's greatest trick was getting people to believe he didn't exist. What if Leander's greatest trick was convincing me he wasn't a liar?

Staring at the lock screen, I tried to figure out what the hell he'd use for a four-digit password. His birthday was too obvious. He definitely wouldn't use either of his parents'. I tried Poe's on a hunch.

Nothing.

I tapped out Lorelei's with a grimace.

Nothing.

He wasn't a birthday person, idiot. He hated birthdays. They were right up there with Christmas and any other family-oriented holiday.

Nor was he the type to use a random code — everything to this man had meaning. So what meaning would he ascribe to his phone — the thing that he used multiple times in a given day? What little daily reminder did he choose to have?

The day he murdered Irene?

Technically also his birthday, but still a giant "Nope."

I tried one of the dates from Puerto Rico.

Nada. Probably too soon. He wasn't the type to change things on a whim. It would have to be a more historic date, so to speak.

Two more attempts before it locked me out.

The day we met?

Nope.

Fuck.

I bit my lip, studying the phone. The screen faded to black again as I held it in my hand. Even though I tipped it up slightly, it stayed black. It did, however, show a flash of fingerprints mostly in the top center of the screen. Bringing it up for a closer look, the phone woke itself up. Grumbling, I forced it to black out again and angled it to the side, catching the kitchen light in the reflective surface.

I'd try one last date. If this was wrong, then the universe was telling me to back the fuck off and walk away, to trust him and tell my self-doubt to take a hike. Plus, it was the only attempt I had left.

After I tapped the last number, the lock screen disappeared, revealing the array of app icons he used to organize his life.

I exhaled, casting a glance upward. Someone out there was messing with me. First the dream, now this.

Shaking off my ridiculousness, I tapped on his text messages and scrolled. And scrolled. Past the numerous conversations with his friends, there were messages back and forth with employees, lawyers, and accountants.

At the bottom was the thread for Lorelei.

I scrolled all the way to the beginning, because I was a fucking masochist. He must have deleted their previous conversation, since the thread was entirely one-sided and seemed to start after our return to the mainland, specifically after I'd called her about the damn cat.

Why he didn't block her was a mystery, but I'm sure there was a reason for it.

Leander, please. Call me back.

Why aren't you answering?

Annabel is fine, but I need to talk to you.

I get it if you don't want to talk, but just let me know you're ok.

Please answer me. You're scaring me.

You don't have to work through this alone. Let me help you. I love you and I'll always be here for you.

The bourbon came up the back of my throat a little bit. I flicked away the messages and moved over to his call log. Dozens and dozens of calls out, but none of them to Lorelei or anyone with an 815 area code. Her name, however, was in red nearly every day, meaning he missed — or avoided — her call.

I tapped on the voicemail icon and waited.

There was only one message from today. I didn't have to listen to it, since the transcription was right below it.

I don't understand why you won't talk to me, why you won't even let me see you. And why do I have to hear about all of this from your lawyers and Olivia? What happened, Leander? Why did you disappear on me? I love you so much and it's breaking my heart that you won't let me be there for you right now. Please, tell me what I can do to help. I *want* to help you. I love you.

Out of curiosity, I checked his deleted voicemails. Sure enough, there were a dozen of them. It was more of the same psychobabble bullshit and teary confessions. At least he was consistent. When he cut someone off, they were all but dead to him. I should know — I was a ghost for months before I somehow managed to get back into his good graces.

How, and why, I still didn't know. All I did was give him a paper flower and a dinner date that technically never happened. Then suddenly we were in Puerto Rico and the rest of the world ceased to exist. It was almost like those months we were separated were erased, except when either one of us was feeling particularly bitter.

Now we were back in Easton, picking up the pieces, trying to make a life together while his ex-lover clung to the hope *they'd* patch things up. Clearly I was hanging on to the past, too, evident by a fucked up dream that had me standing in the kitchen at three a.m., buzzing on benzos and bourbon, snooping through Leander's cell phone.

He, on the other hand, wasn't clinging to anything. Leander wasn't lying to me and carrying on a secret relationship behind my back. He cast her aside. He chose me, just as he said. By all intents and purposes, I "won," like he announced on the plane. But not really. I wouldn't claim that victory until my nemesis was dead and there were no more challengers vying for my place.

Snatching the bottle of bourbon out of the cabinet again, I tossed his phone back on the counter and made my way to the conservatory. There was no way I was going back upstairs. Despite the dual depressants metabolizing in my system, my mind wouldn't shut up or even slow its roll.

I stretched out on one of the wicker couches and folded an arm behind my head, looking up at the glass ceiling overhead. Exhaling, I focused my attention on the night sky beyond. The stars were out, twinkling away without a care as to what turmoil happened here on Earth.

I was still surprised by the date he chose as his password.

February 26.

The first night we spent together. The night all of our barriers came down. They went right back up the next day, for reasons within our control and those forced on us by outsiders. But for that one night, a few precious hours, we were *so* fucking happy. It wasn't just the sex. It was everything. I didn't know anything about soulmates or twin flames or any of that shit, but I knew from that night on that Leander held my heart, my life, my very soul in his hands.

Now I knew he felt it too — the password was proof. Even through the months of separation, the months without me, *that* was the number combination he used to safeguard his phone. Looked like he was also a masochist, giving his heart little cuts every time he had to type out that date, even while he was with *Her*.

He *did* choose me. He chose me first and he *kept* choosing me, even when he thought I was gone forever.

The realization made me smile, whisking away the tension in my body just like that.

The bitch still had to die, though.

So that's where my thoughts carried me. Beneath the bright starlight, with bourbon and Xanax warming me from the inside out, I focused my energy on planning Lorelei's death until sleep finally reclaimed me.

10

BENNETT

The late afternoon sun streamed through the library windows, illuminating the dark wood, its golden undertones shining through. It was warm, made all the warmer for the fact Leander was using my lap as a pillow.

"Have you ever thought of expanding?" I asked, glancing around.

The built-in shelves were jam packed with books, as were the free-standing shelves in the middle of the room. If that weren't enough, there were still *more* books in the attic he didn't display for one reason or another. Not to mention, his ever-growing Poe collection. Why he felt the need to possess as many copies of the same book as possible was beyond me. Then again, my collections involved fine art, where only the original mattered.

"No," he replied, turning a page in his book. He didn't even bother looking up at me, nor did he seem to have any intention of elaborating.

I should have been reading the contract in my lap, but I was too distracted by my hangover and the blonde hair I plucked off of one of the curtains earlier. No matter where I went, she was fucking *there*. I may have felt better after my drunken revelations, but I really didn't want to find pieces of her all over the place for the rest of my life.

"Why not?" I prodded, looking for a distraction from my murderous thoughts.

"I can't go out because of structural issues and I can't go down because of utilities."

"What about up?"

He laid the book on his chest and looked up at me finally, his brows lifted. "The master suite is above us."

"My point exactly. Fuck Irene and fuck her room." I picked up the contract and searched for the spot I left off, trying to keep my tone airy and casual. "Besides, you can always make a new master suite on the west side by expanding into the blue guest room."

Two birds, one stone. Expand the library he loved and demolish the space of the woman he loathed. Meanwhile, renovating the blue room would remove the final trace of his mistress from the property, since Yolanda kindly informed me that was where the annoying doctor spent most of her time after Leander disappeared. Apparently it was just too "hard" being in Leander's room without him.

Although after that dream, I saw Lorelei's dead body every time I went into Leander's room. I loved remembering her dead, but it wasn't an image I wanted to live with — not unless it was a reality and not some fucked up scenario from my subconscious.

If Leander saw the remodeling idea for what it was, he didn't say anything. He simply picked up his book and resumed reading.

Running my hand through his hair absentmindedly, I tried to focus on the fine print instead of the fact it had been exactly twelve minutes and eighteen seconds since his lips touched mine.

My fingers shifted downward, stroking the underside of his sharp jaw. He turned his head slightly, giving me greater access to his throat.

I moved downward, inch by inch, until my hand slipped beneath the collar of his sweater. He arched his back, which put him in a better position to gaze up at me from my lap while my hand splayed across his smooth chest.

"Can I help you with something?" he asked, adopting a demure tone to go along with his polite smile.

"Shh." I cleared my throat, keeping my attention on the contract, or at least pretending to. "I'm trying to get some work done."

"You're incorrigible."

"You love it."

"Will it make you happy?" His voice was suddenly serious.

"Will what make me happy?" I lowered the brief, furrowing my brows at him.

He arched an eyebrow back at me, silently calling my bluff. "You can remodel whatever you like, just don't touch my kitchen."

"I wouldn't dream of it." I smiled and leaned down, kissing him. He dropped his book and reached for me, his fingers slipping through my hair to pull me closer.

The doorbell chimed throughout the house, interrupting the quiet. The deep, booming tone signaled someone was at the front door rather than the back.

We exchanged a wary glance, both looking equally confused. It was safe to assume it wasn't a social call, though, since our friends would have either texted beforehand or simply let themselves in the back door. So God only knew who was here to take one, or both, of our heads off.

Whoever it was, we went to face them together.

The door swung open and the world stopped spinning.

There stood Dr. Lorelei Clayton in the flesh. A block of

ice formed in my stomach at the mere sight of her. Perfect blonde hair, perfect blue eyes, perfect fucking everything. Sadly, that part of the dream hadn't been exaggerated.

For a split second, she stood there, staring at Leander in pure awe. In the next instant, she lunged across the distance, throwing her arms around his neck.

I bit my tongue, literally, as hard as I could between my molars. Forcing my gaze away, I crossed my arms over my chest so I didn't inadvertently strangle her.

Leander, for his part, remained frozen in place, his arms firmly at his sides.

She pushed away after a minute and held his face in her hands. Her eyes were bright, wet with tears, as she gazed up at him like he was the Second Coming. "When your lawyer called, I didn't believe it at first. Where have you been? All this time I thought—"

"Where is Annabel?" Leander took a step backward, out of her hands, his expression devoid of any discernible emotion.

"What?"

"Annabel — I assume you brought her?"

"Who is this?" she asked, suddenly realizing he wasn't alone. She glanced between the two of us, her brows drawn together.

Happy to see I was once again relevant, I turned my gaze to the blonde across from me. "Bennett Reeve," I replied with a tight smile. There was no point in wasting my charm on the likes of her.

A glare shot across her face. Guess she was still sore from our phone conversation. Aw, rats. However was I going to sleep tonight?

She turned back to Leander, her happiness dimmed considerably. "Your lawyer?"

"My husband," Leander corrected, quietly, but as clear as could be.

If I wasn't so skilled at masking my surprise, I'd have been picking my jaw up off the floor. There was no "It's not you, it's me" speech, no hand holding, or "Let's be friends" bullshit. Oh, no. Leander dropped the biggest break-up bomb I'd ever seen and he didn't even flinch. He was *so* getting laid later.

The confusion melted from her face, replaced with something akin to horror. Her golden skin turned an odd shade of green and it sounded like she expelled all the air from her lungs just to push out a single question. "Your *what?*"

"Husband," I repeated, trying not to sound too gleeful. I held up my left hand and pointed at the black titanium band on my ring finger. She must have been a visual learner since she clearly didn't listen for shit. Ironic, considering her profession. She didn't waste any time comparing it to the one and only ring on Leander's hand — a matching band on his left ring finger. "So, where's the cat?"

"You're gay?" Lorelei squeaked the question. She still looked the teensiest bit hopeful, like this was all some sort of a prank. Like Leander was the type to pull asinine pranks. Wasn't this bitch supposed to be able to read crazy people? Even if Leander manipulated the shit out of her, did she not get *any* sense of his real personality?

Leander and I exchanged an irritated look before I rolled my eyes in the opposite direction so hard she probably heard them rattling. I should have listened to Olivia — I should have killed her instead of trying to take the high road. It would have been a lot less aggravating. Explaining the nuances of sexuality to a fucking *doctor* was not on my list of things to do today, or ever. Guess it was a good practice run for Leander, though, since now he'd be facing his fair share of ignorant assumptions.

Forcing a smile to his lips, Leander turned back to Lorelei, answering through his teeth. "No, I'm not. But that is hardly the point."

"Yeah, you're right." She crossed her arms over her chest, glowering at him in earnest. "Maybe I should be more pissed about the fact you're married!" She spat the last word and gave me a dose of her wrath, like I was the one entirely at fault.

Sure, I'd asked the question, but Leander was the one who arranged everything less than two hours after he said "Yes" — *after* we saw Lorelei's fucking news conference, I might add. I never imagined when I proposed that night we'd come home married. *He* was the one who said he didn't want to wait, that he wanted to commemorate our time in Puerto Rico. According to him, what better way than by promising eternity to one another?

Rejuvenated by the warm, fuzzy feeling I got every time I thought about the fact Leander was my husband — *my* husband — I smiled smugly in return.

I know in the dream I stabbed her, but at the moment, I was happily imagining what she would look like if I slit her throat. I'd have to make sure I kept it on the porch. It'd be so much easier to clean the mat outside. Plus, I didn't want to run the risk of ruining the inlaid floor in the foyer.

"Or maybe," she ground out, turning her ire back to Leander, "it's the fact you've been gone for a month and didn't have the decency to let me know you were alive!"

"That was an oversight," he replied evenly.

She barked a short, bitter laugh. "An oversight? And your marital status? Was that another 'oversight?' Have you been married this whole goddamn time?"

Unfolding my arms, I straightened my spine, my right hand drifting nonchalantly to the waistband behind my hip. I was two seconds away from putting a permanent end to this little reunion. But… I didn't have anything pointy on me. Damn it. I'd have to strangle her after all.

A muscle along Leander's jaw twitched. If he knew I was plotting his ex-lover's death, he didn't seem concerned. His eyes were narrowed on hers, as still and silent as a statute. I knew that look. It meant he was in the process of taking whatever positive feelings he ever had for her and warping them, fueling his rising anger with it. Ooo, maybe *he'd* strangle her. I couldn't ask for a better wedding present than that.

"Was it all a lie?" she asked, her voice brittle.

"No." Ouch. Ok. I knew that one was coming. He'd all but told me the same thing on the plane. I wouldn't let it spoil the anticipation of seeing him kill her.

Lorelei scoffed and looked away. "I don't even know why I asked. I can't believe anything you say. I can't believe I ever did."

"For what it's worth, I never meant to hurt you," he said quietly.

That wasn't exactly what I pictured someone saying before strangling their mistress to death… I slid him a curious glance out of the corner of my eye. His expression hadn't softened in the slightest, despite his verbal reassurance.

She dashed a tear away from her face. "No. You just used me for your own sick, twisted game."

And I'd heard about enough of that. I took a step forward, already fantasizing about wrapping my hands around her throat. Her neck was so slim, I could probably do it with just one hand. Two would make it faster. But then again, I wanted her to suffer.

Leander threw his forearm out across my chest, stopping me from crossing the threshold. I looked down sharply before shooting him a quizzical look.

He shook his head and lowered his hand, holding my gaze for a moment. I registered an apology in his eyes before he turned to Lorelei again. His voice was quiet, but rigid. His sympathy was for me, then, not her, a sign of his building anger. "I thought I could love you, eventually, but—"

"Psychopaths don't know how to love," she interrupted, her chin tipping up.

Game on, bitch.

My fists clenched so hard, my knuckles cracked on their own as I took a step toward her.

A dark smile curled the edge of Leander's mouth. He shifted forward as well so the two of us were shoulder-to-shoulder, fixed on the stupid, *stupid* woman in front of us.

"And what does that say about you?" Leander asked, cocking his head to the side. "Professionally speaking? To allow yourself to be *used* by a *psychopath*? To know *you* came to *me*, begging for me to do it all over again?"

The iciness in his voice sent a happy shiver down my spine. Now I knew, without a shadow of a doubt, there weren't any residual feelings for this broad. At least not after this doozy of a conversation, which was thankfully coming to an end based on the subtle change to his demeanor.

"You're sick. You know that right? You need *serious*, long-term help." Lorelei's glare snapped from Leander to me. "Do you even know about the severity of his mental health? All of the disorders he has? Do you think you can handle it when he has another breakdown?"

"I know all I need to," I replied in a clipped tone, leaning forward to brace one forearm against the doorframe. "Just like I know you're dancing pretty fucking close to a HIPAA violation. But by all means, keep talking. What else should concern me?"

"The fact that he's a murderer?" A second too late she

realized what, exactly, came out of her mouth. Her gaze flashed to Leander and she swallowed visibly.

His dark smile returned, accompanied with a dangerous glint in his eye. "You have ten seconds to produce my cat, Lorelei, or I assure you you will not like how this conversation ends."

She stepped backward, her teeth clenched. Snatching a black carrier off the bench on the front porch, she returned with quick steps and shoved it into Leander's arms. "Go to Hell."

Turning from the door with the carrier in one hand, Leander swatted it closed with the other. No "Thank you." No goodbye. Not even a "Fuck off."

I, however, had to lob one last grenade at her. My hand shot out, stopping the door from closing all the way. Taking a step closer to the threshold, I bent my head in Lorelei's direction and lowered my voice. "If I were you, blondie, I would refrain from making accusations you can't substantiate. Call my husband a murderer one more time and I'll make sure it's the last thing you ever do."

She tossed her head, assessing me with a sneer. "How does the bar feel about lawyers fucking their clients?"

I smirked at her brashness. Hell, I might have liked her if we met under entirely different circumstances. "I'm sure the same way the IDFPR feels about doctors fucking their patients."

"I don't know what you think you know about him, but make no mistake, *I* know what he is. I know what he's capable of." Her shoulders squared, strengthened by her self-righteousness.

"Oh, you do, do you?" She didn't have a fucking clue.

"You're out of your depth, counselor."

I gave her a blithe smile, leaning closer. Her perfume was even more noxious in person. It was syrupy sweet to the point I'd inhale a cocktail of bleach and ammonia to get it out of my olfactory system. "Let's see if I can put this in terms you'll understand... Go to the police, or anyone for that matter, and I'll cut your fucking heart out. I assure you, it's not a metaphor — I mean it with the utmost sincerity."

Her scowl tightened, but she recoiled nevertheless, a flicker of fear in her eyes. If she thought Leander was a psychopath, I could only imagine what she thought about me. Maybe one day I would get a chance to show her, up close and personal.

"Ta ta, Doctor." I slammed the door an inch from her pert nose and pivoted on my heel.

Leander was in the kitchen watching the scrawny, orange cat at his feet devour a plate of tuna. "Dare I ask what that was all about?"

Both eyebrows lifted as I passed by. "Hmm? What?"

His eyes narrowed briefly, calling me out on my deliberate refusal to answer.

I continued to ignore him and stepped into the pantry.

"To think, all this time you've been jealous of something that wasn't even real," Leander mused when I reappeared with a jar of peanut butter.

"It was real for her." I shot him a look out of the corner of my eye, fetching a spoon from the drawer. "And I'm not jealous."

"That's not what it sounded like."

"I'm not jealous — I'm..." I squinted up at one of the can lights, waving the spoon in small circles. "Territorial."

"Consider your territory well and truly marked." He laughed and scooped up the cat, scratching beneath her chin. "I hope now you realize you don't have anything to worry about."

"No, but you do." Leaning against the counter, I licked a glob of peanut butter off the spoon.

"What are you talking about?" he asked, nuzzling the cat, completely oblivious to the fact she was shedding orange fur all over him. I could feel my eyes prickling, even from a distance. When they started to water, I made a mental note to have Gavin set up an appointment with an allergist ASAP.

"She all but threatened to expose you."

"She wouldn't dare." His eyes darted to mine over the top of the cat's head.

His faith in her overarching goodness was cute, and entirely misplaced. He did as I asked — he crushed her heart to reassure me of his loyalty, but in the process he obliterated whatever goodwill she might have had. The fact she tried to shock me by divulging Leander's secrets showed how deep the wound actually ran. Had I known how attached she was in such a short amount of time, I would have advised a different strategy.

"Nevertheless, you might want to be prepared. Or... come up with another option." I licked the majority of the peanut butter off of the spoon, arching an eyebrow pointedly.

Kissing the cat on the head, Leander set her on the ground before walking over to me. "Are you planning on killing her?"

"Not *planning* on it, no." I smiled brightly, swiping my tongue over the spoon, cleaning off the remaining peanut butter. It was *planned*. All I was waiting for was a green light, since I couldn't to do away with her ten minutes ago.

He considered me for a moment, nodding to some conclusion in his head. "I'll send Jake up there to keep an eye on her for a while, make sure she doesn't get any ideas."

"Yeah, sure. That sounds like a good idea. Very responsible of you. Speaking of which, do you want to tell me how she *knows* about you?" I forced a pleasant expression to my face, trying not to be accusatory even if I could feel my blood start to boil.

He bit his lips and spun away, suddenly very concerned with refrigerating the leftover tuna.

I jammed the spoon in the peanut butter and set the jar on the counter, hot on his heels. "What did you do?"

"I had a problem. I handled it." He closed the fridge. Instead of facing me, he scurried toward the servant stairs.

I chased after him. "And you *told* her?"

"Not exactly."

When we reached the first landing, I made a grab for him. Spinning him by the arm, I shoved him against the wall and blocked his escape, making the most of the two inches I had on him. "Speaking as one of your lawyers right now, what the fuck did you do?"

His eyes rolled skyward before he caved and looked at me. "I killed Richard's assistant and Lorelei saw me coming back into the house."

I folded my arms over my chest, staring hard at him, waiting for the incriminating part.

"With the crowbar." He winced. "Covered in blood."

"Oh, for the love of Christ!" I gaped at him.

Before I lost my composure completely, it was my turn to dart away, continuing up the stairs. I needed some distance to actually think and not be distracted by his puppy eyes or his pleading.

"Bennett..."

"Do not feed me a line of bullshit right now." I crested the stairs and peeled off for the terrace at the back of the house, trying to talk myself out of following that bitch home and solving *this* little problem right now. I thought she was bluffing. I thought she was referring to the murders he'd been *accused* of. I didn't realize he'd gone and fucking killed someone *else*, someone outside of the plan, someone he didn't tell me a goddamn thing about!

"It's her word against mine." His tone was imploring, a

silent cry for understanding, but I wasn't ready to give it. Maybe when I wasn't so fucking pissed, I'd see his side of the argument.

Throwing open the double doors, I inhaled the evening air as quickly and deeply as I could. So far I hadn't come up with a single reason why Lorelei fucking Clayton should continue to live. She was a walking liability and there was only *one* way to definitively deal with a liability. Even if I somehow got her to sign an NDA, she could break it. She'd already been willing to throw away her career for something as illogical as love. Why should spite be any different?

"She's not a credible witness," Leander continued, stopping next to me at the wrought-iron railing. "If she tells the police how she knows, she'll ruin herself professionally. If she lies about how she knows, you'll destroy her testimony. Or Richard will."

"Where's the crowbar?" I whirled on him so fast he took a step back.

"Gone."

"Gone *where?*"

"Underneath the house. No one will ever find it. I couldn't retrieve it now even if I wanted to."

"And the clothes from that night?"

"Burned." He stroked the length of my forearm lightly. "I promise you. There isn't any evidence left."

"Oh, no? How about the body? Is that in the basement too?" I shouldn't have been so mad, but what.the.fuck? What happened to the man who spent months planning a single event? Now all of a sudden he was whacking secretaries and eloping on a whim? He'd changed during our time apart and the jury was still out whether or not that was ultimately a good thing.

"Dismembered and scattered," he snapped, looking wounded at the line of questioning. Not that I blamed him.

I'm sure he was expecting an entirely different reaction. "Throughout a dozen hog farms, here and across the river. What wasn't eaten was dissolved and buried."

Alright. That *was* a nice touch. My hackles lowered — slightly. He was as capable a killer as I was, and deep down I knew he wouldn't leave anything to chance. "I'd feel a hell of a lot better if that bitch was dead."

Leander softened, slipping his hands around my waist and pulling me closer. "There are people who are relying on her."

He could have only meant the patient he befriended at Parkview, the one whose care he paid for via an anonymous trust. "You mean Martha?"

Nodding, he stretched up and pressed a kiss to the underside of my jaw. Leave it to him to want to protect a paranoid schizophrenic who stabbed her mother to death with a goddamn palette knife.

"I swear to God, my love, if I even get an *inkling* she's gone to the police, I'll snuff her out like this," I said with a snap.

"If she goes to the police, you'll have to beat me to her," he replied before his teeth grazed my throat.

I caught his face between my hands and angled it toward mine, watching for any minute changes to his expression. "You'd really kill her?"

He didn't look away, or blink, or show any emotion other than solemnity. "I won't be separated from you again, mon coeur. I promise you, here and now, I'll kill her or anyone else who tries to tear us apart."

With that declaration, my bloodlust simmered. I closed my eyes and wrapped my arms around his neck, breathing in the scent of his hair.

11

LEANDER

Go to Hell.

Lorelei's parting words circled my brain, day after day. I had Annabel back and Lorelei was gone. The last link between us finally was severed. Or so I thought.

You're sick. You know that right?

Twisting the black wedding band around my finger, I stared at the emptiness in front of me, seeing nothing but the look of betrayal on her face. The anger. Indignation. I hadn't expected her to take the news well, but I was surprised how viscerally she reacted. To which part, I wasn't quite sure — Bennett, or our marriage.

Bennett, because, well, he was Bennett? Because he was a *he*? Because he threatened her femininity? No, not just threatened — thwarted it. That I would choose a "him" over her?

Or was it our marriage that she balked at? That I never professed my love to her during our brief togetherness, only to turn around and announce I was a married man? She knew how I felt about lying, and telling her that I loved her would have been the biggest lie of all. I never did, no matter how much I tried to convince myself that one day, possibly, I might, under the right circumstances.

You need serious, long-term help.

Pressing my hands against either side of my skull, I pushed in, trying to counteract the pain raging inside. It only worked for a moment. Then the vitriol was back, bringing with it a steady stabbing sensation in the center of my brain.

Beneath the pain, Lorelei's voice hissed her condemnation at me. Gradually, it voice morphed into the sound of my nightmares — Irene's voice. Lorelei's words. Together, they were a blend of false concern and barely controlled rage.

Do you even know about the severity of his mental health? All of the disorders he has?

Had Lorelei really tried to turn my own husband against me? Did she think she could scare him off that easily?

And what if she had?

Do you think you can handle it when he has another breakdown?

Another breakdown, thus implying I'd already had one. I knew I had. She knew I had. Sadly, not all of my experiences whilst under her medical care were staged. Some of them were true — flashes of authenticity in an elaborate charade, when I was too weak or delirious to get control of myself.

But Bennett? Bennett didn't know. Bennett didn't know what happened during the time we were apart, that I'd lost my fucking mind without him. He didn't know how utterly destroyed I'd been. And he didn't need to know. Because if he knew, he might choose to leave. He might decide he *couldn't* handle another episode, or that he didn't *want* to. That this life he thought he wanted was just too damn much.

I couldn't bear losing him a second time. I'd barely survived the first.

So, I looked at my ring, trying to convince myself the voices were wrong. But it didn't matter what I did, I couldn't get them to cease their incessant harping. Lorelei. Irene. They both squatted inside my head, like a pair of poisonous toads.

I'd feel a hell of a lot better if that bitch was dead.

Of course, Bennett was right. Killing Lorelei solved a vast majority of my problems. It might not stop her from haunting me, but it would stop the very real possibility that she would go to the police and tell them everything she knew — about me, about Bennett, about all of it. She was a loose end that needed to be tied off immediately.

And yet...

Her only sin had been loving the unlovable, trying her damndest to heal what someone else had broken. I deserved her anger, even her hatred. But did she deserve to die because *I* let her get too close? Because I used her, trying to fill a void in my life?

I picked up the phone and dialed Jake's number.

"Nothing seems out of place," he said as soon as he answered. "Work and home, like usual. Haven't seen any police around. I was still able to log into Parkview's system and she doesn't have anything unusual in her schedule, either."

"Come home, then."

"Are you sure? I can stay another couple of days, make sure she doesn't change her mind."

"No, Jacob. Come home."

"Alright. See you Friday."

Before I hung up, a text message came through from a blocked number.

Done

Exhaling a breath, I leaned back in my chair and closed my eyes. Two things finally checked off the list. Maybe now I'd be able to sleep through the entire night.

12

BENNETT

Friday night dinner arrived with a bang. A literal one, since Cole popped open a bottle of champagne and the cork ricocheted off the stainless steel oven hood, straight into the window above the sink.

"Jesus Christ!" Olivia shrieked and ducked, smacking his bicep.

"Give me that fucking thing before you break something," Elijah snapped, yanking the bottle of out Cole's hands while Leander wordlessly handed him a towel to mop up the fizzing bubbles.

"That thing should come with a warning label." Cole chuckled, wiping his hands before turning to the puddle.

"That's why I use a knife," I said, ducking between Olivia and Cole to snag the hor d'oeuvres plates.

Jake snorted at the far end of the kitchen and rolled his eyes.

"Yes, we all know your affinity for sharp pointy things." Cole shot me a devilish grin.

"Better than poison, right?" I hip-checked Olivia, winking

at her when she teetered on her stilettos. She promptly flipped me off.

Laughing, I carried the platters to the dining room and deposited them on the table between the other place settings. The front doorbell rang, and since I was the closest, I went to answer it.

As soon as I opened the door I was attacked by a bright bouquet of flowers. I grabbed for the stems quickly, juggling them until I got a good grip.

"Oh my God! I don't know how you make that drive as often as you do!" Gavin's voice snapped, somewhere behind the flowers. "Like, these people and their pickup trucks and their country music! Get the hell out of the way already! I would have been here an hour ago if Billy Bob hadn't decided to drive five miles under the damn speed limit. Probably afraid his rust bucket was going to fall apart if he went any faster."

"It's fine," I said, shifting the bouquet to my hip so I could see him. "We haven't even started yet."

Gavin tugged at his white sleeves, only to scrunch them back up onto his forearms. "You know I hate being late."

"You're always late."

"Yeah, but I still hate it."

I rolled my eyes and headed toward the kitchen. "I hope Leander has a vase big enough for these things."

"I was going for a whole sunset theme," Gavin said, trailing after me. The Birds of Paradise flowers certainly did match his bright orange pants.

"I'm sure Leander will appreciate it."

"Anything for him." He made a little giggle that annoyed me more than it should have. For as long as Gavin had known Leander, he'd been in love with him. Well, in *lust* with him, at any rate. If I asked for something, I got twenty minutes worth of backtalk and a motley of huffs and sighs. If

Leander asked for something, Gavin had it done in a matter of moments, served to him with a smile on a silver platter.

"Please tell me you have a vase for these?" I said, hoisting the flowers into view as I rounded the corner to the kitchen. "Or should I just stick them in a stock pot?"

Leander laughed and reached for the bouquet. "I think I have something. Thank you, Gavin."

"My pleasure." He even curtseyed. Gag me. My annoyance was short lived, though. Gavin grabbed my arm and yanked me to the side, lowering his voice. "Oh my God. *Who* is *that*?"

"Who?" I blinked, glancing around the kitchen.

It was the usual crowd. Elijah was doing something with olive oil and seasoned salt at the counter. Olivia and Cole were arguing about some horror movie they watched and who *really* knocked the popcorn over when the killer clown appeared. Since Leander was off trying to find a vase, that left Jake. Sulky, sour-puss Jake, who was playing with Annabel on the servant stairs.

I stared at Gavin, glancing between the two a couple times to make sure I was seeing what he was seeing. "You've gotta be fucking kidding me. Him?!"

"Who is he?"

"That's *Jake*. A royal pain in my ass, although your gay-dar is on point. He's so closeted it's not even funny."

"Oh, I can help with that." Gavin beamed up at me, shimmying his shoulders.

"I don't think he would know what to do if you stripped naked and handed him a fucking manual." It was true. Although I still wanted to punch him in the face every time he opened his mouth, I had to admit Jake could get as much ass as he wanted if he lost the giant chip on his shoulder. He had that good-ol' boy masculinity that made him appear straight, which meant he was man-meat for most of the gay population.

"A fucking *manual*, or a *fucking* manual?" Gavin smacked my chest, biting his lower lip suggestively.

Shaking my head, I held up a hand and waved him off in disgust. "I cannot even deal with you right now." And he had the nerve to call *me* a slut.

Leander saved me by reappearing with the flowers, artfully arranged in a crystal vase. "Help me pick a spot?" He tossed his head down the hallway, which meant it wasn't a request at all.

"Behave." I pointed at Gavin before following Leander to the parlor.

Leander set the vase down on an accent table and took my hands in his, kissing the knuckles on each. "Are you nervous?"

"Shouldn't I be asking you that? I mean... other than Olivia, no one really knows about us."

He winced. "Jake knows."

"He what?!" If it was anyone other than Leander, I wouldn't think they were serious. But since he was serious about everything, I knew it was the truth. "Since when?"

"Remember that loud crash... you know... *that* night?"

"Uh-huh..." How could I forget? It nearly ruined everything. I mean, it did prompt us to go upstairs, so *that* part was a bonus...

"That was him. He saw us."

"Oh. Well, shit. That explains a lot." I replayed every interaction I'd had with the lad since that night. It all made so much sense now.

"Are we going to eat anytime tonight?" Cole shouted from the kitchen. "I'm starving!"

"You're always starving," Olivia snipped.

"Blow me."

"You'd like that, wouldn't you?"

"Hell yeah!"

Elijah was the one to break up the bickering. "Alright children, go sit down."

I pressed a quick kiss to Leander's lips and waggled my brows at him. "Let's go."

Lacing my fingers through his, I led the way into the dining room. When we rounded the corner, Leander tried to tug away, but I held on, shooting him a look over my shoulder. He squeezed my hand, a silent apology. Old habits and all that.

Everyone was already seated, more or less paired off and chatting animatedly. Except for Gavin, who was too busy giving Jake googly eyes while he sipped his spritzer. I couldn't help but notice he somehow managed to snag the seat directly next to the farm boy, despite my warning.

We took our chairs, Leander at the head of the table and me at his left side. Etiquette said I should have been at the other end, but fuck that. I wanted to be within arm's reach of my husband whenever possible.

"About time," Cole said, rubbing his washboard abs as if he was seconds from withering away. "Can we eat now?"

Elijah rolled his eyes and Olivia elbowed him before looking at the two of us expectantly. "How was Puerto Rico?"

Leander and I exchanged a glance, both looking away with a quiet laugh. The butterflies in my stomach were on a rollercoaster, more so for his nerves than my own. I'd been out for more than half of my life. To say this was a turning point for him was a massive understatement.

"Well, it was, umm..." He bit his lower lip, his cheeks flushing more than I think I'd ever seen in a social setting.

"There's something we wanted to tell you," I said slowly, waiting for him to jump back in at any point.

A hush fell over the table as everyone exchanged glances with one another, as well as us, waiting to see who would speak next.

Leander canted his head and smiled at me, giving an almost imperceptible nod.

"We are... together. *Together,* together," I announced. Olivia smiled brightly, but the rest of the table stared at us. Some blinked, some gaped. I cleared my throat and continued. "While we were in Puerto Rico, I asked Leander to marry me."

"And I said yes," Leander added helpfully, reaching for my hand again, this time on *top* of the table. In full view of everyone. If they looked closely, they would have seen his black wedding band.

"And then we did," I said.

"We did," Leander agreed. "We're married."

You could have heard a pin drop until Gavin squeaked, waving his fists in excited little movements.

Olivia shrieked, her chair screeching as she pushed it out quickly. Running over, she threw an arm around each of our necks and pulled us in for a strangling sort of hug. "You guys! I'm so happy for you!"

"I knew it!" Gavin yelled with a laugh, pointing at me. "I knew you called dibs on him!"

Cole and Elijah smiled and said their congratulations, one sounding very confused while the other wasn't fazed at all. Typical Jake was silent, glaring a hole through his plate.

Once everyone settled down, Gavin piped up again. "You *have* to let me help you plan the reception!"

"Uh, I don't think so," Olivia interjected, sliding back into her seat and flipping her dark hair over her shoulder. "If anyone is planning a reception, it's me."

"I got them together!" Gavin snapped.

"I got them *back* together," Olivia countered.

"Ladies, ladies. You're both pretty," I said, holding my hands out to the two of them like a referee. "There's no need to fight because we're not having a reception."

"What?" They gasped in unison.

"Why not?" Elijah asked.

Leander cleared his throat softly. "It's better for business if we keep this between us."

"Business?" Olivia shot me a perplexed look.

"Oh..." Gavin's shoulders slumped. "The Russians."

Leander and I nodded. I was pretty confident Sergei wouldn't jeopardize his contract with Leander's shipping company, but it would definitely be an unnecessary strain to our working relationship. Besides, until the whole Marchese nonsense was over, I didn't need anyone knowing I had a vulnerability.

"So, I have a question," Cole said, leaning forward on his elbows, peering around Elijah. "Which one of you is the chick?"

Before Leander or I could react, Olivia and Elijah both smacked him in the head from opposite sides. He winced and ducked, giving each of them a glare. "Come on! You're all wondering!"

Gavin giggled and swatted Jake's bicep playfully. Jake managed to muster a smirk and rolled his eyes.

Leander and I exchanged a long, knowing look. Giving him a wry grin, I arched an eyebrow at him, waiting patiently with my hand outstretched.

Sighing, Leander pulled out his wallet and fished a hundred dollar bill from the center. He held it to me between two fingers, his jaw shifting as he looked away in defeat.

I chuckled and plucked it out of his fingers, tucking it into my own pocket. "Thank you very kindly, sir."

"What was that for?" Cole asked, eyeing us suspiciously.

"I told him you'd be the first one to ask," I replied with a smirk.

Cole balked at me, but had zero defense because his ass knew it was true.

"And I told him you had more sense than that," Leander added sympathetically.

"Cole? Sense?" Olivia snorted.

Cole gaped at her, looking wounded.

"Wishful thinking," Elijah added with a laugh.

"What is this? Pick on Cole night?" Cole threw his napkin on the table and pushed his chair out. "Fuck you guys. I'm getting dessert."

"We haven't even had dinner yet!" Olivia yelled after him.

"I don't care! I'm eating my feelings!"

Leander chuckled quietly, lacing his fingers through mine again. The smile didn't reach his eyes, though.

"You look troubled," I said, dragging my finger in small circles on Leander's bare shoulder blade.

He shifted his cheek against my chest, further obscuring my limited view of his face. "It's nothing."

"It's something." My fingers continued to skim across his skin, up and down his back in random patterns. Other than playing with his hair or threatening him with bodily harm, it was one of the easiest ways to get him to relax and actually open up. "Tell me."

"Cole."

My hand stopped abruptly. I knew I made a face, not that he could see it from his position. That was the last thing I expected him to say. "What about him?"

"You were right."

"I usually am. What this time?"

Rolling away, he settled onto his back and glared up at the ornate plaster ceiling. His brow was creased and his jaw tight, prompting me to drop the sarcasm.

Shifting onto my side so I could face him, I kissed my way up the side of his arm to his shoulder. "What is it, my love?"

"Our relationship's not like that."

Now I was really confused. I propped myself on an elbow, furrowing my brows at him. "Like what?"

"Where I'm the man and you're the..." He gestured helplessly in the air, way more distraught than he needed to be over a dumb question.

"The chick?" I laughed and scooted closer, nuzzling his neck. "I don't give a fuck what Cole thinks. The only person I'm concerned with is right here."

"But it's not true. You're not. In many ways I'd even say you're more masculine than I am."

"We never answered him, so who cares?" I pulled back with a frown, studying his profile. "Unless you're worried they think it's you?" The whole masculine/feminine debate wasn't exactly something I wanted to get into at the moment, but I knew he wouldn't be able to sleep until we'd dissected every part of our relationship, comparing it to the ridiculous social constructs that meant absolutely nothing in the grand scheme of things.

"It's not that... You know I don't need their approval."

"Then what is it?"

"I haven't quite figured you out."

I rubbed my eyes with my thumb and forefinger, hoping to assuage the dull thumping in my head, a lovely aftereffect of the champagne. "What do you mean? What is there to figure out?"

Leander shifted beside me. When I opened my eyes again, he was looking at me with a befuddled quirk to his mouth. "You've been with women, so you clearly perform that role as well."

"Yes..." I officially did *not* like where this conversation was headed. I had no regrets about my various escapades before Leander, but it wasn't exactly something I wanted to discuss with him either. For someone who gave *me* shit about being jealous, he certainly displayed his fair share since we'd been back and a conversation like this was bound to end in an argument. Personal experience taught me complete transparency involving body counts (the sexy *and* the stabby kind) tended to get ugly.

"What about with other men?" His voice might have been calm, reserved, but the faint beat of his pulse was visible on the side of his pale throat. He didn't want to have this conversation anymore than I did, yet here we were. His curiosity — or maybe his pride — wouldn't let him ignore it now I'd insisted on knowing what he was thinking about.

I propped myself up again so I could see him better and try to decipher what was going on in that head of his. "Why is this even a question?"

"Just answer it." He angled his face toward me, his gaze as solemn as the command.

A sigh escaped me before I could help it. Scratching the back of my neck, I looked away, hoping my response would be sufficient. I mean, it was bound to come up sooner or later, so it was best to get it done and over with. Right? He didn't ask questions often, so it was only fair to answer when he did.

"I'm versatile. Ok? I top and bottom. It just depends." I returned my gaze to his. "Can we drop it now?"

"Depends on what?" Of course not...

"Do you really want to be having this conversation right now?"

"Is there a reason you *don't* want to have this conversation?" His curiosity was tinged with suspicion, tightening the corners of his eyes.

Yeah. Dozens. But I wasn't about to tell him that.

"It depends on a lot," I said, stumbling over the words

while I tried to figure out an answer that would hopefully satisfy him. "My mood, his mood. My size, his size. Does he have a definite role, so to speak. Where we are. How much time we have. How drunk I am." I didn't need the unamused look Leander shot me to know I should have stopped before the last reason, but it was true.

"Do you miss it?"

"Topping?"

"If that's what it's called."

"I mean..." Please, for the love of God, someone come in and kill me so I don't have to answer any more of these questions. "Sometimes. I guess. I don't know. I don't think about it."

"Then why haven't we...?" He rolled one index finger over the other in the air.

"Flipped?" I prompted, raising my brows at him.

He nodded, chewing on the inside of his bottom lip.

"Because I really don't care? Because *that* is not the be-all-and-end-all of a relationship?" The corners of my mouth dipped into a frown, still trying to piece together his line of thinking. "Are you not happy with the way things are?"

"No!" His eyes widened in a flash of worry. "I mean, I don't want *you* to be unhappy."

"I'll never be unhappy with you."

"Yeah. We'll see about that," he muttered, averting his eyes so he could glower at the far side of the room.

"I'm not going anywhere." I wormed myself on top of him, pressing slow kisses to his clavicle and throat.

His hands settled on my waist, but his attention was fixed on some point beyond my head.

"Are you curious?" I brushed my nose against his to get his attention, arching a brow when I finally did.

He met my gaze, but didn't even crack a smile. "That is *not* what this is about."

"No?" Biting my lower lip suggestively, I reached down and gasped in faux surprise to find he was starting to get hard. "I think it is. I think you want to try but you've been too scared to ask."

"You're reading too much into a simple physiological response."

"Oh, I am, am I? You're saying this conversation hasn't piqued your curiosity in the slightest?" I leaned down and dragged my mouth over his chest and shoulder, gripping his cock harder in long strokes.

He closed his eyes and groaned. It looked like he was trying very hard to ignore what I was doing to his dick, but it was a losing battle, especially when his hips shifted upward, trying to get me to speed up.

"I want you to have the option," he said after a moment, looking up at me and, from the looks of it, trying desperately to maintain his composure.

"I don't *need* the option. You are all I'll ever need." To prove my point, I kissed him softly, despite the fact my dick was hard as a rock, pressing into his thigh.

His fingers dug into my hips, pulling me up against him so I was laying flat, our cocks rubbing against one another with each shift and swivel of our hips. The uncertainty was gone from his eyes when he opened them again, replaced by an undeniable hunger. "You're going to make me say it, aren't you?"

"Say what? That you want it?" I chuckled softly, shaking my head. "We can do it, if it's what *you* want. It's ok to be curious. But please don't do it for me."

He brushed my hair behind my ear and kissed me, his hand resting on the side of my face as his tongue slipped into my mouth, caressing mine in long, soft strokes. "Show me," he whispered against my lips.

Tilting my head to the side, I searched his gaze for any

hidden reservation. If there was any, it was expertly hidden behind fervency and a vulnerability I'd only seen in him once before. February 26th.

"Your wish is my command, my love." Planting a trail of kisses down his chest, along his ribs, and tracing the V to his pelvis, I caressed him with my hands as I went. "You'll tell me if you change your mind?"

"Of course."

Ignoring the happy dance going on inside my dick, I focused my attention on Leander's, licking and sucking every inch of it. As the saliva ran down his balls, I palmed it away, massaging them while teasing his crown with my tongue and teeth.

"Oh, Christ!" he rasped.

I stole a glance up at him, pleased he was watching and enjoying the show.

After the third swear word, I figured it was now or never. I retrieved the bottle of lube from the nightstand and poured some into my palm. Instead of going straight in, I went back to playing with his cock and balls.

He whined, swiveling his hips to try and get more… something. Friction, suction, I don't know.

Tracing my finger around his rim, I popped off his cock and looked up at him. "You want this?"

Biting his lower lip, he nodded, but I didn't miss the way his breathing came faster, or the shiver that shot through him.

"Are you sure?"

"I trust you."

Little by little, I pressed my index finger inside him, all the while kissing his thigh. "Relax," I murmured against his skin. "I've got you, my love."

"Mhmm." So convincing. His fingers dug into the sheets,

as if he needed to anchor himself while I worked my finger in and out.

Chuckling, I went back to licking the head of his cock. As soon as I found the spot I was looking for, I pressed against it with the pad of my finger and sucked him into my mouth at the same time.

"Oh my God!" His back arched, which made him grind against my hand even harder. "What the fuck was that?"

"The reason I don't mind being the bottom," I replied, my middle finger joining with the first one. I let him get used to both, sliding in and out slowly, massaging deep inside him, before I went for his prostate again.

Making the "come hither" motion to the bundle of nerves inside, I slid up his body and pressed my lips to his throat.

"Oh, fuck." He caught my face between his hands and pulled me up to his mouth, kissing me feverishly. The harder he kissed, the harder I worked my fingers in and out of him, making sure to stroke along the spot I knew was driving him crazy.

"You like that?" I mumbled against his mouth.

"God, yes."

"You want me to keep going?"

"Yes." He nodded too, his kisses as sporadic as his gasps and groans.

Kissing him once more, I slid my fingers out of him and reached for the bottle of lube again. Coating myself generously, I gave a few lazy tugs to my own dick, taking a moment to wrap my head around the fact that this was really happening. He was really letting me. Not only *letting* me, *asking* me to.

Scooting closer on my knees, I nudged the crown right up against him. As much as I wanted to see it, to watch my cock disappear into him inch by inch, I was focused on *him*. His eyes, his face, his perfectly swollen mouth. Any sign that I needed to stop.

"I want you," he said, reaching for my face. "All of you."

Supporting myself with one hand, I hovered over him, meeting his lips tenderly while I guided my cock past the rim, stopping once the head was inside. His body tensed beneath me, a small cry muffled against my mouth.

"Relax," I whispered, covering his face and throat with featherlight kisses. "Breathe, my love. It goes away. I promise."

When I felt less resistance, I thrust in a little bit more. He breathing sped up again, and his fingers tightened — one hand on the back of my head and the other on my waist. "Fuck fuck fuck."

"You're so fucking tight. Breathe, love." Easier said than done when I, myself, was almost breathless as I slid in deeper, stopping again. It's not that I'd forgotten how good it could feel, but damn. It *had* been a while. "Oh my God… Are you ok?"

"Keep going." He winced, turning his face into the side of my neck.

Lacing my fingers through his hair, I touched his cheek with my thumb, pressing kisses to his forehead, temple, lips, anywhere I could. "You're so fucking perfect," I groaned against his ear, my pelvis flush against him.

He kissed me again, wrapping both arms around me and pulling my whole body down on his. His hips shifted up, meeting each of my shallow thrusts, his trepidation melting with every passing second.

Soon, we fell into a slow, steady rhythm that was every bit as hot as the hard, fast sex we usually ended up doing no matter how gently we started out. Everything was in sync, from the give and take of our bodies to our shared breaths. It was unlike anything I'd ever experienced before. Maybe because I'd never been in love before.

"Fuck, Bennett. I'm going to come soon," he gasped, his gaze locked on mine. His pale green eyes were so fucking beautiful, cheeks flushed and lips reddened.

"God, please do." To help him along in that endeavor, I fisted his cock, matching the strokes to each thrust, increasing the rhythm based on his moans and ragged breaths.

I knew the minute his orgasm hit. Not by the cum jetting out onto his abdomen, but the way every muscle in his body tightened, including the ones my dick was buried inside. If his ass wasn't already tight enough, feeling him come around me was on a whole other level. I was pretty sure I blacked out for a minute. My own orgasm tore through me as I collapsed on top of him, regardless of the fact we were now both covered in sweat and semen.

"Fuck me..." I pressed my cheek against his shoulder in the hopes the world would stop spinning. His heart was pounding so hard, it felt like I had two of my own — each racing and stuttering and trying to come back down from fucking euphoria. Pun intended.

"Is it always like that?" he asked, swallowing thickly. My throat was equally parched. If I had the energy, I'd get my ass up and go get water. But I didn't, so it would have to wait.

"With you? Yeah."

"Fuck... I'm dizzy."

"Me too." Muffling my snicker into the side of his neck, I toyed with his hair. Some curls were noticeably more damp and I could only imagine what a sexy disaster it was going to look like when he finally got up.

Once I could form a coherent thought, I propped myself up on my elbow and stroked his cheek. "Are you ok?"

He gave me a small smile, brushing the hair out of my eyes. "Perfect."

Shifting forward, I kissed him gently, hoping it conveyed the depth of my love, my gratitude. He didn't have to do *any* of that, but he did. Giving up control wasn't easy for him, but in that moment, he trusted me to take care of him. Even if this arrangement never happened again, I would never forget the light in his eyes when he looked at me, full of genuine love.

They said psychopaths weren't capable of love. But *they* were fucking wrong. If this, this whole relationship, wasn't love, then I didn't know what was.

13

BENNETT

Blinking, I inhaled and stretched languidly. When I didn't immediately feel a warm body next to me, I shot upright, looking at the empty bed. Grabbing my phone off the nightstand, I rubbed the sleep from one eye while checking the time. It was just after five thirty in the morning.

"Leander?"

There was no answer.

Yanking on a pair of pajama pants, I darted out of the bedroom and down the stairs. I hopped over Annabel on the final stair and headed for the library.

Sounds from the kitchen drew me the opposite way instead.

Leander looked up with a frown when I walked into the room. He spooned hollandaise sauce over the top of a poached egg, his brow creased. "You should be in bed, mon coeur."

"So should you. Are you ok? I mean, do you feel ok? You're not hurt?" Even though we took our time last night, there was always a chance something could go wrong. And despite our deadly natures, neither of us appreciated actual pain in the bedroom.

He lifted a dark brow at me, spooning out more sauce. "I can't believe I am the one saying this, but please stop worrying."

I sniffed, conceding his point. "Another nightmare, then?"

Ignoring me, he expertly sprinkled bits of chives over the eggs Benedict and added a dash of paprika.

It wasn't worth the argument, so I strolled to his side of the island. Wrapping my arms around him from behind, I kissed the side of his neck, relishing the smell of his skin. "What are you doing?"

He leaned back against me, resting his head on my shoulder. "Trying to surprise you with breakfast in bed."

"Before sunrise?"

"I couldn't sleep."

"Mhmm." My hands slid down his sides, slipping beneath his pajama pants to graze his hips. "I can think of a better surprise."

"I'm sure you could." He glanced at me with a smirk — a smirk I quickly wiped off his face by stroking him with one hand. The other slid up his flat stomach, keeping him pinned to my body.

He let his head fall back with a soft groan.

My free hand drifted northward until my fingers encircled his throat. He didn't need much persuasion to turn his mouth toward me. I pulled back when he tried to kiss me, enjoying his annoyed whimper. Dragging my tongue over his lips slowly, I finally kissed him back, softly and then with a growing intensity.

He broke away first with a scowl. "It's going to get cold."

"Your point?"

"Go sit down so I can bring this to you properly."

I sighed dramatically and peppered his cheek with kisses.

He made a face and shrunk into his shoulder, like a turtle hiding in its shell, trying to limit my access.

"Go!" he said again, pushing me away.

Laughing, I finally did as I was told.

He appeared with a tray, complete with a lily from the conservatory and both newspapers, the *Sentinel* and one from Chicago. Ever since we returned, Leander had been obsessively tracking developments in the Marchese trial. Wordlessly, he leaned down and brushed a kiss to the side of my head.

I unfolded the Chicago paper and actually gasped at the headline.

ALLEGED MOB BOSS MURDERED WHILE IN FEDERAL CUSTODY

There was a side-by-side of Giovanni Marchese's booking photo and one from the incident. FBI agents and prison officials swarmed the scene, a black body bag barely visible between all the legs.

"Did you see this?" I glanced over my shoulder, but Leander was gone.

"See what?" he called from the kitchen.

"Marchese is dead." How the fuck did I *not* know about this? Historically, I didn't get my criminal news from the paper — I got it in a phone call from one of many sources. So, why didn't I get a phone call?

"Oh?" He returned from the kitchen with another tray and sat across from me.

"It says he was shanked in the mess hall. Five times. Jesus." Who the hell got the drop on Giovanni to get in *five* hits? The article said his attacker was a murderer named Don Marsh. Kudos to whoever the hell that guy was.

"You stabbed a man thirty times," Leander pointed out, raising his brows at me as he draped his napkin across his lap.

"Twenty-seven," I corrected. "And it was well deserved."

"So was the five. It should have been five times that amount when you consider what he did to you."

I folded the paper again and tossed it on the table, meeting his gaze. "I did it to myself. I knew the risks when I decided to fuck with the mafia."

"As did he, by living the life he did." Leander lifted his cup in my direction and took a sip of his coffee.

Something in the way he said it, the way the corner of his mouth twitched, gave me a moment's pause. Propping my elbows on the table, I laced my fingers together and leaned forward, watching him carefully. His gaze dropped to his eggs Benedict and he took an extraordinary amount of care cutting through the slice of carved ham.

"Leander?"

"Yes?" Now his attention was conveniently on the English muffin, dabbing up the perfect ratio of egg yolk to Hollandaise sauce.

"Look at me."

He lifted his gaze at the same time he took a bite, eyebrows raised, chewing and conveniently masking his micro-expressions. Damn him.

"What aren't you telling me?" I prompted.

"What do you mean?" He blinked, the perfect picture of innocence.

"If you had anything to do with this" — I pointed at the newspaper — "you need to tell me now."

"Had anything to do with what?"

"Don't do that. Don't pretend you don't know what I'm talking about."

He bit another piece of ham off his fork, slowly, challengingly, looking every bit like a feline savoring its latest kill.

"I know how much you like doling out retribution, my love," I continued, trying to rein in my frustration. "But ordering a hit on a mob boss comes with its own set of rules. You can't just kill whoever you want, whenever you feel like it. There's a certain way things have to be done."

"Marchese had more enemies than you and I combined."

I hit my forehead with my palm lightly. "Oh. Jeez. That's right. How could I have forgotten?"

"Smart ass." He rolled his eyes, taking another sip of coffee. "I don't know why you're not thrilled. The problem appears to have resolved itself, mon coeur."

"Appearances are deceiving." Rather than continue this frustrating dance, I decided to drop it and switch to another equally frustrating topic. "I forgot to tell you — I have to go the city next week."

His fork dropped, clanking against the edge of the plate. "For what? The Bancroft meeting isn't for another month."

His reaction earned him another suspicious look from me. "I got a call from another lawyer up there. They said they had something important to discuss..."

"How mysterious." He picked up the fork again and returned to cutting, so seamlessly I almost questioned what I saw in the first place.

"You know lawyers, never ones to divulge their hand until they're forced to." I smirked. Just like the eccentric millionaires I knew.

"When are you going?"

"Um, Tuesday. I think? Why?"

"So I know what day Olivia needs to re-arrange for me."

"You don't need to do that. I'm not staying the whole day."

He frowned. "You don't want me to go with you?"

"Want you to? Yes. But it's really not necessary. I know how much you dislike anything north of Springfield."

He shot me a fleeting glare. "Sometimes we have to make sacrifices for the ones we love."

"Save your sacrifice for something that matters. I'll take the plane and be back the same night."

He sighed, pushing a bit of muffin around the plate. "I'm sure Del will want to see you, since you're so rarely up there anymore. You might as well stay the night."

I shook my head. "No. I'm coming home."

"I meant what I said. I trust you. In *and* out of the bedroom."

Reaching for his hand across the table, I gave him a soft smile, rubbing my thumb across his knuckles. "One night, then."

"JESUS H. CHRIST. LOOK AT YOU." I stood, opening my arms to the man taking his sweet ass time walking in the door. "About time you showed. Make me come all the way up here and then you're late."

Jerome smirked, clapping me on the back before shoving me away. "You're one to talk. I don't think you ever made it to a ten a.m. class."

"Fuck no. Who wants to wake up that early?"

"That's not early in the normal world."

"When have I ever been normal?"

"Right. Forgot who I'm talking to." Chuckling, he dropped into the chair across from where I'd been sitting. He looked at the table and spread his hands in confusion. "What? No drinks?"

"I'm trying to quit." I smirked and slid my glass of ice water to the side, out of our way.

He busted out laughing. "Since when?"

Since my husband made it perfectly clear he had an issue with it? "Eh." I shrugged. "It was time for a change."

His dark eyes fell on the wedding ring on my finger,

zeroing in on it like a homing beacon. "Well, well. The rumors are true."

My gaze flicked to the ring and back up to his face, scrutinizing every twitch. An uncomfortable prickling spread across the back of my neck even as I forced a small, inquisitive smile to my lips. "Rumors?"

"You know how it goes. People talk. Word was Bennett Reeve actually tied the knot." As he spoke, he adjusted his tie, pulling it away from his throat with an awkward chuckle. And that right there was why he wasn't a trial lawyer. He had too many tells.

I narrowed my eyes, unsure if I should be offended by the fact he thought I was an idiot. "No, Jerome. People *don't* talk because people here don't *know*."

Clearing his throat again, he was saved by the waitress returning with a glass of water for him and a menu. He dove into the drink like a dying man.

The mysterious reason for this meeting was starting to needle at me. That, combined with his knowledge of my marriage prior to my arrival, didn't bode well for the rest of my day. "You called me, remember? So are you going to tell me what's going on, or keep wasting my time?"

Throwing a glance over each shoulder, he scratched the tip of his nose before reaching inside his suit jacket. He withdrew an envelope and slid it across the table quickly.

I unfolded the paper inside and read it beneath the table. It was a letter addressed to the kindly investigators at the Attorney Registration and Disciplinary Commission. My laughter disguised the fact I was two seconds away from upending the fucking table.

"Engaging in sexual relations with a client?" I skimmed the charges again, my blood pressure spiking. "Breach of fiduciary duty. Ooo, this is nice. 'Bringing our noble profession into disrepute.' You've got to be fucking kidding me."

Jerome shook his head. "Sorry, man."

I swore under my breath.

"I just gotta know," he said, lowering his voice. "How the hell did you piss off a judge in another circuit? I didn't think you practiced that far west."

"What?"

"The complaint came from a judge, which is why it got sent to the top of the pile."

I folded the bottom third of the letter back, brows furrowed. The last name of the complainant was Clayton, but it wasn't Lorelei. It was Helena Clayton. "Who the fuck is that?"

"A judge over in Camden County. You remember reading about Daniel Clayton from back in the day?"

"The Federal prosecutor who blew his brains out in the middle of the Connelly case?" Or so the story went. I had a gut feeling there was more to it given some particulars I learned about later, but that was neither here nor there.

Jerome nodded pointedly at the letter. "That's his widow. Looks like she's finally getting revenge for what happened."

I stared at him like he had three heads. "By coming after a lawyer who had *nothing* to do with it? Yeah. Makes sense."

"You represent Connelly Construction."

"Along with twenty other lawyers in the greater Chicagoland area who are into way shadier shit than I am. Not to mention the fact I was *fourteen* when this dude was whacked and not even in the damn country!"

Jerome cocked his head. "Whacked?"

"Died. Whatever. Semantics."

"Then why would she go after you like this?"

Shaking my head, I folded the letter again and stuffed it back in the envelope, holding it out to him. "This isn't her. It's her daughter."

He covered my hand with his, forcing it back down to the

table. Patting it gently, he retracted his own with a quiet chuckle, leaving the letter in my possession. "Why would her daughter be after you, then?"

"The client I was 'inappropriate' with?" I lifted my left hand and pointed at the wedding ring. "She was fucking him too."

"Aw, shit, man." He ran a hand over the back of his head and let out a slow breath.

"It might be her mother's name, but this has that blonde bitch all over it."

"Wow… And I thought I had some crazy exes." He laughed and shook his head.

"Well, she is a psychiatrist, so you know she's just as fucked up as her patients. I mean... clearly."

"Yeah, but you married your client, man."

"Yep." The 'p' popped on the end as I slunk back in my seat. "True love and all that."

"Damn. And it's a guy? For real?"

"As far as I know, he is. If he's not, he had one hell of a surgeon."

He shook his head, leaning back in his seat as well. "Look, I can make this one disappear. Ok? No problem. You know how many letters we get every week? But if she sends another one and another Commission lawyer gets it? Better get your ducks in a row."

"It won't come up again."

"You stole this girl's man! She lost her guy to *another* guy. You think it's over?"

"First of all, he was mine first," I snapped. "She was a means to a fucking end. And second of all, you can't force the willing. No one held a gun to his head and made him marry me. Ok?"

"You know the Puritans at work don't see it like that."

"There is no imbalance of power in this relationship. He

has just as much money as I do and he's the fucking CEO. It's not like he's a goddamn secretary I manipulated into draining the company bank account. So everyone at the ARDC can shove their morality up their ass." I glanced back at him. "Except you. You actually have some common sense."

"All I'm saying is, you better come up with some good precedents as a backup plan." He drummed his fingers on the table, stopping suddenly to look up at me. "When did you know you were gay?"

I leveled a flat look at him. "I'm not gay."

He squinted at me. "Are you *sure* you're not gay?"

"I literally just said…" Bing! Lightbulb. "I am as gay as the day is long. Flaming. Absolutely. All my life."

Jerome nodded slowly, a smile spreading across his face. "And your man is clearly bisexual."

I huffed a sigh, shaking my head and staring wistfully into the distance. "They get such a bad rap when all they want is a little love. Is that so much to ask for?"

"The *bigotry* you must face on a daily basis. And then, when you finally find happiness, the system comes to smack you down."

"Would be a real shame if the ACLU got involved... That's the kind of press our 'noble profession' doesn't need." I shook my head solemnly.

"All because of a crazy, vindictive ex." Jerome shook his head too.

"What a waste of time for the ARDC, a strain on your limited resources, needless stress on my fellow professionals. A political firestorm no one wants to weather."

His smile stretched wider. "Sounds like you got your ducks in a row, after all."

"Speaking of rows... do you think I should go with the club level seats or fifty-yard-line for the Bears/Saints game?" I asked, idly spinning the onyx ring on my forefinger.

He tapped his chin in thought. "Club level. Always."

I snapped, feigning disappointment. "Damn. I just remembered I'm not going to be in town that day. I sure hope I can find someone to use those tickets..."

We exchanged a sly look before breaking down into laughter. Outwardly, I was relieved to have this little problem sorted out. Inwardly, I was fucking fuming.

14

BENNETT

"The stars are beautiful tonight."

The windshield I was laying on provided the perfect angle to reflect on the vastness above me. It was amazing how much you could see outside Chicago without all of the lights polluting your view. It was like Easton. As backwater as that town was, the beauty of it was undeniable.

Leander sighed in my ear. "Why did I stay here again?"

I laughed, switching the phone to my other ear. "Because you hate Chicago and one night won't kill either of us."

"Yes, but snuggling with Annabel isn't quite the same." There was a quiet squeak in the background. I'm sure the princess perked up when she heard her name and was currently in the process of ramming her head into him, soaking up all the love and affection she wanted without me around as competition. "Although, she doesn't steal my pillow."

"Mine fell off the bed."

"Heaven forbid you pick it up."

"Alright, you caught me. It was just an excuse to get closer to you."

"You don't need an excuse, you know. We *are* married."

I laughed, bending one leg to relieve some of the pressure on my back from where the wiper blades were digging in. "Did you ever think *that* would happen?"

"Getting married? Or married to *you*?"

"Both."

He inhaled and exhaled softly. "It's as I've said, I never imagined finding someone like you. And then to realize how much you meant to me? It terrified me."

"You're such a romantic. How could *you* ever be terrified of love?"

"Reading about such things is entirely different than experiencing them. Even now, I can't fully articulate how much you mean to me, Bennett. And I didn't think a feeling like that could ever be reciprocated, not for someone like me, from someone like you."

"You? Imagine *my* surprise. I was in awe of you the first time I met you. I didn't think I ever stood a chance of actually *being* with you, let alone calling you my husband." Hell, I never thought I'd get married at all. You had to have a relationship first and those were something I didn't waste my time on, until Leander.

He scoffed. "I mean, I thought I dropped enough hints. I didn't realize I had to literally spell it out for you."

"Listen, you are *not* an easy read, even for someone like me. That smoldering look of yours could either mean you want to fuck someone, or you're plotting their demise."

He gasped. "I've never once plotted your demise."

"Not even when we were apart?"

"Not even then." I kicked myself when he grew quiet. I'd only meant to tease him, not bring up old wounds. "It doesn't mean it won't happen anyway," he added quietly.

I didn't like the way his tone darkened. Even if he was two-hundred miles away from me, I could feel the shift in his mood, as much as if I was laying right there beside him. "What are you talking about?"

"The curse." He said it so softly, I almost missed it.

I sighed, closing my eyes. "I don't believe in curses, my love. You shouldn't either."

"It doesn't matter if you believe in it — it'll kill you regardless. It gets everyone in the end."

"It won't get me and it certainly won't get you if I have anything to say about it."

"I guess time will tell."

I didn't want to hang up while he was in such a funk, but as soon as I heard high heels clicking on the pavement, I wrapped up the conversation. Hopefully Annabel could purr away whatever melancholy he had while I took care of business once and for all. "I'll see you tomorrow. I love you."

"And I love you."

Shoving my phone in my pocket, I settled into my relaxed position again on the hood of the silver import, counting the approaching footsteps.

"Excuse me?" a female snapped. "What are you doing on my car?"

I sat up slowly, giving Lorelei a dazzling smile. "Hey Doc. Long time no see."

She gripped her leather bag strap, pulling it closer to her body. The stealthy glance around the empty parking lot made me laugh quietly. We were alone and she knew it. The people in the building were too far away to save her and the guard in the shack down the drive couldn't even see us at this angle. There'd be no hero to come save the princess in *this* fairytale.

"What are you doing here?" she asked, holding her ground with a surprising reserve.

"Oh, I was in the neighborhood. Thought I'd drop by. See

how you're doing." I slid down the hood of her car and leapt off, landing right in front of her.

She flinched, but stayed rooted to the spot. "Why?"

"I wanted to have another little chat, clear the air. That sort of thing."

"About what? He has his cat back. What else does he want?"

"Oh, no, this isn't about Leander. This is strictly personal — just between us."

She narrowed her eyes at me. "Then what do *you* want?"

"Honestly? I came to applaud you on your vindictiveness. I didn't know you had it in you. Bravissima, Dottoressa." I gave her a slow clap, accompanied with a dark smile.

Her brow furrowed, her nose wrinkling ever so slightly. "What are you talking about?"

"Getting your mommy to write it was a nice touch."

"What are you talking about?" She ground out each word separately.

I pulled the complaint letter from my pocket, waving it beneath her snooty little nose. "Tattling to the ARDC about me?" I tsked, wagging a scolding finger at her. "Naughty, naughty."

"I don't know what the hell you're talking about. The AR what?" She reached for the letter and I gladly gave it to her. Reading it quickly, her face was mostly passive, except for the hard line of her mouth.

"Look familiar now?"

"I didn't write it and I didn't have my mother write it. She must have done it on her own, which has nothing to do with me." She shook her head and shoved the letter into my chest, sidestepping me.

"Nice try. Covering for Mommy Dearest is sweet and all, but I'm not buying it." I slid to the side, blocking her escape route. Laying a hand on her shoulder, I gave it a gentle squeeze, subtly keeping her in place. "And in my world, snitches get stitches, blondie."

Her brows furrowed again. Before she could ask a question or make another denial, I rammed the knife into her abdomen, angled upward. It didn't go as far as it should have, which was irksome. That's what happened when I rushed — the precision was off. Her gasp of surprise was followed by a strangled moan.

"Oh, God, Doc. I think I hit a bone in there." I jerked the handle, but it refused to go further. "Yep. Definitely got caught. That's the problem with a serrated edge. They don't slip as nicely as a straight blade, but they sure hurt like hell on their way through the skin. In, or out."

She pitched forward against me, shaking, digging her nails into the front of my shirt for some sort of support.

I held her with one arm, pressing my cheek to the top of her head, a mocking inversion of a tender embrace, even as I maintained my grip on the knife. "What should I do? Do I leave it in? Give you a chance to fuck me over in the future? Or pull it out and hope you bleed to death? Tell me, Lorelei. In your professional opinion, what should I do?"

She tried to stand tall, but every movement made her double over again and grab her stomach. The blood seeped out at a steady rate, scenting the air around us.

"Ooo. Maybe the poison will get you first." I ran a hand over her hair, grabbing her by the back of the neck and tilting her face up toward mine. Her blue eyes were wide, frantic, and glazed over by pain. "So what's it going to be?"

I couldn't tell if she was purposely refusing to answer, or if she was too stunned to speak. Either way, my patience ran out.

"Tick tock, tick tock... Fuck it." I yanked the knife out and shoved her away from me. She staggered back a couple steps before collapsing on the asphalt.

Strolling over to her trembling body, I leaned down and swept a lock of hair from her face with a bloody finger. "You know, I still don't see what his fascination was with you. You're like a helpless little lamb, all sweet and stupidly trusting. Guess you forgot you were dealing with a lion underneath all that sadness."

Blood spread over her white shirt, staining her fingers as she tried to press a hand to the wound. Her breathing shifted to short pants. It was either shock or poison. Didn't matter which.

"You rest easy now, Doc. I'll go get help." I winked and chucked her under the chin, standing again.

I stopped by her car, puncturing the front and rear tires, just in case she managed to drag herself over to it.

Whistling as I strolled away, I wiped the handle down and flung the knife over the tall, wrought-iron fence into the cornfield behind the hospital. A moment later, I, too, was over the fence and headed back to the Windy City for a much-needed night of relaxation with Del.

15

BENNETT

It was a beautiful day when I loaded up the car. I had everything all mapped out for my little road trip, including a rough timeline of events. Now all I needed was to grab a coffee and set off. Leander was away on business with Olivia, so it was just me and the open road and... Jake.

As soon as I spied Jake ambling down the sidewalk, I yanked the Maserati to the side of the road and rolled down the window. It was a spur of the moment decision I hoped didn't ultimately end up biting me in the ass. But if there was ever going to be peace in the kingdom, I needed to at least extend an olive branch to the little twerp.

Jake stuffed his hands in his pockets, stopping short with a glare when he saw it was me. "What do you want?"

"Get in, loser, we're going hunting."

Predictably, he made a face and remained exactly where he stood. "I'm not going anywhere with you."

"Come on..." I tossed my head to the passenger seat, slightly disappointed he ignored my Mean Girls reference. "I need you to help me with something."

"*Me*? Help *you*?" He snorted and looked around, like he was expecting cameramen to jump out from somewhere.

"I'm serious. Truce?" I stuck my hand out the window, waiting.

He stared at me, then my hand. If I had to describe the look on his face, it would be something along the lines of pure hatred. Not that I blamed him. We started off on the wrong foot and never had a chance to make it right. So, hopefully this little road trip would do the trick, for Leander's sake.

I sighed. "Look, you're basically on the 'No-Hit' list. So unless you fuck up royally, you don't have anything to worry about." Maybe it wasn't the best way to convince him, but he was screwing up my timeline.

He kept glaring at me, as still as a statute, the little cynic.

"Here. You can even hold on to this if you want." I fished the ice pick out of my waistband and held it out to him. "I just need you for a couple hours. A day, max. Then we can both pretend like it never happened."

Glancing up and down the street, Jake bounced on the balls of his feet before swiping the ice pick. "If you even fucking look at me sideways I'll stab you."

"Fair enough. Hop in, squirt."

"Don't call me that." He gave me the most disgusted look ever before circling the car. Easing into the passenger seat, he gripped the ice pick as if his life depended on it.

"Sport?"

"Shut up."

"Kid?"

Muttering under his breath, he shook his head as I pulled away.

He didn't start asking questions until we got on the highway. "Where are we going?"

"Camden County."

He shot me a confused look. "Why?"

"Like I said, we're going hunting." I grabbed my phone and unlocked it before tossing it in his lap. "You know these two, right?"

He scrolled through the screenshots, his lip curling in recognition. "Yeah. What about them?"

"We're going to pay them a little visit."

"Why?"

I gave him a dark smile and ruffled his hair. "Consider it a wedding present, buddy."

THE MAN STARTED TO STIR, thankfully bringing an end to his snoring and sputtering. Every time he twitched, the hairy gut hanging over the top of his jeans jiggled. He reeked of stale beer and cigarettes. I might have been a borderline alcoholic, but at least I maintained a sense of hygiene for fuck's sake.

I bent over, bracing my hands on my knees, nearly turning my head upside down to see his face clearly. "Oh good. You're up. I've been *so* bored."

The man, Russ Brewer according to my research, jerked his head up, rattling the restraints above him. He yanked at the chains that bound his wrists, trying to lower his arms. They didn't budge — the hook he was chained to was too secure. "What the fuck? Who the fuck are you? What's going on?"

I smiled brightly, extending my hand. "Bennett Reeve. We haven't had the pleasure." Laughing, I retracted my hand again. "Silly me. You're all tied up."

"What the fuck is this?" He yanked against the chains again, like he stood a chance of dislodging them from the rafter. I wanted to give him the benefit of the doubt, that it was the sedative making him so stupid, but I had a feeling I was being too generous.

"Those are chains," I said slowly, pointing upward before spreading my arms wide, indicating the empty pole barn around us. "And this is a kidnapping. Any other questions?"

He blinked rapidly, never taking his eyes off of me. "Who are you?"

"I assume you mean more than my name, since we literally just covered that two questions ago." God, it wasn't as much fun when they were dense. I stroked the underside of my chin in thought, pacing back and forth leisurely. "The context I believe you're looking for is quite simple. Leander Welles. Do you remember him?"

Recognition flashed in Russ's eyes, followed by unbridled hatred. "What about him?"

I took a quick step forward, wagging my finger in his face. "You were not very nice to him, were you?"

"Fuck him. He got me fucking fired and then took everything I had."

"Not everything." A dark smile curled my lips as I booped his nose with the tip of my scolding finger. "Not yet."

Russ swallowed, finally comprehending the seriousness of the situation in which he found himself. I don't know if it was the table full of blades that clued him in, or the fifty-five gallon drum and the bag of agricultural chemicals next to it.

"What do you want?" he asked, his voice shaky.

"Your soul." I smiled again, taking an immeasurable amount of joy from the look that shot across his scruffy face. I could practically smell his regret, his fear.

The large, sliding door at the far end of the barn screeched open. A moment later, a beat-up pickup drove inside and parked. Jake hopped out and closed the door again.

"Perfect timing, squirt." Consulting my pocket watch, I snapped it shut and turned with a genuine smile.

"That's my truck," Russ said dumbly.

Jake shot me a glare before he disappeared behind the stolen vehicle and unloaded something — rather, someone — from the back. Slinging the body over his shoulder in a fireman carry, he trudged to the center of the barn and dumped the woman at Russ's feet. I knew he'd be handy to have around. Why didn't I take on an apprentice years ago to do the heavy lifting? I could have saved myself so much trouble.

"Nora!" Russ's eyes widened. The chains rattled again, but all he could do was sway on his feet. There was no way he could save her, or himself.

"Good job, kiddo! You bagged her all by herself." I smirked at Jake, giving him a round of golf clapping. "Only took you two hours."

"Fuck off." Jake hooked a second set of chains to Nora's wrists and hoisted her unconscious body up into the air. She was more or less standing near, but not too near, Russ.

"Mark?" Russ squinted at Jake. "What the fuck? What the fuck are you doing here?"

"Yeah, bet you didn't think you'd see me again, asshole." Jake turned his glare on Russ as he joined me, actually standing shoulder-to-shoulder with me across from the duo.

I gave the boy a curious side glance. Nothing like a good old-fashioned kidnapping to bring two people together. I always said murder was more effective than therapy. Hatred had the ability to unify people more than any other force on Earth. Love was a tangle of complications. But hate? Hate was simple; a singular, all-consuming energy.

"Safe to say you're acquainted with Ronald here?" I gestured to Russ.

Jake nodded, giving his former co-worker a scathing head-to-toe look.

"Hey man, you got the wrong guy!" Russ sputtered. "My name ain't Ronald. It's Russ!"

Jake and I both ignored him.

"Ok, we got 'em here. Now what?" Jake asked, lifting his brows expectantly.

"Are you familiar with pain compliance?" I asked, tilting my head to the side.

He shrugged, making a face. "Not really."

"They didn't teach you that up at Parkview?"

Jake shook his head.

"Randy here is. It's what he used to subdue Leander on more than one occasion. Except he took it beyond its original intent. You know? The *compliance* part." I followed Jake's outraged gaze to the washed-up guard. "Excessive force is one of the reasons Leander won his lawsuit. Doesn't look so good when one of your patients turns up in court covered in bruises."

"I didn't do anything to that sick fuck!" Russ spat.

Spreading my hands, I cringed and sucked in a hiss through my teeth. "Well, the courts say differently, Ricky. That's what guilty means. That's why you had to kiss your pension bye-bye and your girlfriend over there lost her house."

"I say differently, too," Jake added, taking a step forward, his fists clenching. "I saw him beat on more patients than just Leander. With that bitch's help!" He pointed at Nora in case there was any confusion who the "bitch" was in this grouping.

Tsking Russ, I moved forward slowly and clapped my hands on his shoulders. "Didn't your mother teach you not to pick on people weaker than you? It's really in poor taste."

Holding him steady, I drove my knee into the side of his thigh.

Howling, his legs gave out. The chains jerked tight on his wrists, eliciting a painful hiss to go with his whimpering.

I took a step back, watching Russ swing for a moment before clapping my hands quickly at my assistant. "Come, come, Jacob. Time for your first lesson."

Instead of some smart-ass comeback, Jake stepped forward, his blue eyes bright.

"There's a nerve that runs right through here," I said to Jake, gesturing the length of Russ's thigh. "Hit it hard enough and, as you can see, you'll drop your opponent no matter how big they are. Plus, it hobbles them for the next hour so even if they do get away, they don't make it very far."

Jake nodded, soaking in the information like a sponge.

"I also like this one," I continued, grabbing Russ above his elbow and squeezing hard with my thumb. Russ screamed until I let go. "Immobilizes the arm, which means they can't hit back."

"Focus on the nerves. Got it," Jake said with another nod.

"Oh, no, dear boy. There's more than nerves to play with." I took Jake by the shoulder and steered him around to Russ's backside. "There's muscles, joints, body mechanics. A whole realm of painful possibilities. Let me see your thumb." Snagging Jake's hand, I curled it into a fist, making sure his thumb was sturdy. I maneuvered him into position behind our test dummy and snaked Jake's other arm around Russ's throat in a headlock. "Ok. Now take your thumb and drive it right there. Yep, right under the ear."

Jake did as instructed, resulting in another bellow from Russ. He stepped back with raised brows and a small smile. "Like that?"

I guess I could finally see why Leander liked the little pain in the ass. He was a quick study and eager to please. People like that were useful to people like me. This was officially one of the best ideas I'd had in a while.

I returned Jake's smile with an approving wink. "Just like that."

MY CELL PHONE RANG UNEXPECTEDLY, bringing a halt to the lecture on veins and arteries.

Despite the blood coating my hand, I pulled my phone out of my pocket. It was Leander, which meant I answered immediately. I wasn't planning on talking to him until later, so seeing his name on my screen sent my heart into full-on spasms. "My love? Is everything alright?"

"What are you doing?" he asked, his voice pleasant and completely unperturbed.

I glanced around the pole barn with a small shrug. "Oh you know. Just catching up on work. How is Minnesota?"

"Dull. I wish you were here. Olivia isn't half as much fun as you are."

Russ groaned and his head lolled backward, rattling the chains.

I shot a glare behind me. "I wish I was there too."

"What was that?" Leander asked.

"The TV. Hold on." I strode over to Russ and muted the phone before punching him squarely in the side of the jaw. He fell limp, his head flopping forward on his chest. Unmuting the phone, I forced a smile to my lips. Lies were always more convincing with a smile. "Sorry about that. It's that movie Cole recommended."

"I thought you said you were working?"

"I am. I'm multitasking."

Thankfully he let it go. "Unfortunately, we have to stay another couple of days..."

"Problems?"

He sighed. "Nothing I can't handle. It's just irritating. Anyway, is there anything in particular you would like for dinner on Friday?"

"You know I'm not picky. Everything you make is amazing."

"Yes, I know... but sometimes it's helpful when you throw out suggestions."

Nora started whimpering, her chains clinking with each tiny jerk of her body. Perhaps she mistakenly thought the person on the other end of the line would save her. If she only knew.

"Chicken Marsala," I said quickly, hoping he didn't hear her too. "It's been a while. Is that ok? Kind of in the mood for something heartier. Seasons changing, whatnot. Summer's almost over... that sort of thing."

"It sounds perfect." I could practically hear him brighten.

"I love you."

"I love you. Don't work too hard."

Laughing, I disconnected and tossed my phone on the table. The levity faded into a growl as I turned toward my captives, marching over to them in quick strides.

Fishing a capsule of smelling salts out of my pocket, I broke it beneath Russ's nose. As soon as he stirred, I slapped him for good measure. "Didn't anyone ever tell you it's rude to interrupt a conversation?"

Jake uncovered Nora's mouth and stalked away from her with a disgusted look.

I rolled my head from side to side, cracking my neck. "Now, where were we?"

"Showing Nora the error of her ways," Jake replied.

"Ah, that's right." I walked up to Russ again and yanked the ice pick out of his abdomen. Sauntering over to Jake and his practice doll, I tossed it to him when I got closer. "Your turn."

Jake shifted it in his hand, getting a good grip on the slick handle. Gesturing to Nora's waist with the bloody point, he glanced at me every so often to make sure he was on the right track. "Liver, stomach, spleen. Kidneys and intestines."

"And where's the aorta?" I prompted.

"Here." He pointed, poking Nora just enough so she sucked her stomach in, trying to get away from him. She moaned through her gag, tears and snot running down her red, blotchy face.

"Bravissimo." I inclined my head to him. "The rest is up to you. You can decide how fast, or slow, you want their death to be. Seconds? Minutes? Days? Strike accordingly. For funsies, you can always throw a bit of poison into the mix like I did."

Jake's gaze turned hateful. "This bitch should suffer for days for all the things she said about Leander. She's supposed to be a nurse, for fuck's sake. What kind of nurse treats her patients like garbage?"

"Then aim low, kid." A wicked smile curled my lips. "Let her turn septic and die in agony, thinking about all the ways she's a terrible human being."

Nodding, Jake drove the ice pick beneath her belly button and left it in, tossing a disgusted look at Russ. "What about him?"

I gauged the pool of blood beneath him and the steady dripping from his beer gut. "Oh, his stomach acid and all of those digestive juices are going to wreak havoc on his organs." Taking a step closer to Russ, I bent my head toward him, speaking directly into his ear. "Do you know what it means to get sepsis?"

He grunted, but didn't say anything.

"First you'll get a fever," I continued, softly. "Your heart will race and your breathing will become labored. You'll grow weak as chills rack your body, unable to save itself from the poison in your blood. And then your organs will fail, one by one." I seized a fistful of his hair and yanked his head back. "It will be excruciating."

I shoved his head to the side as I stepped away. Frowning at Jake, I ran my hands over my abdomen. "Are you hungry? Leander got me thinking about food so now I'm starving."

He chuckled and made a vague, unhelpful gesture. "I mean..."

"Good. Let's go get something to eat."

"What about them?" Jake glanced at our two captives with a raised brow.

"Oh. Shit." I turned to face the pair, gesturing between them while I spoke with utter seriousness. "Do you think you guys will be ok hanging out until we get back? Yeah? Cool."

Jake busted out with a real laugh. He clamped a hand over his mouth, as if he surprised himself, and looked at me with wide eyes.

Snickering, I threw my arm around his shoulders and steered him toward the truck. "I think we've turned the corner, squirt."

Instead of shrugging me off, he shook his head and rolled his eyes. "I guess you're alright. But stop calling me 'squirt.'"

"Aw, I appreciate the ringing endorsement, kiddo."

16

BENNETT

"Oh my God, Bennett! It's too big!"

"Just a little bit more."

"No, I can't!"

"Just tilt your—"

"We have to stop."

Sighing, I dropped my end of the desk and stared at Dorian impatiently. "This is why I told you to let the movers handle it."

He laughed between panting, bracing against his side of the desk in the hallway. "They were taking too long. I needed space to see what I was working with."

"As I recall, you have a very vivid imagination." I arched a challenging eyebrow at him.

Grinning, he raked a hand through his black hair, massaging his scalp. "That's swimming in bourbon right now, thanks to you."

I scoffed and folded my arms over my chest. "Are you telling me the infamous Dorian Montclare actually has a hangover?"

"Yes, yes I am." He chuckled and slumped against his side of the desk with a groan. "Could go for a little hair of the dog when this is all done."

"Absolutely. First, we need to get this thing out of the way. So, in or out?"

"Can we switch sides? That might help."

Snickering, I just couldn't help myself. "I didn't know you liked to flip, Dor."

He paused, the double-meaning of what he said sinking in. When he got it, he gaped at me. "Goddamn it! That is *not* what I meant!"

Leander's voice cut through my reply. "What the hell...?"

A second later, he came into view behind Dorian, the planes of his face sharp.

"My love!" I jumped up onto Irene's heavy-ass desk and walked over the top, nimbly avoiding the carved section with the tiny drawers and letter holders. Leaping past Dorian, I angled myself straight into Leander's arms with a wide smile. "You're home early. I wasn't expecting you until Friday."

"We finished early. I thought I'd surprise you." He set me on the floor, his brows knitting together as he glanced at Dorian. "Who is this? And what have you done to the house?"

I hit my forehead lightly with my palm. "Manners, I apologize. Leander, Dorian Montclare — our architect and a friend from the city. Dorian, my husband." I kissed Leander's cheek and took his hand, dragging him down the hall to the west wing. "Come see what we're planning."

Dorian followed after us, explaining his vision for the second floor as we went. I didn't hear a word. My attention was focused solely on Leander's guarded expression.

"We're going to move the master bath here," Dorian said from the hallway, gesturing to the blue bedroom. It had been completely emptied of its furniture already, along with everything from Leander's room and the bathroom. "We'll tear out the old bathroom and combine these two spaces. Now, do you want your reading nook to be on this side of the house, or the other side?" Dorian turned to Leander expectantly.

Leander, in turn, looked at me with furrowed brows, a touch of panic in his eyes.

"Can you excuse us?" I smiled at Dorian and dragged Leander down the hallway again, ducking into the red guest room. I should have re-considered the minute I spied the rumpled comforter and the fact the pillows were all over the ground. I knew what it looked like, or what it *could* have looked like, and I didn't need Leander getting the wrong impression.

"What's the matter?" I asked, closing the door behind us.

Naturally, his attention fell to the bed. I'm sure he'd already taken note of Dorian's suitcase in the corner. His breathing turned shallow, his knuckles cracking as he balled his hands at his sides. The fact he and I had officially moved into his room weeks ago (with the new mattress) must have been irrelevant to whatever he was thinking now.

I bit my lip, but didn't say anything. Instead, I crossed my arms over my chest and waited. Unlike him, I'd been completely honest about my life prior to Easton. If he had a question, he better ask it instead of rehashing our fight from Chicago.

Leander ran a hand through his curls, cupping the back of his neck while he continued to stare at the ground. "I know we talked about remodeling, but I didn't think it was happening right now."

That wasn't what I was expecting him to say, but I was relieved his concerns were only about the house. "Have you changed your mind?"

"I don't know."

"Say the word. I'll tell the movers to bring everything back in, right now."

"What about the trust?" He turned to me, but his eyes were too busy darting back and forth to actually see me. "They're going to know I'm not living here. Everyone in town is going to know. You can't *not* know with a project this big. If Oswald finds out, he'll take me back to court and I forfeit everything. *Everything,* Bennett. I nearly lost it last time with the murder charges. If I—"

"Breathe." I took his face in my hands and met his wild gaze. "Everything is fine. Everything *will be* fine. I've looked over the documents. You're not violating the terms of the trust."

He grasped my wrists, not calming in the slightest. "How do you know? I mean, how can you be so certain?"

"A trust is contract, Leander. And what is my specialty?"

He exhaled a breath, nodding. "Contracts."

I nodded slowly. "The Devil is in the details."

"You're positive we didn't miss something?" he asked, clinging to my wrists.

I stroked his cheek with my thumb, making sure my voice stayed low and even. "Since the house will be uninhabitable during renovation, you're not required to live here. There isn't a judge within a hundred miles who would say otherwise."

"You're right."

"I always am." I gave him a wry grin and slipped my arms around his neck, pulling him against me. "Your most pressing concern now is selecting what wallpaper you want."

He nodded again, his arms tightening around me.

I pushed him away gently, keeping my hands on his shoulders. "Now, let's go get that fucking desk out of the doorway and let Dorian work his magic."

Dorian was sitting on said desk when we returned to the east wing, tapping away on his cell phone. He shoved it in his back pocket when we appeared and jumped to his feet. "Are we good?"

Leander nodded mutely, meanwhile I smirked at Dorian and gave a suggestive glance to the desk. "You want top or bottom, big boy?"

Dorian shook his head with a mock glare. "You're an asshole. You know that?" He hopped on top of the desk and stepped off into Irene's bedroom.

Chuckling, I bent down and picked up my end of the desk. With Leander's help, we were able to maneuver the thing through the doorway and down the hall. Once the movers were back from dropping off our personal effects at the teal Victorian across the river, they could take the desk and deposit it in the basement with the rest of the shit from Irene's room.

"Now that *that* is done..." Dorian dusted off his hands and strolled back inside the master bedroom.

The three of us stood in the middle of the empty room, surveying the massive space. Dorian started pacing around, darting from one side of the room to the next, muttering to himself and holding his hands up every once in a while like he was a filmmaker lining up a shot.

Leander stared at the floor while Dorian discussed various wood densities and undertones. I couldn't help but notice the particular spot that held my husband's attention was where the bed had been. There was a large, circular area, a shade lighter than the rest of the floor.

"Teak is always lovely in a library. The leather smell, combined with the books." Dorian exhaled in delight. "It's also period appropriate."

"If you're basing your decision on smell, then why not

rosewood?" I asked with a smirk, keeping an eye on Leander in my periphery.

Dorian snorted. "How about sandalwood, then?"

"While you're working your way down the endangered species list, why don't you go poach an elephant for an ivory inlay?" I challenged.

Dorian considered it for a moment, probably weighing the cost and the legal headache. "It would be historically accurate..." Biting his lip, he looked at me and raised his brows. If I gave the go-ahead, he was one-hundred percent onboard. We burst out laughing together until Dorian shoved me out of the way. "I'll go get stain samples," he said, still chuckling.

Shaking my head, I turned to Leander, eyes narrowing briefly. He'd been quiet throughout this whole process. Too quiet. I knew he was worried, but usually he was better at hiding it in front of strangers.

"Is everything alright?" I asked, cocking my head to the side as I studied him.

"Mhmm."

"Then why won't you look at me?" He did, defiance hardening his jawline. "Hardly convincing," I said, trying not to sound too bitter.

"You two seem... close." Leander fixated on the floor again, his hands clasped behind his back.

I leveled a look at him, knowing damn well he could feel it. And here I thought I was in the clear of his suspicions. "We were. Once upon a time."

"I see."

"Do you?"

Instead of answering, he chewed on the inside corner of his mouth and let his glare turn up to the ceiling. Just like the floor, there were areas of plaster that were a touch lighter than the rest. It must have been pretty impressive cast-off spatter, but I wasn't about to give him kudos when he was sulking.

When he finally faced me, it was with a frown. "I'm sorry my early arrival disrupted your plans."

"What is that supposed to mean?"

The corners of his eyes tightened, his glare intensifying. "You know what it means."

"Are you asking if I slept with him?" I took a step forward, reminding myself to be the calm one in this ridiculous exchange. It was a bit hypocritical, since *I'd* had the same fear not that long ago... But ever since I took a chef's knife to my arm in Chicago, I thought *he* was past the whole jealous thing.

Before Leander could answer, Dorian's boisterous laugh carried across the room again. "Uh, no. Wrong Montclare." He shoved the stack of stain samples into my hands and turned to Leander with a bright smile. "I'm flattered though, to think I'm appealing to both sexes."

I avoided Leander's less-than-relieved stare, shuffling through the wood chips. Not that I wanted to have *that* conversation with Leander, either, but hopefully now he'd realize there was absolutely nothing between Dorian and I. It would be as gross as fornicating with Del. "How is your sister, anyway?"

"Oh, you know Dru..."

"Is she still playing with corpses?"

Dorian chuckled. "All day, every day. She has control over the whole empire."

"Good for her." I crossed the room and handed the samples to Leander, even though he didn't so much as glance downward. "Dorian's family made their money in the funeral industry."

"Except me," he corrected with a smile. "I'm the black sheep because I work with the living."

"Drusilla works with the living," I countered on her behalf. "She just prefers the dead."

"Don't we all?" Leander murmured, stepping away from me and walking to the fireplace. The wood samples clattered on the carved mantel a second before he braced both hands against it, his head hung.

Dorian shot me a confused look, but stayed silent.

I gave him a reassuring smile and a little wave toward the door. As he exited, I made my way to Leander. Propping my chin on his shoulder, I slipped my arms around his waist from behind. "What's wrong?"

"Nothing."

"If you want to hire another firm, we can. I just thought, since Dorian specializes in historic hous—"

"It's not that. He's fine. *I'm* fine."

"You're not fine. You've barely said two words."

"It's this room," he exhaled in an agonized whisper.

My hands slid up his torso, resting against his chest and pulling him back against me. His heart raced a mile a minute under my palm and he barely took a full breath. "She's gone, my love."

"Is she?" He swallowed hard, his muscles taut against me. "Every time I come in this room, I can feel her, lurking in the dark. As soon as I get complacent, she's going to unleash more evil. I know it. And there isn't a damn thing I can do."

Tightening my arms around him, I pressed a kiss to the side of his face. "I'm right here with you. I'll always be with you."

"Until the day comes that you're not." Turning, he sidestepped, pulling out of my arms. He drifted out the door without another word or a backward glance. I tracked his steps up the servant stairs. Up, not down, which meant he was going to the tower.

For a moment, I worried I'd see his body go sailing past the window, reminiscent of his great aunt's death. Swearing silently, I gave myself a mental slap.

It was this fucking house, that was all. The sooner I got him out of here, the better.

17

BENNETT

One blissful morning while I sipped coffee and enjoyed a cloudless view of Lake Michigan, a notification popped up in my email, interrupting the brief I was in the middle of drafting. It was an update on Lorelei Clayton, of all goddamn people. I'd set up the alert when Leander was taken to Parkview Psychiatric earlier in the year and I'd apparently forgotten to delete it once his master plan was fulfilled.

I never saw an obituary for her, but I never looked, either. Once I left her laying in a puddle of blood in the parking lot of her precious psych ward, I data-dumped that bitch from my brain and moved on with my life. So why the fuck was she in my inbox?

Clicking on the news article out of curiosity, rage immediately flooded every single cell in my body. It wasn't an obituary or a stupid "celebration of life" service. It was a motherfucking article in a psychology journal.

It seemed hell truly hath no fury like a woman scorned. Since she tried — and failed — to take me out, she turned her sights on my husband.

Instead of having the grace to just fucking die, Lorelei somehow managed to live. And instead of quietly accepting Leander's departure from her life, she went DEFCON 1 crazy and decided to publish a fucking case study on Leander.

While good old HIPAA didn't allow her to name names without explicit permission, there was no doubt it was him. The article detailed his horrific childhood, his violent adulthood. She then proceeded to delve into his fascination with Poe, linking the writer's alleged madness with Leander's.

If anyone ever found out Leander was the person behind her patient, "William Wilson," he'd be ruined personally and professionally. She stuck him with a laundry list of diagnoses and predicted a dismal future for him without help. While professionalism dictated she couldn't spell it out in black and white, she all but insinuated Leander would kill himself if his disorders remained untreated. The best hope for him was a long-term stint in another psych ward while being heavily medicated. For life.

The bitch even used his own words against him. Expounding on a book he apparently annotated for her, she cited example after example of how deranged he was. It was literary analysis, for fuck's sake, but she used his opinions on Poe's work to shore up her claim he was one of the most disturbed people she or her mentor had ever treated in their respective careers.

Seething, I slammed my laptop shut and threw it to the side of the couch. My first thought was to call Leander. My second thought was to slap the first thought right out of my head. There was no way I could tell him about this. If *I* was livid, I could only imagine how furious he'd be. He had enough on his plate right now without having to worry about this bitch dragging what was left of his name through the mud.

Snatching my keys off the counter, I marched into the elevator and stabbed the DOWN button.

On my way to the car, I *did* call Leander, but it certainly wasn't to tell him what I was up to. "I'm afraid I have to stay in the city one more night, my love."

"Is everything alright?"

"Of course. I have to take care of something that came up at work last minute." Somehow I managed to say it with an actual smile instead of a snarl.

"Alright... Will you be home in time for the meeting with the estate lawyer tomorrow?"

I scanned the calendar in my head and did a quick calculation of time and distance. "I should be."

He exhaled. "Good. This meeting is a month ahead of schedule, which means it can't be good. It's got to be about the renovation. I told you Oswald would find out."

"I know I'm asking a lot, but please *try* not to worry about it. I have it all in hand."

Papers rustled in the background and it sounded like he shifted the phone to his other shoulder. "Mon coeur, did you have a chance to look at the trust for Martha yet?"

"Remind me again what I'm supposed to be looking for?"

"Why, all of a sudden, the damages from Nora Kelly have been paid in full? There's no way she could afford to settle it on her own."

I swore silently. Why did he have to take such a goddamn interest in Martha? If he wasn't personally keeping an eye on her account, he would have never noticed the giant lump sum of money that was deposited from her measly estate. Thankfully, Russ's family was still fighting for their claim in probate court, so I had some more time to come up with a believable reason. "It's on my list of things to do. I swear."

"You sound awfully rushed."

"I am. I'm sorry. I'll be at the meeting tomorrow, I promise."

"Thank you."

"I'll call you tonight. I love you." I hung up and and shoved my phone in my pocket.

Now that that was taken care of, it was time for another little face-to-face with Lorelei.

LORELEI'S APARTMENT WAS CUTE, clean, and modern. Simple, comfortable furnishings made it feel rather homey, despite the obvious lack of decor. There were a few pictures scattered around either featuring a happy little family when Lorelei was a child, or the obligatory milestone pictures featuring only her and her mother.

The books on suicide and suicidology crammed onto the bottom row of her bookcase reminded me why her father wasn't in any of the later pictures — he was dead. The official story was he shot himself. Rumblings in the Chicago underworld said the Irish got to him and put an end to the federal case he brought against their leader, Patrick Connelly. Daniel Clayton's death was a cautionary tale in law school and in real life — don't fuck with the Irish. Either way, his death obviously fucked up his dear daughter more than she wanted to admit.

Rifling through her dresser drawers, I located a pearl-handled pistol. Based on the investigator's reports, it was the same one Daddy Clayton used to blow his brains out. It was strange she actually kept it. Maybe it was a touch of sentimentality mixed with common sense. After all, she was a single, attractive woman living alone. One could never be too careful — case in point, she had the likes of me prowling around.

Tucking the pistol in my waistband, I continued on with my exploration of her inner sanctum. I'd still never gotten an answer to my one and only question about Lorelei. What was it about her that Leander found so fascinating? She was the polar opposite of him. I mean, sometimes opposites attract, and sometimes they're like oil and water. Try as I might, I could not picture a world where she would ever make Leander happy in the longterm. God knew I pissed him off enough and we were more alike than they were.

I was still pondering the peculiarities of their brief relationship when the front door opened.

Lorelei, oblivious to my presence in the dark, kicked the door shut behind her and slid the chain into place. She dropped her gigantic tote on the floor with a sigh and chucked her keys on an end table.

I let her get halfway across the living room before I flicked on the light next to the chair I'd been occupying for the past three hours.

"Welcome home, honey."

She screamed and nearly jumped out of her skin, whirling toward me with wide eyes. Stumbling on her heels, she backed away from me slowly. "What the *fuck* are you doing here?"

"Waiting for you, of course. I must admit, I didn't think we'd ever have this opportunity again. Guess you're hardier than I gave you credit for."

She swallowed, sliding back another step. Her eyes darted to her bag.

"Don't even think about it," I said, rising from the chair.

I don't know why I expected her to listen.

In the blink of an eye, she bolted, but not toward her bag. She turned the opposite way, sprinting down the hallway off of the living room.

I sprang after her, grateful I'd had the foresight to memorize the layout of the place ahead of time.

In no time, I caught up to her inside her bedroom door. Grabbing ahold of her mandible from behind, I squeezed the bone until she cried out and stopped moving. I spun her toward me slowly, lifting at the same time so she was on the tips of her toes. She grabbed my wrist with two hands, but all it did was make me squeeze harder.

"Before we get down to it, perhaps you can elucidate something for me. What did he find so alluring about you?" I wondered out loud, assessing her with a lifted brow.

Naturally, she didn't supply an answer.

"What did you find so alluring about him?" Walking her backwards, I smiled when her eyes widened and tried to dart behind her, to see what was coming next.

I shoved her onto the bed and climbed on top of her before she could regain her bearings. Settling most of my weight on her hips, I reached across her and snatched her far wrist. Pinning both of them above her head with one hand, I leaned into the soft flesh of her closer tricep with my elbow, rotating the helpless muscle away from the bone.

She screamed and thrashed beneath me, but it was futile. I had her exactly where I wanted her. The more she fought, the more pain I created. This wasn't going to be fast, like last time. I'd spend hours if that's what it took.

"Was it the darkness?" I continued, searching her terrified gaze. "The depravity? Did it *excite* you?"

"I'd never expect someone like you to understand," she said through clenched teeth. An extra dose of anger darted across her face, like she was mad at herself for breaking some oath of silence.

"Understand what? Love? Or a blatant lack of ethics?"

"You'll never get away with it," she declared defiantly, not so subtly changing topics. If she thought she was going to reason with me or negotiate for something, she was mistaken.

"Get away with what, exactly?" I dipped my face close to hers. She turned away, squeezing her eyes shut. Grabbing her jaw again, I forced her face toward me. "What do you think I'm here to do to you? Stab you again? Poison you? Tie you up and fuck you?"

She remained silent, even though her eyelashes fluttered as tears started to build.

Letting go of her face, I skimmed my hand down her body before it darted behind my back, retrieving the gun from my waistband. I withdrew it slowly, cocking the hammer at the same time. "Was this what you were after? Were you actually going to shoot me or was it all for show?"

Her eyes flew open, her breathing quickening. As the gun came closer and closer to her, her wide gaze darted between my face and the barrel.

"Tell me…" I caressed her cheek with the tip of the barrel. "What sort of evil do think I'm capable of?"

Her pretty lips twisted into a scowl, despite the tears slipping out of the corner of her eyes. "If you're anything like your *husband*," she spat the word, her nose wrinkling, "then words can't even begin to describe it."

I considered her assessment, dragging the barrel down her neck, over her exposed sternum, and nestling it above her heart. "Unfortunately for you, *he's* the calm one. I, on the other hand, am a little more... shall we say, unpredictable?"

She inhaled a sharp breath.

Cocking my head to the side, I shifted the gun again, sliding it between her breasts and around to the side, grinding it into her ribcage on the other side of her heart. She yelped, trying to squirm away, but there was nowhere to go.

"Imagine how angry he would be to read your little article." I gave her a dark smile when her eyes widened, finally comprehending the real reason for my visit. "Now triple that anger. It's not even close to the amount of vile atrocities I'd happily inflict upon you."

Despite the tremors rippling through her, she did her best to put on a brave face. "What do you want from me?"

"I want you to retract your article. Immediately."

She gave a small shake of her head.

I pressed the gun into her bones harder, only letting up when she cried out. "Leander told me you were stubborn."

"Funny. He didn't talk about you at all."

"Ooo. Is that supposed to hurt?"

"You'd think he would have at least mentioned you a time or two if you were so important to him."

"Really?" I put more weight on my elbow, digging it deeper into her tricep. "Would you have yielded so easily to him if you knew he was pining for someone else? If you thought for a moment that he didn't *want* to be saved by you? That he didn't *need* you?"

She strained beneath me, trying not to scream until it ripped out of her in a ragged shriek.

I eased up slightly and came nose-to-nose with her. "Retract your fucking article."

The muscles over her collar bones flexed with each shallow breath. "And if I don't?"

"Do you really want to try and take me on a third time?" I dragged the tip of the gun back over her chest, up her throat, and nestled it against her temple. "It won't be a fucking charm for you."

"Tough words for a guy with a gun."

"You should know I don't need a gun to hurt you. In fact..." I lifted it back into view before tossing it to the side. My free hand seized her throat, putting just enough pressure on each of her arteries to make her wonder how long she could stay conscious. "Let me tell you what I have planned so there's absolutely no confusion in that pretty little head of yours."

She squirmed, trying to get me to loosen my grip. Every time she moved, I squeezed harder. If she ended up crushing her own windpipe, then so be it.

"I'll use you in a little experiment of my own, Doctor." I lowered my face closer to hers. My breath, my hair, even my nose caressed different parts of her face as I settled in on top of her. She tried to avoid me, but it was impossible.

"Picture it," I said softly. "You're trapped in an empty cistern in the dark. Cold. Alone. Starving. Your voice is gone from screaming into the void. Your nails torn from trying to claw your way out. Kept alive only by my good graces."

She swallowed hard, staring at the ceiling instead of me.

"You begin to live for my visits, for the meager scrapes of human interaction I deign to give you." A vicious smile pulled the corner of my mouth, watching her expression morph from defiance to dismay.

My cheek skimmed along hers as I shifted forward, my mouth close to her ear. "I will break you, Lorelei. I will ravage your mind until you forget who you were before I put you in that miserable hole."

Her lower lip trembled, but she didn't turn away.

"And then, when I've grown bored with you, you will happily put that gun in your mouth and pull the trigger. Just like your father."

She sucked in a shaky breath, a fresh wave of tears streaming from the corners of her eyes.

I caught a tear on the tip of my tongue, laughing darkly when she shied away with a whimper. "I can kill you without ever lifting a finger," I murmured, pulling back so I could meet her teary gaze head-on.

"You're insane. Just like him," she whispered, trying to maintain her bravado, even though her body betrayed her.

"Believe me, I'm worse." Perched above her, I could begrudgingly see her appeal. She *was* beautiful. Intelligent, sure. But after this little exchange, I knew it was her fierceness that drew Leander in. She didn't cower when she should have, even when every primal instinct signaled imminent danger. "I will give you a week to retract your article and issue a mea culpa. If you don't, I promise I'll be back to fulfill *all* of your deepest fears."

She tipped her chin up and I knew it was the only acknowledgment I'd get out of her.

Smiling serenely, my fingers loosened from her airway completely. She was too busy gasping in a full breath to bother fighting me as I climbed off of her. Snagging the gun from where I tossed it, I kept it aimed at her as I backed away, in case she got any bright ideas. "One week, Doctor."

I gave her a mocking bow and spun out of the bedroom, moving down the hallway in long strides and right out the front door.

A quick jaunt around the block brought me back to my car. I hopped over the door, settling into the driver's seat. Double checking the time, I sped away, swearing. That took longer than I anticipated. God, she was difficult. But hopefully something I said got through to her. I really didn't want to have to come back to this fucking town if I could help it.

I turned off the main road that cut through downtown Stratford and cruised by the police department. There were two squads parked in the back lot, which meant there was a third out and about somewhere.

In such a quaint little town, it didn't take long to find the third guy running radar near the middle school, despite the fact it was almost nine o'clock at night. Perfect.

Popping a U-turn down the road, I tootled past the cop

again, giving a friendly wave when he picked his head up. He gave the obligatory wave back and resumed dicking around on his phone.

I zipped back to downtown, making my way toward one of the ritzier restaurants. Stealing a glance at the time, I slowed down and scanned the sidewalk. A striking, older blonde appeared in the doorway of the restaurant, waving goodbye to her dining companions. I didn't even have to second-guess my target. Lorelei was a spitting image of her.

Despite all of the cars parked along the street, there didn't seem to be any actual people milling around. The closest witnesses were down the block in an outdoor beer garden, which automatically meant their testimony would be suspect.

"Judge Clayton?" I asked, rolling alongside the woman.

She stopped and turned with a polite smile. "Yes?"

I lifted the pistol from my lap and took aim, firing off three rounds in the center of her chest.

A deep, guttural noise tore out of her throat. Her eyes went wide as she lurched forward, trying to catch herself against a light post. In the next breath, she crumpled on the sidewalk, dark red pooling beneath her.

I tossed the gun into the passenger side and drove off, whistling along with the radio. Taking out Lorelei's mom brought two very distinct perks. One was a simple tit for tat. Lorelei came after Leander, so I went after the only family she had left. And two, in case she thought she'd try to call my bluff, this was a little example of the positive punishment I was willing to dole out. The ball was in her court now.

With so much adrenaline buzzing through me, I turned the Maserati southbound and headed home.

By the time I pulled into the driveway of the teal Victorian, I was thoroughly exhausted. The high was great, but the crash was worse than a hangover. All I wanted was a bed covered in black silk and a hand to hold.

After a quick shower, I climbed into bed, careful not to jostle Leander as I slid beneath the covers. Annabel, who was curled up on his hip, opened her eyes and squeaked irritably at me.

"Beat it," I whispered at her.

She blinked slowly, refusing the command, and yawned.

Leander leaned back into me, on instinct it seemed, which disrupted her highness' perfect perch. She leapt to the floor and sauntered away, her tail held high.

"You're home," he murmured, reaching backward for my face.

"I couldn't stay away," I said, pressing his palm to my cheek and curling around him.

18

BENNETT

With a cup of coffee in hand, I settled into the overstuffed wicker chair on the garden patio and opened my laptop. My morning copy of the *Camden Times* was waiting patiently in my email.

I clicked the headline with a smile.

LOCAL JUDGE SHOT IN DOWNTOWN STRATFORD

Such a horrifying, "random" act of violence for such an idyllic little town. According to the police there were no leads, which is exactly how it was going to stay. Since there was zero interaction between myself and the dead judge, there was no way I'd be on anyone's radar. Except Lorelei's. But between planning a funeral and retracting her damn article, she had enough on her plate. Even if she did tell the police, they still had to prove it was me. And as every player in the justice system was well aware, it wasn't what you knew — it was what you could prove. Neither Lorelei nor Stratford PD would be able to *prove* jack shit.

As soon as I heard Leander's footsteps approaching, I closed the laptop and set it aside. There was a whole slew of reasons I didn't want to tell him about my little trip to Stratford last night. I didn't think he'd object to the murdery aspect of my evening — his primary concern would be *why*. Always why. And the why, I just couldn't tell him.

I didn't tell him about the Honorable Judge Clayton filing a complaint against me, nor did I tell him about me getting a little up close and personal with his ex. Either time. The fact I tried to kill her and failed wounded my ego more than I cared to admit. And the reason for the second visit was bound to send him in to orbit. So, for the sake of his blood pressure and not bringing on another migraine, I kept my lips zipped.

Leander appeared a moment later with Annabel weaving between his feet, setting a parfait on the table in front of me before taking his usual seat. He had nothing. No coffee, no tea, and certainly no food.

"Not eating today?" I asked, fishing out a blueberry.

He shook his head, bracing his elbows on the table and resting his chin on his clasped hands.

"Do you not trust me?" I tried not to sound accusatory, but my professional pride was on the line here.

His eyes dipped before coming up to meet mine. "I don't want to fight."

Well that was the biggest "Yes" if I ever heard one. Leaning back in my chair, I tried to school my face into some expression of understanding and not like he just stabbed me in the heart with my yogurt-covered spoon.

He lowered his hands to the table and angled himself toward me, speaking slowly. "I'm *nothing* without my company. I will have nothing. I will *be* nothing. And she'll have finally won."

"I get that you're apparently in the middle of an identity crisis, and I'm sure being married to me doesn't help with any of that" — I shoved my chair out and stood — "but have a little faith that I know what I'm doing."

He caught my wrist. "You misunderstand."

"That you're obsessed with beating a ghost? Nope. Understand it perfectly." I tried to pull away, but he had a vice grip on me and all I accomplished was spinning him in his chair.

Keeping ahold of me, he stood slowly, biting his lower lip. "I want to be worthy of you, Bennett. If I lose my inheritance, the Corporation… what do I have to offer?"

"You!" I stared at him incredulously. "I don't want your money. I don't need your money. You could lose everything tomorrow and I'd give two shits, Leander. *This* is why I'm with you," I said, laying a hand over his heart. "*This* is all I want. Maybe a little bit of this, too." I grazed the front of his pants with a smirk.

He cracked a smile and immediately shook his head. "You're impossible."

"And you're ridiculous. Now let's go see what this idiot wants."

Oswald Farnsworth III was one of the most vainglorious windbags I'd ever encountered in my life. Considering my chosen profession, that was saying something.

For starters, he was late to the meeting *he* called. Once he finally waddled in, he had the balls to try and throw *me* out.

"This is a confidential meeting, sir," Oswald droned. "I'm afraid you'll have to wait in the lobby."

"And I'm afraid you're going to have to get bent, *sir*," I replied with a smile and flicked my business card at him across the long table. "I'm not going anywhere."

Sniffing, he swept the card to the side and pulled a classification folder closer to him. Instead of delving into the heart of the matter, he thought he'd pussyfoot around some more, going over details of the account that could have all been summed up in an email or at least a phone call.

Halfway through it, I kicked my feet up onto the glossy conference room table and leaned back in my chair, rocking back on two legs. For added measure I groaned occasionally and started clicking my pen. If I had gum, I would have been snapping it nonstop, hoping if I irritated this prick enough he'd speed things up.

For his part, Leander remained mostly still and utterly silent. The only part of him that moved was the slow, methodical drumming of his fingers on the table. His pinky went first, down the row to his index finger, and cycling back again.

"As the trustee over the family's account," Oswald said, clearing his throat with a phlegmy cough, "it is my duty to inform you that certain violations have come to our attention."

If it was possible, Leander's spine went even more rigid. His fingers stopped drumming immediately. "What are you talking about?"

"For starters, your recent murder trial has brought into question your mental health — mental health being one of the many conditions—"

"Let's stop right there," I said, clicking my pen once more and pointing it at Oswald. "You don't have the authority to determine the state of his mental health, trustee or not."

"No, but seeing as he was recently evaluated for a *murder* trial, I think it's safe to say the courts would agree with me that these are not the actions of a rational man."

I rolled my eyes. "Determining one's fitness to stand trial

is not the same as a declaration of insanity. You and I both know you're reaching, Ozzy."

"He was *hospitalized*," Oswald challenged.

"For an *evaluation*," I threw back at him with the same snarl, "which has zero bearing on what you're claiming." At that moment, Lorelei's fucking article was front and center in my brain. If she didn't rescind it and this fuckwit got a hold of it, Leander would most certainly be ruined. Then I'd really fucking kill her.

Oswald bristled. "Between his court-ordered confinement and his mysterious disappearance, one can argue Mr. Welles's behavior in general is suspect. Not to mention, he violated the residency requirement by being gone for so long."

Leander glanced at me out of the corner of his eye, his jaw tensing.

"Last time I checked, a vacation doesn't mean you give up residency," I countered.

"Moving out of the family home does."

I raised my brows at the old coot. "Oh, really? He moved? Or simply relocated during the extensive renovations at the 'family home'? I can argue the definition of residency all fucking day. Shall we look at the tax code or the civil code for a definition? Or how about we check in with the goddamn post office to see what address he has on file? I have more than enough ways to prove his residency in whatever courtroom you want to take this to."

Oswald continued blathering on, apparently intent on ignoring all of my counterpoints. "And then there is also the matter of your so-called marriage."

Leander blanched, his hand balling into a fist in his lap.

I, on the other hand, busted out laughing. "Oh, *this* ought to be good. Lay it on me, Oscar."

"After your miraculous return" — Oswald directed his

droopy gaze to Leander — "we sent a private investigator to retrace your movements. He discovered this." He opened another folder and slid a couple documents across the table. Our marriage certificate, along with all of the other records Puerto Rico required.

Leander was barely breathing. He turned toward me, allowing his mask to slip for the briefest moment. His eyes were wide with a small crease between his brows.

I made a show of taking my feet down from the table, one by one. Leaning forward so I could squeeze Leander's hand under the table, I propped myself up on the other elbow, arching a brow at the relic across from us. "Please, tell me, how our marriage — which is, frankly, none of your fucking business — violates any part of this ridiculous trust."

"It's not valid." The lines on either side of Oswald's mouth twitched up in what I think was a smile. It was hard to tell with all of the wrinkles.

I blinked languidly, returning his smug smile with one of serenity. "Hate to break it to you, Waddlesworth, but the Supreme Court says otherwise."

"It's not valid as far as the trust is concerned. Marriage is a sacred union between a man and a *woman*." His chin lifted until he was quite literally looking down his hawkish nose.

"Too bad the trust doesn't *specify* that."

"It is a universal definition."

"Uh-huh. The Bible means jack shit in a court of law. *Obergefell v. Hodges* renders every bit of your argument null and void. And in case you're not familiar with any law passed since 1960, that ruling was upheld a second time by the Supreme Court in *Pavan v. Smith*. But, please, explain your reasoning so I can see how ignorant you actually are."

Oswald straightened in his chair and drew a deep breath, like he was preparing for a filibuster. "At the time the trust was written, gay marriage was illegal. Thus, your marriage, while technically legal under current law, as you so proudly claim, is still deemed invalid by the trust."

Leander's fingers squeezed mine so hard his knuckles turned white.

I rubbed my thumb over his, hoping he'd at least let up a little on the death grip before he bruised my bones against my rings. "The proper term is same-sex marriage and the Fourteenth Amendment says differently. You cannot presume to know the *intentions* of a legal document, or what the guarantor wanted, unless it is stated as such."

"That will be up to a judge to decide, at the end of a long, costly legal battle, of which you will most assuredly lose."

"Are you sure you want to do that, Otto?" I made sure to ask with polite smile. It was only fair to give him an out before I fucking destroyed him.

Oswald feigned sympathy, even going so far as to lay a liver-spotted hand over his cholesterol-ridden heart. "I only have the trust's best interests at heart."

"Bullshit," Leander growled.

I continued quickly, before tempers flared too much. "You know if the terms are violated, the trust defaults to the charities Irene set up. One of them, in particular, has quite the history. Cornerstone Consulting, I believe it is?" I cocked my head, watching the man's jowls start to wobble. "Ah, yes. It should sound familiar. You're the chairman of the board."

Leander leaned into me slightly. He may have been speaking to me, but he watched Oswald like a hawk. "Is that the one without any tangible proof of its existence? Or the one with the suspicious off-shore banking records?" The purr was back in his voice and he finally loosened his grip on my hand.

"One in the same, my love." I edged forward, draping one arm over Leander's shoulder and resting my chin on the one closest to me. "The one with a phantom board that has been siphoning money off of your family trust for years, completely unchecked."

"Fortunately for me, there is one section of the trust that was worded *very* specifically." Leander smirked, reaching up to the hand dangling off his shoulder, lacing his fingers through mine. Our left hands, as it were, with the black bands in full view. "Damned if I can't remember which one. Do you recall, mon coeur?"

"Oh, it's the part where it states the trustee simply has to be a lawyer from Farnsworth & Geller."

Oswald's lips pressed into a hard line. If he saw where we were going, it hadn't quite sunk in yet.

"It seems you forgot one very important aspect of business, Mr. Farnsworth," Leander said, while I tsked him.

The old man's bushy brows lifted. "What is that?"

"Don't fuck over your partner," Leander replied flatly.

I turned to Leander, blinking rapidly and feigning confusion. "Oh, dearie me. Are you saying he's been stealing from your account *and* hiding it from his partners all this time?"

Leander shrugged, a coy smile pulling at the corner of his mouth.

I pulled my pocket watch out and smiled.

A moment later, the door to the conference room swung open. If Oswaldo was expecting Aaron Geller, his penny-pinching partner, he was wrong. In strode Caleb Geller, Aaron's ruthlessly ambitious and extremely pissed-off son.

"We're in a meeting," Oswald snapped.

"Oswald," Caleb said with a tight smile. "It has come to our attention there has been some, mismanagement shall we say, in regard to several of our clients' accounts. I'm here to ask you, politely, to please leave the premises."

Oswald snorted. "You can't be serious."

"I assure you, a full investigation and audit of your files is currently underway," Caleb replied with a predatory smile.

"As of this moment, you are relieved of your responsibilities at the firm and pending the outcome of this investigation, you shall be terminated."

Farnsworth got to his feet, staring down the younger lawyer. "This is *my* firm. You can't fire me."

Caleb smirked and tossed a knowing glance my way.

"See, that's where you're wrong, old chap." I smiled brightly when the bastard turned his glare to me. "Remember when you promoted young Caleb here to *equity* partner? You so kindly sold off ten percent of your share, along with Daddy Geller. That means Caleb owns twenty percent of the company. Aaron owns forty. By my math, they own sixty percent compared to your forty. That makes *them* the majority shareholder and able to do whatever the fuck they want."

Oswald blustered and sputtered, but he knew deep down he was fucked.

I winked at him, which practically made him turn purple as he stomped out.

Leander and I got to our feet, shaking Caleb's hand.

"Gentlemen," he said with a smile. "Thank you for bringing this shameful behavior to our attention. You have my deepest apologies. I can only hope our working relationship moving forward is more fruitful than what you have previously had to put up with."

"I'm sure it will be." Leander inclined his head and headed for the door.

I fist-bumped Caleb on the way out.

In the car, Leander turned to me with an arched brow. "How did you know Caleb would go for it in the first place?"

"I know avarice when I see it." I shrugged. "That kid has something to prove. Rewarding him with a percentage of the money he recovers doesn't hurt, either."

"I don't know how you do it."

"It's a gift."

Leander shook his head before leaning across the console, pressing his lips to mine. Between the remodeling at the mansion and removing the gatekeeper from his trust, I think it was safe to say Irene's ghost was well and truly vanquished.

19

BENNETT

"Shit." Groaning, I dropped my messenger bag on the kitchen table in the teal house. I knew it felt a little too light when I grabbed it earlier. That's what I got for not paying attention.

"What's wrong?" Leander asked, sifting through the mail, throwing most of it in the trash.

"I forgot my laptop at the mansion."

"So?"

"Dorian wants us to pick out light fixtures."

"We'll look everything over tomorrow. He can wait a day. We're supposed to be at Elijah's at seven."

I sighed, swiping my keys off the hook. "No, it's fine. The sooner we make these decisions, the sooner he'll be out of our hair and you can get back to your beloved kitchen."

"This one is... fine." He glanced around the small space, actually managing to keep his distraught expression to a minimum.

"You're so convincing," I said with a laugh. "I'll run and grab it and meet you at Elijah's."

"Alright." He kissed me on my way by, a long, lingering

kiss. I pulled away, but he came with, peppering my lips with kisses despite his devilish smirk. Seizing his jacket by the lapels, I kissed him hard and deep, shoving away at the last second with a wolfish grin. "Goodbye, already."

Ducking out the front door, I jogged down the steps and slid into my car.

A quick jaunt across the river and up the hill and I was back at the mansion. I navigated the car through piles of lumber and stone the construction crew was using and parked around the side of the house.

Hopping out again, I headed for the back stairs, looping my keys around my index finger.

A second too late, I caught a whiff of cheap aftershave.

An arm shot out of nowhere, catching me in a headlock.

I stepped behind my assailant's left leg with my right and threw my arm across his stomach, knocking him off balance. As he fell, I caught his wrist and twisted, putting him into an arm bar behind his back. He landed with a grunt, face-first into the brick driveway.

"What do we have here?" I asked, taking a second to assess him. Overweight. Scruff. Most importantly, no badge or gun. "Can I help you with something?"

"Fuck off!"

"Rude. Who sent you?"

Silence. Well, not total silence. He grunted now and again but nothing I could use as an actual answer.

"Have it your way." I kicked out to the side, connecting with his elbow and snapping it like a chicken wing. Between the dislocated shoulder joint and his broken elbow, his arm flopped to the ground while he howled.

Before I could ask my next question, there was a loud crack behind me. Two red-hot barbs lodged into my skin — one in my shoulder and the other in the small of my back. In the next heartbeat, thousands of volts of electricity shot through me. My muscles seized with a sickening feeling in the pit of my stomach. Collapsing to my knees, I gritted my teeth against the pain and tried, stupidly, to fight the immobilization.

The 'tick-tick-tick' from the taser was unrelenting. I couldn't breathe. I couldn't move until gravity took over and I slammed face-first into the driveway, throwing a whole new shock of pain into the mix.

Chicken-wing was off the ground, holding his broken arm. He dug around in his canvas jacket, withdrawing a needle and syringe. With all the gentleness I'd expect of a man whose arm I just violently snapped, he jammed the needle into the side of my neck.

I'd barely made it through my initial string of curses when the drugs kicked in.

My BACK HURT.

My head hurt.

My fucking neck hurt.

Round Two of riding the lightning was only slightly better than the first time. I didn't smell my own flesh burning, for starters. But I did smell blood. And dirt. Not clean, garden dirt — old, nasty dirt.

I tried to lift my hands, but got zero response. Besides being twisted behind my back, they'd gone completely numb. I pushed against the restraints, trying to get a feel for what it was. Hard, thin plastic. I sighed. They were zip-tied together.

Lifting my face from the cold, dirty concrete, I exhaled a steady breath and rolled on to my back, wriggling my hands under my ass. A couple more shimmies and they popped up in front of me. The returning blood flow made them tingle painfully, but I didn't care. Gingerly touching my eyebrow with my fingers, I hissed the second they made contact with a cut. With my luck, it was probably going to get infected if the grime on my hands was anything to go by.

I'd worry about vanity later. First, I needed to get the hell out of here. Wherever *here* was.

I tucked my legs beneath myself and counted down in my head before springing upward to my feet.

Now for the restraints.

Biting the edge of the plastic tail, I tugged the zip-tie to the side, sliding the locking mechanism to the center of my wrists. Adjusting my position, I bit down further on the excess zip-tie and pulled at it, tightening the little ratchets as far as I could, despite the sharp plastic digging into each wrist.

Once everything was in place, I raised my arms above my head and threw my elbows down sharply. The plastic gave way and my would-be restraints fell to the ground.

"Amateurs," I muttered. Rubbing my wrists gently, I glanced around the dirty little room. Now that I was untethered, I could focus on the next step — escaping.

The floor was concrete; the walls were cinderblock. A basement, clearly. Residential, not commercial. Other than the old, metal piping that ran along one wall, there wasn't anything else in the room.

I patted my pockets. No cell phone or wallet. Big shocker. But the idiots overlooked my ice pick. So, by all accounts, *not* professionals. Good news for me.

Knowing what I had to work with, I wandered over to the windows and yanked on the bars. They didn't budge. I couldn't see beyond the crud-caked glass to even get an idea of where I was, but I knew it was daytime. There was no telling how long I'd been unconscious. At least eight hours, given the fact it was after dark when they jumped me.

We were probably in the middle of nowhere. It didn't

look like any city basement I'd ever been in and even a beginner kidnapper would know better than to take their victim to a populated area.

I turned my attention to the door next.

It was metal, somewhere beneath all the rust bubbling across its surface. There was no handle on the inside to even try to pull on — someone had sawed it off. Assholes.

With nothing else to do and no possible means of escaping, I resumed my earlier position on the floor, sliding the broken zip ties behind me and out of view. I'd just have to bide my time until someone came in to check on me. Whenever that would be.

Raking a hand through my hair, I propped my elbow on one knee, glaring at the floor. This was a new one, even for me. I had no idea who the hell I pissed off this time or what they wanted. There were two obvious answers: revenge or ransom.

If it was revenge, it could have been any one of dozens of people. Literal and figurative bodies littered my path through life. I could draft a list of angry relatives and organizations alphabetically, chronologically, and geographically.

If it was a good old-fashioned ransom, they weren't very smart. Whoever it was wouldn't get a cent out of my mother for my safe return and Allegra's money was tied up in a trust until she was twenty-five. Unless they planned on ransoming me back to Leander, they'd literally kidnapped the only person who could give them a chunk of the Bancroft fortune.

Fuck! Leander.

He was probably losing his mind. I told him I was going to get a laptop and now I was gone, without a fucking trace. Would he realize what happened? Or would he assume I left him — again?

Just the thought hurt more than the taser burns. We went

through so much to get to where we were. I hated that it would all be obliterated in an instant.

What would he destroy this time? The house? His wedding band? My car?

My car!

My fucking car was in the driveway. Unless the assholes moved it, Leander would see my car and know I was there at some point. I went where I said I was going. He would most certainly pull up the security cameras and see what happened. He would see I didn't leave him voluntarily, that I fought to stay.

That meant he'd be out there looking for me.

Still, I wasn't going to sit around and wait to be rescued like a damsel in a tower. As soon as the opportunity presented itself, I was going home to my husband.

20

LEANDER

I looked at my watch for the twentieth time and then checked my cell phone. The results were the same — Bennett had been gone for over an hour. In a town the size of Easton, it didn't take an hour to get anywhere by car. Even if he *walked* from the mansion to Elijah's, he still would have been here by now.

Calls went unanswered.

Texts went unread.

A sickening feeling slithered into my intestines, twisting and knotting with each passing minute. Bennett had disappeared before, right when our relationship crossed from friendship to, well, more than friendship. It wasn't out of the realm of possibility he'd leave again. Even Lorelei presumed he'd cut and run once he realized how damaged I was.

No.

That was before — before Bennett and I made our feelings explicitly known. Before we were married, for Christ's sake. He loved me. I knew it. He wouldn't do that to me again.

Would he?

"I'm going over there," I announced, shoving away from Elijah's dining room table.

"I'm coming with you," Cole said, jumping to his feet as well.

Olivia made a face. "Seriously?"

"Yes, seriously," Cole snapped. "What if something happened?"

"Or what if he just left again?" Jake asked, glancing at me and immediately looking away.

Even Jake knew it was likely, just like Lorelei. They *all* knew it was possible. Probable. Almost a statistical certainty. Bennett Reeve was unpredictable. Capricious. Fickle. He lived for adventure. Being stuck someplace like Easton must have been killing him.

The pressure got to be too much for Bennett. *I* got to be too much. He'd had enough playing house and he wanted his freedom back, so he stole away in the dark rather than try to have an honest conversation with me. Because you can't reason with crazy people. I was, after all, a psychopath. The double-board certified Dr. Clayton decreed as much.

You're sick. You know that right? You need <u>serious,</u> long-term help.

Fuck!

Giving myself a mental slap, I snatched my keys off the table in the foyer and stormed out.

"We'll stay here!" Elijah called after me, right before Cole slammed the door.

"You want me to drive?" Cole asked, holding his hand out for the keys.

"Does it look like I want you to drive?" I yanked open the driver's side door of my car and slid in, turning the key before I even closed the door.

The second Cole's door shut, I stomped on the gas. Each

second that passed, each block we got closer, the knots in my stomach tightened until I could barely breathe.

Flying up the mansion's driveway, Cole was the first to exhale.

"There's his car."

"But where is he?" I parked behind the silver Maserati and climbed out slowly, staring up at the massive house. All of the windows were dark. Considering the house still had electricity, there was no reason for him to shuffle around without the lights on.

Other than the sounds of the river rushing down below the bluff, the entire area was quiet. Silence never bothered me before. Normally, I cherished it. But now? It portended everything I'd come to fear. Bennett wasn't loud, per se, but he wasn't quiet either. He had too much energy to be quiet. Always chattering, laughing, moving around. So why couldn't I hear him now?

Shoving the feeling of dread aside, I took a step toward the house. Something crunched underfoot.

I held my breath before forcing myself to look down.

It was a cell phone.

Snatching it off the ground, my heart stopped as the shattered screen came to life with all of my missed texts and calls. It was Bennett's phone.

"Shit..." Cole cleared his throat and waved me over. "Come take a look at this."

Clutching the phone, I walked over to where Cole was crouched. He shined his phone's light at a spot on the brick driveway and pointed with his other hand.

It was a sizable streak of blood.

"What do you think happened?" he asked, rising to his feet.

Shoving the broken phone into Cole's chest, I bolted up the backstairs and frantically unlocked the back door. I didn't bother turning on the lights as I tore through the hallways until I got to the closet on the first floor that housed all the technology required to monitor the various security systems. Turning on the computer screen, I scrolled backward through the camera footage until I had a shot of the silver Maserati cruising up the driveway.

Bennett arrived, parked, and was almost to the house when someone grabbed him from behind. He disentangled himself with ease, but he was powerless to fend off the second man wielding a taser. As soon as Bennett was incapacitated, the two grabbed him and tossed him into a van like a bag of trash and drove away.

"Holy shit..." Cole stood next to me, staring at the screen in horror. "Who was that?"

I played the footage back, again, and again, and again. Stopping the replay right as the van exited the driveway, I blew up the image as much as I could and pointed at the grainy license plate. "Call Elijah. Find me that owner. Now!"

Cole nodded and pulled his phone out, dialing quickly.

Stalking out of the small room, I yanked at the knot in my tie and loosened it, trying to draw a deeper breath. Any sense of relief I might have had knowing Bennett didn't leave me was crushed beneath the guilt of his capture. If I'd gone with him, if I'd insisted on driving together, this would have never happened. Or if I'd been firmer, telling him to forget the damn laptop, this would have never happened. If I'd done anything at all, except allowing him to leave the house on his own, this would have never happened.

I didn't even realize I'd walked into the conservatory until the smell of flowers and damp earth hit me. The moonlight illuminated the whole room, save for one corner.

Drawn to that darkness like a magnet, I walked straight to the wrought-iron table holding only one plant, a brilliant purple orchid. I cradled the beautiful bloom while it rested, away from the light, just as Bennett instructed all those years ago.

Tears sprang to my eyes. I slammed my hand into the table before I inadvertently crushed the petals.

"Fuck!"

Cole appeared in the doorway, waving his phone at me. "Elijah's on his way."

"What in God's name are you still doing here? Go find them!" I pointed at the door, incredulous I actually had to issue that command. Half the town should have been in flames by now until Cole found *someone* who could tell me something, *anything* that would get my husband back.

"But, we don't—"

"Fucking find them, Cole! I don't want to see you again until you have the owner of that fucking van with you! So help me, God!"

He backed out of the room quickly, hands raised in submission.

I spun and grabbed ahold of the first thing I found, launching it through the air as hard as I could. The antique mister shattered against the inside wall of the house, spraying shards of glass and water everywhere.

Tearing my hands through my hair, I prowled back and forth, my mind racing a hundred miles an hour. I ranked every enemy I'd ever made, theorized the outcome of a dozen different scenarios, and came to the same conclusion — Bennett was going to die *because* of me.

The next thing to shatter was an empty pot. Then a filled pot, scattering soil and poisonous flowers all over the stone floor. Even one of the wicker chairs fell victim to my rage, crashing through one of the panes of glass in the conservatory wall and tumbling out into the garden.

Collapsing where I stood, I drew my knees up to my chest and buried my face in my arms.

"Oh my God! What happened?!" Olivia's voice rang out sometime later, her heeled steps crunching over bits of terracotta and ceramic. She squatted next to me and laid a hand on my shoulder gently.

I lifted my face from my arms and looked at her, unable to do anything about the pitiful tremble in my voice. "They took him. They took him from me, Olivia."

"Who? Who did?"

"I don't know!" The answer, the fucking helplessness, burst out of me with another wave of tears. "If I knew then I wouldn't be here right now! I'd be out there, slaughtering every single person who so much as touched him!"

Olivia wrapped her arms around me and pressed her cheek to the top of my head, holding me tightly. "We'll find him."

"We should call the police," Jake said.

Olivia and I both glared up at him, but she was the only one who spoke. "Are you fucking kidding me?"

"He was kidnapped!" Jake exclaimed, spreading his hands. "They can't *not* do anything. They'll have to investigate."

"And how long do you think that will take, Jacob?" Slipping out of Olivia's arms, I got to my feet slowly. She rose with me, keeping ahold of my forearm. Despite the pressure, signaling me to stop, I kept going. I couldn't help it. Without Bennett, anger was the only thing I had to sustain myself. "How long do you think it'll take for the fine officers at Easton PD to locate him? How hard do you think they're going to look for someone associated with *me*? Do you honestly believe they'll find him in time before those people send him home in a fucking body bag?!"

Jake swallowed and slid backward a step.

"Leander," Olivia snapped, grabbing onto both arms from behind and holding me still. "It's not his fault."

"Let go of me, Olivia."

"Not until you calm your ass down."

"Calm down? Calm down?!" I tried to turn to face her, but she held on, her grip tightening so hard her nails dug through my sleeves. "Do not tell me to calm down while my husband is out there! God only knows what's happening to him! Meanwhile I'm here, unable to do a fucking thing to find him!"

"And how the fuck is taking my head off going to help Bennett?" Olivia let go, taking a step forward and coming nose-to-nose with me when I whipped around. "Or Jake's? Or anyone's? If you want your husband back so goddamn badly, then use your fucking head, Leander." She jabbed two fingers into the center of my forehead and shoved my head back roughly.

Before I could retaliate, she grabbed Jake's hand and dragged him out of the conservatory.

Seething, I stormed back to the closet and pulled up the footage again. There had to be something. Anything. A license plate was good, but it didn't tell the whole story.

Bennett was counting on me to find a breadcrumb, no matter how small. And once I did, these fucking people were done for. By the time I was finished with them, I'd make them wish they'd never been born.

21

BENNETT

An argument upstairs captured my attention sometime after the sun set again. Thus far, no one came downstairs. I could have been dead in here and they'd never know. Which, according to the argument, wouldn't have been good for them.

I tracked the thumping back and forth as one of the men paced above me, cobwebs and a century's worth of dirt drifting downward. The other voice remained stationary.

"This ain't good, man. Not good at all."

"Just tell me what the fuck happened."

"Jesse's arm is broke in two different spots!" *Broken*, hill-rod. Not "broke."

"I don't give a fuck about Jesse. I mean, how the hell did you two screw this up in the first place?"

"Tall, skinny, in a suit. That's who we saw. How were we supposed to know it wasn't the right guy?"

My brows furrowed at that. Not the right guy? If *I* wasn't the target, that meant Leander was. I exhaled my anger so I could focus on the rest of the conversation.

The stationary one, and the one who had to be the

"brains" of the operation, answered in a yell. "Because you were paid to know!"

The pacing stopped. I pictured the man cowering. I didn't know if he was afraid of the man in front of him or the one writing the check.

"I'll make it right," Dumb Dumb said after a minute.

"You better. 'Cuz it's not going to be *my* ass on the line," the other voice snapped before heavy boots thumped across the floor and a door slammed shut.

Learning I wasn't the one they were after was a turn I wasn't expecting. But the fact they wanted Leander made me equally furious. Expelling a sharp breath, I tried to reel my emotions in. I couldn't let anger get the best of me. Even if I was pretty sure I could outsmart Tweedle Dee and Dumb in my sleep, I needed to stay focused so I could get out of here.

The same reasons I was potentially targeted applied to Leander as well — revenge or ransom. He had his own stack of bodies beyond being the most-hated person in Easton. Not to mention his big ass bank account.

But things had been good lately. *We'd* been good lately. We hadn't planned to murder anyone new, nor had either of us actually offed anyone since I took out Lorelei's meddling mother. Lorelei retracted her damn article on the last day of her deadline and forwarded her email to the journal as proof, along with the shortest, shittiest mea culpa known to man.

We removed a corrupt lawyer from his own firm, guaranteeing he wouldn't take advantaged of his poor, unsuspecting clients ever again. With Caleb's help, Leander was able to recover most of the money stolen from the trust over the years.

He also got the remainder of Russ's payout for the damages he won in civil court, which prompted a lengthy discussion of Russ and Nora's untimely demise. I, for one, was simply *shocked* to learn Russell owed money to some rather unsavory people. Wouldn't you know it? Those debt collectors came and murdered Russ and his innocent girlfriend, Nora, and left their tortured bodies in a soybean field before setting Russ's beat-up truck on fire.

Leander didn't look like he bought *any* of my bullshit, but he kissed me all the same and gave me one hell of a blowjob for my efforts. For the first time in weeks, he had a peaceful night of sleep, which meant *I* had a peaceful night of sleep.

Other than sending off a complaint to the Illinois Department of Professional Regulation detailing Lorelei's unethical relationship with both her patient and the prosecuting attorney on Leander's case, I hadn't done anything to anyone. Scout's honor.

The majority of our attention had been focused on the renovations at the mansion, adjusting to a cozier lifestyle in the little teal cottage, and settling into domestic bliss.

So what the fuck was I missing?

THE METAL DOOR swung open with a groan. It could have been minutes or hours after the argument upstairs. Other than a general sense of light and dark outside the window, I had no way to tell the time. All I really knew was the concrete was beyond uncomfortable and as soon as I was out of here I was spending a week at the spa.

Tucking my hands behind my back, I secured my grip on the ice pick and waited.

A man stepped inside, wearing a worn flannel shirt and jeans with dirty knees. From the gunk under his fingernails, he looked like a farmer or a mechanic, not a kidnapper.

"Good, you're awake," he grunted, making his way over to me with a bottle of water.

"Who are you?" I knew the odds of him answering were slim, but I had to try.

He ignored me and unscrewed the cap from the plastic bottle.

"Where are we?"

Still, nothing.

"What do you want? Money?" I ventured as he squatted down in front of me, holding the water bottle out at an angle like I was a fucking gerbil. "I'll double whatever it is they're paying you."

He smirked. "Nice try."

"Are you sure? What if I triple it? Come on. Google me. You know I'll be good for it."

"Not happening."

"Well, if that's your decision." I sighed and looked away, trying to appear crestfallen. My right arm flew out from behind my back, driving the point of the ice pick through his temple.

His brown eyes popped open, along with his mouth, in a stupidly stunned expression.

"Don't look at me like that." I made a face at him, slowly pulling the ice pick back out. "You had a choice. It's not my fault you chose wrong."

His eyes dulled and he crumpled on the floor, that surprised look etched on his face.

Rolling my head to one side and then the other, I sighed with each satisfying crack of my vertebrae. I stood swiftly and stepped over the man, creeping carefully toward the door.

The rest of the basement was cluttered with junk and coated with a heavy layer of dust. It didn't look like anyone had been down here in decades. Shafts of light pierced the dimness through the worn floorboards, allowing me to navigate without tripping over something.

A door squeaked and slammed upstairs.

"Dwight!" a male voice shouted. Brains was back, which meant Dwight was the dummy who fucked up. "Hurry your ass up!"

Cursing silently, I crouched near the rickety stairs. Heavy boots stomped back and forth overhead. It sounded like a chair scraped across the floor and then it got quiet.

I stole a glance up the stairwell. There was a solid door at the top, which was closed. With my luck, it led into the house instead of directly to the outside. Why couldn't there be some nice bulkhead doors instead?

A quick gander around the basement didn't produce any other brilliant ideas or clearly-marked exits. This door was the only feasible way out as far as I could tell. So, I'd have to wait out Dwight's impatient companion.

"I'll be in the truck!" the man yelled. The boots tromped across the floor again. Another door squeaked and slammed shut.

I stayed where I was for another beat, trying to picture the man exiting the house and traversing whatever distance there was to a waiting truck.

When I felt reasonably secure he was out of earshot, I crept up the stairs, pausing now and again to try and listen over my pounding heart. Just a few more steps and I was out of this musty basement. A few more steps and I'd be free. I held my breath, reaching for the door handle.

As I did, someone on the other side jerked it open.

The last thing I saw was the butt-end of a shotgun crashing into the center of my face.

22

BENNETT

"Rise and shine, asshole." Someone kicked the outside of my thigh — hard. Not the head, not the stomach. The leg. Which meant whoever my captors were, they were under orders not to hurt me beyond what was necessary. Hence, the buttstock to the face instead of the barrel.

I jerked myself into a sitting position, except my left hand didn't come with me. The cold, sharp bite of metal dug into my wrist.

Handcuffs. Fuck.

Dwight's body was gone, though I could have easily mistaken the hillbilly in front of me as his twin. Maybe it was the flannel. Or the beards. Or the smell. Jesus.

"I don't suppose you'll tell me what I'm doing here," I said, cautiously touching the gash across my nose. It was swollen and crusted with blood. I'd be surprised if it *wasn't* broken. Dickhead.

"You'll find out soon enough." The new man stayed standing and well out of kicking distance. He tossed a water bottle in my lap, followed by a protein bar.

I made no move to pick up either, even though my throat felt like the Sahara. "Thanks but no thanks. I'm cutting out sugar. Apparently it's bad for you."

"Suit yourself, smart ass." He snorted and turned for the door.

"What are you going to tell them?" I asked, smirking when he stopped short.

"What are you talking about?"

"I can't imagine they're going to be thrilled when they realize how badly your two minions fucked up. Grabbing the wrong guy and all." I sucked in an exaggerated hiss of pain. "Doesn't bode well for you, boss. Might be time to switch sides."

"You don't know shit," he shot back with less conviction than he probably thought he had. His rumbly voice was full of confidence, but the nervous way his eye twitched told me otherwise.

"You should consider your options very carefully. Your friend certainly didn't and look how that played out."

His hand gripped the edge of the rusted door, burly knuckles tightening.

"Oh, sugarplum! You two weren't close, were you? He was a bit of an idiot, truth be told, but I suppose that's what made him so special. *So* special." I sighed wistfully and crossed myself. "May he rest in peace."

He glowered, showing tremendous restraint — unfortunately for me.

I beamed at him, hoping to poke the bear a little more. "Bet it frosts your ass you can't do anything about it, either. You just have to stand there, knowing your kinfolk's killer is going to get away with it. Poor Dwight... No justice at all."

With a low growl, he charged at me. I was prepared for a

boot to come flying at my face, but he stopped suddenly outside of some invisible boundary, his face darkened with anger.

"Aw, come on." I tossed my head, beckoning him with a grin. "Come get your revenge. I'll let you take the first swing." I tugged on the handcuff, trying to tempt him with my vulnerability.

The man shook his head. "You got *no* idea what's coming for you."

"Apparently neither do you."

He blinked before disguising it with a roll of his eyes.

"Quite frankly," I said with a bright smile, crossing my legs at the ankle. "I don't know which should worry you more — what happens when *I* get out of here, or what happens if my husband gets his hands on you first."

The man scoffed, giving me a once-over. "You'll be singing in a different tune in a couple hours, you fucking fairy." Rude.

With that, he stepped out, clanging the door shut behind him. A deadbolt slammed into place on the other side, along with an additional lock of some sort.

As much as I wanted to figure out who the hell Leander or I pissed off this time, time was clearly of the essence.

Jerking my left arm, I tested the strength of the handcuffs against the pipe I was chained to. With my luck, it was a fucking gas line. The pipe was old, but the threads would never give way. Even if I could somehow break through the metal, I didn't want to run the risk of creating a spark or gassing myself out.

That meant the weakness was in the handcuffs themselves.

Casting about for something to help in my endeavor, I tried to stay focused on that task instead of thinking about a thousand other things, namely Leander. Where was he? Was he safe? Dear God, I hoped he didn't think I turned my back on him like before.

Swatting the water and protein bar off of my lap with a sudden burst of brilliance, I unclasped my belt buckle and ripped the leather free. Gavin was getting a raise as soon as I was out of this shithole. Who knew his trendy Christmas present would literally be a lifesaver.

Ok... time to remember what that SEAL in Tangiers said. Pushing past the memories of spearmint tea and perfectly chiseled abs, I picked up the thread of our conversation from fifteen years ago.

Shoving my sleeves out of the way, I slid the handcuff up as far as it would go on my forearm and then forced it even further to make sure it was as tight as possible. The skin on my arm throbbed beneath the metal, but I couldn't think about that since I knew it was about to get a hell of a lot worse.

The pain and the blood doesn't matter. Freedom is what matters, the Texan's voice drawled in my head. Better the left arm than the right, anyway.

Wedging the corner of the belt buckle between the double metal strands, I applied as much pressure as I could, trying to turn the titanium inside the steel. Pain erupted in my arm, aggravated by the hot, sticky blood seeping out of my torn skin. I gritted my teeth and kept going.

Freedom is what mattered — *Leander* is what mattered.

I didn't dare let up on the pressure, even when it felt like my arm was on fire. The strands bowed out, ever so slightly.

A drop of sweat rolled off the tip of my nose and plummeted onto my bloody forearm. Maybe I shouldn't have been so stubborn and actually eaten the damn protein bar. It probably would have helped with the queasiness. Too late now. I wasn't going to let up on the tension for anything.

If all else failed, I was ok breaking my hand to get out of this goddamn cuff.

Thankfully the metal rivet gave way before I had to resort to crushing my own bones. I exhaled a shaky sigh of relief, pulling my trembling hand free from the twisted handcuff.

I tore the bottom part of my shirt off and wrapped it around my forearm to try and stem some of the bleeding before pulling my sleeves down again. It would be fine until I could sit and look at it properly. My jacket was ruined anyway. Assholes. They had no respect for vintage Armani.

Snatching the belt off the ground, I pushed myself into a standing position, leaning against the wall for support. I wrapped the end of the belt around my right hand once and held the buckle loosely in my left. Now, it was time to wait.

And... wait.

Kidnappers were really inconsiderate when it came to timing. I had a husband to get home to, a fuck ton of work to catch up on, and a house remodel to oversee. I didn't have time to sit around, waiting to be tortured.

At last, heavy footsteps tromped overhead. I tracked their movement above me, imagining the layout from the brief glance I got from my first escape attempt. He was walking toward the basement door.

Sure enough, the lock upstairs turned and the heavy boots clomped down the wooden stairs.

I hadn't heard anyone else all day. With any luck, he was still alone and in a matter of minutes I'd be free and clear.

The lock outside my room clicked and the deadbolt slammed open. The rusty door swung inward, screeching on its hinges. I had all I could do to stay where I was and not blow my own element of surprise.

When the man appeared around the door, I lashed the belt buckle at his face. The metal bit into the flesh near his eye, resulting in a rush of blood and a string of expletives.

While he was distracted, I darted behind him and slipped the belt over his head and down to his throat. I pulled back with as much force as I could manage against his sizable girth, bending myself backward until he was practically standing on his toes.

He alternated between clawing at his throat and trying to grab for me, gasping and gurgling and turning an interesting shade of mulberry.

Winded, his body slackened and collapsed. I fell with him, keeping the pressure on the belt for a few more minutes until I was sure the fucker was dead.

Scooting away from him, I took another minute to catch my breath. My sleeve stuck to my left arm thanks to a fresh coating of blood that seeped out during the struggle. The shaking in my left hand had spread to the other now, making it somewhat difficult to thread the belt back through my pants.

Once I managed it, I crawled over to the dead man and rifled through his pockets. The only thing I found was a burner phone and a can of dip. No ID. And sadly, no gun or keys.

Tucking the phone in my pocket, I got to my feet again and made my way toward the stairs.

Creeping up them at a snail's pace, I kept an ear perked for any sound to tell me I wasn't alone. I'd only ever heard the two of them, so I felt pretty confident I was in the clear.

I reached the top of the stairs without incident, but I paused again, listening. Hearing nothing, I darted into the kitchen and slipped out the backdoor.

Inhaling the night air, I stepped off the back stairs with a little spring to my step. Probably adrenaline, but still. I was free and on my way home, once I figured out where I was. All I smelled was manure and all I saw was the dilapidated little farm my captor's house sat on. No matter. I'd find civilization again at some point, or at least a cell phone signal.

I was halfway down the driveway, headed for the truck parked near the front of the house, when a pair of headlights turned off the road and lit me up like a beacon.

"Oh, shit."

The engine revved a second before the tires tore across the gravel. Bullets flew overhead, too quickly to be from one gun. There was at least two shooters, maybe three.

I ducked and spun in the opposite direction. Shouting a string of curses in my head, I made a break for the dark tree-line at the rear of the property.

My heart raced as bullets continued to whizz by. I launched myself over a dilapidated picket fence and cut through an overgrown pasture.

A second too late, I saw a fence post listing to the side. Barbed wire sagged between it and another post down apiece. It was too late. I was committed to my course and plowed straight into the rusty spikes.

"Motherfuck!"

I peeled myself off of the barbs, pressing a hand over the gash on my thigh. Could have been worse, Reeve. Could have been *way* worse.

The SUV on my tail burst through the wooden fence as I hobbled over the barbed wire.

Once I hit the trees, I had no idea which way I was running. I aimed for the darkest part of the landscape and hauled ass, praying I didn't lay myself out by running head-first into a fucking tree or tripping and breaking my ankle like an idiot in a horror film.

Car doors slamming and men shouting at each other echoed through the night. I couldn't make out what they were saying over my racing heart, but I heard at least three voices. It made sense. Three to chase me, while the fourth drove around to try and cut me off. Even if it was only two chasing me, I still had to worry about encountering the SUV if I made it to a road.

Sadly for me, the trees didn't last long. They tapered off, leaving me with a cornfield to navigate. Luckily, the farmer hadn't harvested yet. Thank God for a wet summer.

I dove into the row of stalks. Angling my shoulders to the side, I tried to minimize the rustling as I ran. The musty leaves scratched my face, leaving tiny little stings in their wake. Fucking corn. God, I hated this miserable state! This is why I lived in a *city*.

Mud coated my boots in just a few steps. I was sure each one weighed thirty pounds by the time I doubled over at the edge of the corn, bracing my hands on my knees and trying to breathe. My left arm was fucking killing me. Pain radiated up and down it. I was pretty sure that meant I was having a heart attack, which would be super inconvenient. Call me stubborn or stuck up, but I refused to die in the mud like a peasant.

Refocusing on my escape, I peeked my head out of the last row of corn and peered around. More farmland. Goddamn it. I didn't want to wait here until morning but my options were clearly limited.

A breath away from despondency, the most beautiful sound I ever heard split the night air.

A siren.

Red and blue lights flashed in the distance, illuminating a black and white pickup truck right before it disappeared behind a curve in the road.

A cop!

For the first time in my life I was overjoyed to see the police.

Ducking back inside the safety of the corn, I fought my

way through the rows in the direction the squad went, using the siren and the lights as my guide.

Dropping down to one knee at the edge of the cornfield, I assessed the new terrain in front of me. It was an another open field. Great for running, bad for being a moving target.

Not to mention, I had no idea who the cop had pulled over in the car.

I squinted, trying to make out the vehicle in front of the pickup. There were only two things I could determine — it was small, and it was white. Not an SUV full of people coming to drag me back to a dirty basement for God knew what reason.

Now or never, Reeve.

I burst out of my hiding spot and sprinted across the open field, praying to God the cop didn't leave before I got there and some bullet didn't pick me off along the way.

The deputy was out of the truck, standing on the road, and so was the driver of the little car. They appeared to be in the middle of a field sobriety test, which meant they weren't leaving soon. Thank God for alcoholics.

A light moved in my periphery. I stole a glance in that direction, already fearing the worst. It was another pair of headlights coming down the road at an unusually slow pace — like they were looking for something. Or someone.

Fuck me.

The SUV picked up speed and so did I. It was a race to the squad.

The cop, for his part, held up a finger to the man in the middle of a walk-and-turn test and headed back toward his pickup truck, one hand on his pistol and the other reaching for his radio. His attention, it seemed, was also focused on the SUV barreling down the road.

"Get down!" I shouted.

The cop looked at me before his head whipped back

toward the SUV. It swerved in its lane, aiming right for the poor bastard.

There was a hard, thudding crunch and the unmistakable sound of tires rolling over a body.

Fuckfuckfuck!

The SUV continued on its way without slowing. They didn't even hit their fucking brake lights.

Stumbling up the ditch, I collapsed against the side of the pickup. At the moment, trying to catch my breath seemed like an impossibility. Forcing a swallow down, I peered between the squad and the white car.

A hand reached out of nowhere and grabbed me.

I jerked back with a yelp.

The cop was alive. Holy Mary Mother of God, how the fuck was he alive?!

"Are you ok?" He helped me to my feet, holding me steady when I was upright again. "Are you hurt? Shit, look at your face."

"I'm ok. Are *you* ok?" I looked him up and down, but he seemed fine.

"Yeah." When he pulled his hand away from my left arm, it came back wet with blood. "Fuck. You're bleeding."

I looked down at my bicep. Sure enough there was a hole in the middle of my sleeve. Now that I'd stopped running, blood dripped off of my fingers. "Well, shit." Guess it wasn't a heart attack after all.

Suddenly remembering the other driver, the cop darted around the white car and swore loudly. He dropped to his knees, chattering into his radio at warp speed in a language of numbers and cop talk.

The other driver was sprawled out on the pavement, one leg turned around, facing the opposite direction. His head had been cracked like an egg, brain matter and blood oozing around his mangled face.

I slid down the side of the squad, letting my head thump back against the door panel.

I made it. I actually made it out.

But now? Now it was time for the legal song and dance, which was the last thing I wanted to do. I was so fucking tired and all I wanted was Leander. And a shower. Dear God, I needed a shower.

23

BENNETT

I heard Leander before I ever saw him. I was pretty sure the entire hospital heard him. Whatever nurse was at the intake desk must have threatened to call the police, since he yelled some choice words back at her, ending with, "Ask me if I fucking care!"

Despite the bevy of staff telling him to stop, his footsteps never slowed. I'm sure the look on his face didn't help. A variety of sneakers and Crocs went squeaking in opposite directions the closer he got.

"I don't give a fuck about your goddamn policies! Get out of my way!"

He ripped the curtain open with the force of a tornado, his breathing short and ragged. Working his jaw from side to side in what looked like an effort to regain control after losing his shit on the nursing staff, he froze where he was, his green eyes wild.

"My love." I held a hand out to him, a sense of relief washing over me for the first time in days.

He exhaled sharply, silent tears spilling down his cheeks as he grasped my hand and pulled me into his chest so tightly

I actually winced. As much as I cherished breathing, I wasn't about to tell him to let go.

Once his own breathing calmed down, he took my face between his hands and tipped my head back. His eyes were bloodshot, rimmed with red. Meanwhile, the hollows beneath them were so dark he looked more dead than alive. Between the obvious exhaustion and I'm sure a lack of eating, it was a miracle he was even still standing.

"I thought you were gone," he said quietly.

Again. He may not have said it, but my mind supplied the painful reminder.

"I told you, I'm not easy to kill." I was not in a jovial mood in the slightest, but it was better than breaking down into a blubbering mess. One of us had to keep it together and since he already had at least one meltdown today, I figured it was my turn to be the stoic.

He kissed me once, hard and possessively, before pulling me against him again, his arms tight around my neck. "I've been out of my mind without you. I don't know what I would do if I lost you for good."

"I'm so sorry..."

Jerking back, he cradled my face again, fresh tears in his eyes. "Why are you apologizing? None of this is your fault."

"I'm not so sure about that."

"What are you talking about? Who were they?" His head tilted to the side as he studied my face.

"I don't know," I replied with a small, helpless shrug. "I've never seen them before in my life."

"What did they want?"

"You." I grimaced, my hands tightening around his arms.

He blinked, his brows furrowing. "Me? Are you sure?"

"I heard them talking one night. I guess they made a mistake taking me. Someone sent them there for you."

"Who the hell would want to come after me?"

"I have no idea. But I intend to find out as soon as I get out of here."

"I don't think you're going anywhere. The police said you've been shot." His jaw tensed as his attention turned to my left arm.

I glanced down at my bandaged bicep. "It's fine."

"It's *not* fine, mon coeur."

"It was a through-and-through. All things considered, I've had far worse." I gave him a cheeky grin, hoping it would soothe his hackles.

He brushed his thumb along my cheekbone, frowning at what I'm sure was the most magnificent bruising across my face. "I promise you we'll find them and make them pay. Elijah and Cole are already tracking them down. Their license plate registers to a company out of Blue Springs."

It hurt to arch an eyebrow, so I frowned instead. "The police told you that?"

He frowned right back at me, like I'd asked the dumbest question ever. To be fair, I *was* concussed again. "Of course not. You're not the only one who knows people."

"Was it just a company or was there a name to go along with it?"

"Don't worry about it. You need to focus on resting."

"So do you." I touched his cheek gently.

He leaned into my hand, closing his eyes. I wrapped my arms around his waist and laid my head against his chest, matching my breathing to the steady beat of his heart. "I hate hospitals. I just want to go home."

"Have the police finished getting whatever information they need from you?"

I nodded mutely.

He pressed a kiss to my forehead. "Then I'll go get the doctor."

"Please don't yell at him. I don't need you getting arrested again."

Smirking, he raked a hand through his curls and ducked around the curtain.

I'D NEVER BEEN SO happy to see that little teal house in my entire life. If I could have, I would have hopped out of the car and ran in the front door like a kid at Christmas. As it was, I shuffled up the front steps with Leander watching every step and scolding me when I went "too fast." A turtle could have passed me and he'd still say I was going "too fast."

"You have a concussion," he snapped when I insisted on going up the stairs by myself and — daredevil that I was — did *not* use the railing. After that, I wasn't allowed to go anywhere unsupervised.

"I want a shower," I whined when we finally made it upstairs.

"You have stitches."

"So put a bag over my arm. I'm gross and I'm not soiling the sheets with farm funk."

"I'll buy new sheets."

"What about a bath?"

Huffing out a sigh, he marched me into the bathroom and promptly shoved me onto the toilet. The look on his face dared me to move. For once, I complied without being a smart ass about it.

While the bathtub was filling, he stripped me out of my dirty clothes, inspecting me from head-to-toe despite the fact the doctor and I both told him I was fine. I mean, minus the bullet hole in my arm. Or the concussion, which, yes, hurt like a son of a bitch. But I was fine. A broken nose, some cuts and bruises. All in all not too bad for getting my ass handed to me for the second time in a year.

The first injury to draw his attention was the bruising across my face from the shotgun butt, along with the scab in my eyebrow. Those weren't pleasant, but they were nothing compared to the tiny little lacerations from the corn. Hours later, those *still* stung.

I turned my gaze away from Leander during his scrutiny. The fury in his eyes brought back an enormous amount of guilt, so much that my stomach churned painfully. It was the same look he had after Marchese's men nearly beat me to death. I didn't need a reminder of either of those events — the beating, or its aftermath.

His fingers trailed down my arm, past the gauze on my bicep, to my forearm. Prying the handcuff apart had left a series of deep gashes, which he was now studying. When I looked up, his eyes narrowed in silent question.

"I did that," I said, looking away again. "To get the handcuff off."

He didn't say anything, but his hand drifted down to my lower abdomen and down even further to the top of my thigh, where I impaled myself on the barbed wire. Good thing I was up to date on my tetanus shots.

I didn't bother looking up before supplying the answer. "That was me too. A fence."

He slipped behind me, his hand splaying across the taser mark on my shoulder.

"That was them," I said, glancing behind me. "That's how they got me."

"I know," he murmured. He pressed his lips to my shoulder blade and turned me slowly. "Let's get you clean."

"The cameras?"

He nodded, drifting back to the bathtub and testing the water with his hand.

"I can manage. You should go get some rest." He looked as awful as I felt. Even though it had only been two days, it looked like he'd lost five pounds that he didn't exactly have to lose.

"I'm not going anywhere and I'm not going to argue with you." Both brows lifted, waiting to see what my next move was.

"Then come in with me." I sidled closer to him, kissing his tense jawline.

"Bennett." Shit. I couldn't remember the last time he actually used my name in an angry way.

Acknowledging defeat, I eased into the water carefully, propping my left arm up on the towel he draped over the edge.

Kneeling next to the tub, and sadly still dressed, Leander wet a sea sponge and dabbed behind my ear. I winced and jerked away, but he held me in place with one hand threaded through my hair.

"You have blood in your hair," he murmured. Confirming his observation, swirls of dark brown stained the water when he squeezed the sponge to clean it.

I stopped his hand and angled myself so I could see him. "Promise me we'll handle this together."

He shifted further behind me so I couldn't see him as he continued sponging the dried blood off of me. A not-so-subtle way of ignoring me.

"Leander..." Two could play the name game.

"You've done enough."

I scoffed. Enough as in let myself get kidnapped and shot? Yeah. My contributions to the group project were stellar.

"The police said you killed two of your captors," Leander continued. "Not to mention, you freed yourself. I'd say your participation in this endeavor is over."

"I mean it," I said, ignoring the body count. I didn't know

if he somehow felt a need to catch up to me, kill-wise, or was trying to make me feel better by pointing out I wasn't a fucking damsel in distress. "I don't want you doing anything without telling me."

"Is it because you want your own revenge or because you don't trust me to take care of you?" His voice may have been quiet, but I detected a sharpness all the same.

I turned to face him, my brows drawn together sharply. "Neither. Why would you even say that?"

He gritted his teeth and looked away.

Touching the side of his face, I guided him back toward me gently.

He put off answering as long as he could before it came out in a rush. "I wasn't there for you before, Bennett, and I nearly lost you. Now this has happened and I nearly lost you again. If I do, I may as well end it all. There is no life for me without you. I tried to live without you once and it broke me. You are the reason my wretched soul continues to exist. So, no, mon coeur. Don't sit there and expect me to make promises you know I won't keep. I will *not* put you in harm's way again. I will not—"

I pressed my lips to his, silencing his outburst.

He pulled away and exhaled, resting his forehead against mine.

Lacing our hands together, I nudged him with my forehead. "What have I always told you?"

"I don't know. You talk nonstop, it's hard to keep up with."

I pulled back with a mock glare, gaping at him.

A wry grin pulled at the corner of his mouth, even though his eyes were still clouded with worry.

"Together," I said loudly, giving him a pointed look. "We're unstoppable."

"Just like we handled Mr. Brewer and Ms. Kelly together?" He arched an eyebrow. "Go ahead and deny it. I know you killed them."

I made a face, sputtering out a few noises before finally answering. "That was totally *different*. And besides, Jake and I are cool now because of that whole thing. I mean, he hasn't given me half of a best-friend necklace yet, but I'm sure it's coming. He's just waiting for the right moment. I can tell."

Leander rolled his eyes, spinning me away from him and adding soap to the sponge. "Where do you propose we start?"

"One of them had a burner phone. I need to get it to my guy in Chicago and hopefully he can get us some answers."

"Didn't the police confiscate it?"

"Oh, I'm sure they would have. Too bad it's in the lining of my jacket."

He resumed dabbing at me with the sponge, running it over my shoulder and down my left forearm. "I thought it felt unusually heavy."

"I wasn't going to give up the only lead we have." I reached across myself and caught his wrist gently, dragging his arm across my chest.

He took the hint and wrapped his other arm around me too, nuzzling the side of my head. "I mean it, mon coeur. I don't know what I would do if they killed you. I can't live in a world without you."

"You'll never have to. I swear, I'm not going anywhere."

24

LEANDER

Even after Bennett's relatively safe return, I didn't sleep. I couldn't. The nightmares were back with a vengeance, only this time they switched from my own demons, to his — unknown men taking the only thing that mattered to me. My brain conjured a variety of outcomes, ways his kidnapping *could* have gone, each ending more terrible than the last.

His physical wounds healed a little more every day, while the ones in my mind continued to fester. The only thing that brought any form of relief was being with Bennett — knowing he was alive, and safe.

So, I lived on coffee and the updates from Elijah and Cole as they worked tirelessly to find me the remaining kidnapper, the one Bennett hadn't been able to kill.

The company van, sadly, was a dead-end. The van had been stolen the day of the incident and from all of the information we were able to unearth, there was no connection between anyone at the company and Bennett or I.

Our break came, days after Bennett's return, in the form of a local obituary.

"That's him," Bennett said, stabbing a finger into the photograph of an unremarkable man. "Dwight! I'll never forget that stupid look on his face."

Taking the paper from him, I skimmed the rest of the text. "It says he had a farming accident."

"Sure. If you want to call an ice pick to the brain a 'farming accident.'"

"And his brother Maynard died unexpectedly at home?" I turned the paper around again and showed him the second picture under the fold. "Was he the other one?"

Bennett nodded. "Yeah. That's the one I strangled."

"Galigher…"

"What?"

"Galigher!" Shifting to the edge of my chair, I dropped the paper on the table between us and grabbed his wrist. "Edna Galigher. Did we, or did we not, acquire that property last year at a sheriff's sale?"

Furrowing his brows, his gaze fell to the paper. A moment later, his eyes flicked up again, once he'd cycled through his incredible memory. "Galigher. A three-hundred acre farm outside of Blue Springs, went to auction after the old woman died because her sons neglected to pay the property taxes. It was an absolute steal."

Leaning forward, I cupped the back of his head and pulled him closer, pressing my lips to his. I stood quickly, kissing his forehead as well before darting toward the stairs.

"Where are you going?" he asked, spinning in his chair.

"To pay my respects."

It wasn't hard to find the Galigher's only living brother, Jesse. In such a small town, even a blind man would have found his address easily enough. With the family name painted on the mailbox, he may as well have rolled out a welcome mat.

For this venture, only Elijah and Cole were with me. They flanked the front door, in the shadows, while I stood in the center. I cocked my head, taking in the wall behind Elijah. It was decorated with antique farm implements, a perfect complement to the rusted-out tire leaning against the porch and the broken-down tractor, half-sunk into the side yard, overgrown with weeds and flowers alike.

Chewing the inside corner of my mouth, I considered my options. The scythe was the obvious choice. Or the saw. At the last second, I opted for the T-shaped stake.

"What the fuck is that?" Cole whispered.

"A dibber," I replied, wrapping my fingers around the handle and getting a feel for the weight. "You use it to plant seeds. Or, you used to, anyway."

Elijah chuckled and shook his head. "Only you would know that shit."

"And Jake." I smirked at him as I raised the dibber to the front door, knocking loudly with it.

When the shuffling inside got closer, a male barked out, "Yeah, I'm coming," as the locks turned. As soon as the door swung open, Cole threw his elbow out, slamming right into the center of Jesse's face.

The man stumbled back into the house and Cole rushed after him.

"Who the fuck are you?" he asked, scrambling backward and holding his gushing nose with his one good hand. The other was trapped in a sling, courtesy of Bennett snapping his elbow.

I declined to answer while Elijah secured the front door. Cole was able to dart around behind the man and grab him in a headlock, wrestling him down to his knees.

"Look, I'm sorry! You can have the money back! I don't want no trouble!"

"Oh, I'm not here for your money." I leaned down and stuck the point of the dibber underneath his chin, forcing his head up. "But tell me, Jesse, who do you not want trouble from?"

"Who are you?" he asked again, his eyes wide and watering from the blow.

I gave him a polite smile. "I'm the husband of the man you just kidnapped."

If it was possible, his eyes widened even more. "Look, mister. I'm sorry, ok. It was a mistake."

"A mistake which I am here to address." Straightening, I cracked my neck and nodded at Cole.

Cole pulled the stun gun from his waistband and drove it into the man's back. Jesse yelped and fell forward, writhing in place until the electricity stopped.

I nodded again and again Cole pulled the trigger, eliciting another howl.

"Put him over there," I said, gesturing to the kitchen table.

Elijah and Cole scooped him up and dragged him over to the chair. They secured him in place with zip ties, making sure each limb was held in place individually. He could struggle all he wanted to. Without enough force, friction, or a blade there was no way he would be able to free himself.

Dragging one of the other chairs over, I sat across from him, tapping the dibber against my knee. "I'll cut to the chase, Jesse. Who hired you?"

"I don't kno—"

Before the lie even finished forming, I stabbed the dibber straight down into his thigh.

He screamed and clawed at the air, trying to reach the tool.

"I ask again." As soon as I yanked the stake out, blood surged out of the hole and cascaded down the side of his leg. "Who hired you?"

"We never used names! Ok? Just a phone!"

"Where's the phone?"

Breathing hard, he squeezed his eyes shut and shook his head frantically. "I don't have it."

Clucking my tongue, I shook my head as well and drove the dibber into his other leg.

"Fuck, man! I don't have it! I swear! Maynard had it! He did all the talkin'."

Well, at least that was favorable news. The fact we were already in possession of the phone put me in a slightly better mood. Bennett assured me he knew someone who would be able to get the necessary information off of it. And once this interrogation was over, that's exactly what we were going to do.

"Did they tell you who you were supposed to kidnap?"

"Leonardo something. I don't know! I told you, Maynard had all that!"

"Leander?" I ventured, my brows raised slightly.

His eyes widened again, stupidly hopeful, like if he gave me the right answer I would stop making him bleed. "Yeah. Yeah. Leander."

Elijah tapped Cole on the shoulder and tossed his head to the side. They disappeared silently, leaving us alonc now that I had the information I wanted.

"How unfortunate for you, then, that you kidnapped Bennett by mistake… Leander is so *very* protective of his husband." The information sank in slowly. When it clicked into place, Jesse sucked in a breath at the same time I drove the dipper into his abdomen and up at an angle, through his diaphragm.

"And to make sure this never happens again" — I smiled, twisting the stake up even further — "I'm sending your employers a very succinct message."

Jesse gurgled and gasped, his stomach heaving as the blood oozed out of it, coating my hand.

"Your brothers got off easy. You're going to die slowly, Jesse, anticipating each moment until death finally comes. Do you smell that? That gas? You know what will happen when it fills this place up." I leaned closer until we were nose-to-nose. Another smile graced my lips, as dark and delighted as ever, before I whispered the answer. "Boom."

Tears streaked down his face, leaving track marks through the crusted blood from his broken nose. "I'm sorry! We needed the money! After the county took our..." He hiccuped and looked at me with sudden realization. "You. It was you, you son of a bitch! You stole our farm!"

Ignoring his self-righteous outburst, I stood and wiped my hand with the handkerchief from my front pocket. Cole and Elijah returned from different parts of the house, each nodding that their tasks were complete.

Elijah cocked his head at me. "Did he just mention the farm?"

"He did." I wiped the last of the blood away and flung the handkerchief at Jesse with a wrinkled nose before heading toward the front door.

Cole was the last out, pulling the door shut and making sure it was secured. "What are the odds a family that's more pissed off at you than usual is the one who gets paid to kidnap you?"

"Coincidence?" Elijah asked.

"I don't believe in coincidences," I replied.

Plenty of people had motive to hate me and my company — and they did, passionately. It was one of the hallmarks of being born into the Welles family. Wealth, power, and a burning hatred in the eyes of nearly everyone you meet.

But who was smart enough to use that hatred against me?

Hopefully Bennett's associate in Chicago could provide the answer.

25

BENNETT

"You trust him?" Leander asked, folding his arms while I knocked on the apartment door.

"More than most."

"Do I want to know how you two know each other?" He arched a brow at me, the corner of his mouth ticked up in a smirk.

"Down killer. I used him on a few cases. That's all." And he said *I* was jealous. Jeez. Now that I was mostly feeling better, we were back to that whole pot/kettle thing.

Kai opened the door with a dazzling smile. Wearing a formal black-and-white ensemble, topped off by black headphones, he either looked like he was a waiter or going to prom. The black cat ears and fingerless gloves really pulled the whole thing together. "Bennett! I can't believe it. I got your message and I said to myself 'Kai, darling, I told you not to worry. He would never cast you aside and find someone new. See? Good things come to those who wait.' So where have you been? It's been ages. Don't tell me you went straight."

"I've been busy," I replied flatly. Normally I didn't mind

his faux-English accent or his cattiness — no pun intended — but my head was throbbing. I blamed the rapid pressure changes thanks to the flight.

Kai's almond eyes narrowed as he took a step closer, zeroing in on my face. I mean, it was pretty hard to miss. The bruises were obvious, as were the scabbed-over cuts. "Oh, yes, I can see. Did you forget your safe word?" He turned to Leander, giving him a sweeping look. "You look like you can wield a paddle with some authority. Who might you be, handsome?"

"None of your business," I interjected. "All you need to know is he's not interested. Besides, crowbars are more his thing."

Leander's lips twitched, ever so slightly, when he slid his gaze in my direction.

Kai clutched the black collar on his throat, the tiny silver bell jingling. "Oh, my. I have *so* many questions now." I didn't appreciate the repeated once-overs he was giving my husband, but before I could say anything, he refocused his attention on me. "Are they dead? The people who...?" He pointed at my face, waving his finger in random zigzag motions.

"Two of them are. I need to know who's pulling the strings." I slipped the burner phone out of my pocket and held it up. "Can you do anything with this?"

Snatching it out of my hands, he turned it over and over like it was a rare treasure. "Only one way to find out." He pirouetted before slinking off back into the apartment.

I fished Leander's hand out from where it was folded against his chest and held it, leading him into the apartment. I knew he constantly questioned himself, trying to decide when to show scraps of public affection and when to be wholly reserved. If he couldn't tell by now, Kai was the absolute least of our concerns when it came to judging sexuality.

Leander pulled away regardless and started nosing through Kai's haphazard bookcase. It was crammed with as many books as it was notebooks and random computer parts. "How, exactly, did you two meet?"

"The asshole hacked my bank account."

Leander shot me a curious look, his brows lifted.

"I know. It surprised me too." I chuckled, holding my hands up in defense. "But I figured a guy like that was someone I should play nice with. Once we came to an understanding, we've had a very pleasant working relationship."

Kai returned with an armful of gadgets. Sweeping a pile of graphic novels out of the way, he dumped the electronics onto the coffee table. He'd lost the headphones, but the cat ears were still firmly in place. "If, by 'understanding,' you mean you threatened to cut my balls off, then yeah. It's been great, bruh. Really appreciate the Christmas gifts every year."

Leander raised his brows at me again.

I shrugged and smiled innocently, easing into the oversized chair across from Kai. When Leander walked by, I grabbed him by the hips and pulled him down onto my lap. He shot a look over his shoulder, which I promptly ignored. Even though he didn't relax, *at all,* I kept my hands on his hips.

"How long is this going to take?" I asked, shifting to one side so I could see what Kai was up to. "I've got a masseuse scheduled at five."

"Shit, darling, bring her here." Kai wired up the phone to a small box, which he then hooked into his laptop. "I could use with a little relaxation."

"Mexico wasn't refreshing enough?"

Kai looked up, eyes wide. "How do you know about Mexico?"

"The tequila on the counter," I replied, cocking my head. God only knew what nefarious activities he'd been up to.

Judging from his reaction, I probably didn't *want* to know — from a legal standpoint. "It's from that from that little place outside Guadalajara, right?"

A throaty laugh escaped him while he shook his head, literally waving away whatever concern he'd had. "You always did know your alcohol."

"It's one of my many talents."

Leander snorted, but refrained from commenting.

"Something to add, husband?" To punctuate my question, I squeezed his hip bone. He squirmed and elbowed me in return, still keeping his remarks to himself.

Kai's attention snapped up again, a smile stretching across his face. "Husband? You guys are married? Aw, that's awesome!" He threw the laptop to the side and darted across the loft to the kitchen, snagging the bottle of reposado. "We're definitely having some now."

"It's really not necessary," Leander demurred.

"The hell it isn't." I made a face at him. A little alcohol might be the cure for my pounding headache.

"Then give me your oxy," Leander said flatly.

"I left it at home."

Leander's hand dove into the inner pocket of my jacket, withdrawing the orange bottle with an irritated scowl.

Damn it.

Before he could actually scold me, Kai handed us each a glass and held his aloft. "Congratulations. Statistically you have a higher chance of staying married, so good job, fellas."

We clinked our glasses and took the obligatory sip — not a shot, like you would with shittier tequilas.

"Damn it. The sangrita." Kai snapped and rushed back to the kitchen.

Leander held his glass out to me. I happily took it and dumped it into mine, giving him the empty one back. It wasn't oxy, but it was a good enough sort of compromise.

Kai strolled back to the living room and set the sangrita on the table next to me. "Oh good! It's done." He almost sloshed his drink as he jumped over our feet and slid onto the couch, tapping a few things on the keyboard.

Leander's hand drifted down from his lap and found mine. Instead of giving me a concerned look, he had a death grip on my fingers.

I squeezed him back, hoping it conveyed my understanding and reassurance. Even though Kai looked like he leapt out of some anime book, with his shock of silver hair and chipped black nails, he really did know his shit. In all of my shady dealings, I'd never found a better hacker.

"You want me to email you this file?" Kai asked, clicking through a variety of screens as they popped up. "I mean, there's not much here since it's a burner, which you already knew. But I've got the list of incoming and outgoing calls. And some of these dodos used a real phone number, not a spoofing program." He laughed and then sighed dramatically, muttering to himself about how stupid people were.

"Can you trace them?" Leander asked.

Kai grinned at him over the laptop. "I can get you their favorite color if you give me enough time."

Leander's hand relaxed in mine.

"What are you going to do when you find them?" Kai asked, typing away. "Please tell me it's something naughty."

"What do you think?" I shot him a pointed look.

He ignored it and kept working. "What ever happened to that doctor? I haven't seen anything else pop up online from her, so she must have gotten the hint."

Leander swiveled in my lap, narrowing his eyes. "Doctor? What doctor?"

Unfortunately, Kai and I answered at the same time.

"It's nothing, my love," I replied with a brilliant smile.

"Just some crazy psychiatrist," Kai added helpfully.

I was going to strangle him with that fucking collar. Still, I did my best to mask my true feelings when I turned my face up toward Leander. "As I said, it's nothing. It was for another case."

Leander's mouth pressed into a hard line. "You're lying. What happened with Lorelei?"

"It's really nothing," Kai said on my behalf. "I just scrubbed a couple things from online. That's all."

Leander slid out of my lap, glaring between the two of us. "What things?"

Sighing, I got to my feet and reached for his hand. He jerked it away from me, purposely folding his arms across his chest.

"How can I put this?" I hoped it would buy me some time, but all it did was piss him off further.

"As quickly and truthfully as possible!"

"She published a case study on you. Anonymously. But..." I winced, trying to find the gentlest way to give him what he wanted while getting myself out of hot water. "You know what? It doesn't matter. I got her to retract it. And Kai did whatever it was to the journal's server to make sure it was well and truly gone."

"What sort of case study, Bennett?" Shit... there was my name again, in *that* tone.

My fingers tapped against my thigh while I tried to think of the best way to phrase it, but even a sonata wasn't helping come up with anything brilliant.

"Bennett!" When I still didn't answer, Leander unfolded his arms and pulled out his cell phone. I thought maybe he was going to call her, or send a text message, in a desperate attempt to get to the truth. But a moment later, his jaw almost hit the floor and he stared at me. "You shot her mother?!"

"Do you hear that?" Kai asked, popping up to his feet. "Is

that my phone ringing? I definitely think that's my phone." Without waiting for an answer, he practically flew out of the room, his cell phone laying in plain view on the side table.

Brows furrowed, I bit my lips, trying to think of the appropriate response to the new predicament I found myself in.

Leander didn't give me a chance. "Why in God's name would you shoot her mother? She's a judge, Bennett! The police aren't going to sweep this one to the side. They're going to keep investigating until they have a suspect!"

"It's fine. I promise. There's literally nothing that links me to her anymore."

"What do you mean *anymore*?" Fuck. I was just digging myself deeper and deeper.

"There's some things that came up, that I didn't share with you... because I didn't want you to worry! It's been dealt with it so there's no need to drag it up again."

"What kind of *things*?"

"Nothing important."

"You honestly expect me to believe that? How stupid do I look to you?"

An unexpected thread of anger wound its way through my insides. By the time it reached my head, it was poised to overtake any sort of rationality I may have started the conversation with. "Just so we're clear, are you mad about the fact I hurt your precious Lorelei, or the fact I didn't tell you?"

He stiffened, looking like I'd slapped him. "Hurt Lorelei? Did you shoot her as well?"

The air went out of my lungs, each syllable like a series of chains wrapping around me. Still, there was no way he was going to win this fight. Not this time. Fuck the high road. "*That* is your concern? Really?!"

Instead of replying, he continued to hold my glare.

"No, Leander, I didn't shoot her," I snarled, taking a step

closer to him. "I fucking *stabbed* her. But I'll be God damned, she lived! And then the bitch turned around and published an article that could ruin you. So yeah, I shot her mother as a little nudge to do what I told her. And before you go crying about poor Helena Clayton, you should know she filed a complaint about me to the ARDC. Neither of them are innocent, so don't act outraged that I did what was necessary to protect both of us."

"I'm 'outraged' that you continue to withhold things and yet expect *me* to go over every single thing *I'm* doing!" He'd started pacing in a tight circle while I defended myself, prowling about Kai's living room, and it didn't stop once I was finished. "I have told you time and time again not to lie to me. *Not* telling me things *is* lying, Bennett! Have I not been abundantly clear? All I've ever wanted from you is the truth!"

"Seriously? How understanding would you have been if I told you I tried — and subsequently failed — to gut your girlfriend?" He shot a scowl in my direction, so I held up my hands and rectified it for him. "Oh, that's right. You never 'labeled' it. My bad. Regardless of the fucking title, you wouldn't have been ok with my decision, even though I've only ever had your best interest at heart."

He raked a hand through his hair, throwing me another heated look while he continued to pace. The wheels in his brain were definitely turning, probably going over every single conversation and unexplained absence since we'd been back in Easton.

I plowed on anyway, each new point throwing another log on the fire. "How happy would you have been to learn she took every single thing you ever told her and put it out in the world for everyone to read? Your thoughts. Your fears. The misery that keeps you awake at night. She dissected every part of your brain, every part of your life, and turned you into a fucking monster."

"I *am* a monster," he snapped, jerking to a halt in front of me. "An aberration, wrought from decades of bloodshed and corruption, as you well know. You cannot stand there and tell me I'm not, no more than you can swear *you're* innocent."

"You know what your problem is? You believe Irene. You believe her minions. You've internalized all of their venom your entire life. *They're* the monsters, Leander, not you."

He scoffed. "So I'm to be the hero now? Is that what you're saying? I should rise from the ashes of my childhood trauma like a fucking phoenix? You sound more like Lorelei than you think."

"No, that's *not* what I'm saying," I shot back, disgusted he'd even lump me in with that woman. His eyes narrowed at the viciousness of my reply. "I didn't fall in love with a hero — I fell in love with a villain. So be a fucking villain! Stop debasing yourself because you only hear that miserable bitch's voice in your head. Every single word in that article is an insult, not only to you, but to *us* — our marriage, everything we've accomplished. A little fucking gratitude wouldn't hurt, you know."

"What would you have me do?" He unfolded his arms and spread them wide. "Kill Lorelei in front of you? Would that finally put this whole thing to rest?"

"Yes! God, yes! Please!" I clasped my hands together in prayer and fell to my knees in front of him. I'd go back to church every Sunday like a good little Catholic if he'd make that one wish come true.

"I told you — she has people who rely on her." Leander started to turn away from me, but I grabbed onto his belt and clung to it with both hands.

"I'll find Martha the best psychiatric facility there is. I swear! I'll petition the court and get her transferred as soon as I can file a motion in Camden County."

"Get up," he said, rolling his eyes skyward.

"Are you going to kill her?"

"Bennett..." My name came out as a sigh, weary and pained.

"Are you going to kill her?"

"I'm going to kill *you* if you don't get off your goddamn knees."

"Why?" Smirking, I pushed the end of his belt through the buckle's frame. Winning was winning. Frankly, I didn't care how I achieved it. "I thought you liked me on my knees?"

"Oh my God. Stop." He swatted my hands away before I could get the prong out of the hole. "You don't get to *tell* me off and then *get* me off in the middle of some stranger's apartment."

I grabbed onto his belt again, giving him my best puppy eyes. "Is there nothing I can say or do to get you to change your mind?"

"About a blowjob or killing Lorelei?"

It was my turn to roll my eyes. I let go of him roughly and got to my feet again. Before I could offer a verbal rebuttal, Kai was back.

"Is it safe to come out?" he asked, peering around a bookcase.

This time it was Leander and I who answered at the same time. He said "Yes," while I said "No."

"Ok, well, that's not the least bit confusing." Kai cleared his throat and took a dramatic step into the room. "Is there anything else I can do to help?"

"Do you have a copy of whatever it is you deleted from that journal?" Leander asked.

I sliced a glare at Kai, silently channeling all of my energy into telling him to shut the fuck up via telepathy.

He most definitely caught the look on my face because he immediately snapped his mouth closed, giving the worst vague shrug of his life.

Leander took a step closer to him, moving past me and not-so-subtly blocking me with his shoulder. "Don't look at him. Do you, or do you not, have a copy?"

I shook my head vehemently behind Leander, mouthing all sorts of silent threats and pantomiming the various ways I planned to kill him if he said yes.

Kai looked away quickly, turning his attention to his cell phone. I darted forward, fully intent on making good on my threats.

Leander grabbed a handful of my coat from behind and held me in place. "Don't even think about it." His cell phone chirped a second later, indicating Kai air dropped the file to him. He let go of my coat to reach into his pocket.

I made a grab for Leander's phone, but Leander was faster. He ducked under my outstretched arm and sprinted across the loft to the bathroom.

Swearing, I raced after him. The door slammed a millimeter away from my face.

"Leander!" I pounded on the door. "Listen to me! Do not open that fucking file! I know you *think* you want to read it, but you don't! It'll do more harm than good!"

Of course, there was no answer.

"Do you have any idea what you've done?" I snarled over my shoulder at Kai.

"You'd want to know," Kai said simply with a small shrug.

"Why the fuck did you keep a copy of it? The whole reason I paid you was to get rid of it! Forever!"

He rolled his eyes. "Everything gets backed up in, like, three places. It's not like a did it on purpose."

"Well, you didn't have to give it to him!"

"If any part of what that doctor said is true, I don't want to end up on the dude's hit list."

Ignoring him and the fact he fucking read it, I went back to slamming my fist against the door. "Leander, open the door before I kick this fucking thing in! You have five seconds!"

I made it to three when the door swung open.

Looking as regal as ever, chin lifted and shoulders squared, Leander met my gaze dead on. "Patience is a virtue. Now, if you've done everything you need to do, I have a dinner at seven."

"A dinner? With whom?" Before he went into that bathroom, we had zero plans. How the hell did he come out with a new schedule for the evening?

"No one you need to concern yourself with." He gave me a tight-lipped smile and slid past me, making a point not to touch me, even in passing.

I stayed where I was, one hand clutching the doorframe to the bathroom, listening to his footsteps cut through the loft. The door opened and closed again, as quietly as ever. No slamming. No shouting. Not even a polite goodbye to Kai, which was probably the most un-Leander like thing of all.

What the fuck just happened?

"I'm so sorry. I—"

Raising a hand sharply to cut off his sympathies, I turned on my heel slowly. "Email me everything you find from that burner phone, no matter how small. Got it?"

"Got it."

Stalking out of the loft, I jogged down the three flights of stairs, using the time to try and figure out what was going on in Leander's brain.

When I popped out onto the sidewalk, I expected to see Leander standing there, or already in a waiting car. He wasn't. In fact, he was nowhere to be found in either direction.

Muttering under my breath, I pulled out my phone and called him, glancing up and down the street in hopes of hearing it ring.

It rang twice before he sent me to voicemail. The prick.

I called again, and again it went to voicemail. Not after one ring, indicating the phone was off. After *two* rings, the giant, electronic "Fuck You."

Growling to myself, I scheduled an Uber and waited, impatiently, for Omar to swing by in his white sedan. On the way to my new destination, I canceled the masseuse and then called Del.

"You busy?"

"Uh, no. I don't think so. Why? Are you in town?"

"Yeah. Meet me at Delirium."

He laughed. "Seriously? What time?"

"Now," I said icily.

Papers shuffled in the background and I heard a computer logging off. "Hasta luego."

Hanging up, I tipped my head back against the seat and closed my eyes.

Leander was right about one thing. This city *had* turned into a cesspool. Every time we were here, we fought like cats and dogs. Not that Easton shielded us from all of our problems, but it was never anything like this. So hopefully after he was done with his mysterious "dinner" and I polished off a bottle of alcohol with Del, we could go home to Easton and forget this whole fucking trip happened.

26

LEANDER

Fury emanated from every cell in my body. Instead of carbon dioxide, I exhaled a cloud of rage and betrayal, so much so that I actually lied to my husband. Not that he believed me for one second. I didn't have dinner plans. The idea was laughable. With how tightly my insides were clenched, I knew I wouldn't eat for a week. Even the thought of food made me nauseated.

I did, however, have a meeting. A very important, last-minute meeting that needed to be conducted without him hovering nearby.

Speeding down the tollway in a rental, I checked the time, comparing it to the schedule that had been imprinted on my brain for however brief a period. Given the hour and the day of the week, I knew exactly where I was going — St. Mary's Hospital in Stratford.

It was late, but not late enough that they'd locked the main doors of the hospital yet. I was able to slip in and up the stairs, glancing around the deserted lobby just to make sure I didn't miss my target moving about on some errand.

Like a bloodhound on the trail, the smell of muguet and bergamot led me straight to her.

I spied a curtain of blonde hair through the sidelight of her office door before throwing it open and slamming it shut again.

"Leander!" Lorelei jumped to her feet, blue eyes wide.

We stared at each other across the space, eternity ticking by in each passing second. I could practically see her muscles tense a second before she lunged for her desk phone.

I launched myself at her and grabbed a handful of hair before she made it. She knocked the handset off the phone as I yanked her away from her desk, dragging her the three steps to the wall.

Wrapping my fingers around her throat, I slammed her back into the wall as hard as I could. I squeezed, hard, keeping her pinned against it. I'm sure she remembered the first time I grabbed her like this. And the second. If she thought it would end the same way, she was sorely mistaken. This time I wasn't here to manipulate *or* seduce her. I was here for fucking answers and I had no qualms in killing her if she refused to give them.

"You're hurting me!" she squeaked, clawing at the hand on her throat.

"Give me one good reason why I shouldn't snap your fucking neck!"

"Leander, please!"

"Tell me why, Lorelei!" Hundreds of tiny needles pricked my eyes, burning with anger and the tears that started to well. "Tell me how you could, in good conscience, write something like that! You *know* what would happen if people found out! I'd be ruined! I'd lose everything! Is that what you want? You want me to lose everything I've fucking worked for? Everything I've bled for? Nearly fucking died for?"

Her own tears slipped down cheeks. "No, of course not!"

"Then why?!"

"You need help."

My grip tightened so hard her face started turning red. "So that gives you the right to betray me like that? To use me to further your career? I didn't tell you those things as my fucking therapist, so you could turn around and expose me to the world!"

"No? Then who did you tell them to? Your puppet? Just some chick you banged while your *husband* wasn't around?" Her lips twisted into a bitter smile. "Yeah. That's what I thought. You think *I* betrayed *you*? I love you, you asshole! I was willing to give up everything for you! But you didn't care. Not one bit. It was just a fucking game to you!"

Swallowing thickly, I loosened my hold on her and staggered backward, more stunned by her words than her anger.

I love you.

Not "loved," *love*.

Present.

Current.

Fuck.

"I did care, Lorelei," I said quietly, turning away from her and covering my mouth with my hand. At the moment, I didn't trust myself not to throw up all over her office.

"I don't believe that. I *can't* believe that, as much as I want to. You are sick, Leander. Do you hear me?" She closed the distance I managed to gain and took my face between her hands, forcing me to look at her. "Forget the article and listen to me. I am truly worried about you, about your quality of life."

"No, you're not." I covered her hands with mine and dragged them downward, off my face. "You're worried about your own failure. If I commit suicide, you'll have failed. Again. And you don't want that on your conscience."

She shook her head, blinking back tears. "I don't want

you to die, Leander. By suicide or any other means. Look at you. I can tell you're under stress. You need—"

"Don't." I pivoted away from her, putting more distance between us while also backing toward the door. This was a mistake. Coming here solved absolutely nothing.

"Don't what? Care?"

"Yes!"

She advanced again, reaching for me. "I'll never stop caring about you. Even after everything that happened. I *can't*. I can't turn that part of myself off."

I retreated further. "I'm not yours to care about, Lorelei."

She scoffed and looked away. "*He's* part of the reason I'm so worried about you. Your precious husband. He tried to kill me, Leander! Did he tell you? And when that failed, he murdered my mother! What's going to stop him from killing you? Or Elijah? Or anyone else in your life? He's dangerous, Leander. I know what you've done, but it was never with malice. You have a good heart, in spite of everything you went through. Can you honestly say the same about him?"

Shaking my head, I closed my eyes and did my best to tune her out. As furious as I was with Bennett for lying, I knew in my soul he would never hurt me. *Ever*. Just as I could never hurt him. The thought alone was unfathomable.

Her perfume rushed over me a second before her hands landed on either side of my face again. "Leander, look at me."

I did, grudgingly, and only because it was the quickest way to get this conversation over with.

"I can help you," she whispered, her blue eyes shining with dampness. "Please, let me help you. Just stay here for a little bit. We can try some new medication and see—"

Anger exploded inside of me. The mere mention of medication reaffirmed what I already knew — that Bennett wasn't the right "choice." There'd never been a choice at all.

Lorelei would never see me for who I was. I'd always be this broken thing she had to save, to pity.

I shoved her away from me as hard as I could. "I told you, I'm not your fucking lab rat!"

She stumbled back on her heels, crashing into her desk before she stabilized herself. "Oh, that's right. Medicine is for the weak!" she spat back, glaring at me. "I remember. Well, too fucking bad because you need it! A *lot* of it! For the rest of your life. Or your darkness is going to consume you and that scares the hell out of me."

"It already has." My gaze fell to the floor, away from the hope in her eyes. With nothing left to say, I turned and strode to the door, my fists clenched at my sides.

"It's not too late."

I didn't answer her, even when her signature heels clicked across the floor behind me.

"Leander, it's not too late! Please!"

Closing the door on her entreaties, I moved down the hallway at an unhurried pace. The sound of her sobbing bounced off the pristine white walls, echoing in the recesses of my mind.

27

BENNETT

"Where is he?" Olivia yelled, slamming through the back door of the teal Victorian with zero regard for whatever was happening on the inside of our temporary abode.

Leander and I looked up from our dinner plates, equally confused. We exchanged a glance, brows raised or furrowed accordingly. In the span of three seconds, we had an entire conversation and came to the same conclusion: we had absolutely no idea what Olivia was talking about.

"Who?" Leander asked, setting his utensils down on the edge of his plate.

"Cole! He's been ignoring me for the past three days." She put her hands on her hips, staring both of us down.

I raised my hands and leaned back in my chair. "We just got back from Chicago yesterday. Remember?" And not that I would ever admit in front of my less-than-sympathetic husband, but I was still feeling the effects of my hangover from Delirium.

"That doesn't mean you didn't send him off somewhere!" Olivia snapped.

Between all of our feuding over Lorelei's stupid case study and following up on the information Kai sent from the burner phone, I don't know when Olivia thought we'd have time to hang out with Cole for a clandestine boys' night *or* task him with some nefarious activity.

In fact, this dinner was the first time we'd had a civil conversation since Leander up and disappeared on me at Kai's apartment.

He never told me where he went, which I assumed was an attempt to give me a taste of my own medicine. I had a sneaking suspicion he met with Lorelei. Or hell, maybe it was Martha. It's not like he had that many connections that far north. But whoever it was, he didn't throw it in my face. Nor did he scold me for coming home blitzed. Maybe it was because Del was with me, or he realized it was a pointless argument, just like I realized it was pointless to grill him on where he went.

"I haven't talked to Cole all week," I said, glancing at Leander for backup. "Last I heard, he was driving down to Mississippi to pick up some pocket doors or some shit."

Leander nodded. "It's true. For the renovation at the mansion."

"Why do you think he's ignoring you?" I asked.

"He left the read receipt on his text messages. And he stood me up for movie night," Olivia growled, her eyes narrowed.

"Maybe he didn't like the movie you picked?" I offered. A second later, Leander kicked me under the table. Wincing, I rubbed my shin with the opposite foot.

"Call him." She crossed her arms over her chest, jutting her chin toward Leander. "Let's see if he answers for you."

Leander slipped his cell phone out of his pocket with a resigned sigh. Putting the call on speaker, he kept his attention on Olivia. It rang four times before it went to Cole's voicemail. He hung up without leaving a message and spread his hands.

She turned to me, brows raised expectantly.

"Are you serious?" I blinked at her.

"Yes. He fucking ghosted me, Bennett. I want to know where he is and what sorry ass excuse he's going to try to give me."

Rolling my eyes, I, too, called Cole's phone. After four rings, I, too, went to voicemail. However, I opted to leave a message in an English accent as my way of letting Olivia know how ridiculous I thought she was being. "Cole, darling. Do give us a ring when you get this. The missus is quite beside herself. Frankly, I fear for the safety of my testes if you do not establish some line of communication in the near future. Hoping you're merely out of cell range. Cheerio."

"You're a dick," she sneered as I hung up.

"What more do you want from me? He's apparently ghosted all of us. Feel better?"

Leander pushed his chair out and stood, dropping his napkin in his empty seat. "Let's see if he's home."

"Seriously?" I made a face at him and gestured to my half-eaten chicken scampi.

"I already went by there. He's not there," Olivia said with a huff.

"Then we'll wait, seeing as it means that much to you." Leander arched a brow and swiped his keys off the hook by the back door.

Groaning, I stood and followed them out of the house.

We drove to Cole's together in absolute silence. Olivia oscillated between looking pissed and looking ill. She twirled a lock of hair around her finger the entire time, staring out the window.

I stretched my arm out and draped it across Leander's shoulder as he drove. Running my fingers through the bottom of his curls, I tapped the back of his neck three times. I didn't need to ask the question out loud — he was already thinking it, judging from the way his brows slanted.

His gaze slid over to me before shifting to the backseat. "I'm sure there's a perfectly reasonable explanation."

Olivia snorted but withheld a comment as the car rolled up in front of Cole's house.

It was dark and quiet. There was a pile of newspapers in the middle of his driveway. Considering Cole devoured the sports section on the daily, I doubted he would let them keep sitting there.

Climbing out of the car, I wandered over to the detached garage, looking up at the row of small windows in the top of the door. "See if his car is there," I said to Olivia, lacing my fingers together and stooping down. Nodding, she stepped into my hand and I boosted her upwards.

"I can't believe it!" she growled. "He *is* here!"

Unlacing my fingers, I caught her around the waist as she fell. I set her on the ground gently, squeezing her ass in the process. She shouldered past me to follow Leander and when she turned to flip me off, I blew her a kiss, swaggering after them.

By the time I got to the back door, they were already inside, courtesy of a spare key Leander must have known about.

An old, yellow lab ambled toward us, wagging its tail slowly.

"Since when does Cole have a dog?" I asked, patting its head as I passed.

"Since Leander murdered his owner," Olivia replied flatly, marching into the living room.

"Did you murder Annabel's owner too?" I asked Leander with a smirk.

Not even deigning to answer, he tossed a glare my way before trailing after Olivia.

Seeing the dog's stainless steel bowls were empty, I took a moment out of the manhunt to fill them with food and water. Scratching behind his ear one last time, I met up with the others in the living room.

Everything looked to be in order, but it still felt off. Cole's house had always been tidy, but lived in. This was *too* neat. Too clean. The distinct scent of bleach lingered in the air, turning my stomach.

"Guys! Come here!" Olivia yelled.

We followed the sound of her voice down the hallway, locating her in Cole's room.

Unlike the living room, the bedroom was a fucking wreck. The mattress was askew, the sheets half-ripped off. The bedside lamp was broken, dried blood smeared across the wooden floorboards.

"Do you know if he has cameras?" I asked.

Olivia shrugged. "Probably. After what happened to you, we were all a little paranoid. If he does, they'd be hooked up to his laptop."

I slipped past her and headed back to the living room in search of it. It wasn't anywhere that I could find. Not on the couch, under the couch, or near the TV.

I finally found it in the kitchen, underneath a stack of mail and a bunch of blackened bananas.

Flipping it open, I grumbled when I saw it was password protected. No matter. I had my own personal geek at the ready. Pulling out my cell phone, I dialed Kai.

"Can you hack a laptop remotely?" I asked without introduction.

"Oh my God. Did you really just ask me that? What do you take me for?" he sputtered.

"Not in the mood, Kai."

"Ooo, meow." He actually hissed at me, accompanying the sound of speed-typing in the background. "I'm assuming you're right in front of it?"

"Yes."

"Don't move. I'm using your cell location to hop on the network."

After another minute of clicking and typing, the laptop came alive and the lock screen faded.

"Don't let it time out, or I'll have to do the whole thing again."

"Thank you."

"Always happy to help."

I carried the laptop to the kitchen table and sifted through the collection of icons until I found one for Cole's security system. Clicking it, I went through the recording history, starting a week ago, on the day Cole was supposed to leave for Mississippi.

He did leave, as we'd said. And he returned in a matter of days, as we predicted. However, Day Four is when it went to shit.

There were three of them; dark, male figures I couldn't really make out no matter how big I blew up the screen or tried to zoom in. In a matter of moments, they picked the lock on the front door and let themselves in after midnight when Cole and his ferocious guard dog were probably sound asleep.

With no interior cameras, I could only imagine the struggle that took place. Based on the wreckage in the bedroom, it wasn't an easy snatch-and-grab. It required all three of them to carry out Cole's unconscious body. They disappeared from view around the corner of the house. A minute later, a dark SUV rolled down the street.

An SUV with damage to the front passenger side and a very familiar streak of white paint transfer.

It was the same people who shot me when I escaped my dopey kidnappers. Except *these* were professionals and they had a significant head start.

I exited the security system and scrolled over to Cole's cell phone app. Clicking on the very convenient "Find my phone" feature, I drummed out a nocturne on the table while the circle spun.

The map popped up on the screen and a blue pin dropped south of Chicago.

"Fuck me," I exhaled.

"Where is that?" Leander asked, leaning over my shoulder.

Jumping, I shot him a glare. I hadn't even heard him walk up behind me. Jesus. Either I was slipping or his ninja skills were improving.

He braced one hand on the back of my chair and the other on the table, fixing me with a concerned look. "Where is that, Bennett?"

"Nowhere Cole should ever be."

28

BENNETT

Olivia, still clinging to hope, insisted time was of the essence, so we took the plane to Chicago. As we approached the industrial building, I felt nothing but dread. While it wasn't a location I had cause to visit with any frequency, I still knew it. It was part of the logistics network Marchese used. The two times I'd been here, I witnessed two executions.

Security was nonexistent. They didn't need any. Everyone in the area knew not to interfere with the comings and goings of Romano Inc.

Since there were no lights on inside, we made our way with our cell phones until I found a light switch. Flicking it on turned on a row of fluorescents along one side of the warehouse.

Cargo containers and semi tractors filled the interior, but there wasn't much else. Thankfully, there weren't any people, either. This time of night, I figured there wouldn't be.

"Do you hear that?" Olivia asked, grabbing my sleeve.

I did. It was a faint humming that sent a fresh wave of chills down my spine.

The sound was coming from a huge, walk-in cooler.

Olivia reached for the silver handle on the cooler.

I grabbed her wrist and pulled her away, shaking my head. "Stay with Leander."

"But, I—"

"Stay!" I snapped, pushing her into Leander's arms. To make sure she listened, I held up a finger like a scolding parent and waited until Leander had her securely in his grip before turning my back to her. Facing the door, I drew in a breath and opened it, slipping inside and pulling it shut before she tried to glimpse past me.

It was mostly empty. There were a couple cardboard boxes stacked in one corner, covered in import stamps, and a large, plastic tarp tossed in a heap at the far end of the metal container. Steeling myself, I walked toward it with slow, measured steps, hoping against hope I was wrong. There was no arguing with smell, though. Even if it was thirty-five degrees in here, something was rotten.

Kneeling next to the tarp, I tried to ignore the shaking in my hands as I pulled the plastic back.

It *was* a corpse — but it wasn't Cole.

Exhaling, I closed my eyes and rocked back on my heels. It was just some schmuck with a receding hairline and too much chest hair, not even close to the person we were looking for.

But if Cole wasn't here, where the hell was he?

Olivia's scream shattered my relief.

Springing to my feet, I flew out of the cooler. Neither Leander nor Olivia were where I left them.

"Leander?!" I darted through the containers, like a rat in a maze. "Where are you?!"

"We're by the loading docks."

Once I got my bearings, I rushed to the back of the building, pulling up short as I burst into the open space near the shipping and receiving office.

Cole was seated in a chair, completely motionless. His head hung backward, jaw slack and eyes half-closed. Even at a distance I could see the giant blotches of antemortem bruising beneath his ripped t-shirt. Livor mortis set in on his hands, which were tied behind the chair. Given how he was positioned, I knew more than a few bones were broken. Italians were old-school like that. Their torture techniques were basic, but effective. They'd shot out both of his knees before they ultimately shot him in the head.

Olivia was on her knees beside him, draped across his lap. She sobbed hysterically into his thigh, grasping and clutching at his waist and hips, regardless of all the blood.

Leander was as still as a statue, his gaze locked on Cole.

I laid a hand on Leander's shoulder. He didn't even flinch let alone break his stare. There was a tremor every now and again when he inhaled or exhaled a ragged breath, but that was it.

Giving his shoulder a gentle squeeze, I carried on to Olivia. Kneeling behind her, I slipped my arms around her waist and tried to pull her away. "You shouldn't see him like this."

"No!" Her protest was more of a shriek, her fingers digging into Cole's bloody shirt so hard she ripped it more.

"We have to go," I said to her, tightening my grip.

"No! I'm not leaving him!"

Leander's voice came next, quiet and barely controlled. At first I didn't even realize it was him speaking, he sounded so foreign. "Yes, I need to report a murder."

My head snapped up. His phone was pressed to his ear, his eyes closed and his cheeks slick with silent tears.

"Yes," he hissed into the phone. "I'm sure of it. He's dead."

Olivia wailed again and readjusted her grip on Cole's hips.

I let her go and sat back, staring at Leander, unable to even comprehend the man in front of me.

Never call the cops. It was Rule Number One in the criminal code. And there he was, chatting away with dispatch, telling them what he knew.

Leander disconnected and exhaled audibly before opening his eyes and turning toward me. "The police are on their way."

"Perfect." I closed my eyes and rubbed my temples in small circles. "Just perfect."

Leander's voice was still sharp and alien. "We can't cover this up, Bennett."

Dropping my hands, I stared up at him. "With the police after them now, the murderers are going to go to ground. They're professionals, which means we've just lost our fucking chance. They could take months or years to resurface," I said, rising to my feet, holding his glare with one of my own.

Leander's face twisted darkly, unfazed by the silent challenge presented by me standing. "They've been monitoring his phone this entire time. They know we're looking for him, but there is no way they could know we found him this quickly." He stalked over to Cole's body and nudged his foot carefully with the tip of his shoe. It moved, but barely. "They're only a few hours ahead of us."

"You don't think the police are going to have questions when they get here? Our friend was just kidnapped, driven four hours north, tortured for days, and fucking murdered in a warehouse with mob connections. And then we miraculously find him six hours after he's been killed? You don't think that's going to set off some alarm bells?"

"Control the narrative," he spat back. "*You* taught me that.

We can spin this however we want and use the police to our advantage."

Shaking my head, I shoved my hand into my pocket and pulled out my cell phone.

"Who are you calling?" Leander asked. More like demanded.

"We're going to need a fucking lawyer. A *criminal* lawyer."

Olivia's muffled cries continued behind me as I gave Del the briefest rundown ever in the history of a client consult. Leander turned his attention to Olivia, but he had no more luck prying her away from Cole than I did. Once he gave up, he knelt next to her, rubbing her back gently.

"Neither of you say a goddamn word to anyone unless Del or I are with you. I don't care if they have a badge, are a medic, or a fucking chaplain. Not a *single* word." I rubbed my face with both hands, trying to shake off my shock and get into lawyer mode. "For the record, I object to every part of this."

"Noted, counselor," Leander retorted.

While we waited for the police to arrive, I opened one of the shipping doors and made myself comfortable on edge of the concrete dock. At least I finally had an answer as to who kidnapped me — someone with a connection to Marchese. Even though he was good and dead, he was still a pain in my ass. Typical Giovanni.

But Sergei and his men killed all of the major players in the Marchese outfit. Anyone who was still alive was low-level and didn't have the power *or* the money to pull off something like this. It could have been his cousin from New York, but in all the years I'd hung around Giovanni I never got a strong sense of family loyalty. I heard "Fuck those pricks" more than I heard any praise directed toward the east coast branch of the family biz.

So who the hell was settling the score for Giovanni?

No doubt whoever it was originally intended to use *Leander* as leverage against *me,* which was the exact fear I had the first time my interests ran counter to what the mafia wanted. When I escaped, they didn't hesitate to try and kill me, which meant my death was authorized by whoever was footing the bill — as long as it was *them* that got the pleasure of killing me and not the rednecks they hired. It was only a matter of time before they tried again. Cole was proof of that.

But Cole? He hadn't done anything. Other than be a friend and employee of my husband's company, he didn't have any mob connections. If they were going to snatch the next closest person to me, it would have been Gavin. Or Del.

Cole was such a random choice, I couldn't make sense of it. He was the strongest of the group, therefore the biggest physical threat? No... Even that explanation didn't jive, considering how many bodies Leander and I dropped between us. Muscles weren't everything when it came to murder. And it's not like Elijah or Jake were wimps, either.

So, yeah. I got one answer out of this whole mess, and a fuck ton more questions.

29

LEANDER

Cole was dead.

No matter how many times I repeated it in my head, it never quite sank in. The mantra, combined with Olivia's heartbroken sobs, circled in my head on a never-ending loop.

I was numb to it now — the crying. It didn't draw out my own tears or make my throat close like it used to. I watched Olivia cry and all I could think about was how this entire thing was my fault.

Perhaps if I hadn't killed Jesse Galigher, his mystery employers would have never retaliated and taken Cole.

Perhaps I went too far.

Perhaps I didn't go far enough.

Running my thumb along the handle of Bennett's straight razor, I felt something at last. A little rush. The tingle of something forbidden and unnatural. An answer. A solution.

Pocketing the razor, I left the bathroom and made my way to the garden patio. The sun was setting, casting pink and orange light over the purple sky. It wasn't the same view I'd known my whole life, living atop the bluff in my very own, multi-million dollar prison, but the view from the Victorian cottage was beautiful all the same.

Annabel raced me to the table and chairs, leaping into her preferred seat and meowing loudly at me.

I stroked her head lightly as I dropped into the other chair, the weight of all my guilt wrapped around me like heavy chains. Glancing back at the house, I imagined Bennett inside, trying to console Olivia for the hundredth time.

Even if he tried to hide it, it went without saying my husband didn't like Annabel. They fought over me in a way no one ever had before. Bennett chased her out of my lap when he wanted attention and she wedged herself between us on the couch or in bed, glaring at him and twitching her tail. It would have been comical any other time in my life, but now it left me saddened.

Thankfully Olivia didn't share Bennett's feelings toward Annabel. Olivia would take care of her, especially since Elijah took custody of the old yellow lab Cole insisted on adopting once its owner was bludgeoned, dismembered, and scattered to the four winds. I wouldn't have to ask her to step up to the responsibility — she just would.

Slipping the razor out of my pocket, I unfolded it slowly, drawing out the rush of adrenaline. My fingers trembled as I held it lengthwise, studying the grooves in the wooden handle. The blade caught the dying light, flashing orange while it could, before it was coated in crimson.

The decision before me was simple. So simple I couldn't even recall when I arrived at the conclusion. At any rate, my mind was set.

Bennett was taken because of me.

Bennett was hurt because of me.

Cole was taken because of me.

Cole was dead because of me.

And Cole would be the last to die because of me.

If I sent a message once before through Jesse Galigher's murder, then my self-murder would send an even bigger message.

I closed my eyes and laid the razor against my wrist, surprised and comforted by the cold steel all at once. At the very least, it was a familiar feeling. After not feeling anything for so long — not hunger, or exhaustion, or grief — I latched on to the feeling, the last shred of my humanity.

"What the fuck are you doing?!"

My eyes flew open. I nearly jumped out of my skin at the sound of Elijah's voice.

Before I could register that it was really him, he was across the yard and in my face, hauling me out of the chair by the front of my shirt.

"Are you fucking kidding me right now?!" He wrenched the straight razor out of my hand and flung it into the darkness.

"Elijah, I—"

He shoved me in the chest, his face contorted with rage. "We just lost Cole and you think *this* is the fucking answer?!" Instead of keeping his distance, he reeled me in again, his hands twisted in my shirt, and came nose-to-nose with me. "You think I want to bury you too? Did you stop to think at all, you selfish son of a bitch?"

A surge of anger replaced any guilt I had in a flash. I pushed him away from me before he could try to reclaim his hold. "Don't start with me, Elijah! You don't know what you're talking about!"

"The fuck I don't! How many times have I bandaged you up? How many times did I have to nurse you back to health, whether that sick bitch poisoned you or you just fucking refused to eat? And now when *I* need *you*, you're trying to fucking leave me too?!"

"If I'm gone, these people have no reason to come after

any of you, *ever* again." I threw my hands out wide. "Selfish son of a bitch that I am, I'm trying to keep the only fucking family I have safe from the danger *I* put you all in!"

"Yeah? Did you leave us letters, like last time? Or do I have to go in there and tell your *husband* that he wasn't worth sticking around for? Hmm? You want me to break Olivia's heart all over again and tell her you're bleeding to death on the fucking patio, but it's ok because you did it for her?"

Even if I'd wanted to reply, Elijah kept going. "You know how you keep us all safe? Find these assholes and fucking destroy them. Between you and Bennett, you can find a way to get to anyone. So do it! Not this self-sacrificing bullshit!"

The back door creaked opened and Bennett stepped out halfway, his brow furrowed. "You guys ok?"

Turning away from him, I folded my arms across my chest, unable to even look at Bennett after everything Elijah said. Bile rose in the back of my throat, but I forced myself to swallow the burning shame.

Elijah, on the other hand, snorted. "Yeah. Just great."

"K... well, I made dinner, if you're hungry."

"I don't have much of an appetite," Elijah replied. He crossed the yard toward me. As soon as he was close enough, he squeezed the back of my neck and pulled me against him, none-too-gently. "You're no good to us dead."

Nodding, I blinked back the tears before he saw them, keeping my gaze downcast.

Elijah gave my neck a final squeeze and walked away. He murmured something to Bennett and disappeared inside, presumably to find Olivia.

"My love?" Bennett was still in the doorway, but from the confusion in his tone I knew Elijah didn't tell him what he interrupted. If he had, Bennett would have been in the yard screaming at me, too, in a plethora of languages. "Dinner?"

"I'm not hungry." Still without looking at him, I scooped

up Annabel from the chair and cradled her against my chest. I held her close, absorbing the vibrations from her purring, and made my way toward the house.

Bennett stepped outside all the way and held the door open for me. The heat of his gaze followed me inside, only dissipating when I climbed the stairs, Annabel's tail swishing behind me.

30

BENNETT

The days following Cole's murder were grim, to say the least.

Elijah threw himself into trying to determine the identities of Cole's kidnappers, using whatever extralegal resources he had. I gave him Kai's number and a blank check to buy whatever he needed, whether it was information, technology, or a murder-for-hire.

Jake stepped up and took care of the actual business while Leander and I were preoccupied making all of the funeral arrangements.

Fearing for her safety as well as her mental well-being, we brought Olivia back to the teal house. Even if I was the one they were ultimately after, she was still safer with Leander and I together than staying on her own.

She didn't eat for days. Neither did Leander. The two of them survived on liquids, refusing even the most basic meals I tried to coax them into eating.

Leander hardly spoke, unless it was about funeral arrangements. Olivia didn't speak at all. She could generally be found crying at all hours of the day and night, though the location varied.

The first time she crawled into bed with us, I thought it was a dream. It was me, of all people, she came to first. Lifting the covers, she slipped beneath them and squirmed back against me, draping my arm over her shoulder. The similarity to my own situation a few months back wasn't lost on me, except my heart had only been broken — not ripped out of my chest and smashed into a thousand pieces.

In the morning, Leander gave her a quizzical look, but he didn't say anything. I certainly didn't — I had zero room to talk. When I hit the lowest of low without Leander, it was Olivia I'd gone to. It was only fair I return the favor.

The next night she fell asleep between us, once again using my arm like a blanket. She clung to Leander's hand all night, even when he tried to roll over. It seemed the only time she slept was if one of us was with her, whether it was in bed or on the couch, and even then it was a toss up if it was going to be restful or not.

"I'm worried about her," Leander said one night after she'd fallen asleep on his lap in the living room. He stroked her hair gently, his mouth downturned. "The only time I've seen her like this was when her mother died."

"I'm worried about *both* of you," I said softly.

He sighed and reached for my hand. "I'm sorry. For all my melancholy, I don't handle death very well."

"Gee, I can't imagine why." I ran my thumb back and forth over his knuckles.

"What I don't understand is..." He tipped his chin toward Olivia.

"Were they...?"

Shrugging, he looked as clueless as I felt. "I thought you'd know."

I held a finger up and ducked into the kitchen, retrieving

Cole's cell phone from where I'd stashed it. After the police dumped the data, they gave it back. The rest of his personal belongings, however limited, were still in evidence.

Scrolling past the scores of angry texts from Olivia in the days leading to Cole's death, I whistled low.

Leander perked up. "What is it?"

I handed the phone over to him so he could see for himself.

His eyebrows lifted higher and higher the more he scrolled. "Well then..."

Apparently the two had been committed to one another for quite a while and we were either too dumb or distracted to see it. It was hard to say.

One thing was clear — Cole was head-over-heels for Olivia. He told her as much in one of his last messages. He wanted her to move in with him, to make it official, to tell the rest of us. She said "No," with no explanation. True to his nature, Cole told her he'd wait as long as necessary for her to be comfortable... and then cracked a joke about jerking off to her picture, like he used to do when he first met her. Predictably, she flipped him off with an emoji.

Then he stopped answering.

"Why didn't they say anything?" I asked, shaking my head.

Leander shrugged again, handing the phone back. "Olivia is intensely private. She was probably worried about what the rest of us would say."

"I would have told them congratulations," I said sadly, watching Olivia's brow furrow in her sleep.

"As would I."

One night after dinner, Olivia disappeared abruptly. Leander and I exchanged a look before I inclined my head and stood. It was my turn to try and comfort her. *Try* being the keyword, since she wouldn't talk about anything. But at least she was finally eating.

I found her in our bed again, curled up in the middle, hugging a pillow.

"Hey," I said softly, crossing to my side of the bed and laying down next to her. "You ok?"

She shook her head mutely.

Suppressing a sigh, I ran my fingers through her hair, pulling it away from her neck and smoothing it across the pillow.

She tossed the pillow she was holding to the side and rolled over, hooking her leg around mine and using it to drag herself closer.

I wiped a tear from her face with my thumb. "Hey, beautiful."

Her dark lashes fluttered, blinking away more tears. She swallowed visibly and opened her mouth, but only a squeak came out.

"I miss Cole too," I said quietly, wrapping my arm around her.

No one had said his name since the night we found him, at least not to each other. The only ones who spoke about him were the people involved in business transactions — the funeral, the bank, the DMV, etc. Another account to close. Another name to strike off a list. And no one, I mean *no one*, had mentioned the connection between him and Olivia.

Simply saying his name unleashed the floodgates. The sobbing renewed in earnest, soaking through the front of my shirt as she buried her face against my chest.

"Everything ok?" Leander asked from the doorway.

I didn't know what the hell to say since the last thing that came out was clearly the wrong thing, so I laid there with my mouth hanging open like a guppy.

Pushing off of the doorframe, he crossed the room in a few strides, edging onto the bed and rubbing small circles on her back. When her crying tapered off to sniffles, he finally spoke up. "We want to help you, Olivia. But we don't know how."

I followed his lead, nodding along as he spoke. "Tell us what you need, Kitten."

She sat up, wiping her eyes with the edge of her sleeve. "I'm so tired of feeling this." Her hands gnarled around some invisible ball of grief. "I don't want to feel anymore. I don't want to feel anything."

Leander leaned forward, brushing a lock of dark hair behind her ear. "Turning it off doesn't make it go away."

"I don't care. I just want it to stop." She collapsed against him, sobbing onto his shoulder.

He wrapped his arms around her and pulled her into his lap, stroking her hair.

"Why is this happening?" she choked out, her fingers digging into Leander's shirt. "Why did they kill him? Why *him?*"

His gaze swept past her head, landing on me. The guilt was clear as day in his eyes. He may as well have had a neon sign pointing at him.

"You?" I asked in French, blinking at him. *"Why do you think it's because of you?"*

He shook his head, turning his attention back to Olivia and whispering softly to her. A poem, from the fragments I could hear.

As soon as she was asleep, curled up between the two of us, I reached over and flicked Leander's hand.

He picked his head up, arching a silent eyebrow at me.

"What the fuck?" I stared at him expectantly.

"Shh!" He glanced pointedly at Olivia. I didn't know if he

was shushing me because of the volume of my voice, or the fact it was in English.

"Why do you think you're to blame?" My French was never as good as my Italian, but it was passable. And hopefully he'd be a little more forthcoming if he knew Olivia wouldn't understand us.

It took him a while to reply. I was beginning to think I'd lost my grip on the language entirely and bumbled the question when he finally spoke.

"You know my relationship with Marchese was never the best. The FBI used the contract with my company and the shipping manifests as evidence for their case."

I wasn't buying it. It was a flimsy argument at best. A lie, at worse. *"But why take Cole?"*

"They knew they couldn't take you a second time."

"Then they would have taken Elijah. Or Olivia. Someone closer to you than Cole."

He shrugged, not even believing his own explanation, it seemed.

"The original kidnappers wanted _you_*,"* I continued. *"That leads me to believe I was a happy accident, that their original plan was to use you to get to me."*

It was his turn to look unconvinced. *"After all is said and done, it doesn't really matter does it? Cole is still dead."*

I wasn't going to argue with him, mainly because he wasn't wrong. Cole was dead, for reasons unknown. But one thing was for certain — we weren't going to stop looking until we had an answer for Olivia.

31

BENNETT

The day of the funeral was cold and windy, a sign summer was over and fall was here to stay.

Leander chose to bury Cole in Holyrood Cemetery, in one of the vacant plots his father earmarked for all the children he and Eleanor never had. It was fitting, since Cole and the rest of Leander's friends were the family he'd been denied for so long.

Having been purchased by a Welles, it was a pretty spot in the older, picturesque part of the cemetery with a beautiful view of the river. Cole would have liked it.

The funeral was a private affair. A dozen or so other people, mostly from work, came to pay their respects. Cole's mother was dead. He had a half-brother, somewhere, that he hadn't talked to in years. There was no other family except for us.

That was precisely the reason I first took note of the burly man standing off to the side, watching us from a distance.

Since Olivia was standing between Leander and I in our attempt to shield her from the wind, I couldn't speak to him directly. I reached around her and tapped the small of his back.

He looked at me over the top of her head, brows furrowed.

I flicked my gaze toward the scraggly man wearing all denim.

Leander's jaw tightened and a murderous look crossed his face. He gave a slow shake of his head before glancing at Elijah. Elijah was oblivious to both the man and Leander, staring at Cole's casket with a startling intensity, like he might float away if he broke eye contact with it. Jake was also focused on the casket, only moving to reach up and lay a hand on Elijah's shoulder gently.

After the service concluded, Leander turned his back on the stranger, offering Olivia his arm. She slipped her hand in the crook of his elbow and leaned into him as they headed for the car.

"I'll be right back," I said, peeling away from them.

"Bennett!" Leander growled, but it was too late. I was already committed to my course and the man saw me coming.

He glanced from side to side, clearly debating his next move, as if running was even an option for a man his size. I had no idea why he'd be nervous in the first place. He probably had seventy-five pounds on me and looked like he'd been in his fair share of fights from the broken nose and the way he carried himself.

"Can I help you with something?" I asked as I approached.

The stranger cleared his throat, shoving his hands in his pockets. "That was Cole Holliday, right?"

"Who are you?"

"I'm his dad."

My spine straightened as I took the man in once again. If you knew what to look for, you could see the resemblance to

Cole, particularly in their large build and sandy-colored hair. "What do you want?"

It wasn't a secret his father had been out of his life for quite some time. Even when he was around, he wasn't worth a damn. Given the few memories Cole shared, I wasn't about to put the man up for a Father of the Year award just because he managed to drag his ass to his son's funeral.

"Look, I didn't come to cause trouble," he said, shifting on his feet. "I just wanted to see if my boy left anything for me."

I narrowed my eyes, replaying his words in my brain one more time to make sure I heard him correctly. "Excuse me?" My family were greedy fucks, but Jesus! They could at least wait until the will reading before they ran to the trough. "You came to his funeral — not to bury him — but to see if he left something for you?"

"Yeah. Like an envelope or something?"

"An envelope of what? You think he wrote you a letter before someone blew his brains out?"

He expelled a sharp breath, shaking his head and muttering to himself. "I told him not to fuck around with those people. And now they've gone and killed him."

"Who?"

"The Marcheses."

I reeled back as sharply as if he punched me. "What the fuck do you know about the Marcheses?"

The man looked me over from head to toe, his bushy brows knitting together. "What are you? A fucking cop?"

Fury bubbled up inside me. Having put my friend in the ground not but five minutes ago, I was not in the mood to play Twenty Questions with some shitbag who turned up out of the blue. For all I knew, the Italians got someone with a vague resemblance to Cole to come here, just to fuck with us.

Determined to get to the bottom of his murder once and for all, I kicked out with my right heel, directly in the center of the man's kneecap. There was an audible crunch and his leg bent in the most unnatural way.

He collapsed to the ground, screaming and trying to clutch his fractured knee. The denim and extra weight around his midsection made the task of self-soothing a little difficult.

Before he could even think about getting up, I stepped on his knee, forcing it to the ground.

"Do I look like a fucking cop?" I shouted over the top of his screaming. "Now answer the goddamn question! What do you know about Marchese?"

"You broke my fucking knee!"

"That's not all I'm gonna break." I leaned more of my weight on his shattered kneecap, until sweat broke out across his brow and his face turned dark red. His screams tapered off into pitiful squeaks of pain.

Elijah and Jake rushed up behind me, yelling my name as their boots pounded across the manicured lawn.

"What the fuck—oh. *You.*" Elijah seethed when he saw who was sprawled in front of me on the ground. "What the fuck are *you* doing here?"

"He knows something about the Marcheses and he isn't being very forthcoming." I let up on the asshole's knee. "Feel like talking yet?"

"It don't fucking matter what I say," the man panted. "They're going to kill you. All of you! And you're never gonna see it coming."

"I've got the chains in the truck," Jake offered helpfully.

While I appreciated his enthusiasm, Jake really needed to learn to be a bit more subtle.

Elijah surprised me by delivering a swift kick to the man's girthy ribcage. "Fucking talk already, Dale!"

When he was done grunting, Dale held his hands up toward Elijah. "Ok! Ok! Cole asked if I still had buddies on the inside! Asked if I could make an introduction. That's it."

"An introduction for *what*?!" Elijah yelled, pulling his leg back for another kick.

"He wanted someone who could get to that fat fuck in Chicago. You know, that mob guy who's been all over the papers? Said he'd give me ten grand to make it happen."

"Who was the contact?" I asked.

"It don't matter. He's dead."

"The name!" I leaned on his knee at the same time Elijah kicked him again.

"Marsh," Dale croaked out. "Don Marsh."

Lifting my foot, I took a step back, trying to process the new information in light of everything else. The ground swayed beneath me, to the point where I had to lean against a tree for support, re-evaluating everything I thought I knew about the past few months. The past few years, for that matter.

Cole asked his shitbag father to get him in touch with another shitbag in DOC. The second shitbag, Don Marsh, was housed with Giovanni. Don Marsh, as in the man responsible for stabbing Giovanni Marchese to death.

Cole ordered the hit on Giovanni. No, not Cole. Leander. Cole was just the go-between. And now Cole was dead. Don Marsh was dead. How much longer before they got to Leander?

Leander.

They're going to kill you.

Seeking him out across the cemetery, I searched for his dark shape against equally dark trees and tombstones. I finally spied him near the main drive, where the line of black cars were waiting to take us home.

All of you!

Cole wasn't just a link in the chain leading to Leander... He was bait.

And you're never gonna see it coming.

Italians were old school, I said so myself.

Fear exploded in my chest as Leander reached for the door handle.

I screamed Leander's name at the same time I broke into a run.

The scene in front of me unfolded in slow motion.

Leander opened the rear passenger door of the car.

Olivia ducked inside.

The driver stopped and spoke with Leander. When they finished, the man circled around the car and opened his own door.

Leander stepped into the cabin, pausing to glance over the top of the door frame.

The driver closed his door.

The next time I blinked, a bloom of orange appeared beneath the car. It exploded in all directions, a burst of white and orange flames, lifting the car off its wheels.

The shockwave knocked me backward. A shrill ringing flooded my ears. I shook my head in a vain attempt to re-orient myself. I could hear muffled screams, but everything sounded like it was underwater.

Fire caught my attention as soon as I was on my feet again.

The car was on fire. *Leander's* car was on fire. Thick, black smoke rolled out from the interior. The windows were completely shattered and flames danced on the inside.

I lurched toward it anyway. The closer I got, the worse the smell became. Burning hair and charred flesh. Scorched metal and heated motor oil.

Covering my nose with my forearm, I staggered toward the rear, trying to see into the backseat. Something.

Anything. But it was impossible to see through the wall of fire.

I sank to my knees, staring at the car. I saw it, yet I didn't believe it. I *couldn't* believe it, even with the unbearable heat on my face.

People yelled behind me. All around me. They hadn't stopped yelling.

Vaguely, I thought I heard someone shout my name. I didn't bother moving, but somehow the ground beneath me shifted. Someone grabbed me, dragging me away.

It was Elijah.

He hauled me to my feet and spun me by the shoulders, pushing me forward, toward the gravesite and away from the car.

We were only a few steps away when another explosion knocked us forward.

Elijah recovered first, pulling me to my feet and asking me questions. I stared blankly at him. He may as well have been speaking Greek for as much as I understood.

Getting nowhere, he resorted to grabbing my sleeve and leading the way. There was a little cluster of people near Cole's grave: Jake, Madison, and Gertrude, the little old lady who ran the historical society with an iron fist.

Jake knelt on the ground, his head bowed. When we got a little closer, he turned toward us, shouting something to Elijah. I couldn't hear what. I was too focused on the lump of black behind him.

It was Leander.

Sitting upright, Leander was propped against a headstone, holding his arm. Gertrude stooped beside him, pressing an embroidered handkerchief to the side of his face. Jake was talking to him, but Leander didn't respond.

Shoving past Elijah, I sprinted the rest of the way. Jake

wisely got out of my way when I collapsed to my knees, seizing Leander in a hug.

Blood dripped from his ear, along with a dozen tiny cuts on his face. His left arm, cradled against his chest, was covered in flash burns from his hand down his forearm. His suit was destroyed but otherwise he seemed to be in one piece, at least on the outside.

Gertrude said something, but I ignored her.

"Where's Olivia?" I asked, holding on to a thread of hope. By the grace of God, he made it out alive. So did she. She had to. "Leander?"

Leander blinked slowly, lost in his daze.

I repeated the question louder, making sure to enunciate.

Still, he said nothing. He did, however, lift his right hand and point a shaking finger at the car.

The last bit of hope snapped completely.

Closing my eyes, I buried my face against his unburned shoulder and exhaled an unsteady breath.

Of course, I was furious Olivia was dead. I was sick. Heartbroken.

But like the asshole I was, I thanked whatever god there was that Leander was still alive. If I had to trade every single life in this cemetery for his, I would — mine included.

32

BENNETT

They say tragedy has a way of bringing people together. In some ways, it was true. For the first time in the history of Easton, the town actually sympathized with the Welles family. Easton PD, Leander's historic nemesis, displayed an altogether different side following the explosion. Even Chief Albrecht showed up to offer his sympathies.

At the hospital we learned Olivia and two other people were dead — our driver and one of Cole's construction workers. Three others, including Leander, were wounded. Meanwhile the rest of us were in utter shock.

Leander's physical wounds were mostly superficial. Nurses plucked crap from the explosion out of his face and carefully wrapped his burned skin. His perforated eardrum, they said, would heal over time, as would the concussion and sprained wrist. The doctor told me all of this with an encouraging smile and a pat to the arm. It was well and good, but it wasn't his body I was most worried about.

After Leander was discharged from the hospital, and after he'd given a brief statement to Easton PD, we went home to the mansion. Despite the fact it wasn't entirely finished from the renovations, it felt more secure than the teal house in town, with its wrought iron fencing and security cameras. Under threat of physical pain, Elijah and Jake came too, though they wisely chose the apartment over the garage rather than stay under the same roof as Leander.

The days in the immediate aftermath were mostly a blur.

We drifted around each other like ghosts. Leander didn't speak, even after I knew his eardrum healed and he could hear me just fine. He refused to eat. It didn't matter if I did the cooking, or if it was Elijah. To make matters worse, Leander didn't sleep, either. At least when Olivia had been mourning Cole, I knew what stage of grief she was in at any given time. With Leander, I had no fucking clue, and that was unnerving.

I often found him awake at odd times, in odd parts of the house, doing particularly odd things. Cleaning, re-organizing the library, sorting through a hundred and fifty years of photographs and family documents, repotting plants in the conservatory and outside in the garden shed. Anything, it seemed, to keep from sleeping. Anything that was a solitary activity, I should say. If it could even remotely involve me, he promptly found a way to remove himself from the situation and hole up in a different part of the mansion.

I learned to orbit around him, taking different stairs when I heard him coming, even making sure I stayed on a different level. It was easier to hide from him than to face the devastation on his face.

Keeping my distance in the conservatory, I was halfway through another bottle of bourbon when I heard the first glass break. Freezing in place, I waited to see if it was an accident. But then Number Two and Three shattered.

By the time I made it to the kitchen, all of the teacups were destroyed and he'd started in on the the saucers. Since I was more of a coffee guy, I let him have at it. Besides, it would be easier to replace the whole set than try and match a couple of pieces.

Leaning against the archway, I took another pull from my bottle, watching him hurl a tiny plate against the wall.

When he saw me, he spiked the remaining plate on the black-and-white tiled floor. "Don't!"

"Don't what?" I spread my arms, itching for a fight. It might not have been the healthiest coping mechanism, but if he was screaming at me, then at least I'd know what he was thinking, what he was feeling. It was better than the cold darkness I'd been living with.

"Stand there and say 'I told you so.'"

"What the fuck are you talking about?"

"Marchese!" Leander shouted the name, tears running down his face. "This is *my* fault. This whole fucking thing! *I* paid for Marchese's death which means *I* got them killed!"

His admission hit me hard. I wanted to believe him when he said he wasn't involved in the hit on Marchese. But then again, he never *said* he wasn't involved. He simply said the problem fixed itself. Because *he* fucking fixed it. Even after Cole's funeral, I didn't want to believe Leander was responsible for any of this. I'd refused to ask him, preferring to live in denial. But now, he ripped that away from me too.

Anger unfurled inside of me, igniting on the fumes of the bourbon. I nodded, fixing him with an accusatory glare. "Yeah. You're right. You *did* get them killed."

The next plate came at my head. I barely had time to turn my face from the shards of china flying through the air.

"But *you* knew!" he screamed at me, hurling another plate. It, too, shattered on the wall next to me, flinging fragmented bits everywhere. "You knew and yet you stood by! You didn't do a damn thing about it!"

"What was I supposed to do?! You lied to me without

lying. Your trademark move." At least I was able to bite my words off before "Fucking hypocrite" came out of my mouth. The cocktail of tranqs and painkillers, mixed with the bourbon, made my movements slower than usual. So when I shrugged with a feigned helplessness it was at a mockingly slow pace.

"You have connections! You could have stopped it! Their blood is on your hands just as much as mine!" Leander shouted, prowling back and forth in a circle. "And *you're* the one who brought Marchese into our fucking lives to begin with!"

"Yeah, maybe I could have done something. Except… I told you so. I told you you can't just kill a mob boss. Right over there." Squinting one eye, I pointed at the dining room and gave him a shitty smirk before gulping down another mouthful of bourbon.

If I'd been sober, I could have blocked his attack. Hell, if I'd been sober, we wouldn't be having this fight to begin with. But, I wasn't. So when he launched himself at me, I was completely unprepared.

We crashed to the floor together, his hands twisted in my shirt. The bottle shattered right next to me, sending a shower of glass and alcohol over us both.

I tried to push him off, but he wouldn't let go. We rolled over one another, straight into the broken glass. Jagged shards pierced through our clothing, compounded by the sting of alcohol. I ended up on top, but not for long.

Leander threw his elbow against my jaw, sending me flying to the side. As soon as my weight cleared him, he was on top of me again, one hand holding me down while the other punched repeatedly at any spot he could find.

I blocked what blows I could with my forearms, but he was wild and unpredictable. As soon as I was able, I arched my back and threw my hips up and to the side, knocking him off. I rolled with him and straddled his waist, trying to ignore the chunks of glass digging into my knees.

Grabbing his shirt with both hands, I yanked him up before slamming him into the ground. It might not have been the best thing for his concussion, but I needed a way to end this without actually doing serious damage. Besides, he could afford to lose a few brain cells. Might even the playing field between us.

The fight went out of him, along with whatever air was in his lungs. His hands fell to the sides and he squeezed his eyes shut, his chest heaving.

"Are you fucking finished?" I panted, preparing for the next hit all the same.

He swallowed thickly, but didn't answer.

Climbing off of him slowly, I scooted backward and slumped against the wall.

Without me on top of him, Leander rolled onto his side and curled into himself, despite the fact he was in a puddle of blood and bourbon and broken glass.

"I'm going to find them," I said, touching the tip of my tongue to my split lip, licking away the blood. "And I'm going to kill them."

"You don't know who they are," Leander said, his voice hitching. "*I* don't know who they are. No one does."

"Doesn't matter. If I have to kill every fucking Italian between here and Chicago, I will. "

He pushed himself into a sitting position, wiping his face with the back of his hand, his jaw tightening. "Not if I get to them first."

33

BENNETT

"As I live and breathe," I said, halting dead in my tracks. Agent Craig Diefendorf, of all people, stood right in front of me on the sidewalk. If we were in Chicago, I wouldn't have been so shocked. But smack dab in the middle of Easton's charming little downtown? Fucking floored. "I never thought I'd see you in Easton ever again."

Craig grimaced, adjusting his grip on his briefcase. "Trust me, I'd rather be anywhere else."

"Then what are you doing here?"

He tossed a wary glance over his shoulder. "Is there someplace we can talk?"

I made a face at him but nodded mutely. His arrival, combined with his cautious concern, made me forget all about being a smart ass. This wasn't good. I thought he came down here to razz me about the Calaveras again, or some other criminal enterprise. By the look on his face, I knew it wasn't anything as simple as that.

"This way," I said, tossing my head down the street. We set off for the office together, not even bothering with the typical chit-chat.

For the first time since Olivia's murder, Elijah managed to drag Leander into the office. The two of them were in the conference room going over who knew what when Craig and I walked in.

Leander looked up sharply from a pile of papers, drawing himself up to his full height, eyes narrowed.

"You might want to bring your boss too," Diefendorf said, gesturing to Leander.

I cocked my head at the suggestion. Turning toward Leander, I met his furious gaze through the glass and nodded toward the stairs.

He said something to Elijah and slipped away, his eyes trained on us the entire time.

"Agent Diefendorf has something he'd like to talk about," I said when Leander approached, his fingers brushing my palm.

"We can use my office," Leander replied in a clipped tone, making his way up the stairs.

I gestured for our guest to go first. Glancing at Elijah, I gave him the OK signal with a furrowed brow. His dark gaze darted to the second floor briefly before he shook his head. Great. So a return to work wasn't soothing the beast the way we'd hoped. And I'm sure whatever Diefendorf was going to drop on us wasn't going to help matters either.

Closing the door behind me, I assessed the two of them as I cut across the room to Leander's side.

Leander leaned against his desk, arms crossed and head canted, watching Diefendorf like a hawk. Diefendorf, on the other hand, set his briefcase down on the table by the window and faced us with a grim expression.

"I'll cut to the chase," Craig said, popping open the briefcase and pulling out a handful of photographs. He handed them over and I flipped through them quickly. They featured a dark-haired young woman, mostly. Sometimes she was alone, other times she was flanked by group of men I'd peg as Italian mafia from a mile away. "Do you know Gianna Scardato?"

Leander and I exchanged a glance. We both shook our heads as I returned the photographs to him.

"You never heard Giovanni mention her?"

"No. Why?" I asked.

"She's his daughter. Illegitimate, but still. She grew up with her mother and Giovanni's cousin, Marco, in New York. Sounds like he left them behind when he relocated here."

"Ok...?"

"She's in Chicago," Craig said simply.

Leander shifted closer to me, ever so slightly. My heart rate kicked up a notch. Could it be as basic as that? The missing link we'd been searching for?

"Why are you telling us this?" Leander asked. His tone may have been quiet, but it was sharp and untrusting.

"Even though Giovanni is dead, we're still running an investigation on the rest of his crew. What's left of them, anyway," Craig replied, shifting his weight to his back foot. "I was going through the surveillance transcripts from the other day and Easton came up."

"What did they say?" I asked.

Diefendorf grimaced, hesitating for a minute, like he was weighing the pros and cons of his honesty. "Gianna's right-hand man, Paulie Esposito, was talking about placing an order."

Fuck.

Leander's dark brows dipped down. "What does that mean?"

"It means she took out a hit on us," I answered, still looking at Craig. There was more. That little wince he did when I confirmed the hit meant he was holding something back.

"And you came all this way just to tell us that?" Leander stood up straight, unfolding his arms. "I'm not sure if you're aware, Agent, but someone blew up my friend at a goddamn funeral. I'd say we're well aware someone wants us dead."

Craig didn't even flinch at news of the bombing. "We found ties between your kidnappers" — he nodded at me — "and the ones who killed your employee at the Romano warehouse. I put two and two together. But not soon enough, apparently."

Leander bristled at the mention of Cole. I leaned into him slightly, hoping it would remind him to take a breath.

Diefendorf continued, lowering his voice. "You two need to be extremely careful. You don't know what these people are capable of."

I knew he was trying to be helpful, but I couldn't help but smirk. Did he forget who he was talking to?

"*When*, exactly, did you put two and two together?" Leander asked through his teeth, his molars clenched so hard the muscle in the side of his jaw popped out.

"About two weeks ago. I was—"

"Two weeks ago?" Leander's spine straightened even more than I thought was possible. He took a step forward, staring at Craig with unchecked rage. "Did you say *two* weeks ago?"

I straightened as well, sensing danger on the horizon. "Leander..."

"Two weeks ago you knew Marchese's daughter was behind Bennett's kidnapping and Cole's murder? Two weeks ago would have been *before* the funeral," Leander said, taking another step closer to Diefendorf. "*Before* Olivia was blown into a dozen pieces." He seized the front of Craig's suit jacket and shoved him into the bookcase. "If you would have called two weeks ago, she might still be alive!"

Diefendorf held up his hands defensively, not even bothering to try and guard himself.

I grabbed my husband from behind and hauled him off the agent before he did something stupid enough to land his ass in prison for real. "Easy... He's not the enemy this time."

Leander ripped himself out of my hands and stalked to the far side of the room, positively seething.

My attention snapped back to Craig, eyes narrowed. "Leander's right. A phone call would have sufficed at any point. Why wait? And why the four-hour drive?"

"It's complicated, ok? This was the earliest opportunity I had to get away and I didn't want the information to fall into the wrong hands," Craig replied, tugging on the bottom of his jacket to straighten it. Picking up the scattered photographs, he tossed them into his briefcase and smacked the lid shut.

"And by wrong hands, you mean your bosses?!" Leander interjected with a snarl, surging forward again. "Are they in on this too? We all know the mafia makes deals with everyone, even law enforcement!"

"Listen, I took a risk coming here," Diefendorf spat. "But I did it because it's the *right* thing to do, despite everything you put me through." That time, he threw his glare in my direction.

I caught Leander by the elbow, pulling him back to safety and squeezing gently before facing Craig with a perfectly pleasant expression. "And I appreciate the warning. Are you staying in town long?"

He snorted. "I'm out of here first thing in the morning."

"Do you have a place to stay?"

Craig shook his head. "I saw there's a hotel down the block."

"Perfect," I said with a dazzling smile. "It's one of the businesses Leander owns. We'll get you sorted." I gave Leander's elbow another squeeze, making sure I pinched the nerve to get his attention.

Thankfully his reaction was almost nonexistent. Leander drifted away from me, back to his desk, and hit the speaker button on his phone. In two rings, Madison answered. Her voice, while pleasant, was still jarring for the simple fact it wasn't Olivia.

"Yes, sir?"

"Can you block off a suite at Walker House tonight?" Leander asked.

"Oh and make dinner reservations at Bellavia's!" I added from the background. "Say, seven? On us. Of course."

"Yes, Mr. Reeve. Anything else?"

Leander lifted his brows at Craig, who promptly shook his head. "No, that's all. Thank you." He disconnected and turned his full attention back to the agent. "There. It's all settled."

"You really don't have to do any of that," Craig said. "We're not supposed to accept favors."

"I insist," I replied, walking Diefendorf to Leander's office door. "After all, you came all this way. The least we can do is pay for a room and dinner."

"I'll be in touch." Craig paused, blatantly frowning. "Until then, don't do anything... Just, don't do anything. Let us handle it. Ok?" He gave me a pointed look before walking through the door.

I forced a bright smile to my face, patting him on the shoulder. "Have a good night. And you drive careful tomorrow morning. Call me when you get home, so I know you made it safe. Ok, sweetie?"

Craig rolled his eyes and walked out, closing the door behind him.

As soon as he was gone, Leander whirled on me. "Want to tell me what that was all about? Why you're suddenly playing nicely with the FBI after everything that's happened?"

I bit my lower lip and stepped closer to him, trailing my fingers along the edge of his belt. Even if neither of us was in the mood, hopefully it would be enough of a distraction to calm his ass down. "What did he just show us?"

"What?"

My other hand slipped around his waist, curving downward to grab his ass. "Think, my love. What did he just show us?"

"Pictures." His huffed reply came out with a little more force when I yanked his body against mine.

"And where was he keeping those pictures?" I asked quietly, my teeth grazing his earlobe.

He pulled back, meeting my gaze as the corner of his mouth ticked up in a smile. The malice was gone from his face, replaced with a calm understanding now that he finally saw the bigger play. "You're going to break into his room at the hotel."

I returned his smile with a devilish one of my own. Planting a kiss on his cheek, I swatted his ass as I moseyed away to put my plan into motion.

34

BENNETT

Shortly after seven, we strolled into the hotel like we owned the place — because we did. Leander was known for popping in and out of his businesses at random, forever keeping his employees on their toes. So no one questioned us when we cut through the lobby and took the elevator to the fourth floor. Even if they saw us up there, either in person or on the security cameras, they wouldn't dare question what we were doing.

With the master keycard in hand, we simply waltzed into Diefendorf's room.

I expected a scavenger hunt. I thought for sure we'd be up to our elbows in vents and flipping over mattresses to find what we were looking for. Nope. The briefcase was sitting on the table next to the TV in plain view.

Leander and I shared a wary glance.

"It can't be that easy, can it?" he asked as I pulled my phone out and snapped a picture of its exact position.

Rule Number One in snooping: make sure everything gets put back in place *perfectly* because there were assholes like me who lined things up a certain way to see if their shit had been messed with while they were gone. More than one frat brother learned the hard way after I broke their fingers for prying.

"Maybe he thinks he's safe in a small town? Something you Chicagoans seem to have in common." Leander squatted in front of the briefcase and took a picture of the locking mechanisms, including what numbers they'd been left on.

"I don't trust anyone for that very reason." I smirked and flipped the briefcase upright. "Hand me that paper over there?"

Leander grabbed the notepad from the nightstand and offered it to me on the flat of his palm. "Why does this not surprise me in the slightest?"

"I'm sure there was a compliment in there somewhere, my love." I tore off a piece of paper and got to work, fiddling with the dials and using the edge of the paper to feel for the telltale groove.

After a few minutes, the locks popped open.

"Unbelievable," Leander murmured beside me. "When did you study lock picking?"

"You can learn anything on the internet."

"Like how to poison people?"

Scoffing, I feigned the most insulted expression I could manage. "No, love, that I got from the Medici archives. I told you. There's an art to it."

Sadly, all of my work on the locks was for naught. Aside from the usual pads of papers, receipts, and pens, there wasn't anything important or relevant inside. No massive file on New York and Chicago mob bosses. No telephone or address to lead us straight to Gianna fucking Scardato. Nothing.

"Knew it wasn't going to be that easy," I muttered, closing the lid again and rearranging the numbers accordingly.

Guess we were tossing the room, after all.

"He didn't take it with him. We would have seen him when he left," Leander said, heading over to the bed. He slid his hands under the mattress, in the pillowcases and behind the headboard.

While he took the bed, I checked underneath the nightstand and dresser drawers.

Nada.

The ceiling was solid and all of the vents appeared secure. Nothing in the bathroom. Nothing in the living room area or the kitchenette.

"Where the fuck would he have put it?" I growled, stalking around the room again, trying to think of a better hiding place.

Leander opened the closet door and checked in the folds of the extra blankets. Before he closed the door, I stopped him.

"Is that supposed to be hung?" I asked, pointing at the ironing board.

It was currently leaning against the inside of the closet, not hanging on the metal holder above it. Hauling it out, I unfolded the contraption and set it upright. The imprint of a file-sized rectangle sat in the middle of the padding, just beneath the cover emblazoned with Walker House across the center.

"Clever fox," Leander said, grabbing me suddenly and kissing me. Even though we were still working against the clock, I didn't want to rush this moment. It was the first time he'd actually kissed me since Olivia was killed. In fact, it was the first time he'd shown *any* emotion other than anger or grief. I was going to savor every second of it, because who knew how long it would last.

He pulled away after a moment, his green eyes finally sparkling again. "Let's get what we came for."

Nodding, I fished the folder out from underneath the

cover and spread it open. There was something to be said about people who were still analog in a digital world. While it may not have had as much information as a database full of reports, Craig had enough in this one folder to build a pretty decent background of Miss Scardato and her New York kinfolk. Kai could fill in the rest.

Leander and I photographed every scrap of paper we could, as quickly as we could. As soon as we had it all, we filed it back in the folder, just as it was, and returned it to its hiding place in the closet. One quick glance around the suite ensured everything was in order before we ducked out.

Strolling down the hallway as if nothing happened, we made our way back to the elevator. At the last second, I called an audible.

Fishing the keycard out of Leander's front pocket, I swiped us into one of the other suites.

"What are you doing?" he whispered as I shoved him into the room. "Someone could be in here!"

"The parking lot is practically empty. You know we have another two weeks before the tourists come back." I kicked the door shut behind me and advanced on him. "I'll bet you a hundred dollars no one else is even registered on this floor."

"You brought me in here to make a wager?"

"No. I brought you in here to have hot, dirty, hotel sex with you."

"Bennett, I—"

His next words were covered by my hard, demanding kiss. His protest died completely when my mouth coaxed his open, our tongues commingling at long last.

"God, I've missed you," I panted when we finally pulled apart, stripping one another of our suit jackets.

"I'm sorry." He didn't even bother unbuttoning my shirt the rest of the way before he tugged it over my head and tossed it aside. Kissing and licking my skin, his hands roamed my body, pulling my hips against his.

I shed my pants and stripped him of his. Taking our cocks together in my hand, I stroked them from base to tip in languid movements. Just feeling him was almost enough to make me come on the spot.

"Promise you won't pull away from me again," I said, sucking in a breath when he bit my neck.

He ran his hands through my hair and drew me close, kissing me, and *not* answering. The avoidance wasn't lost on me, but I pushed it to the side in favor of enjoying this connection to him, shallow and inappropriate as it may have been. We should have been focused on revenge, on murder, on retribution for all we'd lost.

Instead, we brought each other to the brink of orgasm and stopped, again and again, a revenge of an entirely different sort. We punished each other just to have some semblance of control in a situation where we had none.

But tonight was the first step to rectifying that.

"Fuck, I'm going to come," I groaned. Leander's grip on my cock tightened, timing his strokes with each thrust. "Don't you dare stop this time!"

Smirking, he leaned down and captured my mouth in a kiss. I knotted my hands in his hair so he couldn't pull away completely.

All of the sensations built on one another — his hot, wet tongue in my mouth; his hand stroking my length; and his dick hitting the perfect spot — until the warm, tingling in my lower abdomen exploded so hard I saw stars.

"Oh, God!" Leander collapsed on top of me, his hips jerking as his own orgasm rolled through him. Burying his face in the side of my neck, his breaths came out hard and sharp before tapering off into a normal rhythm. "Thank you..."

"You're welcome?" I tried to angle myself so I could look at him, but he latched on tighter, keeping his face where I couldn't see it.

"You didn't leave. I gave you every reason to… but you didn't."

"And walk away from the other half of my soul?" I shook my head, even if he wasn't looking. "Impossible. I'd rather throw myself from the top of this building than live one more moment without you."

He lifted his head, meeting my gaze hesitantly. There was a profound sadness in his eyes, illuminated by the unshed tears. Still, after all this time, after everything we'd been through, he didn't quite believe me when I told him how much he meant to me.

I hid that stab of pain behind a smile, brushing his hair out of his eyes. "As much as I love holding you, we should probably get in the shower and get out of here. After all, we have a slew of new murders to plan."

35

BENNETT

I thought learning all about Gianna Scardato and planning her excruciating death would be enough to keep hold of Leander, to keep him from slipping back into melancholy, as he called it.

It wasn't.

When the insomnia kicked in again, I knew I was losing him. He didn't isolate me completely as he had in the immediate aftermath of Olivia's murder, but I could tell he was channeling enormous amounts of energy into faking it.

One afternoon Leander's voice carried out into the hallway as I came down the front stairs. It was still too distant to make out what he was saying, but the tone sounded... off. I hadn't heard anyone come into the house. I figured he was probably on the phone, as he had been a lot lately.

When I turned the corner to the library, he was standing with his back to the door, staring out the massive window to the gardens behind the house. As I'd guessed, he had his phone pressed to his ear.

I walked up behind him and slipped my hands around his waist, pulling him backward. He didn't turn to look at me.

He didn't cover my hands with his. He didn't do anything, except remain as unyielding as possible in my arms.

"I assume that won't be a problem?" His attention was completely dedicated to the phone call, his gaze fixed on some point beyond the glass. "No, I'm sure."

Circling around to his frontside, I furrowed my brows and crossed my arms. He continued to avoid even glancing in my general direction. The world outside of that conversation had apparently ceased to exist. He didn't blink. He didn't twitch. He was as frozen as the statutes outside.

"Oh, and one last thing," he said, his voice dropping even lower, barely above a snarl. "When you find him, you send him to me — alive."

Tears glistened in his eyes, turning them a brighter shade of green, but they didn't spill over. He disconnected without further instructions and exhaled a slow, steady breath.

"My love…" I tilted my head and reached out, caressing his cheek. Like waking a sleepwalker, I was mindful of his hands and any sudden movements. "What did you just do?"

As if he was in a fog, his gaze slid toward me slowly, like he was just now aware of my presence. Instead of lighting up in recognition or happiness, or even anger, his eyes remained dull and dark. Whatever emotion he might have felt failed to register anywhere in the sharp angles of his face or in his rigid frame. The only time I'd ever seen that wraithlike look was in the moments before he was arrested. Seeing it again made the hair on the back of my neck stand on end.

Unable or just unwilling, he didn't give me an answer. Bowing his head, he swallowed hard before turning and drifting out of the room, leaving me standing there with a sinking feeling in the pit of my stomach.

I had no idea who was on the phone and I had no idea what bargain they struck, but I knew it wasn't going to be good.

Then the boxes began to arrive.

First it was one.

Then two.

All from a kosher deli in Chicago. A *Russian* kosher deli.

I only saw the cardboard boxes, never the contents or any packing slips. There certainly wasn't any pastrami in the fridge and the only bagels I could find came from the local grocery store. Delivered day or night by a portly man in a white, unmarked box truck, there was no pattern to their arrival. Sometimes it would only be one box. Sometimes a couple.

I asked, of course. Leander refused to answer. After that, he didn't let me get within five feet of any box before he whisked it away to a different part of the house. He made sure I couldn't follow him by locking one or more doors behind him, as if he thought I would stoop to picking the locks... which, I totally would have if he ever left the house and gave me the opportunity.

Failing to get an answer from my husband, I called Misha with my inquiry. He was as clueless as I was, or claimed to be. I knew better than to try to ask Sergei. Even if he knew what was going on, he'd never say and I didn't want to weaken my standing in his eyes by not knowing something going on with my own "partner."

So, I did what any suspicious spouse would do — I told Leander I was working late and then snuck into the house like a burglar to catch him in the act.

The first thing that hit me was the smell — woodsmoke and meat. Normally, those types of smells would have been fine if Leander was the backyard barbecue kind of a guy. But he wasn't. He wasn't even close.

Not to mention, the smell was coming from the library, which was even more disconcerting.

Creeping around the corner, I found him sitting on the

floor in front of a roaring fire. There were half a dozen open boxes scattered around him. Beyond the scent of something odd roasting, the next thing I smelled was blood. A *lot* of blood. That copper smell was absolutely unmistakable.

I didn't bother hiding my presence anymore or waste time trying to ask questions. Marching over to one of the boxes, I ripped the lid off of the styrofoam cooler inside, putting an end to the secrecy bullshit he claimed to hate so much.

Inside the cooler lay a pair of hearts.

I wanted to believe they were bison hearts for some new bizarre recipe, or pig hearts for God knew what. But the size, the shape, even the number of pulmonary veins all stared back at me, indisputable proof.

They were human hearts.

"Leander." I carried the box over to him, about to ask more when I saw he was already holding something. At first, I thought it was a plum. But there was no mistaking the shape.

It was another heart, only it was *much* smaller than the ones in my box.

The cooler dropped to the floor a moment before I sank to my knees next to him. The smoke curling out of the fireplace seemed to have a stranglehold on me; I could barely force out my next words. "Leander, what did you do?"

He was staring at the flames, but his fingers curled instinctively around the little heart, as if I was going to snatch it away. His dark lashes fluttered and I thought he might say something, but he didn't. In fact, he did the opposite by pressing his lips together even harder.

"Children?" I breathed the word, still struggling to believe it myself.

He didn't blink or turn his head. Other than that one

protective gesture, he didn't acknowledge my presence at all. His silence was infuriating.

"Leander!" I grabbed him by the shoulders and shook him hard, hoping to jar him out of whatever Hell his mind was trapped in.

His gaze dropped to his hand. Uncurling his fingers, he stared at the heart for a minute before flinging it into the fire. It landed amongst the charred logs, popping and hissing.

"It had to be done," he said, so quietly I almost missed it.

I shook my head, refusing to believe what was in front of me despite a literal pile of evidence. "This isn't you."

"Yes, it is."

"No, it's not."

"It is."

"It can't be, because *you're* not you. You're not thinking clearly."

"I am."

"No. You're not. You don't do this." I gestured helplessly at the boxes of carnage all around us.

"I do."

"Not *this*." I hurled the pair of hearts into the fire after the little one, styrofoam cooler and all. "You don't kill the innocent! You never have."

"There is no such thing as innocence." His head turned toward me slowly, his gaze vacant. The dried tear marks on his face caught the light, but his eyes were empty now.

At a loss, I simply shook my head again. I could have the most logical argument in the world and it would fall on deaf ears. Knowing there was nothing I would be able to say or do to get through to him was both incensing and absolutely crushing.

Without saying another word, he rose to his feet and padded out of the room, leaving me in the midst of his bloody boxes and his broken soul.

36

BENNETT

Elijah and Jake appeared in the kitchen one night, unannounced and unexpected. They were still living in the garage apartment, so their presence wasn't entirely out of place. It was the looks on their faces that unsettled me.

"What's wrong?" I asked, already dreading their answer.

Ever the eldest, Elijah spoke first. "Is Leander around?"

"He's resting."

In the days following my gruesome discovery, Leander resumed his hunger strike. On top of it, his insomnia was particularly brutal. I think he was on Day Three of no sleep before he finally crashed. Literally. He collapsed in the hallway and I had to drag him to bed.

Elijah frowned, shoving his hands in his pockets. "I know it's been rough, but you might want to go get him."

"Why? What's happened?"

"He's here," Jake said, as if I was supposed to know what that meant.

"He who?"

It was Elijah who answered, looking even more grim than before. "The bomb maker."

I swore under my breath. It all made sense now. Leander hadn't been in a hurry to go after Giovanni's daughter because he had other plans — like working his way through Gianna's associates and their families until someone gave up the identity of the man whose device killed Olivia.

"You didn't know?" Elijah's frown deepened.

I shook my head. "No. He hasn't exactly been chatty lately."

Elijah nodded. Thankfully, he was all too familiar with Leander's moods, so I didn't need to elaborate.

"What do you want to do?" Jake asked.

"Where is this guy?" I asked.

"The Young property," Jake replied. "In Missouri."

"Give me a couple hours. We'll meet you there."

They nodded and left again. The sooner we got rid of this fucker, the sooner we could fully commit to giving Gianna her just desserts. Then, hopefully, Leander could move forward.

When I went upstairs, Leander was still fast asleep, his hand draped across Annabel, who was curled up in the curve of his stomach. He didn't look like the ruthless man who ordered the execution of entire families. For once, he looked peaceful instead of the tortured specter I'd been living with.

I let him sleep for another hour before I went in to wake him. Sliding into bed next to him, I caressed his face. "My love. You have to wake up."

He stirred, only to shake his head and roll away from me, curling up tighter around the cat.

"I know you're exhausted," I said with a sigh. "But you really need to wake up."

"Why?" he groaned.

"Because your bomb maker is here."

For a moment, time seemed to stop. Given his lack of reaction, I assumed he didn't hear me. Then he sat up slowly, giving me a wary look, like he expected me to take his head off at any moment.

I tried to smile, but I knew it was nothing short of bitter. "Yeah, I know about him."

He ran a hand through his hair, casting his gaze downward.

"Why didn't you tell me?"

"Because you wouldn't approve." Leander looked up at me again, his eyes finally clear.

"It's not that I wouldn't approve..." I cocked my head, trying to keep the frown off my face and appear as understanding as possible in this impossible situation. "It's simply because children are different."

Jaw clenched, he shook his head. "No, they're not. They just have to wait longer for their vengeance. I ensured we aren't waiting along with them."

"It's the *guilt* that is different." I took his face in my hands gently. "You already carry so much, my love. You don't need this on top of it."

"It was the only way."

"But why didn't you tell me?"

"I didn't want to burden you..."

"That's my job, in every facet of my life — as your husband, as your partner, your lawyer. Lean on me. I promise I won't break."

"I'm afraid I will," he whispered, tears welling in his eyes. "And I'd never forgive myself if I destroyed you in the process."

The minute I wrapped my arms around him, a sob racked his body. He clung to me like a life preserver, while I ran a hand over his hair and whispered small assurances.

This was the part about being a villain that no one ever

saw. You already knew what you were doing was wrong by society's standards, but you did it anyway, be it for love or hate or whatever fucking reason you came up with.

Leander claimed he was a monster, but monsters had no conscience. Monsters destroyed everyone and everything around them and went to sleep peacefully at night. They were brilliant liars, *especially* to themselves.

If I'd never met Leander, or if I'd walked away after he was arrested, none of this would have ever happened. Cole and Olivia would still be alive. Leander would still be in one piece. Life would have carried on as usual for so many different people.

But I stayed. I refused to give up the love of my life for entirely selfish reasons. I knew it was wrong, and I did anyway. I was also the one who slept peacefully at night.

Guess I wasn't a villain, after all.

I was the fucking monster.

37

BENNETT

Driving for what felt like hours to the middle of bum-fuck Missouri in the dead of night was not how I envisioned my evening. Following Leander's sporadic commands, we finally turned off the road and bumped along a hard-packed drive to a pair of silos. If I would have known we were basically going off-roading, I would have insisted on taking Leander's SUV and not my poor Maserati.

Jake's truck was there, along with Elijah's SUV.

The car was barely in park before Leander bailed out the passenger door and ducked into one of the silos.

In a surprising flash of déjà vu, I was reminded of my bonding time with Jake up north. Instead of a drunk has-been security guard, another man was strung up before me in the center of the silo. Chained around the waist with his arms pinned to his sides, he dangled from the beam overhead. He was bleeding profusely from his face, but he was still alive.

Elijah and Jake were on the opposite side of the silo, glaring daggers at the human pendulum. Both of them were wearing leather gloves, perfect for a beatdown.

"This is the piece of shit," Jake said when Leander got closer. He emphasized his point by punching the man in the kidney.

The man cried out, swinging back and forth with the force. "Look man, I just make 'em! Ok. I don't know who they're for or why!"

Jake responded by punching him again, this time in the other kidney. I nodded approvingly of the choice. It seemed he really did retain the knowledge I passed along with the Parkview employees.

"He says he didn't plant it," Elijah added with a sneer. "He *mailed* it to an address."

"An address where?" Leander asked, his voice surprisingly calm.

"I don't know."

Jake stepped up behind him and drove a screwdriver into the man's thigh. Plucking it back out, he snuck a glance at me. I gave him a thumbs up.

"Fuck! Ok! It was in Illinois!"

"Wonderful," Leander growled, shifting his dark gaze to me as well. "There's only twelve million people in Illinois. Should we start alphabetically or geographically?"

Jake lifted the screwdriver, feinting another blow to his leg.

The man yelped and closed his eyes. "No, no! I remember the name! Holliday. The guy's name was Holliday!"

Leander surged forward, shoving Jake out of the way and grabbing a handful of the man's shirt to stop him from swinging. "Cole Holliday? You're telling me you mailed a fucking bomb to Cole Holliday?"

The guy shook his head, cringing. "No. No. It was someone else with that name. Dan. David."

"Dale?" Elijah asked, stepping forward out of the shadows.

The bomb maker nodded emphatically, tears and sweat pouring down his face. "Yeah! Yeah, that's the guy! Dale Holliday!"

Leander's teeth clenched and I watched as anger transformed to pure fury. He shoved away from the man, taking three unsteady steps backward.

I exhaled a long, slow breath, putting it all together. That's what that fucker was doing there Holyrood. He wasn't after a payout from Cole. Or maybe he was. Either way, he was there planting a bomb for Gianna Scardato in an attempt to wipe us all out at his son's funeral.

"He was there," Elijah said, his voice hollow. "He was fucking *there*, Leander! He killed her. For all we know, he fucking killed Cole too!"

"I know. I'll handle it," Leander said, his voice eerily pleasant considering the look on his face. "Do it."

Upon command, each of them took a gas can and sloshed it over the man. Diesel *and* gasoline. The smells were unmistakable. It was so wicked, it made me all warm and fuzzy inside.

The man continued to scream and plead for mercy, sputtering when Jake splashed the fuel directly into his face. It fell on deaf ears all around.

As soon as the pair emptied their gas cans and tossed them to the side, Leander reached inside his coat pocket and pulled out a small book of matches. I couldn't help but notice they were from the coffee shop next to the office, the very same coffee shop Leander first met Olivia at. Maybe it was a coincidence.

"No! Please, for the love of God!" The man screamed. "I'll tell you whatever you want! Just please don't do this!" When bargaining didn't work, he switched to straight up groveling. "I'm sorry! I'll do anything you want! Please! I'm so sorry!"

"Oh, I'm sure you are," Leander replied, his brows dipping

in understanding. "Unfortunately for you, it's too little, too late." To emphasize his point, he struck a match and held it aloft. Without even blinking, he flicked it at the man.

The tiny flame caught the gasoline fumes and 'whooshed' upwards, spreading over the man's body.

Stepping up to Leander's side, I laced my fingers through his and squeezed his hand. I may not have been part of this plan, but I was immensely proud of how it all turned out. I was even happier he got justice for Olivia. Hopefully it would be one less ghost to haunt him.

Together, we watched the man twist and writhe in front of us. His screams turned to howling as his skin blistered and popped, charring as the fire sat on top of the slow-burning diesel.

It was an excruciating way to die. I didn't feel one ounce of remorse for the man.

"Change of plans, gentlemen," Leander said, rolling his head from side to side to crack his neck. "You're going to have to finish here. Jake — your keys."

Obediently, Jake tossed his keys over.

I stepped in front of Leander as he turned to go. "Where are you going now?"

"Go home. You'll have plausible deniability."

"I can't believe I am actually telling you this, but you can't just charge in there and kill someone. We need a plan, Leander."

He shook his head and darted around me, striding to Jake's truck. "That man dies tonight. I don't care if I go back to jail."

"Well *I* fucking care. I just got you back!" I snapped, hurrying after him. "Can we take a second and think—"

Leander spun quickly, his fist flying outward. Not toward my face, thankfully, but right in my diaphragm. Fucking asshole.

"Je suis désolé, mon coeur," he whispered as I doubled over, trying to breathe. Sorry, my ass!

By the time I could stand upright again, he was speeding down the road, angry dust clouds spewing out behind him.

Wheezing, I stumbled around the side of my car and flopped into the driver's seat. I didn't bother calling him. I knew where he was going and I knew what was going to happen once he got there.

DALE HOLLIDAY LIVED in the same decrepit trailer Cole spent a quarter of his childhood in, in the same rundown trailer park on the outskirts of Easton. Half of it had been ripped away in a tornado a few years ago. Cole lamented it didn't take his father too. Leander was on his way to rectify that.

I caught up to Leander once we made it back across the river, speeding and swerving along behind him as he tore through the sleeping countryside. There was no stealth involved. No swapping cars or wearing different clothes. None of the intelligence either of us typically used in our crimes.

Nope, we drove right up to Dale's trailer at the end of the row and parked like we were there to drop off a fucking casserole.

Leander kicked the driver's door open and snatched something out of the bed of the truck while I was still trying to put my car in park. He didn't acknowledge my presence before he rushed inside, as dark as a shadow.

I didn't even bother closing my car door. I bolted after him, in time to hear a thud, a surprised "oof!" and an even louder thud.

When I burst through the door, Cole's dad was sprawled on the floor. Leander stood over him, holding something long in his hand. Dale didn't ask any questions — it seemed he knew the reason for our visit. That didn't mean he was going down without a fight.

Thanks to me breaking his kneecap, the asshole wasn't able to move very fast. But he was still a sizable man, so when he punched the side of Leander's knee, it dropped him like a sack of potatoes. Once they were more or less level, Dale swung a beer bottle at Leander's head. The brown glass shattered, knocking Leander to the side.

Dale heaved himself onto his belly and started crawling away. Where he thought he was going, I had no idea. I didn't give him the opportunity to get very far before I stomped on the back of his knee, right where I'd broken it previously.

He roared in pain, freezing in place.

Leander was on his feet again, favoring his left leg. Blood dripped down the side of his face, but he didn't seem the least bit concerned. Hefting something in his hands, he brought it down on the back of Dale's head in one heavy blow.

Dale's skull split like a watermelon, splattering gore everywhere. When Leander lifted it a second time, I finally saw what it was. A sledgehammer. Way more effective than his usual weapon of choice, I'd give him that.

After the third hit, Dale's head ceased being a recognizable object.

A pile of pulverized goo was all that remained by the time Leander's arms gave out. Gasping for each breath, he dropped the sledgehammer a second before he collapsed.

I caught him from behind and dragged him back, out of the circle of carnage. Blood and sweat were smeared across his face. His hands, likewise, were dark and wet. His whole body shook like a leaf and I really hoped Jake had some hillbilly snack in the truck like jerky, or seeds of some sort. I'd take anything to keep Leander from passing out.

"You're not supposed to be here." His scolding was far less effective when he had to speak between labored panting.

"Oh yeah? Where am I supposed to be?"

"As far away from me as possible. Somewhere safe."

He tried to pull out of my arms, but I held on to him, nuzzling the side of his face. "Don't start with that curse bullshit. I don't believe in curses and even if I did, I'm not going anywhere. You'll have to get rid of me the old fashioned way."

"Murder?"

I laughed, squeezing him just a little bit tighter. "I was going to go with divorce, but yeah, that works too, I guess."

When his breathing finally slowed and his heart rate returned to normal, I loosened my grip. "Let's go home."

Still shaking, Leander got to his feet and hobbled toward the door. He paused at the threshold, glancing over his shoulder. "Aren't you coming?"

"Just a sec."

Wandering into the small kitchen, I ran a finger along the top of the dirty oven hood. Wiping twenty-five years' worth of grease and hair off my finger on a towel, I turned and grabbed a crusty pan from the sink. I snagged a package of bacon from the fridge and tore into it, dumping the entire slab into the pan and turning the flame on high.

Whistling to myself, I bounced on the balls of my feet, checking the time on my pocket watch. Given the late hour, all of the volunteer firemen were guaranteed to be home, snuggled warm in their beds. Even if a neighbor saw and called right away, there was no way they were getting dressed, to the station, on a rig, and out to this shithole in time to save it. Their primary concern would most definitely be the neighboring trailers.

Once there was a good amount of grease in the pan, I angled it toward the flame. Just like the bomb maker, the fire 'whooshed' over the bacon and sparked up like a bonfire.

"Oh, goodness. Whatever shall I do?" I said to myself in faux horror. I shoved the flaming pan to the back of the stove, near the wall, and grabbed a cup full of water from the sink.

I preempted my toss by turning my face away and angling most of my body in the opposite direction. As soon as the water hit the grease, it splattered sending flaming droplets everywhere.

Refilling the cup, I took a couple steps back before launching the next round at the sputtering fire.

Success.

The flames lurched up onto the wall and raced to the disgusting oven hood. From there, they went straight to the ceiling. Tossing the cup over my shoulder, I headed for the door.

Exiting the trailer quickly, I waved away a plume of black smoke from my face as I descended the stairs, trying not to cough and accidentally inhale the toxic cloud.

Leander was in Jake's truck with the window rolled down. The concern lining his face didn't dissipate until after I leapt up onto the running board.

Hanging on to the door frame, I leaned in the window, pressing my lips against his. He tasted like beer and blood, with just a hint of smoke.

"You need a shower," I said, bonking my forehead to his.

"You're one to talk." A hint of a smile curled the edge of his mouth. "You smell like bacon."

Smirking, I kissed him again and hopped off the side of the truck. "I'll race you home."

38

BENNETT

Once Leander effectively dealt with his demons surrounding Olivia and Cole's murders, it was time to double-down on Gianna. Between the information Kai tracked down and what we lifted from the FBI, we formulated our plan down to a T.

In celebration, I actually managed to talk Leander into going *out* for dinner. Grudgingly, he chose the steak house in Clairsville and away we went.

"You know I make better," he muttered between bites of his filet.

"Yes, my love, but I don't feel like doing dishes tonight."

"What *do* you feel like doing?"

Cocking my head, I shot him an incredulous look from across the table. I couldn't quite tell if he was messing with me or not. From the way he smirked before sipping his wine, I quickly figured out the answer.

Wiping my mouth with my napkin, I hailed the waiter as he floated by. "Check please."

"It was *your* idea to go out," Leander murmured.

"If you would have clarified what was on the menu,

perhaps I would have chosen differently," I said as I stood and pulled out my wallet, throwing down a couple hundreds instead of waiting for the man to come back with the bill.

"Perhaps?" He raised his brows at me.

"You can be such a smart ass sometimes." Grabbing Leander's hand, I hauled him out of his chair and yanked him toward the door.

"Are you the pot today, or the kettle?" he asked with a chuckle.

As soon as we got to the car, he pushed me up against the side of it, slanting his mouth over mine. I was surprised, more for the fact he was being so openly affectionate in public, but I wasn't going to stop to point it out.

"How fast is this thing?" he asked, fumbling behind me for the door handle.

"Zero to sixty in four point seven seconds," I mumbled against his lips right before he pushed me down into the driver's seat.

"Good." He licked his lips and shut my car door. As soon as he was in the passenger seat, I put the four hundred fifty-four horses to the test.

We were halfway between Clairsville and Easton when a flash of red in my rearview mirror caught my eye. Squinting at the sudden glare of headlights, I adjusted the mirror, trying to get a better look at the vehicle. It pulled out when we passed, which wouldn't have been strange were it not for the fact they were speeding to catch up to us. "Check out that car behind us."

Leander adjusted the side mirror. "Weren't they at the restaurant earlier?"

"That's what I thought." I punched the gas and sped off down the road, turning at the first intersection I came to. At the next intersection, I turned again. A quarter mile later, the goddamn road turned to gravel. It better not fuck up my undercarriage.

"Do you know where you're going?" Leander asked.

"Not a clue."

"Turn left up here."

I did as instructed, looking back the way we came and swearing. Not only was the red car still there, it was catching up. It went from an odd coincidence to bad news, just like that.

Trying to accelerate, the tires ended up throwing more gravel than anything. "Get us the fuck off of these roads!"

"The next road turns to blacktop again. Turn right."

I whipped the car according to his instruction, keeping an eye on the headlights gaining ground.

As soon as the tires touched smooth pavement, the Maserati surged forward and I let out the breath I'd been holding.

"I think they're gone," Leander said, looking behind us.

"Let's hope—" I yanked the wheel to the right, narrowly avoiding the front end of a black car that screamed into the intersection from my left. "That fucker just tried to T-bone us!"

"This isn't good, Bennett." Leander was watching the side mirror, gripping the arm rest on the door. "The red car is back."

"Get us to the highway and I can lose them."

The speedometer climbed higher as I sped down the road. Every time the black car tried to pass, I swerved to block them. I was not about to let these assholes box me in.

"Persistent, aren't they?" Leander mused.

"Who knew date night would be so exciting?"

The red car caught up, meanwhile the black car fell back so they were driving side-by-side. A curve in the road meant I had to slow down or flip. They took the opportunity to lurch forward, the black car to my left and the red car right on my ass.

The railroad crossing up ahead lit up like a beacon in the darkness. The warning bells dinged rhythmically, accompanied by the flashing red lights.

"Hold on," I said, flooring it.

Leander braced one hand on the dash, staring straight ahead with wide eyes. "Bennett..."

The black car dropped off and fell behind, but the red car was still in pursuit.

The train and I raced for the crossing. It barreled in from the west, while I floored it from the south.

Clenching my teeth and the steering wheel, I tried to ignore Leander's panicked breathing next to me. I had faith in my car. He needed to have some in me. Back to that whole trust thing we needed to work on.

"The train," Leander spit out, shrinking into his seat.

The conductor must have seen us coming, since he laid on the horn. Sparks flew as he threw on the brakes, but we all knew there was no way it would ever stop in time.

"Bennett, for fuck's sake! It's physics!"

"Memento mori," I said with a small smile.

The Maserati's engine roared.

The train horn blasted.

The front of my car smashed through the railroad arm.

The Maserati sailed across the tracks, clearing the front of the train by a hair.

I let the car decelerate for a bit before I applied the brakes and pulled over.

We made it.

We fucking made it!

As much as I wanted to cheer, I knew my enthusiasm wouldn't be well received. Swallowing hard, I turned to

Leander to apologize, but he threw the door open and hurled himself out of it.

He was still on his hands and knees, vomiting up the remnants of dinner on the side of the road, when I finally freed myself from my seatbelt and rushed over to him.

"Breathe," I said, shaking out my handkerchief and wiping his mouth with it. "You're ok. We made it."

"Don't!" He all but snarled, pushing away from me roughly. "You're going to fucking kill me one of these days!"

I frowned, watching him get to his feet slowly and stagger back to the car. He didn't even let me close his door for him. That maneuver was probably worse than Venice, admittedly, but it's not like I *planned* it. It just worked out that way.

Cringing, I slid into the driver's seat. "Guess your math was a little off, huh?"

For the first time in my sober life, I was actually afraid when Leander turned his gaze on me. I was fairly certain sex was *off* the table for the rest of the night. Probably the rest of the week with how pissed he was. Maybe the month...

We continued down the road in silence. Every time I wanted to say something, I thought better of it. I could practically feel the heat rolling off of him.

I was so preoccupied with formulating the appropriate apology in my head I wasn't even paying attention to the fact a pair of headlights appeared in the rearview mirror until they were too close for comfort.

Gradually applying more pressure to the gas pedal, I tried to accelerate without Leander noticing. I mean, he was staring out the window, but that didn't mean he was actually seeing anything in the blackened landscape.

The headlights kept coming.

"I know you're mad at me right now," I said quietly, stealing a glance at him. "But we're not alone anymore."

His head whipped up and he turned in his seat. "You've got to be kidding me."

"I wish I were."

"Take the next right. We can lose them right after Salsberry Bridge."

Nodding, I braked hard and drifted around the corner.

The black car did the same thing.

Just like the train, it was a race to the bridge. Except, the black car had a better engine than I would have liked since I couldn't gain much ground.

The headlights behind me jerked to the left suddenly. His front end smashed into my rear quarter panel and the cars ground together, despite the fact the needle on the speedometer shot over seventy.

In that moment, I knew what he was doing and there wasn't a damn thing I could do to stop it.

"Brace," I said as the back end of my car swung out to the side.

"What?"

"Brace!"

The black car steered right into us, whipping the Maserati into a spin. I yanked the wheel to the side, steering into the skid. My arms felt like they were going to break from the force, but I couldn't stop trying to undo that asshole's pit maneuver.

It didn't matter in the end.

The world turned upside down, literally, as my car flipped. I saw the ground at least three times as the car rolled into the field. The only saving grace was that we didn't plummet into the river.

Glass shattered and metal groaned. The airbags exploded, burning my hands and releasing a haze of powder into the cabin. The seatbelt tightened to the point where I couldn't breathe. My head cracked against the window, along with my left arm.

When the car finally came to a stop, it was on its roof.

Coughing, I clawed at my seatbelt, trying to disengage it.

"Leander?"

There was no answer.

I groped at the buckle until I found the release button. Landing with a thud on the roof of my car, I hissed as shards of glass ground into my palms. "Come on. We gotta go."

Dangling from his seatbelt, blood dripped from his hair. He didn't move, and he still didn't answer.

My head was killing me, but it didn't even come close to the fear crushing my heart. I did my best to support him as I hit the release on his seatbelt. He dropped to the roof limply.

"Leander." I pulled his head into my lap, patting his cheek. "Wake up." I felt for a pulse, but my hand was shaking too much to tell if I actually found one or not.

"Wake up!" Something wet rolled down my face, blood or tears or both. I grabbed his jacket and shook him, panic twisting inside of me. "Leander!"

He didn't move.

Someone grabbed me from behind and yanked me out the shattered window.

"No!" I tried to kick them off and hang onto Leander, or the steering wheel, the seatbelt. Something. Anything. But my fingers kept slipping with the blood and the person behind me was too strong.

The hands wouldn't budge, ripping me away like I was nothing.

I only caught a glimpse of black boots before I was shoved face-first into the ground. Someone drove their knee into the middle of my back, practically crushing me. In the midst of it all, there was a familiar stabbing sensation in my arm, followed by nothing.

39

BENNETT

The next time I woke up, it was on a concrete floor. Again. For someone used to a supportive, memory foam mattress, it was getting really fucking old. But, unlike the first time, my hands weren't tied. In fact, as far as I could tell, I wasn't restrained at all.

I pushed myself into a sitting position and looked around, deflating again. Another one of Giovanni's warehouses. Fucking perfect.

As soon as I spied a heap of black off to one side, my heart seized.

"Leander?"

Between the pain and the sedative, getting to my feet was a bit of a struggle but I managed it. Staggering over to him, I dropped to my knees and rolled him over. There was dried blood on the side of his face, along with a dozen new cuts from the glass.

"Leander!"

At least he was warm. Just to be on the safe side, I settled his head in my lap and checked for a pulse anyway. It was there. Thank God.

His eyelashes fluttered, but he didn't open his eyes.

"My love." I cradled him gently, grabbing one of his hands and folding it over his chest to make it easier to hold. "Wake up. Please, wake up."

He squeezed my hand weakly.

A wave of relief crashed over me. Tears stung my eyes as I pressed my lips to his, trying to keep myself from bawling like a baby.

He tried to kiss me back, but his breathing was more of a wheeze. Our lips touched for no more than a second before he pulled back with a grimace.

Helping him into a sitting position, I wrapped my arms around him, guiding him backward to lean against me. "Are you ok? Tell me what hurts." I tried to rake through his dark curls to see if there were any serious head wounds to tend to, but they were even more unruly than usual thanks to dried blood and dirt.

He pressed a hand to his head and sucked in a pained hiss.

"Talk to me!" This was *not* the time to be stoic about anything. If we were going to make it out of his warehouse, I needed to know what kind of condition he was in.

"I'll live," he replied, his voice raw.

"Not for much longer," a female voice said, accompanied by the sound of high heels tapping across the floor.

Easing away from Leander, I made sure he could sit upright on his own before I got to my feet slowly, assessing this newest threat.

The woman in front of me was none other than Gianna Scardato, flanked by Paulie and two of her other goons. Our game of cat and mouse had come to an end at last. Unfortunately for us, it was on her turf, which put us at a serious disadvantage.

She strolled forward with a smirk, her platform heels grinding on the concrete with each exaggerated step. Her hands were tucked inside her fur coat, more than likely pointing a gun right at me. She would have been an idiot if she came to this little meet-and-greet unarmed.

"I can't believe it," she said with a laugh. "The infamous Bennett Reeve. In the flesh." One hand slipped out of her pocket, empty, and caressed the side of my face. "Finally."

At six feet, I wasn't the tallest person but I easily dwarfed the Italian princess. Seizing her wrist, I dragged her a step closer, bending down so she could hear me clearly. "Touch me again and I'll break your fucking arm." I sent her staggering backward with one shove and immediately squared off against the goon who rushed forward.

Leander appeared at my side, somewhat evening the odds, even though he didn't look like he was in the best fighting shape.

Regaining her footing, Gianna laughed and waved off her dogs. "Easy boys. You'll have your fun soon enough."

"If you're going to kill us, just kill us. You've been trying for months, so get it over with," I spat, looking Paulie up and down. He was a meaty fellow. He wouldn't go down easily. "Otherwise, quit wasting our fucking time."

"Not if, sweetie. *When.*" Gianna flashed a smile, all bright-white teeth and matte, burgundy lips. "I wanna talk to you first."

"Aw, shucks. I'm not in the mood."

"I think I can help with that." She turned to Paulie, pointing a long nail at Leander. "Start with that one."

"No!" It was my thought, but not my voice. In fact, the scream came from the last person I ever thought I'd hear.

Lorelei fucking Clayton.

Appearing from the direction of the office, her eyes were wide, her breathing rapid either from the sprint or a sudden dose of panic. Probably both.

"That wasn't the deal!" she said to Gianna, swallowing thickly.

Excuse me, what? Did that bitch just say *deal*? I stole a glance at Leander. He gave me a nearly imperceptible shrug. Great. This obviously wasn't something he cooked up behind my back, which meant neither of us knew how it was going to play out.

"He wasn't supposed to get hurt. Remember? You said he was bait and that you'd let him go." Lorelei's voice may have lowered, but I heard enough. She used my husband as fucking *bait* to get to *me*. I might have admired her tenacity if I wasn't two seconds away from ripping her throat out.

"He was. Two for the price of one," Gianna replied with a sickeningly sweet smile. "Thanks Doc. You turned out to be a real catch. I'm glad Paulie here did a deep dive into Reeve's background, otherwise we probably wouldn't have found your man over there. Or, ex-man I guess."

"Please, Gianna." Lorelei was actually crying now. Unbelievable. "Don't kill Leander. I'm begging you. He's already suffered enough. Let me take him out of here and you'll never have to worry about him again. I promise."

I didn't bother holding back a snort. There's no way in hell Leander would ever walk away and leave Gianna alone after this fucking cluster. Lorelei was a fucking idiot for even trying to lie and say that he would.

Gianna sighed dramatically and looked over at Paulie. He raised his brows at her but didn't say anything or give any obvious clue as to what he was thinking.

At last, Gianna clapped her hands. "I got it. Since Mr. Reeve is so fond of deals, I've got one for you."

I didn't like the glint in her eye when she turned back to me, continuing with a sugary cheeriness that made me want to slap her. "One of you *will* walk out of here. Alive. Which one will depend entirely on you two. The choice is yours."

Leander moved closer to me, his fingers brushing mine.

"What are you talking about?" I asked, slipping my hand into his completely.

Strutting over to Paulie, she whispered something and held her hand out like a spoiled brat waiting for her weekly allowance. He coughed up whatever she wanted, but it was too small to see what it was. Sauntering back to us, she tossed it at my feet with another plastered-on smile.

It was a switchblade.

"You two can decide who lives and who dies. The choice is totally yours," she announced brightly.

Neither Leander nor I moved.

Pouting, Gianna gestured to Paulie, who lifted his gun, pointing it at Leander. "Let me be clear, boys. One of you *will* kill the other one, or you'll *both* get a bullet in the head. Along with everyone else you've ever cared about. Elijah?" She looked pointedly at Leander before her gaze flicked to me. "Allegra?"

"Well, what are you waiting for?" I asked, spreading my arms and calling her bluff. She knew their names. Big deal. Threatening someone across the Atlantic without actual proof you could pull it off was an amateur move. Her uncle should have taught her better 'cuz Lord knows her father didn't. "Let's get this massacre underway."

Before my brain could even comprehend what it was seeing, there was movement in my periphery. Leander stepped forward and swiped the knife off the ground. Releasing the blade as he lifted it to his throat, bright red spilled down his pale skin.

Lorelei and I both screamed "No!" in unison.

I threw myself at him and wrestled his arm downward before he could cut any deeper.

"Let go of me," Leander growled, trying to either shake off my hand or bring the blade back up to finish the job.

"So you can kill yourself? Absolutely not!" I glared at him with a combination of anger and betrayal, driving my thumb into the pressure point in his wrist. It made zero difference in getting him to drop the knife or even loosen his grip.

"Better me than you. I'm half-dead anyway."

"Don't say that."

"I'm not afraid, Bennett. Let me do this for you."

I didn't answer him, because I knew he wasn't lying. Nor was it some romantic gesture. He wasn't afraid of death, he never had been. Not like me. And he was using that fear against me now to be the fucking hero — the *last* thing I ever wanted him to be.

"'The boundaries which divide Life from Death are at best shadowy and vague. Who shall say where the one ends, and where the other begins?'" he continued, his gaze imploring.

I shook my head vehemently, molars grinding together. I wouldn't be swayed by Poe any more than the sad expression on his face. "No. Don't even say it."

"You *have* to." He pressed the knife into my palm, forcefully squeezing my fingers around the handle. "You have to live, Bennett, for both of us. Or this has all been for nothing."

"There is no living without you." The thought alone nearly struck me down where I stood. I couldn't go along with this ridiculous fucking demand. I *wouldn't.*

Leander cupped my face with his bloody hand, brushing his thumb across my cheek. "Memento mori, mon coeur."

"Don't make them do this," Lorelei said to Gianna, grabbing hold of her with both hands. "Please. Please, I'm begging you."

Gianna tugged her hand free, her nose wrinkled. "You can go now, Doc. Your part is over. Unless Reeve is the one who bites it. I know you really wanted to see that happen."

My glare snapped at Lorelei, but Leander caught my face and turned it toward him again.

I couldn't see him through my tears. Even though I kept shaking my head, it didn't stop him from pulling my hand, and the knife, closer to his abdomen.

"I love you," he said softly, nodding in encouragement.

There really was no alternative. In the span of seconds, my mind churned through hundreds of scenarios, as his presumably had as well. This was it. This was the only way one of us would make it through and make sure the other was avenged.

"I love you," I whispered against his lips. I kissed him gently, then harder in the hopes of distracting him as the blade pierced his abdomen.

He inhaled sharply and exhaled a painful gasp. The hand guiding mine tightened, while his other clung to my shoulder.

"Again," Gianna commanded.

"No!" Lorelei yelled.

"Zip it," Gianna snarled at her before turning to me. "Again. In fact, make it five, just like my dad got. If Mr. Welles can dish it out, he should be able to take it."

Leander's eyes were already glassy, but he held my gaze and nodded.

Swallowing hard, I pulled the knife out. Before he had time to feel the full agony of its removal, I plunged it into him.

Biting his lip, he leaned against me and buried his face into my chest.

"I'm sorry," I whispered, holding him tightly as I sunk it into him again.

Blood poured to the ground, splattering like crimson paint over our shoes. Never before had the smell of copper and salt nauseated me so much.

His grip on my jacket started to falter and I prayed I had the strength to keep him upright. Every agonized gasp he took was like I was stabbing myself. Every ragged breath that escaped him, escaped me. He refused to scream or make any noise beyond an anguished whimper now and again.

After the fifth stab, I left the knife in. What good it would do, I didn't know. It was like putting a bandaid on a gunshot wound at this point. Who cared if one wound was stoppered while four others bled freely?

Lorelei sobbed behind us, but I couldn't afford to think about her and the hell that was coming her way. There would be plenty of time for that later.

Leander shook violently as I lowered him to the floor. Pressing his own hands over the wounds, I hoped he didn't realize how badly mine were trembling. He was counting on me to be the strong one. I couldn't lose it now, even as the blood oozed out between his fingers. With each passing second, his pale skin turned more ashen beneath the beads of sweat dotting his forehead.

"I'm so sorry," I whispered, cradling him against me.

His eyes drifted closed, his breathing so shallow it was practically non-existent. The blood continued to drain out of him, the sheen on his black suit spreading by the minute. The hand furthest away from me fell limp, another rush of blood chasing after it from the uncovered wound.

I bit back a scream, refusing to give either of those bitches the satisfaction.

"Aw, isn't that sweet," Gianna said with a laugh, snapping her fingers at her oversized dogs. "It's like a fairytale. Except no singing and way more blood."

Rough hands seized each of my arms, ripping me away from Leander. They dragged me backward, streaking his blood across the concrete, before they finally lifted me to my feet. I didn't fight them. All I could do was stare at the love of my life and the crimson puddle seeping out beneath him in an ever-widening radius.

"Go on. Get out of here. Both of you. Before I change my fucking mind," Gianna said, waving Lorelei and I away with a flick of her wrist.

Instead of leaving, Lorelei darted forward, shoving past Gianna. She fell to her knees next to Leander and immediately got to work, stuffing her wadded up coat under his feet. Fabric ripped, hers and his. She tore open his shirt and rent the sleeves off her own blouse as makeshift gauze.

"You're not doing this to me again!" Lorelei said, pressing the fabric over his wounds.

A gunshot rang out. Lorelei screamed.

I didn't even turn my head. The emotions inside of me died in the wake of that blast, flicked off like a light switch.

Throwing off the hands holding me, my right fist flew outward, aimed at the man on my left. It landed directly in the center of his windpipe. He gasped and clutched his throat, dropping to his knees and out of my way.

The second guy grabbed the back of my jacket and slung me around like a rag doll. I crash-landed against a shipping crate. He advanced swiftly, kicking me in the abdomen. Luckily I had enough time to exhale, absorbing most of the blow even though it still hurt like a son of a bitch. I caught his boot on the second kick, slowing most of the force, and yanked it forward. He lost his footing and toppled over, landing hard on the concrete.

I lunged at him while he was still flat on his back, clamping my fingers around either side of his trachea. He tried to push my hands away, gasping and gurgling, but I dug my fingers in deeper until the cartilage crunched and collapsed. I would have torn the whole thing out, except for the boot that kicked me away from the dead man.

Scrambling to my feet, I came face-to-face with Paulie. He had a gun leveled at me, but I didn't care. Even if he got a shot off, it wouldn't be well-aimed and it certainly wouldn't be enough to stop me unless he somehow managed to plant one in my brain.

Closing the distance on him quickly, I grabbed the gun in my left hand, seizing his wrist with the other. I twisted the gun downward and to the side, adding additional pain to the pressure point I'd tried to use against Leander earlier.

Like a twisted dance, Paulie spun in the direction I was pushing, trying to alleviate the tension I was putting on his gun-hand. In the midst of it, he head butted me. The angle was off and he missed his mark, but his forehead still connected solidly with my cheek. A burst of pain sparked in my face but I shook it off quickly.

Fueled by rage and impatience, I heaved my weight downward. The effort was rewarded with a loud "snap."

Paulie screamed and let go.

I ripped the gun off of his mangled finger and promptly put a bullet in the center of his forehead. The first guy, having regained control of his breathing, made a beeline for the exit. He got one in the back of the head before I turned the gun to Gianna.

Breathing hard, I canted my head as I studied her. "Well, well, princess. Bet this wasn't the happily ever after you were expecting."

Gianna had her own gun drawn, but it hung uselessly at her side. Black tracks ran beneath both eyes and her lower lip quivered.

Leander stood behind her, one hand around her throat. In his other, he clutched the switchblade, still glistening with his own blood. His mouth was lowered against her ear and his lips were moving, but I couldn't make out what he was saying. Whatever it was made her cry harder.

"My family will come for you," Gianna said, the waver in her voice betraying the confidence of her words.

"They can try," I replied with a dark smile.

Leander and I locked eyes, electricity simmering between us.

"'The death, then, of a beautiful woman is, unquestionably, the most poetical topic in the world,'" he murmured against her ear with a chilling calmness. I thought he was going to finish off Poe's essay, but he didn't.

He lifted the switchblade and drove it into the side of Gianna's neck. With one quick motion, he pushed the blade forward, slicing through her trachea and her vocal cords. Blood sprayed in front of her in an arc, gushing out so fast it sounded like someone turned on a faucet.

As soon as she collapsed, I surged forward and seized Leander's face between my hands, claiming his mouth with frantic kisses. He dropped the knife and clung to my jacket, gasping for breath between his return kisses.

"Sit down," I said suddenly, pushing him onto a crate.

He hissed, clutching his abdomen. It did little good. He had too many wounds and not enough hands. Blood continued to drip beneath him wherever he moved. "Where's Lorelei?"

"Fuck if I know and fuck if I care. If that bitch isn't dead already, she's going to be soon enough." I ripped my jacket off and pressed it over his stomach. The makeshift bandages Lorelei tied in place were already soaked through.

"There," he said, tipping his chin.

I touched his cheek gently, keeping my frown to a minimum. I wanted to tell him "No," and that I could give two shits about her, but I couldn't refuse him anything after the torment I just put him through. Clenching my jaw, I walked over to where Lorelei's heels were sticking out from behind a junked vehicle.

Sadly, she was alive. The gunshot I heard earlier was meant for her, not Leander. Except, Gianna was a terrible shot and only got the bitch in the shoulder instead of the head.

When Lorelei saw me, her eyes widened. She tried backing up, but there was nowhere to go.

"You stupid, self-righteous fucking bitch." Grabbing her by the throat, I hauled her to her feet like a fucking life-size Barbie.

She screamed, a combination of surprise and pain that ended in a strangle cry the harder I squeezed, hopefully cutting off her air and her blood flow. Fear radiated out of her so strongly I could practically smell it.

Dragging her back to Leander, I threw her at his feet like I was paying tribute to a conquering warlord.

"What do you want to do with her, my love?" I asked, sorting through the punishments in my mind. "Stab her five times? Shoot her in the fucking head? Or how about I take her down to the river and drown her?"

She turned her terrified gaze to Leander, tears welling again. "Leander..."

I dropped to one knee behind her and snatched a handful of her hair, yanking her head back. "I'll make it quick this time. Promise. I won't do you dirty like you did to us."

She shrieked and clawed at my hands.

Leander watched the two of us, silent pain etched into his face. He needed to get to a hospital, not dick around with this bitch anymore. She'd already cost him enough.

"I'm sorry," Lorelei said. "Leander, please. I'm *so* sorry. I didn't know she was going to do this. You have to believe me. She said she only wanted him! She only—"

I pulled even harder on her hair. I don't know what planet she was living on, but an apology would never suffice for a betrayal like that. "What the fuck did you think was going to happen?!"

"It was just supposed to be *you*!" she screamed back at me, hatred lacing every word. "*You* were the only one who was supposed to get hurt, you fucking asshole!"

I laughed darkly. So much for that fucking plan. "I'm going to enjoy watching you die."

Leander lifted his gaze to mine. He blinked slowly and shook his head once.

"You wouldn't be here if it wasn't for her," I snarled in response, my fingers tightening in her hair.

He gave me a sad smile. "I know. But you would have, and you would have been alone."

"I had no idea—" Lorelei's defense ended in a squeak when I jerked her head back even farther.

"Shut up," I growled. "You don't get to play the victim."

Tears streamed down her cheeks. She whimpered, but didn't say anything. She'd probably worked out she was safer that way.

Leander's voice cut through my rage. "Mon coeur..." When I looked up, he held his hand out to me, palm up.

I begrudgingly let go of Lorelei. And by let go, I mean I shoved her away from me as forcefully as I could and stepped over her trembling body to get back to my husband. Taking his hand, I helped him to his feet and looped an arm around his waist to keep him steady.

"Let's go home," Leander murmured.

"But, she—"

He shook his head, silencing my outrage. "She saved my life. If not now, then before." His gaze fell to Lorelei, his ashen face hard. "I'll give her this one reprieve."

I glowered, my molars grinding together. That was *not* what I was hoping he would say. Not even fucking close.

"But," he continued, reigniting hope. "You would do well to keep your distance. If our paths cross again, Dr. Clayton, in *any* capacity, I will let Bennett do whatever he wants to you for as long as he wants to do it. Understood?"

Lorelei nodded meekly, her lower lip trembling.

It wasn't an immediate green light, but I was willing to take a rain check. She wouldn't be able to stay away. I could tell that from the first time I saw her look at him.

We limped toward the door as quickly as Leander could go. I snagged one of the Italian's cell phones on the way out and called Gavin. In no time, he picked us up around the corner from the warehouse, probably breaking about fifteen different traffic laws along the way. I definitely owed him another raise.

"Oh my God! Is that blood?" Gavin said, eyes wide as Leander slumped across the backseat.

"Hospital. Now," I replied, shutting the door.

"No hospitals," Leander wheezed.

"You need a fucking hospital."

He laced his fingers through mine, squeezing his eyes shut. "No. Too many questions…"

I kicked the back of Gavin's seat to get his attention. "Call Molly O'Brien. Have her meet us at my apartment."

"On it."

I pulled Leander against me, stroking his face lightly. "Hold on, my love. Please hold on…"

40

BENNETT

Two weeks later

Rolling over onto my side, I stared at the empty space next to me in bed. My hand skimmed across the cold sheets, but my otter wasn't there to hold it. Without him, I was adrift once more.

After a moment, I pulled Leander's pillow closer and inhaled his scent. It wasn't the same thing. It wasn't even close. On top of that, it felt wrong — being *alone* in bed with only a lumpy pillow and faded cologne for comfort. I would have even taken that damn cat at the moment, allergies and all.

Seconds, or hours, later, I swatted Leander's pillow off of me and threw back the sheets. I couldn't take it anymore. The silence. The emptiness. I needed him like I needed air and right now I was suffocating.

I trudged down the hallway and down the circular stone staircase. Padding toward the living room, I lingered at the threshold as my eyes adjusted to the dim lighting, courtesy of the moon over the water.

Leander was asleep on the couch, his bare chest rising and falling rhythmically. One hand rested on the large bandage across his abdomen, while the other dangled off the cushion. A book was laying on the floor beneath it.

Making my way over to him, I knelt on the floor and set the book on the coffee table. Like a creeper, I propped my elbow on the edge of the couch and held my head, watching him sleep. I'd come so close to losing him for good that I needed continual reassurance he was fine, even if that meant watching over him like a teenage vampire in the middle of the night.

All I could say was thank God for Molly O'Brien. Of all my mob connections, she soared to the top of my Christmas list for the rest of her life.

A bonafide trauma surgeon by day, she helped out the Chicago mobsters on the side as needed. She was kind enough to stitch up my arm after my insane declaration of love and she'd been a fucking godsend from the moment she stepped into my apartment and saw Leander bleeding out on the floor. Between a field transfusion and suturing all of his stab wounds back together, she managed to pull Leander back from the brink of death. Again.

"He's lucky," she said, slapping a bandaid on my arm from the needle stick. "They didn't hit any major organs. I gave him antibiotics to be on the safe side and enough pain killers that he'll probably be asleep for the next couple days."

Lucky. Yeah. That's not what I'd call being stabbed by my husband five times, but I saw her point.

He accused me of being a lunatic, yet *he* was the one who devised the horrible plan to play possum. I didn't want to, clearly, but he insisted through all of his little quotes — a language in and of itself to anyone who knew him. As much as I hated it, there really was no other option and we both knew it.

Going low and slow, as it were, I'd hoped the knife would slip between his intestines without doing permanent damage. The trade off, however, was ten times the pain. It was a sacrifice he was willing to make because when it came to revenge nothing deterred Leander Welles, not even his own mortality.

The wind shifted off the sea, breezing through the balcony doors. A damp chill rolled through the room. I hopped to my feet and hurried over, securing them against the cold.

By the time I returned to Leander's side, he was awake, pulling a blanket off the back of the couch to cover himself.

"What are you doing?" he asked, his voice husky from sleep.

"Watching over you."

"Again?"

"I couldn't sleep." I snagged an extra pillow on my way by the overstuffed chair and resumed my spot on the hard tile.

He gave me a small smile. "You say that every night."

"Because it's true. I don't know why you won't let me bring the bed down here."

"Doctor's orders. Besides, I'll be able to use the stairs soon enough." He ran his fingers through my hair, brushing it away from my face.

"Or I can just carry you upstairs." I waggled my brows at him.

He smirked, stifling a chuckle. "*That* goes against doctor's orders too."

"Does it? I didn't hear her say that..." I slid my hand under the blanket, running my fingers up and down his leg.

"She said no undue exertion." He gave me a warning look. "You're lucky she even agreed to let me fly in my condition."

"But the Mediterranean is where people come to convalesce." I blinked innocently at him while my fingers walked up the inside of his thigh. "That's what we're doing. Convalescing."

"And here I thought it was to avoid the inquiries into Gianna Scardato's death."

I feigned offense. "I would never purposely avoid the FBI. And even if I was, I wouldn't come to Malta. They have an extradition treaty."

He shot me a look.

"The Maldives don't," I added with a smile.

"Mhmm."

"Are you not relaxing, my love?"

"Your idea of relaxing is wholly different than mine," he said, glancing pointedly at his leg before he met my eyes again.

"I don't think it's all that different. I mean, they both involve a bed. Or, the lounge chairs on the roof… or the sail boat... or—"

"Need I remind you," Leander interrupted, his tone as unamused as his face. "I ripped a stitch open the last time we tried relaxing your way."

"I don't know about you, but I took that as a crowning achievement. The orgasm to end all orgasms." I did a little chef's kiss and grinned at him. "You're welcome."

"If you're this rapacious while I'm wounded, I shudder to think what you're going to be like when I'm fully healed."

"I'll be gentle. I promise," I purred, slipping my hand inside his pajama pants. I gasped, eyes widening as my hand wrapped around his hardening length. "What? What is *this*? Why, I never… What do you have to say for yourself, Mr. Welles?"

He glared at me at the same time his hips tipped upward,

stroking himself against my hand. "You have the worst bedside manner I've ever seen."

"Or the best. Depends on your point of view."

"You are impossible."

"It's why you love me."

"Is it?" A dark brow arched slightly, the corner of his lips curling into a smirk.

I gave him a mocking glare before biting my lip and ducking underneath the blanket.

"Bennett..." He tried to swat me away as I crawled up onto the couch, wedging a knee between his legs and straddling his thigh. "Don't you dare! Don't you—"

Popping out from beneath the blanket, I perched above him carefully, making sure to balance my weight so none of it was on him. "Were you saying something, my love?"

Brushing my hair out of my eyes, he gave me *that* look, a small smile pulling at the corner of his mouth. "Kiss me."

He didn't have to tell me twice. It's all I ever wanted to do, now and for the rest of our lives.

41

LEANDER

One year later

The golden light of another day gone slanted through the windows, illuminating the rows of books. I shelved the last of my stack and headed toward the cash register where Luciana was tallying the day's sales.

"Did you ever hear from the buyer in Rome?" I asked, leaning against the antique counter.

"Yes. He's flying in at the end of the week to sit down with you."

"Perfect. Thank you."

A bell chimed from the front door, despite the CLOSED sign hanging in the window. Suppressing a smile, I turned and folded my arms over my chest, adopting a serious expression. "I'm sorry sir, the store's closed."

"Does that mean I have to come back tomorrow?" Bennett asked, sauntering forward, his head canted to one side.

"If you'd like."

"And the day after that? And the day after *that*?" He bit his lower lip and stopped right in front of me.

I lifted a brow, smirking at the sly grin on his face. "All of eternity?"

"And then some."

Linking my fingers through his, I threw a glance over my shoulder at Luciana. "See you tomorrow."

"Goodnight you two." She smiled and shook her head, disappearing into the back room with the money and the ledger.

As soon as she was gone, Bennett yanked me against his chest, his mouth crashing against mine. I wrapped my arms around him, ridding any possible space between us while he kissed me deeply.

Pulling away with a small sigh, I ran my hand through his hair and rested my forehead against his. As much as I enjoyed our nightly routine, if he didn't stop kissing me soon, it was going to be hard for either of us to walk home unhindered.

"I've missed you," he whispered. "Maybe I should move my office here. What do you think?"

"That neither of us would get any work done."

"So?"

I pulled back to look at him, shaking my head. "Let's go home, mon coeur."

"Let's." He took a step away and offered me his arm. "I'm famished."

"Good thing the stew has been cooking all day," I replied, threading my arm through his for the short walk to the door.

The streets of Valletta were slowly emptying as the sky overhead continued to darken. A soft breeze swept through the city, carrying with it the clean, salty smell of the sea I'd come to love.

Slipping my arm around Bennett's waist, I leaned into him as he slung his arm over my shoulders. Neither of us spoke as we strolled through the quiet streets. We didn't need to. Each look, each touch, said it all.

Life in Valletta was everything I'd ever wanted and never thought I would have — a life of my own making, with someone who loved me beyond measure.

Of course, running an American business from overseas wasn't always the easiest thing in the world, but we made it work. Whenever either of us had to return to the States, we made the trip worth our while, staying for weeks on end before packing up and returning to the sanctity of our palazzo.

Us.

We.

Ours.

Words that still seemed foreign, even though the proof was there on my hand — the black titanium band that would never, ever leave my left ring finger. The proof was in the way Bennett looked at me. The way he kissed me. Even the way he killed for me. Though, that hadn't been much of a problem in Malta, thankfully.

Here, we were safe from all of our demons.

"I'll grab the post," Bennett said, kissing my cheek before peeling away to check our mailbox.

Nodding, I headed upstairs to finish dinner.

I'd just poured the wine when Bennett reappeared, setting a wrapped parcel on the kitchen island. It was addressed to me in a handwriting I didn't recognize.

"What's that?" I asked.

Bennett shrugged. "I have no idea. I figured it was another book. Aren't you expecting that first edition from London?"

"It's rather large for a book." Tearing through the brown

paper, my nose wrinkled when a box came into view. It was a simple, wooden box save for the fact it was covered in dried mud. A dark red stain colored one corner.

Sliding around the side of the island, Bennett leaned down toward the box, his brows drawn together. "My love, what is that?"

"I have no idea." I reached for the lid, but Bennett grabbed my wrist and shook his head.

"I don't have a good feeling about this."

"We can't very well ignore it." As soon as his fingers loosened, I undid the antique closure and opened the box. There was a piece of paper, folded, laying inside. Beneath it was a pair of small, bloody forceps. The kind used to extract teeth.

"Are those...?" Bennett turned slowly, his hazel eyes wide.

"Teeth," I confirmed in one breathy word.

Rattling along the bottom of the box was a pile of bloody teeth. Thirty-two adult teeth.

Unfolding the paper, I only had to read the handwritten note once to know immediately what the package was referencing. My legs trembled a second before they gave out entirely.

Bennett caught me on the way down, easing my fall to the floor. "What is it? Leander?" He didn't wait for me to answer, instead snatching the note from my hand. "Latin?! Fuck. Um, 'My companions told me—'"

"'If I would visit the grave of my friend, I might somewhat alleviate my worries,'" I whispered the rest of the quote, trying to slow the whirlwind of my thoughts. Rising nausea, wrought by the box and the lie I just uttered, crept up the back of my throat like acid. The true quote read as "the grave of my beloved," a fact Bennett either chose to ignore or overlooked in his hasty translation.

"Who the fuck would send you a real-life version of *Berenice*? And whose teeth are these?"

"I have no idea…" I shook my head, pressing the heels of my hands into my eyes until I saw black and white dots. Bennett rubbed my leg gently until I lowered my hands and looked at him. "We have to go home."

"The hell we do. This could be some sort of a trap. Until we know who sent this, we—"

"It doesn't matter, mon coeur," I interrupted with a shake of my head. "They already know where I am. I need to make sure Elijah and Jake are alright." I handed him the note again and tipped my chin toward it. On the back was another message.

See you soon.

He nodded, despite the worry written clearly on his face. "I'll make the arrangements, then."

As soon as he was gone, I hauled myself to my feet and stared at the box of teeth. Thirty-two brilliant white teeth, now dulled by dirt and stained by the blood of their painful removal. Teeth I would know, even without the rest of the face. Teeth that were once part of a beautiful, kind smile — teeth that bit with passion and want.

"'Misery is manifold,'" I murmured, hanging my head. Slamming the lid down, I shoved the box away from me, squeezing my eyes shut. "I'm sorry, Lorelei… The darkness claimed you after all."

The End

PLEASE DON'T FORGET to rate/review if you enjoyed the book! Every rating helps indie authors, more than you know.

ABOUT THE AUTHOR

Award-winning dark romance author Ashlyn Drewek has always been a hopeless romantic. She's also fascinated by the dark, macabre things in life (you can blame a love of Halloween and Edgar Allan Poe for that one).

Most of her time is spent making up stories in her head or researching some obscure topic just because she's that much of a nerd. The degree on the wall says she's a historian, but the paycheck says she's a first responder.

Ashlyn lives in Northern Illinois with her patient husband, fearless daughter, and a house full of animals.

For information on news and upcoming releases, check out her website at www.ashlyndrewek.com to sign up for her newsletter or follow her at any of the social media options below.

ALSO BY ASHLYN DREWEK

The Leander Welles Series:

THE MYSTERY OF LEANDER WELLES — a dark, psychological romance about a criminal psychiatrist who falls in love with her patient. Finalist for Suspense in the 2021 Next Generation Indie Book Awards.

THE RATIONALE OF LEANDER WELLES — a dark, psychological romance about an alleged murder who falls in love with his psychiatrist… or does he?

THE DAMNATION OF LEANDER WELLES: OR, THE DEATH & LIFE OF BENNETT REEVE — a dark, romantic suspense about a cutthroat lawyer and an enigmatic millionaire and what happens when two dark souls join forces. A prequel to Book I and II.

THE WRATH OF LEANDER WELLES — a dark, romantic suspense about love, revenge, and how far a psychopath is willing to go for both.

THE FALL OF LEANDER WELLES — TBD

The Solnyshko Duet:

THE KIDNAPPING OF ROAN SINCLAIR — a dark MM romance

about an American college guy who is kidnapped by a Russian criminal.

THE VENGEANCE OF ROAN SINCLAIR — a dark MM romance about love in the aftermath of trauma and finding your new normal. Coming 2022

Paranormal:

OUT OF THE DARK — a slow-burn paranormal romance about vampires and Chicago cops and what it means to fall in love when you're not supposed to.

MALUM DISCORDIAE — A dark, paranormal MM romance about witches, Necromancers, and a blood feud that has lasted centuries. Coming 2022

www.ingramcontent.com/pod-product-compliance
Lightning Source LLC
LaVergne TN
LVHW041106080826
845145LV00007B/1705
9781955211031